CONRAD EDISON

AND

THE BROKEN RELIC

OVERWORLD ARCANUM
BOOK THREE

JOHN CORWIN

FOREVER BROKEN

When Conrad learns of an ancient artifact that might be able to reverse death, he dares to hope it might return Cora from the grave.

The Broken Relic, however, is highly sought after by collectors though nobody knows exactly what it is. After being kidnapped, chased, and nearly killed, Conrad realized he and his friends will be lucky to survive the preparations for the quest, much less the quest itself.

But the Seers, an organization that gathers prophecies, offers him a dire warning: If he seeks the relic, he may doom the Overworld.

ISBN- 978-1-942453-08-6

Printed in the U.S.A.

RAVEN HOUSE

Books by John Corwin:

The Overworld Chronicles:
Sweet Blood of Mine
Dark Light of Mine
Fallen Angel of Mine
Dread Nemesis of Mine
Twisted Sister of Mine
Dearest Mother of Mine
Infernal Father of Mine
Sinister Seraphim of Mine
Wicked War of Mine
Dire Destiny of Ours
Aetherial Annihilation
Baleful Betrayal
Ominous Odyssey

Overworld Underground:
Possessed By You
Demonicus

Overworld Arcanum:
Conrad Edison and the Living Curse
Conrad Edison and the Anchored World
Conrad Edison and the Broken Relic

Stand Alone Novels:
No Darker Fate
The Next Thing I Knew
Outsourced
Seventh
Mars Rising

For the latest on new releases, free ebooks, and more, join John Corwin's Newsletter at www.johncorwin.net!

Chapter 1

I jerked awake on a cold slab of stone, the coppery stench of blood in my nose.

Something tight around my neck strangled the gasp rising in my throat. Sitting up, I felt a leather collar squeezing the flesh just below the Adam's apple. Blood soaked my shirt. *Where am I?* I tried to remember where I'd been, what I'd been doing before this. I peeled off the shirt and threw it to the floor in disgust.

My breath came in pants, stress and the choker on my windpipe doing their best to deprive me of air. *Think, Conrad, think!*

I took a long deep breath and held it a few beats. Before I could think, I had to be calm. My thudding heart carried on its panicked race, but eventually it began to slow. Some shred of rational thought finally penetrated the haze of desperation.

"My name is Conrad," I croaked. The choker made it difficult to speak. I swallowed hard against the dryness in my throat and conserved my breath.

I remembered my name. I knew that I was attending my second year at Arcane University, and that my best friends were Maxwell Tiberius and Ambria Rax. It seemed my long-term memories were intact. The last thing I remembered was leaving Golem's Gourmet, having eaten fairy pies with my friends and leaping from the top of the building only to drift slowly to the ground since the ingredients made a person light as air.

After that, Max had left for his uncle's house on his broom. Ambria and I had boarded the saddles on our brooms and flown for the house on the corner of Dowling and Bucket Streets. Beyond that, I remembered nothing, no matter how hard I squeezed shut my eyes or tried to remember the way home. How long ago that had been, I couldn't even guess. Had I slept here for a night, or longer?

Now that I'd determined the distant past and the recent past, it was time to evaluate this most unpleasant present time. *Whose blood is that?*

The sight of so much blood might make most people go weak in the knees or toss up a recent meal. I'd seen worse—much worse. I'd seen a demon devour a werewolf. I'd killed the wardens of my former orphanage. I was only thirteen, but I'd seen more than enough blood for one lifetime.

Apparently, someone didn't agree.

A thin layer of blood coated my chest and stomach, crimson streaks running down my ribs where the blood had seeped through my shirt. I ran my hands over the sticky mess and found no wounds in my skin. I checked my other extremities, looked down my blood-soaked pants, and found no cuts. I gingerly fingered several bruises, especially on my right arm and shoulder.

Four walls, a ceiling, and a floor of slick gray stone made my prison. The stone slab that had served as my bed was polished to a sheen barely reflective enough for me to see a shadow of my face looking back. Blood spattered the edges, leaving an outline of my upper body where it had collected the blood.

I felt for cuts on my head and neck and found nothing, except—there, on the right side just below my ear, the flesh tender and puckered. A small scab covered what could only be a puncture wound. A dart perhaps? It might have delivered a dose of potion that knocked me out as I flew down the winding roads of Queens Gate toward home. That would explain the bruises.

The blood did not appear to be mine, which meant—icy claws gripped my heart. Had the kidnapper taken Ambria as well? Had he done something awful to my friend? My heart raced. I tried to breathe, but a vice of despair squeezed my ribs.

I ran to the steel door embedded in the stone wall. I pounded, my small fists hardly making a sound against the dense metal. "Let me out!" My voice came out as a harsh whisper. I clawed at the rough leather of the choker. A metal clamp locked it. Try as I might, I couldn't pry it loose. My panic turned to claustrophobia, fear choking off my air supply. The room went dim and I teetered on the edge of consciousness.

Calm yourself, you little fool. Della sighed loudly in my head. *Ambria is dead.* My eyes burned with tears. I curled up on the cold floor and cried.

Crying certainly won't bring her back, Della said.

I ignored the voice in my head. After some time, I cried myself out and lay on the floor, spent. I felt calm and absurdly relaxed, as if I were not the prisoner of someone who had killed my best friend and poured her blood on my chest.

Why would anyone do such a horrible thing? Why were they not in here gloating over my misery?

I did not have many friends. Most of the other kids at school kept their distance. I had nearly as many enemies as friends. Harris Ashmore hated me because my parents had murdered his. My parents, Victus and Delectra Edison had used me as a demonic vessel to store their souls. After they'd been resurrected, parts of their souls had stuck to mine. Even now, they wanted me dead because my death would restore those soul shards to them.

I doubted Harris capable of kidnapping me and murdering an innocent. It seemed more likely he would prefer to beat me up and humiliate me as he'd tried to do in the past. My parents, on the other hand, were evil enough to do something like this. Perhaps they hadn't yet killed me because they enjoyed toying with their prey. Beyond the usual suspects, I couldn't imagine anyone else would go to the bother.

Sometimes the soul shards spoke to me, usually to berate me. I'd nicknamed them Vic and Della after their corporeal counterparts. I waited for them to chime in on this situation, but they remained quiet.

I huddled in the corner of the room, shivering in the chill, but unwilling to put back on my blood-crusted shirt. *How long does it take blood to coagulate?* Not long, I suspected. That meant little time had passed since the kidnapper poured it on me. It meant he timed it so I would wake up with wet blood on me. It meant he knew I was in here suffering, sick with worry about the source of the blood, and questioning everything.

Why hadn't the kidnapper introduced himself yet? Was he watching me?

In this new calm state, rational thought came much easier. To gain entrance to Arcane University, I'd been subjected to tests, both physical and mental. I had to view this experience as yet another test designed to make me fold.

I took another long look at the room. The door was smooth iron—no lock or handle on this side. The walls had no markings, the floor had no drain, and the ceiling had no vents, only a glowing orb providing the light. There seemed to be no way out.

I went through my pockets but came up empty. The chain my foster mother Cora had given me with her stone was gone from around my neck. My heart caught in my throat at the thought that it might be gone forever. I took a deep breath and calmed myself. The only way I'd recover it was if I escaped. I once again looked for options.

My only assets were a bloody shirt, my pants, and shoes. I bumped into the sharp corner of the stone table and winced. As I rubbed my sore skin, I realized the corner might be an asset.

Holding a finger to the leather next to the locked buckle on the back of my neck, I lined it up with the corner of the table and worked it up and down until my legs grew tired. My fingernail found a nick where the stone had worn through. It was a small victory, but at this point I was willing to take whatever I could get.

Once I felt rested, I resumed my labor. Three more rest periods later, the leather finally parted. I tore off the choker and threw it to the floor.

"Hello." I tested my raspy throat with a few more words until my voice sounded dry but normal. It felt good to be free of the constricting strap, but it brought me no closer to being free of this room. My parched lips begged for water, and I felt the urge to use the bathroom. It seemed that whoever trapped me in here wanted me to suffer in all ways possible.

I finally gave in and urinated in the corner of the room. Right after I finished, I regretted not having something to store it in. I'd read stories of people drinking their own urine to survive. Then again, what good would it do to drink my own waste water? I could only recycle it once, and that would barely delay my dehydration.

Somehow, I had to find a way out of this room.

I went back to the door and traced my finger along the seams. There were no hinges on this side, and the crack at the bottom was too narrow to look beneath. I found a slight gap on the right side of the door, and through it, a sliver of light. Something halfway up the door blocked the light. The latch? It looked about an inch wide, but I couldn't make out how thick it was.

If only I had something to pry at it.

My eyes wandered to the discarded collar. The metal buckle was thin on the ends where it was stitched into the leather. I picked it up and tried to bend the leather away, but the thick hide was too stiff. I went back to the table and worked the inside of the collar against the sharp corner of the stone table. I worked feverishly, sweat dribbling into my eyes, and finally cut through the leather.

Tugging hard, twisting the leather back and forth, I finally tore it free from the buckle with a grunt of effort. The thin metal was tougher than it looked, and didn't bend when I tested it. Now to try it on the latch.

The blade of metal slid into the groove. I pulled up and felt it catch on the latch. It jiggled but didn't move so I increased the pressure. Still it resisted. I lowered the makeshift jimmy and slid it up fast. It dinged against the metal, but the latch didn't give in the slightest.

Maybe it moves in a different direction.

I'd thought this door similar to the ones in Arcane University where they used a latch that flipped out and down to lock into a notch. Perhaps this one was more like the ones used by normal people—the noms.

I pressed the tip of the jimmy against the latch closest to the door frame and then pried it to the left. The latch moved ever so slightly. My body trembled with excitement. *I can do this!* I nearly congratulated myself but the second I tried to slide the pry bar back to the right, the sliver of progress slipped back into the jamb. My shoulders slumped. Apparently this was harder than I'd hoped.

Once again, I positioned the jimmy and moved the latch to the right. I knew the moment I tried to adjust the angle, the spring-loaded lock would go right back into position. I needed another piece of metal, but I had no way of cutting the buckle in half.

I might as well wish for a blowtorch.

The keyhole looked relatively simple, but I had nothing that might be used as a lock pick. That meant I had to come up with another way of holding the latch in place, but what would work? All I needed was a bit of pressure to keep the spring in the door from pressing the latch back into place. There was really only one option.

I braced my feet against the floor and pressed my shoulder against the door. When I moved the jimmy, the latch stayed in place. I felt a grim smile on my lips. *This will work.* I pressed the jimmy into place, removed my shoulder from the door, and worked the latch another fraction to the left. Using my body weight against the door, I held the latch in place once again.

My hands ached and the metal bit into my fingers as I worked the jimmy back and forth, the latch barely moving with every effort. Minutes ticked past and I soon wondered if the latch was moving at all or if it was my imagination. Blood trickled from a cut on my left index finger, and my joints ached from the strain.

I gave myself a moment to rest and then resumed the grueling work. Slide, pry, hold the door. Slide, pry, hold the door. My movements became so automatic that when the latch clicked and the door swung outward, I fell to my knees and the buckle clattered to the floor.

Freedom!

Chapter 2

A glance into the hallway beyond told me that wasn't nearly the case. Four more steel doors with levered handles were on the opposite wall from mine, and three more were on my side. The corridor dead-ended on my left, but a short hallway to my right led to a stairwell.

I left the door to my cell hanging open and cautiously tested the other doors in the hallway. None were locked, and all opened to rooms identical to mine except they held no occupants. I crept up the stairs at the end of the hall and found another hallway of cells. These too were empty. The next level up was different. Wooden doors lined a corridor that stretched from left to right. An open doorway a dozen paces down was the only break in the monotony of this dungeon. I heard a faint cough and froze with dread.

Someone was inside that room. I certainly wasn't strong enough to fight someone, especially not with my exhausted hands. Stealth was my only option. I retreated back down to my cell where I picked up the buckle, the leather choker, and my bloody shirt. My assets were so few that I couldn't afford to leave anything behind.

Once back upstairs, I treaded softly, pressed my back to the wall, and sneaked up to the open doorway. A man in black Arcane robes sat inside small living quarters, his profile to me. Yellowed parchment filled a box on one side of his old wooden desk. Leather-bound books weighed down sagging shelves against the back wall, and next to the shelves was a small wooden bed with rumpled sheets. Behind it was a closet filled with more robes.

Though the man could glance right and see the hallway at any moment, his full attention was on a sheet of parchment where he scrawled with a feather quill. He faced in the direction I needed to go if I planned on proceeding down the hallway. Despite being preoccupied, his peripheral vision would spot me in an instant if I tried to pass.

It seemed prudent to turn around and go the opposite direction, so I did. The door at the end of the hallway was locked. I tested the other doors. Those that were unlocked opened into living quarters like the one occupied by the man. It seemed I had no choice but to go back the other way.

I returned to the open doorway and peeked around the corner. A wand hung from a holster at the man's side, and a compact rod of wood about ten inches long and slightly thicker than a broom handle sat on the desk.

If only I had that wand.

I had to get my hands on it. Unfortunately, there was no way to slip inside without detection. The man might be distracted with his paperwork, but any movement was bound to attract his attention. My only hope was that he got up at some point and put his back to me.

Time ticked away, but the man seemed intent on writing a book in one sitting. The moment he reached the end of one parchment, he grabbed another and continued to write. The longer I waited, the more antsy I became. What if there were more guards? What if the man got up and came to check on me?

I'd closed the door to my prison, but that didn't guarantee they wouldn't look inside to make sure I was still there. At any moment, the man in the room might get up and put his back to me, but he was just as likely to come my way. Then I'd have no choice but to run.

Since the desired situation hadn't occurred organically, I decided to force it. I peered in and waited for the man to work his eyes from the left side of the parchment to the right as he wrote. When his head

9

began to shift my way, I ducked behind the corner and tossed the leather choker down the hall.

He made a confused noise. "Hagan, that you?" Wood grated across stone and footsteps came toward the doorway. The man leaned out and looked down the hall away from me. "Hagan, this better not be one of your jokes." He flinched and looked down at the leather collar. "What the bloody—"

I swept my blood-soaked shirt over his face, held the corners, and jerked back, using all my weight. Despite my smaller size, he wasn't prepared and fell over backwards, hands windmilling for balance. His head bounced off the floor. I leapt on top of him and swung both fists down at his face. His head lolled to the side and his body went limp.

There was a chance he might recover so I quickly nicked his wand and prepared a spell. He remained still, breath wheezing from beneath the bloody shirt. I plucked it off his face. Prodding him with my foot elicited no response and a sense of mild relief eased the knots in my stomach.

I gripped him beneath the armpits and dragged him down the hall and the stairs. I was huffing and puffing by the time I got him into one of the cells on the floor below. I didn't bother putting him on the table and closed the door behind me.

On the way back up the stairs, I flicked the wand through a pattern and said, "*Illumus.*" A small globe of light appeared at the tip. I snuffed the spell, satisfied that the wand wasn't charmed to refuse the commands of another spell caster.

I took the man's staff and flicked it out to full length. It rose half a foot taller than me, making it awkward to aim, so I reduced it to compact size and stuffed it in my back pocket.

Though I now had magical means, I was merely a novice. I knew only one offensive spell and one for defense. If there were other people in this dungeon, I would do well to avoid them.

The parchment the man had been so intent upon caught my eye. I shuffled back to the first page and found the title: *5002 Analysis by Seer Paul Plinth*. I didn't understand what about a number needed analyzing and read the introduction.

Foreseeance 5002 has been a subject of great debate. Should action be taken, or should events take their course?

I argue for the former.

Arcnology may pave a path for the subject to become stronger much faster than a traditional Arcane education. It may also lead to another Overlord scenario or worse. We cannot discount the dark influence on an impressionable mind.

Remember this dire warning: Dark specters shall herald the destruction of worlds.

I believe it means all the realms will suffer if we leave the future to chance. Overt action is justified and required.

The third paragraph sent ice spiders crawling down my spine. The Overlord was the name Victus had adopted once he forcibly took control of the Overworld. It appeared this fellow didn't know my father had risen from the dead on the back of his own son.

I wished to read more, but there was no time. I had to make my escape.

After searching the desk and the pockets of Plinth's robes in his closet, I found nothing else that might aid my escape, so I crept back out into the hallway and along the wall. More stairs were around the corner. I walked up to the top and found three doors. Only one was unlocked so I eased it open and peered through.

A wide room with neat rows of bookshelves was on the other side.

"How odd," I muttered. This was a strange place. Why were there living quarters on the floors just above the dungeon? I wondered if all those levels had been converted from one use to another at some point, or if this was some sort of dormitory.

After listening carefully for several seconds, I felt confident there was no one inside the library, so I ventured in and faced three doors. I'd crossed halfway through the room to the door straight across from me when I heard a snort and loud sniffs. I froze and felt the hairs on the back of my neck stand on end. The clack of claws echoed against the stone, coming closer and closer.

Bookshelves blocked me on both sides. I had nowhere to run but forward or backward. Unfortunately, I didn't know where the sound originated. I readied the wand and waited. A huge black dog wearing a collar like the one I'd woken up in stepped around the corner in front of me and growled. I turned to run back the way I'd come, but the growling went from mono to surround sound. Another dog blocked my retreat.

What a conundrum, Della said in an amused voice.

Any advice? I asked.

Run, Vic said dryly.

My parents' soul fragments weren't much for offering helpful advice. *Where do you suggest I run to?*

There was no reply.

The dogs stalked closer, teeth bared in angry snarls. I pressed a hand against the bookshelf to my right, heart thumping. It was solid wood, sturdy, nearly immovable. Before the dogs came any closer, I shoved books off the shelf and clambered up. The dogs charged.

I pulled my feet up to the fourth shelf just before canine jaws tore into my ankles. I'd hoped the cases had open backs, but whoever built these hadn't cut any corners, and solid wood prevented me from slipping through to the next row. I reached the top of the bookshelf and lay on my back, facing the ceiling. Sweat trickled down my forehead and my heart pounded like a frightened rabbit's.

Four feet separated the case from the ceiling—more than enough room for me to crouch-walk. The dogs paced below, ready to pounce the moment I returned to the floor. Though they continued to snarl and growl, they didn't bark. That surely would have alerted anyone in nearby rooms.

I looked across the tops of the other bookshelves at the other doors. The aisles were just narrow enough for me to jump, so I did. I hopped left, going from shelf to shelf until I reached the other side. The dogs whined in confusion as they searched for me. I clambered down from the shelves and tested the two doors on this wall. Both were locked. Clacking paws told me I had no time to jimmy the doors, so I went back up to the top of the shelves just as the dogs rounded the corner.

I hopped my way to the other side of the room, once again throwing the dogs off my trail. The three doors on this wall were also locked. I took a moment to inspect the latch, but it appeared to be a deadbolt. Before the dogs reached me, I climbed back to the top of the bookshelf. Falling books thudded to the floor behind me.

It wouldn't take much in the way of brains for anyone who came in here to realize that someone unauthorized had been in here. I took a book from the top shelf and examined it. Surely there must be valuable books in this library to warrant guarding them with dogs.

This book was about an organization called the Illuminati. Apparently, they'd been quite powerful, judging from the summary, but had been nearly wiped out by Templars and other organizations. I hopped over a couple of aisles and found a tome about a man named Peter Evans, a once prominent Arcane. As I leafed through more books, I realized many were like spy dossiers on individuals and organizations.

A few books down from the book about Peter Evans, I found three books with my family name. My book came before the ones about my parents, and it was short—more of a leaflet than a book. In its few pages, it described my life as a child. I was so entranced with it, I nearly forgot I was in the middle of an escape.

I folded the pamphlet and stuffed it in my front pocket. I wanted to take the ones about my parents, but escaping with my own hide intact was challenge enough without carrying books. This library was a treasure trove of information. It made perfect sense why the owners would so zealously guard it. This place was obviously home to an organization that spied on everyone and everything.

The most glaring incongruity was why they'd kidnapped me.

My next challenge was to test the final door in this room and pray it wasn't locked. To do that, I had to elude the guards.

They're just dogs, Della said. *Even you should be able to outsmart them.*

I sat down and shifted uncomfortably due to the metal buckle in one back pocket and my bloody shirt in the other. I took out the bloody shirt and one of the dogs whined and licked its muzzle. Though the dogs had probably been asleep when I came in the room, it was no wonder they'd known there was an intruder.

The blood on my shirt probably smells like a feast to them. I walked along the top of the book case to the side of the room I'd entered on and the dogs followed as if I dragged them on an invisible leash. The open door to the cells was twenty feet away. I wrapped a book in my shirt, cocked my arm, and threw the shirt through it. It landed on the top of the stairs.

The dogs raced toward it and began a vicious game of tug-of-war for the bloody prize. I clambered down so quickly my teeth clacked, ran to the door, and closed it before the dogs could come back through. I took a deep breath of relief to celebrate being one step closer to freedom, however far away it might be.

14

Conrad Edison and the Broken Relic

Now that I had a moment to rest, I retrieved the books on my parents and skimmed through them. The highlights of Victus's evil career seemed to span from cover to cover. My mother's started off much differently.

Though Delectra is often seen as the cold, ruthless wife of the Overlord, she was once a very promising student. Mentored by the once peerless Galfandor, she quickly rose to the top of her novice class and beyond. He described her in his journal as a brilliant light in a room of dim candles, and yet a gentle soul, filled with empathy.

This was before Victus set his sights on her. As the brightest star of Science Academy, many of his peers disdained his obsession with Delectra. What none realized was that he was also secretly studying magic, most notably, demon summoning.

Through our studies of Victus's secret journals that we found after his death, we discovered that Delectra's gentle nature was destroyed by demonic inversion. He slowly destroyed her and rebuilt her into the ruthless woman that he needed her to be.

Chapter 3

My insides felt hollow as I continued to read the impersonal observations about my twisted evil mother. Had she truly once been a kind and gentle person? Why had Galfandor never told me he mentored my mother? My face burned with rage, but regret doused the fire and left me feeling cold inside.

Lies, Vic said. *I only brought out the real her.*

Is this true? Della said.

Vic didn't reply.

Whatever Victus had done to Delectra, it had been thorough. She'd wasted no time trying to kill me shortly after Rufus Cumberbatch had resurrected her and Victus.

My thoughts came to an abrupt halt as I read the next passage.

It was rumored that Galfandor sought the Broken Relic of Jura to cure Delectra. He apparently abandoned his search once he realized in the wrong hands, the relic could be, as he noted in his journals, "a dreadful weapon."

On a related note, it was rumored that Victus sought the Eye of Jura. Some reports claim he found it, but if that was the case, why did he not use it to escape death? Underborn's collection is by far the largest of all the relic hunters', though Stella Tiberius was not far behind. (For more information, please see Relics of Jura).

What was this Broken Relic of Jura? How could it cure my mother? I held onto my parents' dossiers and ran to the R section. There I found a slim book with the referenced title and tucked it with the other books. I wished I had a backpack. There was probably one in the living quarters, but since the dogs were now trapped in that hallway, I didn't dare go back.

I'd wasted enough time in this library already. It was only a matter of time before someone else came through here and discovered the escaped prisoner. I tested the final door in the room and discovered it was just as locked as the others.

I'd searched Plinth and hadn't found any keys on him. How had he gotten in and out of this place without a key? I closed my eyes and visualized the desk and everything on it. I didn't remember seeing a key lying around. That meant he must have gained entrance in another way.

It meant—I reached into my pocket and withdrew Plinth's wand. Once inserted into the keyhole, the tip elicited a click as the deadbolt withdrew. I opened the door and found a long corridor. The other doors revealed two closets, a bath house, and another long hallway. I went to the end of one hallway and found a kitchen.

Hunger gnawed at my insides. I tore chunks from a loaf of bread on the counter and gulped it down. A pantry with a cooling enchantment held pails of milk which looked as if they'd just been filled. I was too thirsty to look for a glass and slurped straight from the pail.

Several packages of meat bundled with twine sat on a shelf opposite the milk and in the back of the room were fruits and vegetables.

I didn't allow myself to eat anything else. Running would be hard if my stomach was full to bursting. I exited the cooler and looked around.

The kitchen windows looked out into a large green field, and a door led outside to a woodpile. A tall stone wall with sharp iron spikes guarded the perimeter. Though I didn't see any people, that didn't mean there weren't more dogs running about. I went back into the cooler and unwrapped the twine from the meat then used it to bind the books together so I could sling them over my back. The meat would be the final key to my escape, provided there were dogs outside.

I resisted the urge to race outside and took a moment to survey the landscape. The wall was too high to climb, and I saw no gates. My heart sank. I'd come so far only to reach a dead end. The situation left me with no alternative but to go outside and sneak around the perimeter to the front where there surely had to be a gate.

The doors in the kitchen weren't locked and I discovered a larder, the entrance to a dining hall, and a private dining room with a blackened hearth. I heard voices echoing through the dining hall, though the room appeared to be empty. The private room had no other doors. I would probably have to backtrack and investigate the other rooms for a route to the front of the castle.

The voices drew closer, accompanied by the clomp of hard-soled shoes on stone. I risked another peek into the dining hall and saw two men in black robes coming my way. I dashed through the opposite door and down the hallway leading to the library. Shouts rose from the other side of the door and dogs barked in response.

They know I escaped!

Fighting knees weak with fear, I ran back into the kitchen and considered my last two options. Either run outside where I'd surely be cornered by dogs, or find someplace to hide in the private dining room. I ran inside the private room and looked up the chimney. It appeared wide enough for me to shimmy to the top, but the square of light looked very far from here and my bare back would be rubbed raw from the stone.

It was the only avenue left.

Before I began the climb, I went back into the kitchen and squeezed blood from the meat and onto the floor, leaving a trail to the back door. Then I took the chunks of meat and threw them outside. It wasn't very far, but it would give me a little extra time. I rinsed my hands in a bucket of water and grabbed a handful of dried and crushed lavender from the window sill to rub over my body to help counter my scent.

The footsteps sounded much louder now. I had only seconds left. As I turned for the private room again, I saw another small door built waist-high into the wall. I jerked it open and found a dumbwaiter inside. Designed to carry large trays, it was large enough to accommodate me. I made a split-second decision and went with my gut.

I shut the door to the dumbwaiter. Seconds later, the kitchen door opened and the men entered.

"…got word he escaped," one man said.

"Impossible," the other replied. "Even if he got out, he'll never get past the moat."

A moat? Unless I could scale the wall around the compound and ford the moat, my odds of escape looked slim.

"I'd like to know how he got out of the cell," the first man said. Another door slammed shut and their conversation faded.

I pulled on the rope and the dumbwaiter inched up. I expected a great struggle to lift my own bodyweight, but found progress to be relatively easy. It occurred to me that there must be a counterweight built into the design. Otherwise the food would plummet straight back down the moment anyone released the rope.

I reached the second floor and the wooden box clicked into place. I cracked open the door to a hallway lined with doors. A man in black robes appeared from a stairwell at the end and might have seen me had his nose not been buried in a book. He vanished inside one of the doorways.

This definitely wasn't the floor I wanted, so I continued up to the third floor. The platform refused to go any higher, so I assumed this was the top level. A peek through the door revealed an opulent bedroom. Tapestries and paintings adorned the walls, and a large four-poster bed with a richly embroidered comforter sat against the far wall. An old man in black robes stared serenely out from one of the portraits. He held a staff topped by a circle of gold in which hung an unblinking silver eye. Something was inscribed at the bottom of the frame: *Quod visum non videntur.*

What has been seen cannot be unseen, Della said.

"What does that mean?" I hissed back at the voice in my head.

They have been watching you, she replied. *Foolish boy.*

The hairs on my neck pricked at the thought. "What do you mean?"

There came no reply.

How typical! Why did she tease me with such frightening information and leave me suspended?

I listened intently for a moment then disembarked the dumbwaiter and scurried through the room. The study next door was overstuffed with ornately carved wooden furniture, marble-topped tables with crystal vases, and richly bound leather books in glass display cases. A book with a golden cover sat directly in front of the window behind the desk.

The plaque on the case read: *The Golden Standard.*

Surprisingly, the case had no lock and the door opened with a gentle tug. I tentatively touched the book, afraid it might have a charm that would set off an alarm. When nothing terrible happened, I took the tome and opened it.

Foreseeance 4311 – The Gold Standard

Despite attempts by third parties to prevent the knowledge in this volume from being properly recorded, we were able to collect that which was feared lost. Though we have foreseen many important events over the past few millennia, few compare with the accuracy and the importance of Foreseeance 4311.

What was seen came to pass and will not be forgotten. Despite the foreknowledge gained by the subject, it was agreed that most came to pass as it should have.

The pages were thick, the letters embossed in gold. It was obvious these people were extremely proud of whatever it was they'd done. The first few pages waxed philosophical on whether it was a good thing or not that the subjects of foreseeances were given the details of their futures.

This book spoke of Justin Slade and the Second Seraphim-Eden War, as the writer titled it. The first section about the foreseeance was a collection of snippets from various foreseers around the world. Most of them were so vague they hardly seemed connected to Justin Slade.

The next section was reserved for the foreseeance that had been written by one of the foreseers in this organization. It was also vaguely worded, but the author praised it as being precise and thorough.

The few moments I spent thumbing through the book were probably foolishly spent, especially if people were looking for me. On the other hand, I needed to know more about my captors. I replaced the heavy book in its case with a much better idea.

"Kidnapped by prophets," I muttered. Why would they do such a thing?

It really didn't matter. All I needed to know was that they'd callously knocked me from my broom and whisked me away to their dungeon. Since the other cells were empty, it seemed they hadn't taken Ambria as well, or at least I kept telling myself that. I still didn't know whose blood stained my clothes and I dreaded finding out.

Turning from the glass case, I spotted a bundle of items on a small table on the opposite side of the desk. My heart leapt at the sight of my broom, wand, and arcphone. I grabbed the most valuable item—the chain with a green pebble attached. Cora had left me the stone and even if it were nothing more than a rock, it would still be my most prized possession in the world. I turned on the phone. "Phone, has anyone else used you today besides me?"

"Two people attempted unauthorized access," it replied. "Both were denied."

I didn't know why, but that made me feel less violated than before. Relief soothed my nerves when I tested the broom and it worked. Neither wall nor moat mattered now. All I had to do was leap out a window and fly away. I stuffed the books about me and my family into the saddlebag on the side of my broom so I'd no longer have to carry them across my shoulder.

The windows in the study were locked and Plinth's wand did nothing when I pressed it to them. I tested those in the bedroom with the same results. The sitting room had a large balcony with a magnificent view of a wide green lawn between rows of neatly sculpted trees. The colors red and blue wound through the rose gardens and a brown cobblestone path ran inconspicuously to the tall wall a hundred yards away.

More conspicuous were the people in black robes combing the bushes and rushing toward the end of the road where a thick iron gate guarded the only way in or out of this estate. It was all so tantalizingly close, but the balcony doors didn't respond to Plinth's wand. It appeared the only lax security measure on this floor was the dumbwaiter.

Rather dumb of them, I thought.

The pun failed to bring a smile to my face. I opened the final door in the sitting room and found a stairwell. Voices echoed from below. I quickly shut the door and backed away. Sweat beaded on my forehead. Before long, I'd be cornered, with no way out.

Since the windows wouldn't open, I had only a few remaining choices. I went into the study, picked up a heavy marble bust of a serious-looking bearded man and threw it at the glass door to the balcony in the sitting room. His head left a divot in the glass. I picked up the bust and smashed it again and again into the glass. It was obviously charmed not to break, because after giving it everything I had, a spider web of cracks spread across the surface, but the window refused to yield.

Heart thudding, sweat dripping down my face, I dropped the bust and groaned. Leaden arms hanging by my sides, I leaned my forehead on the stubborn glass. "Why won't you break?"

Glass shattered, clattering to the floor like a pile of porcelain plates. I fell forward, catching myself inches before impaling my throat on a shard of glass. An alarm wailed and shouts sounded from outside. The people searching the lawn spun around, eyes locking onto the balcony and me.

Freedom!

I hopped on my broom saddle and darted out the window before veering sharp left toward the nearest section of wall. People in black robes ran below, crying out for me to stop.

When I soared over the wall, I quickly realized we weren't in Queens Gate. Forest stretched out as far as the eye could see. I hooked right and paralleled the wall, keeping low to avoid prying eyes from the inside, and remaining in the clearing between it and the forest to avoid the trees.

The driveway inside the castle grounds had to lead to a road. That was my path back to civilization. I smacked my forehead as I remembered the greatest tool in my arsenal. "Phone, show me where I am."

"Location unavailable," the phone replied. "Would you like me to resolve the problem?"

"Yes!" I shouted back. "Resolve it quickly."

It went silent for a moment. "There appears to be a jamming spell preventing a signal to the aethernet. Please disable the jamming spell so I can reestablish a connection."

Unsurprisingly, my hosts wanted to remain off the radar. I could fly in any direction and eventually find civilization, but the road seemed my best bet. Wind whistled in my ears as my broom hit top speed. The gray wall blurred to my right, green and brown foliage to my left. Three figures zipped over the wall ahead, each of them on brooms. I looked back and spotted another group flying in pursuit.

Forget the road, it was time to take to the forest.

Chapter 4

I pressed hard on the left stirrup and the broom tilted sideways while I dove lower to get beneath the tree branches. My pursuers outnumbered me, but now I was in my element. My mother had been an expert broom racer. Thanks to her soul fragment and inherited talent, I was no slouch myself.

Spells sang through the trees. Branches smoked, broke, and fell. Bark exploded from the trunks of hardwoods. Every shot flew wide. Either the people chasing me were poor shots, or they weren't trying to hit me. I dodged between tree trunks and the occasional broken branch. My pursuers stayed above the tree tops and easily gained on me since they had no obstacles.

I should have stayed high.

A section of thick canopy shaded the forest floor from sunlight and blocked the view from above. I leaned hard left and turned sharply. My bare shoulder scraped against the tree. Blood welled in the scrape but the wind quickly dried it. For several long seconds I didn't see or hear the shouts of the pursuers.

Climbing higher, I poked my head out of the treetops and saw them circling the area where I'd turned. My gambit had worked. I went back below and sped away, gaining as much distance as possible before they spotted me.

My phone vibrated in my pocket. I leaned back so I could slide it out. *Aethernet access* flashed on the screen. I flicked to the map and breathed with relief when I saw that I was nearly forty miles southwest of London. Not long after, I saw houses nestled among the trees, stone walls, and narrow roads.

I stopped at a small country house of gray stone. A clothesline provided me a damp shirt designed for a man many times my size, but it was better than flying around half naked with dried blood on my chest. I tucked it in and flew back into the trees, skirting civilization, but before long, I'd reached a point where flying my broom would expose me to noms—the normals.

Since I didn't wish to get in trouble with the Overworld authorities, I settled down next to a bubbling stream and waited for the afternoon to fade into dark. Leaning against a tree, I closed my eyes and tried to rest, but every crack of a twig, or the susurrus of wind in the leaves jolted me awake with a mild panic attack.

My kidnappers were out there somewhere, possibly still looking for me. I had to be careful. Ambria didn't have an arcphone, and Max's older brothers had recently broken his—their cruel idea of a joke. I rang his number just in case, but it went straight to voicemail. Galfandor didn't have a phone either since Arcane University frowned on such arcnology, as Seer Plinth called it.

That left me very much alone until I made it back to the secret entrance to Queens Gate in London—unless…I pondered the other contact on my phone. Esma Emoora had taken me aside and taught me magic outside of class. She'd helped me fight Naeve, the Glimmer Queen. Perhaps she could help me out of this tight spot.

I dialed the number. "Hello, Professor Emoora—"

"Conrad?" Her voice cracked with surprise.

"Yes, Professor." I swallowed nervously. "I need your help."

"Tell me what's the matter." She sounded in control again. Esma was quick to adjust to new situations. Then again, she was the Magical Defense teacher.

"I was kidnapped. I escaped, but I'm outside of London and waiting for dark to fall before I fly back." I checked the map. "I was held in a rather large castle in an estate southeast of the city, but they jammed my aethernet connection so I couldn't get a precise lock on the location."

"Conrad," Esma said in a disbelieving tone. "You tell me you were kidnapped, yet you sound as if you've just come from a leisurely stroll."

I hadn't really thought about it. I'd been frightened to death at first, but now that I'd escaped, I just wanted to go home. "I'm sorry. I could sound more frightened if that would help."

She laughed. "I suppose you've been through worse, child. Some pass through the crucible, forever scarred and burned to the core. Others are forged into new beings. Perhaps you are the latter."

"I just want to go home," I told her, allowing that scared part of me to peek through.

"I can be there well before dark," Esma said. "I'll leave right away and we can fly back together, okay?"

My insides melted with relief. "Oh, thank you, Esma—I mean Professor."

"Esma is fine when you're not in class, Conrad." She had a smile in her voice. "Being called Professor all the time makes me feel old." She laughed. "I'll see you soon."

I gave her my precise coordinates and put the phone back into my pocket. With Esma on the way, I felt safer already. I picked up a flat stone and skipped it across the water. It hit the muddy bank on the

27

other side after two skips. I amused myself this way for a while, then checked the time on the phone.

"Conrad Edison."

I leapt and spun, dropping my phone in the process.

Two men in tight black robes stood feet away, wands drawn and pointed at me.

"Who are you?" I said. "What do you want?"

The man on the right shook his head.

I slowly moved my hand toward my wand, but someone came up behind me and gripped my arm. He snatched Plinth's wand from my grasp and took the staff from my pocket. "None of that, now," he said.

How had they found me? I'd lost them miles ago.

Four more men whisked silently across the stream on brooms and dismounted. Instead of robes, one wore a black cloak over matching shirt and pants. He handed his broom to one of the others and stepped forward.

"You're a very resourceful boy, Conrad." His voice had no malice, despite the stern look creasing his brow. "Unfortunately, you must come back with us."

I backed up a step, fear sickening me. "No!"

"I cannot give you a choice in the matter, boy." He nodded at the two men aiming their wands at me and they moved toward me.

"What do you want from me?" I took another step back, my foot at the edge of the stream. "Just tell me!"

"It's very simple," he said. "We need your soul."

28

One of the men flicked his wand. A jet of green smoke flew at my face. I stumbled back into the stream and splashed into the shallow water. The moment I scrambled to my feet, the same man reached the bank and hit me full in the face with the spell. My limbs went weak and my eyelids grew heavy. I fell backward with a splash.

Water washed over my face and then I bobbed back to the surface, legs bent at an awkward angle, my back pressing uncomfortably against a stone in the cold water. The two men bent down to retrieve me. There was a shout. Something blurred past. The men cried out and splashed face-first into the water next to me.

Flashes of light and explosions rocked a tree. Dirt flew into the air and gravel splashed all around me. More shouts, and then men sped away on brooms. I could barely move a muscle, but I tried anyway. I slid off the stone propping up my back and water rushed over my face. I choked and sputtered, but I didn't have the strength to pull myself up. I was going to drown and there was nothing I could do about it.

A silhouette stood at the stream bank, features blurred by the water over my eyes. For what seemed an eternity, the person seemed to watch me, though I couldn't tell if they were looking at me or if they were more worried about another threat.

My lungs burned and my body begged for me to breathe. I couldn't hold my breath a moment longer. The figure reached down and pulled me from the water. I sucked in a lungful of air. Esma smiled, not a lock of her curly blond hair out of place after presumably beating back my attackers.

"There's not much on your bones but skin," she said, "but you're heavier than you look." She waved her wand over my chest then tapped it to my ribs. A flush of heat spread through me and suddenly my limbs were once again mine.

I climbed to my knees and saw the two men lying face down in the water. "Are they dead?" With much effort, I flipped them on their backs.

"Not quite drowned," Esma said matter-of-factly, "but nearly."

"We can't let them die." I wished I could be callous enough to leave them to their fates, but I had enough blood on my hands. "Is there something you can do to revive them?"

Esma raised an eyebrow. "Really? After they tried to kill you?"

They said they wanted my soul, but hadn't tried to kill me. I decided not to voice that argument and chose another. "I want to question them."

"Well, just one will suffice for that," she said. "Choose."

Esma was short and adorable for a grown woman, but her callous nature frightened me sometimes. "Please save them both," I said. "One might not be willing to answer."

She shrugged. "As you wish." With a flick of her wand, large hands of energy appeared and pounded their chests. Water spewed from their mouths. Esma flicked her wand again and again, the hand pressing rhythmically against their chests as she gently sang, "Staying alive, staying alive. Ah, ah, ah, ah, staying alive."

The men drew breath, gasping and floundering like fish on the shore and Esma smiled. "I believe we'll have answers soon."

"Over here!" someone shouted. "I swear I saw explosions from the creek!"

We looked downstream and saw a group of locals running our way.

"Oh, bother." Esma took the wands from the recovering men, then found their broomsticks nearby. She incinerated them with a quick spell. "Questioning will have to wait."

I grabbed my belongings and got on my broom. Esma spun her wand in a circle and the air around us blurred. "Are we invisible?" I asked.

She laughed. "No, merely cloaked. They will see a ripple in the air unless they get within a few feet." She pointed up. "Let us away, Conrad."

I followed her lead and we soared high into the overcast sky and the clouds.

When we reached cruising altitude, she folded her arms and looked at me expectantly. "I would love to hear the details of today's tribulations, child."

I reached across the gap between our brooms and touched her hand. "Thank you."

Her rosy cheeks went a bit pale. "Of course." She withdrew her hand and patted mine almost apologetically.

I told her the story from beginning to end, though I didn't mention the dossiers about me and my family. That information felt too personal to divulge to her. I did tell her about the Broken Relic in the hope that she knew more about Jura.

"Why would you be interested in the relics of Jura?" she said. "Did your kidnappers have any of them?"

I shrugged. "I don't think so, but they sound powerful."

"So I've heard." Esma pursed her lips. "It is said some of those relics could break the world."

"Vic and Della didn't say anything either."

She laughed. "Vic and Della?"

"That's what I call their soul fragments." I sighed. "I can't call them Mum and Dad, now can I?"

"What's it like sharing your mind with them?"

I considered it for a moment. "They don't speak often, and when they do, it's usually just to be mean."

"But you have gleaned valuable knowledge from them?" Esma watched me intently.

"My mother was an expert broom racer," I said. "I think I got that from her."

"And your father?"

I shrugged. "He's good with technology and demons, but I'm not really interested in either."

Esma flinched at the mention of demons and her eyes grew haunted. She seemed to withdraw into herself before breaking free with a shudder. "I suppose you enjoy broom racing?"

I felt a grin stretch my lips. "I love it." I thought back to what I'd read about Delectra and heavy sadness weighed down my heart. "I wish my mom was a good person. I think if she'd never met Victus she'd be really fun to know."

Esma stared at me with deeply troubled eyes. "You shouldn't think that way, boy. Delectra would kill you in an instant. She and Victus desperately want their soul fragments back. Without them, they are weakened."

I swallowed the lump in my throat. "I know, but it would be nice to have a family again."

"Again?" Her eyebrows arched.

"Cora was the closest thing I had to a mother."

Esma's jaw tightened. "You're only punishing yourself, Conrad." She pressed a hand to her chest. "Find your strength here and never submit to fantasy or whim. They will be your undoing."

We flew in silence for a while. I considered Esma's words, but also wondered what had happened to her to make her so skeptical. She was a lovely woman, full of smiles and vigor on the outside, but her warm friendly surface guarded a core of ice. *Esma just wants what's best for me.* She was my teacher and my friend.

Galfandor, on the other hand, had a lot to answer for. He'd never told me he was my mother's mentor, or about how he thought she could be saved. I didn't know if confronting him would be productive. What I needed was more answers about the Broken Relic. Galfandor might tell me, but he was just as likely to remain elusive with his answers.

I didn't understand why the man was so helpful at times, and so secretive at others.

"You're not thinking of looking for the Broken Relic, are you?" Esma's question caught me off guard.

I hadn't told her it could cure Delectra, but I had mentioned it in the hopes that she knew more about the relics of Jura. I fumbled the answer. "Uh, no, of course not."

She nodded. "Good."

It was dark when we landed in a London alley, protected by the cloak spell. Esma lifted it and we walked into the tunnel next to the Queensway Subway entrance. Esma activated the hidden levitator and we dropped with gut-wrenching speed into the parking deck far beneath the earth. We stepped into the massive cavern, the Queens Gate waystation. An Obsidian Arch towered over a nearby stable. Energy crackled through its thick columns and thundered into a portal leading to another part of the world.

Esma ignored it as if she'd seen it a thousand times and headed for the large double doors leading into the city of Queens Gate. I spared a few glances for the elephants emerging from the portal, ornate platforms on their backs bearing riders.

We skirted around a gold carriage with silver spoked wheels as it rolled unmanned into a parking space and stopped.

"Gaudy." Esma wrinkled her nose. "Such wealth, and people waste it on trivial things."

"What would you spend money on?" I asked.

She stopped, eyes distant, then shook her head. "There's no use indulging in fantasy, now is there?"

We went inside the doors and a wide green valley spread before us and into the distance. I drew in a deep breath and smiled.

I was finally home.

Chapter 5

Though I'd seen the sight a thousand times, it was still so odd to find an entire world seemingly buried a mile beneath the surface. What most people referred to as a pocket dimension was actually where Eden touched the broken realm holding all the realms together—the Glimmer.

My foster mother, Cora, had once been Naeve, the Glimmer Queen. The anchor stone had been torn from the foundation of their realm and formed into a moon that kept all the realms from drifting further apart. While it granted her people, the Lyrolai, immortality, it stripped them of emotion, of humanity.

She'd traveled to Eden seeking a cure, but found death instead. The demon magic binding my parents' souls to me was so malevolent, it had killed people around me, including her after she'd taken me in as a foster child.

Images flashed before my eyes, like flickering frames in an old movie.

Cora stands far above on a ship with wings. At my side are Delectra and Victus.

Mum hugs me and smiles. "Have fun, dear."

Victus pulls her away. "Wait here."

"But—"

He shakes his head and takes my hand. "Come Conrad."

Mum takes my favorite toy and I feel lighter, happier. The blurry gray world brightens.

Cora greets us with a smile. She is every bit as lovely as I remember. She kneels in front of me and gives me a hug. "Hello, Conrad."

My eyes burned with tears.

Esma rests a hand on my shoulder. "Are you okay?"

I nodded. "I just remembered something I'd forgotten."

"Was it unpleasant?"

I shook my head. "It was beautiful." I wiped my face. "I got two hugs in it."

Esma laughed. "You certainly have no need for riches if that's all it takes to make you happy."

We flew our brooms up the towering cliffs on the left of the green valley where the city of Queens Gate sat. The city appeared part Roman, other parts British countryside, the architecture a testament to the age of this place.

Arcane University sprawled atop the cliff, a splendid castle of towers, spires and a library with a great crystal dome. Closest to us were the uniquely structured keeps, Graeven, Moore, and Tiberius.

Graeven Keep was all squares and rectangles, from the main building to the towers at each corner. Tiberius Keep was a plain red-brick manor, though many also likened it to an asylum one might stumble upon in a horror film. Moore Keep stood out perhaps as an example of what not to do when designing a building. Turrets sprouted seemingly at random from the main building, making it nearly as confusing to navigate as the university itself.

In the center of the cobblestone roundabout was a clear pool. Coins and other objects twinkled at the bottom of the water where hopeful individuals had requested the services of the wishing pool. While the pool might not actually grant wishes, it had helped me rid this world of Cora's evil reflection, Naeve, banishing it back to the reflected world.

I rubbed the green pebble and wondered what I'd find if I used its powers to take me into the other world. Would the Glimmer Queen be waiting on me? I shuddered at the thought. She was Cora's clone in every way except her evil twisted heart.

"I would not tempt fate," Esma said. "A woman such as Naeve plots revenge and waits an eternity if she must."

"I know." We landed next to the wishing pool and got off our brooms. I hadn't planned on coming back to the keep since Ambria was probably at the house in Queens Gate, but Max might be here.

Esma looked at me as if considering something and spoke after a brief pause. "Shall I inform Galfandor about your little adventure?"

"I can do it," I said a bit too quickly. If Galfandor withheld secrets about my mother from me, why should I run and tell him everything?

She nodded. "Rest well, Conrad. I'll see you in class tomorrow."

I resisted the urge to hug her. She didn't seem to like being touched. "Thank you, Esma."

A brilliant smile flashed across her face. "You're most welcome." She boarded her broom and flew away.

I raced inside Moore Keep, up the stairs and into the common room between the boys' and girls' dormitories. I didn't see Max or

Ambria, but the students lounging in the room saw me and stared. No doubt the huge shirt and bloodstains on my pants were out of the ordinary.

I ignored them and ran up the stairs to the left and into the common room of the male dormitory.

Yan Yung barked a laugh. "Couldn't find a shirt that fits, Edison?"

Without reply, I continued through and went upstairs to the room I shared with Max. A groan escaped my throat. I only wanted to shower and rest, but if I didn't let Ambria and Max know I was okay, they'd be furious. It seemed I had no choice but to go back to town. School had just started and we were required to live in the keeps during the school week, but Ambria preferred staying in the house on Dowling and Bucket on the weekend.

A shower first. Then I'll go to town.

I gathered fresh clothes and soap for the washroom, but my phone rang before I left the room.

The phone displayed, *Private Caller*. Dread snaked around my heart. Did the kidnappers know my number? Had they somehow tracked my arcphone? It would explain how they'd found me when I thought I'd lost them.

"Phone, record this call," I told it.

"Recording started," it replied in a robotic monotone.

"Hello?"

"Gah! I got him, Ambria," Max said.

"Conrad, where are you?" Ambria said.

"Get out of my face, girl." There was the sound of scuffling and a clatter. "I hope you didn't break my mum's phone!"

"You are a rude, rude boy," Ambria shouted back. More scuffling and then Ambria spoke again, this time more clearly as the phone was closer to her. "Conrad, I've been worried sick about you."

I grinned. The dread melted away, leaving behind a warm, comfortable sensation. "I'm fine, but I didn't think I would be."

"Did you run off?" Max said. "Ambria says you vanished without a word."

"No." I set fresh clothes on the bed. "Look, can we meet for dinner in a few minutes? I need to shower."

"Of course," Ambria said. "I was going to cook shepherd's pie, but Sonia screamed at me."

Max laughed. "Because you're an awful cook and vampires have sensitive noses."

"Sonia is overly sensitive to everything," Ambria complained.

I squeezed my words between their arguments. "I'm going to shower. Meet you at the house soon."

"Okay, but—"

I disconnected before Max could finish his statement. Otherwise, I'd never get off the phone. After showering, I reveled in the blessed comfort of clean clothes and the joy of fresh socks against my feet. I retrieved my broom and looked out of the window and into the night sky. I wondered if Cora's spirit was out there watching me, or if when she'd died, all of her essence had transferred to Naeve.

What if even now, my beloved Cora was trapped in the shell of her reflection? What if her consciousness was subdued but alive? What if the Broken Relic could cure both of my mothers? Hope

39

swelled my heart until it felt ready to burst. I dared not believe it could be true. Better to expect the worst so I wouldn't be devastated by disappointment.

I flew the broom out of the window and across the university grounds to the cliff. A few minutes of reckless flying carried me to the house at the corner of Dowling and Bucket where I found Ambria and Max pacing in the front yard.

Ambria rushed over and hugged me. "Conrad, why did you leave me like that? One minute you were there, and the next you'd completely vanished!"

I tried to remember what had happened, but recalled nothing more than before. I let the hug linger. Ambria smelled so good, like flowers and fresh tea leaves. She was such a different person than the girl I rescued from Little Angel Orphanage. If I hadn't acted, she might have been sold into slavery or worse.

"Let's talk about it over food," Max said. "I'm—"

"Starving," Ambria and I said together. She and I burst into laughter.

I backed away reluctantly from Ambria, wishing I could enjoy the comfort of a hug a little longer. The memory of the hugs from Delectra and Cora teased me with a fleeting shadow of their warmth.

Max huffed. "Well, I'm a growing boy."

"Perhaps you could mix it up a little," Ambria said. "You could say famished or ravenous, for example."

"Why would I say that when I'm starving?" Max said. "Let's go eat." He patted me on the shoulder. "Glad to see you're okay. You had us worried."

"Agreed." Ambria squeezed my hand in both of hers. She sighed. "Well, let's go eat before Max collapses and dies."

Max led us to the Copper Goose restaurant, a name which literally described the aesthetics of the building, though it was much larger than the average goose. We entered the doors in the goose's breast. The host, a teenaged boy by the name of Rory Culpepper glowered at us. He'd put on some muscle over the summer and was no longer the tall lanky boy who'd threatened me in the dorm last year.

When he'd tried to disqualify me from trying out for Kabash, I'd turned the tables and he'd lost his chance instead. This time, I didn't have Stephan here to back me up if things became unpleasant.

"When did he start working here?" Ambria whispered.

"He started working in the kitchen during the summer," Max said. "I heard my brothers talking about it. I can't believe they let him serve as host though!"

Rory continued to stare as we walked up to the host station. He forced the words through clenched teeth. "Table for three?"

"Y-yes," Max said.

"Right this way." Rory bit off every word like a hunk of tough jerky. He seated us and left without another word.

Max put a hand to the side of his mouth and leaned toward me. "I guess he still doesn't like you."

"Duh," Ambria said. "It's his own fault for being a bully."

A nice waitress took our order and brought us tea. I saw the expectant looks on my friends' faces and began the tale of my adventure. It took longer than expected thanks to Max's constant interruptions, but then the food arrived and his mouth was too full to speak.

"I feel awful!" Ambria said. "You and I were talking and you fell a little behind me. When I looked back, you were gone!"

41

"You didn't see or hear anything?" I asked.

Her hand rested on mine. "No, Conrad." A tear formed at the corner of her eye. "What if you hadn't escaped? I'd have never known what happened."

Max said something but the food in his mouth muffled his words.

"We flew all over town looking for you," Ambria continued. "We even went to the old mansion behind the Fairy Gardens."

"Your favorite hiding spot," Max managed to say before stuffing a biscuit into his mouth.

"I only went there to spy on my parents when they were going into the Glimmer." With the defeat of Naeve, Victus and Delectra were supposedly blocked from that realm by Cora's daughter, Evadora.

"I'm rather curious about the Relics of Jura." Ambria leaned forward. "Who is Underborn and why does he have them?"

Max swallowed hard. "Underborn's the sort you don't want to mess with. He was the Overworld's most notorious assassin, and maybe he still is." He waved his hands imploringly. "Stay away from this one, Conrad."

"Underborn might know where I can find the Broken Relic." I certainly didn't expect the people who captured me to help. "If there's even the slightest possibility I could cure Delectra or revive Cora, I have to try."

Ambria folded her arms and gave Max a cross look. "I agree. It certainly can't be any riskier than waiting around for those goons to kidnap Conrad again."

Max dropped a biscuit dripping with gravy. It looked as if he'd suddenly lost his appetite. "You're both completely mental. What

42

makes you think Delectra wants saving? Besides, she's murdered so many people I don't see why you'd want to."

"Because it wasn't her," I shot back. "Victus did something horrible to her."

"He maimed her soul with demons," Ambria said.

"What makes you think the Broken Relic could revive Cora or turn Delectra's evil soul good?" Max shook his head sadly. "I think you're hoping for way too much."

His words struck me, a dagger in the heart. He might be right. My mothers might be beyond salvation. Seeking a secretive assassin for answers about Jura sounded like a fool's errand. Though I felt terrible for what Victus had done to my biological mother, I had no love for her. Cora, on the other hand, was my heart. If there was even a sliver of a chance to help her, I would gladly risk death.

"Gah," Max threw down his napkin. "I can see by the look in your eyes that you've already made up your mind."

I nodded. "We need to find out all we can about Jura and Underborn."

"What about classes and schoolwork?" Max said. "And aren't you supposed to be on the Kabash team again?"

"I received the invitation," I told him.

"But did you accept?" Max's forehead pinched with worry.

"Oh, bother." Ambria sighed. "It's a stupid game, Max. I think Conrad has a lot more to worry about than bashing down towers with a disc."

"I haven't decided," I admitted. I felt torn. Kabash was fun— something I was good at. During a game was the only time when

43

people didn't look at me as the son of the evil Overlord, Victus Edison, unless, of course, they were rooting for the other team.

"It might just be a game," Max said, "But I think Delectra would be proud to know how good you are at it."

"Maxwell Tiberius!" Ambria slapped him on the arm. "How dare you play that card."

He threw up his arms to ward off her blows. "It's true!"

I wondered if Cora would be proud of me too.

After dinner, we flew back to the university. Max and I said our goodnights to Ambria and went into the male dormitory. As I lay down to sleep, I couldn't stop thinking about Cora's soul, possibly trapped in the body of the mad Glimmer Queen, Naeve. I didn't want to hope, but I couldn't help it. I might once again have a true mother who loved me.

Chapter 6

Cora stands at the helm of her massive ship. Unlike the other Mzodi ships, it is made of wood and vines. Unlike the Mzodi, she is not Seraphim. She is Lyrolai, the folk of the wood. Even though my younger self does not know this, my current self does.

Cora rests a hand on my shoulder. "Do you like the Evadora, Conrad?"

"It is the most beautiful thing I have ever seen," I tell her. It's no lie. My days are dulled to gray by whatever evil lurks inside my favorite toy. I did not suspect a thing all those years ago, but the older Conrad knows Victus is prepping this young body for something terrible.

Victus stands across the deck, deep in conversation with one of the Mzodi. Cora whisks me below decks to a secret room that contains a forest and night sky filled with stars. I stand in awe at the spectacle. My soul is slowly recovering from the effects of the evil toy. Something about this place lifts me from the depths and makes me feel alive.

"There is something about you, Conrad." Cora sits and a chair of vines forms beneath her. "You remind me of my daughter."

"But I'm a boy," my younger self says.

A tear forms in the corner of her eye. "You are a lost soul, child." She tells me of her daughter, Evadora and the sad tale of Cora's banishment from the Glimmer.

She dries her eyes and shakes her head. "I'm sorry to burden you with such things."

I take her hand. "I like hearing your stories."

Cora laughs and continues the tour of the ship. I have the best time of my life. When Victus finds us, a terrible weight settles back on my shoulders. My older self knows that the happiness is about to be taken away.

As we head down the gangway, I notice a man and woman step through a portal. The man is tall and muscular with thick dark hair. The woman is beautiful, long black hair falling over creamy skin.

Victus growls at my side as we walk down. "Can't wait until that arrogant Slade boy is trapped here forever," he mutters under his breath. He fakes a grin at the man and woman and leaves me with my Mum while he goes over to talk with them.

A genuine smile spreads across Delectra's face. She drops to a knee and hugs me. "Did you enjoy yourself, son?"

"Yes, Mum." I can barely contain my excitement. I want to tell her all about it. "It's a flying ship!"

Delectra and I walk, hand-in-hand toward Victus and the others. "He had a wonderful time, Victus. Can he do it again soon?"

Victus wears a strained smile on his face. "I don't know, dear. Why don't you give him his toy and we'll be going?"

"But I thought—" A single hard look from Victus stops Delectra from uttering another word.

She reaches into her purse and hands me a spiky blue toy. The bright colors of the world begin to fade and something dark wraps around my soul.

We step through the portal and arrive back in another place. The dulling mind of my younger self tries to remember the name. My older self knows we have arrived back in Eden.

"Serena is ready," Victus says as we walk through a room filled with black arches of all shapes and sizes. "She failed to find the Eye of Jura, but I think the Hand will suffice." He takes out a small doll that looks eerily like my mother and runs his hand over the eyes.

Something cold and reptilian sweeps over her features. Her eyes go black as pitch. She releases my hand abruptly and a sneer twists her lovely face. "Serena is a fool. We should have never let her search for the eye alone."

"The hand is enough." Victus puts the doll away and stares at Delectra. "You become too sentimental when I let the boy off his leash. Remember, he is a tool, our insurance policy if things go awry."

"Of course I remember," Delectra says haughtily. "It is your fault you didn't extinguish the soft parts of me. There is still a part of the weak, pathetic girl I once was hiding inside me."

"It will die soon enough," Victus says. "Once we control the Overworld, there will be no room for weakness."

I try to listen to more of their conversation, but the words grow muffled and the color fades until all is black and white. My younger self is once again shrouded in a poison cloud of demon magic.

Eyes crusted with sleep, I wakened to a blurry world. The imagery of my dream remained sharp in my mind. The dreams of Cora and a ship were too vivid to be mere products of my imagination. It meant I'd actually met her long before she became my foster mother. It meant I'd overheard Victus plotting to trap Justin Slade and his army in Seraphina.

I jerked upright. "He used a relic of Jura!"

Max leapt out of bed at my outburst, his wand at the ready, though he staggered, still drunk with sleep. "Who is it?" He stumbled against the wall. "Are we under attack?"

I laughed. "No, I was having a dream." The sun peeked through the window and my phone informed me it was time to get up anyway. Excitement heated my blood. "You won't believe what I dreamed about."

Max flopped back in bed, his wand arm dangling over the side. "I can't believe you woke me up so early."

I shook him. "Get up, Max. I remembered something important in my dream."

He mumbled something and rolled out of bed. "I hope it's good. I was dreaming about pancakes."

As I showered, I thought about the doll Victus touched and how Delectra had gone from being happy to evil in an instant and complained about being weak. Did that mean there was still good in her? Victus seemed convinced he could kill the good in her. If that was true, it meant she might be beyond redemption. It meant even the Broken Relic might not be able to fix her.

I showered and dressed then went to the common room between the dorm towers where Ambria waited.

"Where's Max?" she asked.

"Slow as usual," I said.

He met us a few moments later and we set off to eat. The roar of conversation quieted noticeably when we entered the dining hall, and the weight of stares felt heavy on my shoulders. I stiffened my back and pretended not to notice. Some students looked curious while others outright glared at us—some more than others.

Then I saw the terrible trio. Harris Ashmore stood up, his long brown hair slanting sideways across his angry green eyes. He'd obviously spent a great deal of time styling it in dramatic fashion this morning. His friend Baxter Troy emulated him, his thick red hair a messy curtain against his pale freckled forehead. Lily Crown remained seated and smiled at us.

"I don't understand that girl," Max grumbled. "Wish she'd just be mean to us and get it over with."

"Conrad's parents killed Harris's parents, not hers," Ambria said. "Just because Lily is Harris's friend doesn't mean she has to hate us too."

I winced at the reminder.

We found an empty table and took a seat. Moments later, wooden golems dressed in servant livery delivered steaming plates with sausages and eggs.

Ambria took a sip of tea. "Conrad, did you have a chance to read those books you took from the kidnappers?"

I shook my head and swallowed food. "No, but I have something exciting to tell you."

"About your dreams?" Max quirked his lips.

"More like memories." I told them what I'd seen.

Ambria's eyes widened. "Your parents used a Relic of Jura to disable the Alabaster Arches?"

I nodded. "We have to find out what the Hand of Jura does."

"Is it literally a hand?" Max said. "Sounds disgusting."

I shrugged. "I guess so."

Ambria frowned. "Maybe we should talk with Galfandor."

"He never told me that he was Delectra's mentor." I felt angry at the old headmaster. "If he kept that from me, he might not tell us everything we need to know about Jura."

"We need to start somewhere," Ambria said. "I wouldn't even know where to start looking for these relics."

Max nodded. "The headmaster has been helpful before. It can't hurt to ask."

I didn't want to agree, but they were right. Galfandor might have good reasons for not telling me about mentoring Delectra. We finished eating and made our way through the maze of halls to a classroom for our first class, Intermediate Spellcasting. The dark hardwoods creaked under my shoes in the empty room.

"Are we the first ones here?" Ambria checked the time on her watch. "We're only ten minutes early."

"What's this?" Max pointed to a piece of parchment taped to the chalkboard in the front of the room. "It says, 'To find the class, perform this spell; if you don't, you'll surely fail.'"

I groaned. "Professor Grace doesn't believe in making things easy."

"What was that noise?" Ambria looked around.

Max shook his head. "I didn't hear anything."

"Sounded like a laugh." She shrugged. "Probably my imagination."

Holding out the parchment, Max flicked his wand through a pattern and said, "*Decreptis!*"

Ambria turned in a circle, looking around the room. "Well, that's a rather profound lack of results."

Max blew out a breath. "Can't expect me to get it perfect the first time." He tried it twice more and had no more success than the first time.

Ambria snatched it from him. "Let me try." She squinted at something. "There's a drawing of bookshelves at the bottom of the page. Why didn't you mention that before?"

"I thought it was just decorative," Max said in a defensive tone.

"Professor Grace doesn't believe in decoration." She pointed the wand at the bookshelves on the wood-paneled wall. "You're not very good at seeing clues, Max."

Max threw up his hands. "Then you do the bleeding spell!"

Ambria sniffed. "I will." She practiced the pattern a couple of times, said the magic word, and flicked the wand at the bookcase. The wooden shelves creaked, groaned, and promptly collapsed in a heap. Books scattered across the floor, pages spilling out from loose bindings.

We jumped back at the unexpected literary carnage. The parchment burst into flames. Ambria squeaked and tossed it away. It vanished in a puff of white smoke.

"What spell did you use?" Max said. "I was expecting some arrows to point the way, not collapsing bookshelves!"

"What is the meaning of this?" Gideon Grace stood just inside the classroom, his thin lips peeled back in a snarl. "Is this your idea of a joke, Edison?"

"Me?" I poked a finger against my chest. "There was a parchment with instructions on it."

"A parchment?" His sour voice rose an octave. "Where?"

Ambria swallowed hard. "Well, it sort of burned up after I cast the spell."

"A likely story," Grace growled.

Max smacked his forehead. "We've been tricked."

"Let's see how much you enjoy detention," Grace said.

Ambria's eyes flicked to a corner of the room and narrowed. Without a word, she picked up a leather bound book and threw it across the room. It thumped something before it hit the corner, eliciting a loud grunt. The air shimmered ever so slightly, but enough to tell me that something wasn't right about that dim corner of the room.

Grace's lips pressed tight as he stared at the corner. "Come out this instant."

Harris and Baxter appeared as if someone had dropped a curtain. Behind them stood Lily, a guilty look on her face.

"Was that a camouflage veil?" Grace said.

Lily nodded. "Yes, sir. I've been practicing all summer."

His lips tried to smile, but his face said no. A sneering grimace replaced his dour look for an instant. "Most impressive, Miss Crown."

She smiled sheepishly. "Thank you."

"What was the spell on the parchment?" he asked.

Harris and Baxter looked at Lily again.

She sighed. "*Decreptis*, sir. It weakens objects."

"That's a rather advanced spell." Grace tried to smile again. "You've obviously spent your summer productively."

Ambria flashed me an annoyed look. "Does that mean I also did well, Professor? After all, I was able to cast it."

Grace's nose wrinkled, lip curled into a sneer. "It was an act of stupidity, Miss Rax. You should never cast a spell if you don't know what it does."

Other students began filing into the classroom, curious eyes darting back and forth between us, the books, the professor, and Harris. It was obvious to anyone with half a brain that something bad had happened, if evidenced only by the pile of books on the floor.

Ambria's face burned bright red and her fists clenched by her sides. She seemed to barely restrain a retort, but it would be unwise to antagonize Grace. He'd proven on more than one occasion that he despised our families. Though Ambria had never known Cyphanis Rax, a man who'd usurped and abused power, sharing the same blood was enough for Grace to dislike her.

Max tried to make himself smaller, shoulders slumping, eyes on the floor. The attempt didn't work.

"I'll see the three of you for detention after school today," Grace said to us.

"What?" Ambria jabbed a finger at Lily. "She tricked us! We thought it was a test."

"A test you failed," Grace said. "No one made you destroy the bookshelf. You and your *friends* will clean up this mess and construct a new one."

My face heated and my hands tightened into fists. I felt something in my hand and looked down to see my wand. *How did it get there?* I didn't even remember pulling it from my pocket. I met Harris's delighted eyes. He looked at the wand, eyes eager for me to try something. After all, he was the child of destiny, the one who was supposed to destroy me.

I wanted nothing more than to punch him in the face. Once again, we were being unfairly targeted because of our rotten parents.

Chapter 7

Weak boy, Della said. *Do not fight when you can be clever instead.*

Clever? I didn't see how my brain could get me out of this one.

Other rules were broken, Della replied.

It was the most she'd said to me in a while. Helpful advice was not something Della offered. Then again, she probably hated Gideon Grace as much as he hated her. An image of parchment flashed through my mind. *A rulebook.* It was the rules and regulations of Arcane University that we'd had to read and sign before being admitted.

I closed my eyes and saw it with perfect clarity.

Spellcasting shall not be allowed on university ground without direct professorial approval and supervision.

Under no circumstances are students to teach other students advanced spells without professorial supervision.

I might have been viewing a photograph. The list of rules was so long and complex, I doubted anyone could remember them all, much less see an image of the pages in their minds. Since I didn't have photographic memory, I wondered if Della was showing this to me.

I swallowed the anger and forced a smile. "Professor Grace, perhaps I could refer you to paragraph twelve, subsection three of the university rules on spellcasting without supervision."

Grace's brow pinched with confusion. "What are you getting at, Edison?"

I quoted the paragraphs. "As you can see, Lily and her friends cast their veil spell without approval or supervision, and then instructed us how to cast an advanced spell as well." I shrugged. "I believe the punishment for such offenses is detention or worse."

Harris's mouth dropped open.

"He's lying!" Baxter shouted. "There's no such thing."

Lily turned pale. If anyone in that group knew what rules existed, it would be her. She was obsessive about knowing everything. Then again, most girls claimed to know it all. Perhaps she was just smarter than others.

Max gripped my shoulder and whispered in my ear. "How'd you know that?"

I didn't answer. The other students seemed entranced with the unfolding drama. Some seemed to be placing bets on the outcome.

Liana Augustus leafed through one of the thick tomes that had fallen off the bookshelf. "Conrad is right, professor." She hefted the rulebook off the floor and put it on her desk. "Would you like me to look up punishments?" An innocent smile spread across her face.

My head flinched back with surprise. I barely knew Liana, having seen her in the common room at Moore Keep a few times, perhaps greeted her on my way out to Kabash practice. I certainly never would have expected her or anyone but my closest friends to back me up.

Grace clenched his teeth, eyes shooting daggers at me and Liana. "It appears Harris, Lily, and Baxter will be joining you for detention."

He spun toward a gaggle of girls rushing into the room and roared, "Get in your seats!"

The girls screeched and hurried to sit down, even though they were a minute early.

Graced raked his eyes over us and Harris's group. "I want the six of you to move those books out of the way this minute."

Moving the books proved considerably harder than it seemed. Many were damaged by the *Decreptis* spell and pages spilled from the covers unless we were careful to squeeze them tight while carrying them. Harris and Baxter scowled at us the entire time. Lily giggled nervously as if this were all some huge misunderstanding that would be cleared up shortly.

We still hadn't cleared the entire mess when Professor Grace ordered us to our desks and started the lesson. Coincidentally, the lesson was on advanced wand patterns and why they mattered. He demonstrated how precise movements earned more powerful iterations of the same spell even though his patterns looked equally precise each time. It was a relief when the gong chimed in the distance and class was over.

Professor Sideon was surprisingly on time for our next class, Intermediate Enchantments. He seemed particularly focused on a rugged leather-bound text on his desk and didn't look up once as students poured into the room. The minutes ticked past and it wasn't until Harris cleared his throat that Sideon looked up and blinked with confusion.

He sighed and muttered something as he stood. "What's the most powerful enchanted object?"

Lily's hand shot upward. "The Sword of Shanria!"

"Wrong," Sideon said. Rory Culpepper chuckled and drew the professor's attention. "Do you have an answer?"

Rory Culpepper snorted. "Everyone knows the Swords of Power are the most powerful."

"They don't even exist," Anna Greene said. "Besides, my father always said the Alchemist's Ring is the most powerful. It could turn people into stone or gold."

Sideon's eyes flashed. "Yes, now that was a powerful enchanted object. What else?"

"The Crown of Knowledge," Lily said, apparently willing to give it another go.

The professor nodded. "Knowledge is power, but there are other enchanted objects that offer more."

"An arcphone," Max said.

Sideon offered the barest of smiles and then he locked eyes with me. "What do you think, Edison?"

I felt intense discomfort looking into this man's gaze. His shaved head and lean narrow face reminded me of a weasel. I didn't want to answer him, but before I could control my nervous lips, I said, "The Broken Relic."

The murmur of conversations faded to a chorus of confused exclamations.

"The Broken Relic?" Lily said querulously. "I've never heard of it."

Baxter snorted. "Making things up again."

Sideon's tiny smile spread across his weasely face. "Edison is not making it up. The Broken Relic is very real, students." He leaned on his desk. "I'd be most curious to know where you heard of it."

My mind scrambled for an answer. "My great-grandfather was a relic hunter."

Yes, he was, Della said.

That's the truth?

She didn't answer. I could only surmise that she'd put the answer in my head.

"How interesting." Sideon drawled. "What other relics do you know of?"

"Uh, I don't remember." If I'd hoped Della would provide me with more answers, I was disappointed.

"What is the Broken Relic?" Lily asked.

"That is a very good question," Sideon said. "Some say the Broken Relic was once something whole that broke into many pieces, all of which are valued relics in and of themselves. Others say the name is metaphor and that broken may refer to an emotional state." He paced in front of the room, unusually animated for a man who typically sat behind the desk and made us read our textbooks without actually lecturing. "While there are many powerful relics, the most powerful and useful arguably originated with Jura, also known as Juranthemon."

"I've heard of that," Lily said. "Justin Slade used the Map and Key of Juranthemon to lead Templars out of Colombia so he could fight an army of vampires."

"Yes, yes!" Sideon said. "The map is capable of linking two doors anywhere in the world. When opened with the key, the door will lead to the linked destination."

"Why not just use portals?" Baxter said.

Sideon didn't seem to hear him. "We're going to try something new this year, class." He rubbed his hands together. "Instead of reading this useless textbook, we're going to seek out and find an ancient relic of power, be it from Jura or elsewhere."

A chorus of oohs and aahs rose from the students as the most boring class suddenly became the most interesting.

"That means we must comb texts and search for clues." Sideon sat on the edge of his desk. "Do any of you know relic hunters?"

Rory and Liana raised their hands.

"My father is in El Dorado looking for old Seraphim and Siren artifacts," Rory said. "He wants to find out how the Sirens built the arch systems so we can build more of our own."

Sideon pursed his lips. "Interesting. Has he ever sought any relics of Jura?"

Rory nodded. "Yeah, but he stopped after someone almost killed him."

"Do go on," Sideon said.

Rory bit his lower lip. "It all started about eight or nine years ago."

Clothes rustled and desks creaked as the other students leaned in to hear the story.

"Someone hired him to find the Hand of Jura," Rory said. "It was a woman, but he never found out who she was."

If I'd been a dog, my ears would have perked. Max and Ambria looked at me, both bitten by the same thought. *Serena hired him. Rory's father was working for Victus!*

Rory looked uneasily at his audience. "It took him months to track down the first solid lead. The whole time he was looking, other relic hunters would come by our house asking questions. My mom thought they were probably trying to find out where Dad went so they could get the relic first."

"Naturally," Sideon said. "Relic hunting is a dangerous trade. Need I remind you of those brave souls who died in places like Thunder Rock and El Dorado before the ghouls who haunted the ruins were driven from them?"

"Justin Slade did that," Lily said in a matter-of-fact voice. "They were husked angels and he revived them."

Sideon dismissed her comment with a backhanded wave. "Yes, yes, child." He nodded at Rory. "Please continue."

"Um..." Rory looked up as if recalling from memory. "Dad found the Hand of Jura in the lost city of Sukhothai. Before he could leave Thailand, he was ambushed, beaten, and left for dead. He survived and made it home then swore he'd never search for another Relic of Jura ever."

"What does the hand do?" Ambria asked.

"The hand can untie or unbind magical energies," Sideon said. "It is particularly useful if you wish to defuse hidden wards or enchantments."

"Is it a right or left hand?" I asked.

He raised an eyebrow. "Rumor has it that it seems to be both a right and left hand at the same time."

"Impossible," Ambria said. "How can it be both?"

Sideon ran a hand across his shaved pate. "A better question would be *why* does it unbind magical properties? How was it enchanted in the first place?"

"How can you affect magical energies if you can't see them?" Lily asked.

"Just because aether is invisible to the naked eye doesn't mean there aren't ways to see it." Sideon turned to Liana. "Who in your family is the relic hunter?"

"My big sister, Gwyneth." The girl flashed a smile. "She majored in Enchantments and minored in Treasure Hunting. She did so well in her first few hunts, the Reliquisti Order invited her to join them last year."

"Impressive," Sideon said. "The Reliquisti are highly selective. Perhaps she would like to come here and share a story with us."

"I think she'd love to!" Liana said. "When would you like her to come?"

"Why, as soon as possible," Sideon said. "Perhaps she can help us decide what the object of our first relic hunt should be." His face looked more than ever like a weasel as a grin stretched from ear to ear.

Max cupped a hand to his mouth and whispered, "Sounds like old Sideon is doing his best to get out of teaching again."

"I don't know." Ambria frowned and watched the professor speak with Liana. "He seems awfully excited."

He's not the only one. Sideon's sudden interest in relics was fortuitous for me. I barely knew where to start on my quest for the Broken Relic, but Liana's sister might be able to help. I certainly couldn't go to Rory's father, and I doubted my great-grandfather, the relic hunter, was still alive.

Vic and Della remained silent on the matter.

After class, I lingered outside the room. Max and Ambria were so busy arguing about relics that they didn't realize I wasn't behind them.

Conrad Edison and the Broken Relic

I knelt in the hallway, pretending to tie my shoe in the hopes Liana would pass me and I could talk with her. I heard a giggle and looked behind me. Liana stood just outside the doorway, an amused grin on her face.

"Having trouble, Conrad?" She stepped to my side. "You've been working on that shoelace for nearly a minute."

I stood and tried to speak, but the smile in her blue-gray eyes disarmed me. My lips parted, but whatever I'd been prepared to say evaporated from my mind like morning mist caught in the rays of the sun. I found myself admiring the dimples in her cheeks instead of uttering anything worthwhile.

"Conrad?" Her smiled faded. "Are you okay?"

Della expressed her displeasure with my state. *Gird yourself, boy! Don't let feminine wiles distract you.*

I took a deep breath and cleared my throat. "Um, hello, Liana."

She sighed in relief. "You're not brain dead after all."

"No, not yet." I managed a smile. "It seems we both have relic hunters in the family."

"Yes, your great-grandfather, was it?" She started walking but motioned me to come, so I paced alongside her.

"Yes," I replied.

"Is he still alive?" she asked.

I shrugged. "I don't know."

Her dark eyebrow arched. "You haven't kept in touch with him?"

The questions were venturing into rocky territory for me, but since she had to know the truth about my parents, I didn't see any point in lying. "I never knew him. I only heard about him from my mother."

"Ah." She touched my hand. Her skin felt soft and smooth and instantly made me forget how to walk.

I stumbled and nearly dropped my satchel. I looked back at the floor as if something there had tripped me. Liana giggled again.

So far this meeting wasn't going anything like I'd expected. I'd faced my murderous parents and fought the Glimmer Queen, but nothing was quite as unsettling as a pretty girl. I steeled myself and skipped to the real question I'd intended to ask her. "My great-grandfather was searching for the Broken Relic." I didn't know if that was true, but it segued nicely into my request. "Does your sister know much about it?"

Liana's eyes lit. "She might. Would you like to meet her?"

I nodded. "Yes, very much."

"She'll be in town this Thursday. Perhaps you could join us for dinner at the Copper Goose."

"Sounds delightful." I nearly walked into the doorframe outside Magical Defense class because I couldn't stop looking at her eyes.

Liana stopped just inside the room and leaned toward me. "I think Harris is wrong to judge you by your parents." She frowned. "The trick they played on you this morning was just mean."

I couldn't stop a grin from stretching my face. "Thank you." A voice somewhere in the back of my head whispered a warning. *Remember Blue. She was nice, and then she betrayed you.* I involuntarily stiffened at the memory. Harris and I had once been, if not friends, at least on good terms. That was before he'd discovered my true last name, thank to Blue.

Liana sensed my sudden discomfort. "Did I say something wrong?" Her dimples vanished and her forehead wrinkled.

"No." I forced a smile. "I just wish Harris didn't hate me."

She nodded. "There's too much hate in the world already." Liana walked across the room and took a seat next to two other girls who looked back and forth between me and her, eyes alight with the possibility of scandalous gossip.

Ambria did some looking of her own, a deep frown indicating her misgivings. "Did you stay behind to talk to Liana?"

"Obviously." I tried to act as if it was no big deal. "I asked if her sister could give us some advice."

"I wouldn't trust anyone in the Augustus family farther than I could throw a mule," Max said.

I dropped into my seat, heart heavy with his words. "Why would you say that after she helped us with Gideon Grace?"

"Her parents were big admirers of the Overlord—your father." Max scowled. "That makes them about as trustworthy as my parents."

"You should listen to Max," Ambria said. "Remember what happened with Blue."

Her echo of my own misgivings nearly made me change my mind about Liana. But what if the Broken Relic could save Cora and Delectra? I would do anything if it meant having Cora back. If Liana couldn't be trusted, then I'd have to be extra careful.

I had to be ready for anything.

Chapter 8

An explosion rocked the classroom. Students screamed and ducked under desks for cover. I reflexively flicked my wand and a shield formed over me and my friends.

Max stared at me with astonishment. "How—how did you do that without saying the words?"

"The words?" The floor quaked and dust drifted from overhead, running down the sides of the translucent shield. Everything had happened so fast, I couldn't remember if I'd said anything. "I thought I said them."

Ambria hunched next to me. "You didn't."

Light flashed, and we braced for another explosion. Instead, the dust and debris vanished and the classroom was once again in pristine shape.

Esma Emoora stood in the doorway, tutting disapproval and making marks on a piece of parchment. "This is not the performance I'd expect from intermediate students."

I looked around the room and saw Lily cowering beneath a small shield. Harris locked eyes with me from behind a shimmering barrier of his own and smirked.

"If I call your name, you had better be fast," Esma said. "I promise the consequences will not be pleasant."

One of Liana's friends looked at the professor with huge frightened eyes. "Fast at what?"

An evil smile spread across Esma's face. "Jessica Hale." Her wand flicked out and a bolt of red energy zapped out.

The spell hit Jessica in the shoulder. Shrieking, she stumbled backwards and fell on her backside.

Esma didn't stop, calling out Liana next. Liana held her wand defensively, like a sword parrying a blow and shouted, "*Parrano!*" The spell ricocheted and sparked off the wall.

"Excellent," Esma said. She spun. "Maximus Tiberius!"

Max spun his wand and cried out, "*Soros!*" The red energy shattered the shield like thin glass, but thankfully none of it reached him.

Esma continued randomly calling names. Ambria passed. Lily, Harris, and I had little problem countering the spell. Four more students felt the stinging pain of Esma's magic—a pain I was all too familiar with since she'd taught me how to shield myself by attacking me. She even called out Jessica once more. This time the poor girl managed to parry the spell.

The professor hung the parchment on the wall in the front of the classroom with the names those students who'd failed her impromptu test. "If you see your name up here, you will report to me after school for remedial training." She regarded us with a cool expression. "I will not tolerate lackluster performance in my class. If you fail two more pop quizzes, you will be demoted back to the Elementary Magical Defense class."

Students shared uneasy looks with each other. Max blew out a long sigh of relief. "Man, I'm glad I practiced."

After class, Esma motioned me to her desk. Ambria and Max watched with concern, but I motioned them to go ahead to lunch without me. Liana lingered at the back of the room with Jessica, a curious look on her face, then followed her friend out of the door.

"I was impressed with your shield, Conrad." Esma tucked away her wand, much to my relief, since she enjoyed surprising me with random attacks to keep me on my toes. "Who taught you to cast without words?" There was an edge to her voice—something resembling jealousy.

"No one," I hurriedly assured her. "It just happened."

A smile broke the ice. "Yes, I see you're learning to think magic and not just translate it."

"Translate?" I scratched my head. "I don't understand."

"Word is merely form, Conrad." She took out her wand. Her smile broadened when I tensed in preparation. Instead of zapping me, she rotated her wand in a pattern. Her voice dripping with sarcasm, she said, "Here at this *vaunted* university you are taught that spells are made from wand patterns and words."

I resisted interrupting and let her continue.

Esma planted her small fists on the desk, and leaned toward me. "The very fact that you could cast a complicated shield spell without uttering a single word makes me believe that you could be ready for something far more advanced."

I could barely contain the elation ignited by her kind words. Of all the teachers, Esma had been the only one to take extra time out of her schedule, to help me hone my skills. She cared even more than Galfandor. If I were to defeat my parents, I needed advanced training.

"Yes," I said, "I'm ready."

"I thought so." She put her wand back in its holster. "After school today, I'd like to introduce you to someone."

I grimaced. "I have detention with Professor Grace."

Her lips peeled back into an adorable snarl. With her bouncy blond curls and petite figure, Esma Emoora looked anything but threatening. Having witnessed the way she'd dispatched my abductors and nearly killed them, I knew better than to be deceived by her outward appearance. "Gideon Grace is a disgraceful grump who isn't fit to teach."

I completely agreed with her, but kept my opinions to myself. It was one thing for a professor to say such things, but completely another for a student. "Perhaps tomorrow?"

She shook her head. "I'll speak with Grace. Perhaps he'll let you serve your detention with me." Esma's eyebrows rose as she turned her gaze on me. "What, exactly did he deem deserving of detention?"

I told her about the trick played on us. She didn't seem amused.

"How delightful—the good Professor Grace laid bare his favoritism for the golden boy, Harris Ashmore." Esma backhanded the air. "I will speak with him. Meet me in my office after school."

"What if he doesn't agree?" I said.

"He will." Esma clasped her hands together. "I will see you later."

"Thank you, Prof—Esma." I picked up my book bag and hurried to the dining hall where I met my friends and told them about the meeting with Esma.

"I wonder what she has in store for you," Ambria mused.

Max cast a frightened look at me. "Better be ready to defend yourself. It might be one of her pop quizzes."

I laughed though deep down I knew he might be right. After lunch, we went to our next class, Arcane History.

I expected to see the squat figure of Eleanor Beetle waiting inside. Instead, a beautiful woman with lustrous black hair and creamy fair skin watched me enter. Asha Fellini's red lips smiled at me, and dread turned my knees into water. Though the woman had never raised a hand against me, she so closely resembled Delectra that I couldn't help but fear her.

"Good day, children." Her dulcet voice bore the hints of an exotic accent that hearkened to some faraway land.

"Where's Professor Beetle?" Ambria asked.

"I was told she's not feeling well," Asha replied.

Liana came in behind us. "Professor Fellini, I thought you taught prophecy, not history."

"One cannot see the future without the past." Asha smiled. "Take your seats, please."

I chose a desk near the back, to be as far from those unsettling features as possible. Asha bore far too close a resemblance to Delectra for my comfort. I dared a glance toward the front and met the professor's eyes. I looked away first.

Where Eleanor Beetle preferred to read straight from the history text, Asha Fellini told riveting tales that held me and the other students in thrall. Using her wand, she conjured illusions of Moses, the first Arcane, and told us how he was involuntarily drafted into the first war against the Seraphim.

A chorus of groans sounded when the class ended on a cliff hanger.

"Why did Daelissa kill Thesha?" Max said. "Can't you tell us a little more?"

70

Asha smiled with great satisfaction. "I'm afraid you'll have to show up for class if you want answers, Max."

Ambria couldn't stop speculating about what might happen next on our way to Rhona McTrask's potions class. "Do you think Kenshu will live? He was so close to the blast zone, I don't see how it's possible."

"I'm positive he's alive," Max said. "He's my favorite character."

I chuckled. "It's history, not fiction. They're people, not characters."

"Oh, you're no fun." Ambria slapped me lightly on the shoulder. "I don't know why you're still afraid of Asha. She's a wonderful professor."

A shiver ran down my spine. "I know, but she looks so much like Delectra."

"Did your mother have sisters?" Max asked.

I shrugged. "I hardly know anything about my family."

"We know your great-grandfather was a relic hunter." Ambria squeezed my arm and let go. "At least that's something."

It was something, but not nearly enough. I wondered if the books I'd taken had any information on my family tree. Reading them would have to wait until after my meeting with Esma.

Headmaster Galfandor stepped around the corner ahead of us, his tall frame looming over the children. His beard looked several inches shorter than the last time I'd seen him, and he seemed to have fewer wrinkles in his face. He smiled at us, bright blue eyes twinkling. "Hello, children."

"Hello, Headmaster," Max said in his most respectful voice. "How are you today?"

"Quite well, young Tiberius." He removed a pair of spectacles and polished the lens on his long gray robe, but his eyes remained on me. "Conrad, I require a moment of your time."

"Yes, what is it?" I couldn't hide the annoyance in my voice. I knew I shouldn't show disrespect to the headmaster, but why had he kept his mentorship of Delectra a secret from me? What else was he hiding?

Galfandor raised a bushy eyebrow. "Is something the matter?"

Max and Ambria stood where they were, eyes wide at my disrespectful tone.

I allowed myself a moment to cool off. "No, sir. I just don't want to be late for Professor McTrask's class."

"Ah, yes." He chuckled. "She doesn't abide tardiness." Galfandor perched the spectacles back on his long crooked nose. "Perhaps we can speak later."

His abrupt dismissal caught me off guard. "What was it you wanted to talk about?"

Galfandor stopped in mid-stride. "It's likely nothing, young man, but there are troubling rumors that there are people in town who have been asking a lot of questions about you."

My heart skipped a beat. "When?"

"The past few weeks." He stroked his beard. "I only found out about it while dining at the Dancing Pig a few evenings ago."

"Where is that?" Max asked. "I've never heard of it."

"Jack Lamont, the owner of the Laughing Dog in the Grotto, just opened a new public house here." Galfandor turned back to me. "I asked Shushiel to take you a note since you were staying in town, but she's been dealing with family issues and couldn't break away."

Ambria shuddered. "What sort of family problems does a giant spider have?"

"More than you'd suspect," Galfandor replied. "I know you remain alert for danger, Conrad. After all, few students have parents who wish them dead. Until I discover more about these people, you should not go anywhere alone."

Max snorted. "Too late for that."

I gave him a sharp look, but Galfandor's eyes narrowed. "I take it you've encountered them?"

"Oh, just tell him, Conrad." Ambria huffed in exasperation. "Someone kidnapped him, Galfandor. They locked him in a dungeon and he barely escaped with his life."

The headmaster's lips and eyes tightened. "Is this true, Conrad?"

"Yes, it's true." The tension in my chest deflated. "I really don't have time to talk about it now. We're already going to be late to potions class."

"I'll walk with you and explain your tardiness to Professor McTrask." Galfandor turned and led us down the hall. "Tell me what happened."

I told him what I'd told Esma, leaving out the parts about the dossiers. His relationship with my mother was a subject for another time.

"The people who took you are called the Seers," Galfandor said. "What I find most troubling about this incident is that they rarely, if ever, interfere with what they perceive as the natural progression of events."

"Is there something we can do?" Max said. "Arrest them?"

"I can speak with the Templars," Galfandor said. He looked down at me. "Was the blood on your shirt in a pattern?"

"No." I didn't even have to think about it. "It looked as if they poured it on me."

"A ritual of some kind." Galfandor tapped a finger on his chin. "What I wouldn't give to have that shirt for examination."

McTrask's Irish lilt drifted out of the doorway ahead. Galfandor seemed to steel himself before stepping inside. "Good day, Professor."

"Can't you see I'm in the middle of class, Galfandor?" McTrask said.

The headmaster cleared his throat. "I'm afraid I inadvertently delayed three of your students, Professor."

Her sharp eyes settled on us as we stepped through the door. "I don't appreciate this interruption one little bit. Perhaps the next time you have cause to delay my students, you'll do me the favor of advance notice!"

"Yes, yes, of course." Galfandor bowed slightly and backed out of the door. "Carry on." Before she could respond, he vanished around the corner.

Max snorted, drawing a glare from McTrask.

"I won't repeat what I've already said, so you'll just have to catch up on your own," the professor said. "Now find a table!"

Ambria and Max took one empty lab table. Since each table was designed for only two people, I had to look around for one with an opening. Liana waved me over to her table. I crossed two rows and joined her while McTrask droned on about the day's assignment.

"There are no shortage of spills and messes that must be cleaned while learning potion making," McTrask said. "Ordinary soap won't do the trick, so you must create a magical cleaner using the ingredients written on the board." She turned an hourglass on its other end. "Begin now."

I noticed Jessica and Liana's other female friend, Gertrude, partnered at the table behind us. "Did your friends leave you?"

Liana shook her head. "I wanted you to be my lab partner."

Any other time I might have been flattered. Considering what Max had told me about her family, I felt suspicious instead. "Why is that?"

"You're an interesting person, Conrad." Liana pointed to a black cast iron pot. "Can you start some water boiling?"

I hefted the heavy pot and took it to the water pump on the other side of the room to wait my turn. I filled it and placed it over the magical heat rocks Liana had already warmed with her wand. An uneasy silence took over as we waited for the water to boil. I didn't know what to say, and Liana seemed content with crushing ingredients with a pestle and mortar.

"Can you hand me the toasted slugs?" she said.

I opened a drawer. "How many?"

"Four."

I removed the crispy slugs and handed them to her. She dropped them in the water and stirred. Liana continued mixing ingredients, pausing only to consult her notes. She seemed sure of herself and there was an easy way about her that I admired. When we poured the mixture into the strainer, a thick milky liquid dripped from the other side.

Before long, our glassware was filled with magical soap.

Liana bit her lower lip and smiled. "Want to test it?"

Professor McTrask had stained a cloth with potions and cut it into pieces. I took a strip and rubbed the slick soap on it. Liana dipped it into water and the stain lifted and peeled away like a sticker.

"We did it!" Liana held up her hand and I high-fived it.

I didn't want to like her or trust her, but the look of delight in her eyes lightened my heart. I felt the soft skin of her hand close around mine for all too brief a moment, and then she let go. The rest of the room fell out of focus and all I could think about was touching her hand one more time.

Chapter 9

A surprised shout from Max told me he and Ambria weren't doing quite as well. In fact, the situation quickly went from bad to worse. Black liquid bubbled and frothed in their pot. Max tried to turn off the heating stones, but the potion boiled over, spilling down the table and onto the floor.

It spread quickly, raising cries of alarm and sending students scattering in all directions to avoid the dark tide. Rory didn't move fast enough. The moment the inky potion touched his shoes, he fell and slid across the floor as if it was made of ice.

Professor McTrask glared across the room. "What's the meaning of this, Tiberius?"

"I don't know!" Max shouted as he ran from the spreading slick.

Students climbed atop their chairs and tables to escape. Others joined Rory on their backsides, sliding across the floor and desperately grabbing for something to anchor them. Anything coated by the potion was too slippery to hold onto.

I grabbed our potion and poured it on the oily slick. The magical soap cut through the grime, dissolving it into a dark puddle. Others who'd successfully made the cleansing potion followed our lead and soon the floor was covered in foul-smelling water.

Professor McTrask twirled her wand and a small funnel of air formed. It whirled across the liquid like a mini-tornado, sucking it up and pouring it into a large kettle at the front of the room. When it was done, the floor practically sparkled.

"I don't know what I did," Max groaned.

"You added peppered snails instead of toasted slugs." Ambria hid her face behind her hands. "Our grade is ruined!"

Rory squeezed water from his shirt and walked over to Max. My friend backed up a step, wary of the larger boy. I stepped between them, ready to help if Rory wanted a fight. Instead, he looked at the oily substance on the lab table. "The only thing you did differently was add peppered snails instead of toasted slugs?"

Max's forehead wrinkled. "Uh, yeah. The second I added the crushed ingredients, it boiled over."

Rory nodded and went back to his lab table where he scratched out something in his notes and wrote something else down.

"An interesting concoction," McTrask said. "While you and your partner receive a failing grade for the day, you can take some comfort knowing that you just discovered an unknown substance, Tiberius."

"Unknown?" he said. "B-but it was just one ingredient."

"A failing grade?" Ambria's lips trembled. "Oh, Max, how could you?"

The professor handed Max a piece of parchment with a wax seal on it. "This is your certification of authenticity. Take it to the Department of Magical Verification and have them make sure this potion recipe has never been filed."

Max's mouth dropped open. "You mean, I invented something?"

"Perhaps," she said. "I suggest you have it verified first."

"Yes, Professor." He tucked it into the folds of his potions book, a stunned look on his face.

Liana clapped her hands. "How exciting!"

I didn't know if I felt more excited for Max or sad for Ambria. Then again, a bad grade for one assignment wouldn't cause her to fail the class.

When class ended, Max could hardly wait to go to the verification office. "I'm going to run it by before I report to detention," he said, and raced away.

I patted Ambria on the back. "I'm sure everything will be fine."

"He can be such a moron, Conrad." Ambria's shoulders slumped. "Liana, would you like to swap Conrad for Max?"

Liana laughed. "Maybe you should keep a closer eye on your lab partner."

We gathered our belongings and went into the hallway. "I have to report to Professor Emoora," I told Ambria.

"Lucky you." She shivered. "I wish I could go with you instead of reporting to Professor Grace." Her eyes narrowed with suspicion when she looked at Liana, and I could tell she wanted to warn me away. Her lips pressed together in an obvious effort to keep her mouth shut.

I waved. "See you later."

"Bye." Ambria slowly turned and walked away.

"Why do you have to report to Professor Emoora?" Liana asked, pacing me down the hallway.

I almost told her about the private tutoring, but switched to a half-truth. "She didn't tell me exactly. Some sort of alternate detention."

"Interesting." Liana tapped a finger on her lower lip, eyes lost in thought.

I stopped outside Esma's office. "Why are you so interested?"

She seemed caught off guard, and stammered out a reply. "There's something different about you."

"I'm the son of two murderers," I said more harshly than intended. "My parents were evil, and half the school hates me. Why do you want me around you?"

Her eyes grew very large, shimmering pools of innocence. "I don't hate you, Conrad. I think you're very interesting."

Don't be a fool and make her angry, Della said. *If you want help finding the relic, remain on good terms with her.*

Why do you care? I asked.

Relics of Jura are powerful, Vic replied.

I should have known they'd only care about power. They were right, though. If I wanted a chance at finding the Broken Relic, I needed Liana so I could meet her sister. I adjusted my attitude with a fake smile and a nod, as if accepting her reply at face value. "Thanks." I waved goodbye and left her there. Maybe Max was right and Liana was just playing games with me. Maybe she couldn't be trusted. Even if that was true, why did I feel so dirty for going along with it?

I had to protect myself. The only people I trusted not to betray me were Ambria and Max. Esma looked up from her desk when I entered and smiled. It occurred to me that I trusted her nearly as much as my best friends. She was a hard teacher, but that was only because she wanted us to learn.

"Was that your girlfriend, Conrad?" The professor looked delighted. "She's very pretty."

"Uh—" I tugged at the collar on my shirt. "She's just a friend."

Esma tried to sit on the corner of her desk, but her legs were too short to make the attempt look dignified. She scowled and leaned on the desk instead. "Has anyone spoken to you about girls?"

My throat felt tight and my palms felt damp. "No. Is it really necessary?"

"It is," she said with absolute certainty. Esma crossed her arms. "First, you must never let a girl keep you from your dreams. They will try to lure you, and make you their little manservant." She waggled a finger. "Girls possess a particular magic boys find very hard to resist."

I wanted to disagree, but thinking about the way Liana's simple touch made me feel, I found myself nodding in agreement. "She just touched me," I said. "All I wanted to do was touch her hand again."

"Precisely my point, Conrad." Esma squeezed my shoulder. "You are a genius with great potential—the sum of powerful parents. If you do not learn how to govern your feelings, you may be diverted from the path of greatness."

Her high praise made me feel uneasy. "Am I really a genius?"

"I have seen it in you before as I saw it today." Esma smiled at me tenderly. "If you ever need advice about girls, ask me. I was once a girl myself after all." Tears pooled in her eyes. She stiffened and wiped them.

I took her hand. "Are you okay, Esma?"

She slipped her hand away, a cool mask replacing the warm vulnerability. "Quite." She glanced at the time on an antique wall clock. "Let's go. We don't want to be late." She opened a broom closet and removed two high-performance brooms, one of which she handed to me.

I wanted to tell her that she didn't need to hide her feelings around me. I wanted to hug her and tell her that everything was okay and that I wouldn't judge her for whatever hid behind that mask of hers. But the moment was lost, so I followed Esma and kept quiet.

"Are we going into town?" I asked when we got outside.

Esma climbed on her broom and shook her head. "No, we're going across the valley."

I looked out over the valley toward the shining chrome buildings of Science Academy. "We're going over there?"

"Have you never been?" she asked.

I shook my head.

"Well then, you're in for a treat." Esma watched as I hopped on my broom. "Have you been practicing your flying?"

"Every day." It was one of my favorite pastimes.

"Excellent, then you should have no trouble beating me in a race." She leaned forward. "Ready, set, go!"

She streaked forward and I jetted in pursuit. Delectra had once been a broom racer and her soul fragment had imparted skills and knowledge that might have taken me years to master otherwise. I hugged the broomstick to lower wind resistance and positioned myself directly behind Esma and into her slipstream.

I shot forward and was about to slingshot around her, when she waggled the broom, disrupting the suction and causing me to lose ground. It was a maneuver few fliers knew, and even fewer could master. Then again, Esma had played Kabash and raced brooms as well. She looked over her shoulder, a smug look on her face.

Conrad Edison and the Broken Relic

The waggle maneuver might have cost me the slipstream and an easy way to pass her, but it also cost her some speed. I angled my pitch to match hers, rotating my broom back and forth each time she waggled, making it impossible for her to keep me from her slipstream. Before she realized what I was doing, I catapulted around her.

Now I was in the lead.

I looked back and offered a smug grin of my own, but Esma wasn't done yet. She rolled into my slipstream and began to gain. I didn't bother waggling, instead, veering side-to-side and up and down so she had to fight to remain behind me.

We were nearly to the other cliff when Esma gave up trying to stay in my slipstream and simply streaked past me. She held up her hands in victory when she crossed the edge of the cliff and hovered in place to wait for me.

"How did you do that?" I asked. "Did you cheat? Is your broom faster?"

Esma shrugged. "Perhaps I'm simply better than you." She turned and flew across campus.

I had my doubts about her claim, but the Science Academy campus was more than enough to take my mind off the race. The largest building rose from the earth at an angle, its sides flowing in liquid curves to a slanted dome at its peak.

Stainless steel towers rose nearby, thick metal discs segmenting them every few feet with shiny spheres perched at the tops. Blue electricity arced between the towers, snaking up to the spheres where the energy dissipated into the heavens. Next to them stood a glass building with a narrow base and a spherical top, resembling a massive lightbulb. Behind them stood a third building shaped like a twisting ladder of DNA. They looked so familiar, I could almost—

I stand on a floating platform gazing out at the two buildings. "Our father was weak," I say grimly. "How could he let Lab Edison sink so low?" The sound of my voice is deep and familiar. I looked down at the hands of a man. At my side stands a thin man with black hair and a pointed beard. He looks similar to Victus, and yet is not him.

"He had no vision, unlike you, Victus." The other man claps me on the back. "After what Tesla did to him, I will do anything to destroy them."

I feel a grin stretch my face. "Then you're with me, Theodore?"

"I am, brother."

"You will not like this, but it is the only way to beat Tesla," I say.

Theodore sighs as if he knows what's coming. "Magic."

"Arcnology," I say. "Magic and technology are stronger together than apart."

I blinked and was surprised to be back in the present, my broom still gliding after Esma. I looked back at the buildings we'd passed. *Tesla and Edison Labs.* They were the Science Academy equivalent of keeps. The third building was Lab Curie, named for Marie Curie.

I trembled, my nerves still unsettled by the strange flashback.

Students riding moving sidewalks looked up at us, foreheads creased with confusion or mouths twisted into grimaces at the sight of flying brooms in this sanctum of science. Chrome-plated robots patrolled the grounds and more students perched on shiny rocket sticks flitted past, some of them slowing to watch us pass.

"Pay them no mind, Conrad." Esma made a shooing motion at two children who flew too close to us. "There is a mutual mistrust between those who respect only magic, and those who worship science."

The children zipped away when Esma drew her wand and aimed it at them threateningly, their eyes wide with fright. Esma laughed and tucked her wand back in her robes.

We continued on to the far back of campus where a plain rectangular building of gray stone sat apart from everything else. It stood out if only because it looked so mundane compared to everything else here.

"What is this place?" I asked.

"Something different." Esma glided to an easy landing and hopped off her broom.

I joined her on the ground and followed. A plain sign hanging above the door read, *Arcnology Lab*. The passage I'd read in Seer Plinth's essay flashed before my eyes. Was this a place that combined magic and technology? A breath caught in my throat as I wondered what marvels might wait inside.

The front doors slid open and we entered a wide atrium. Esma consulted a directory board on the wall and headed right. Pounding echoed from ahead. A metal door buckled and a spiked metal ball burst into the corridor. It rattled past us, swerving drunkenly around obstacles. Two students raced down the hall after it, one of them punching a red button on a remote control, all to no avail.

Esma continued on as if nothing had happened. She took a left into a corridor and stopped outside an office door which she rapped on once with her knuckles and then opened. A man with his shirt hanging open was enthusiastically kissing a woman perched on the edge of his desk. My face burned with embarrassment.

The woman broke her lips free and shrieked when she saw us. The man groaned. "Don't you know how to knock?"

"I did knock." Esma raised an eyebrow at the woman. "Don't you have something better to do than sit around gawking?"

The woman hastily buttoned her lab coat, face red, eyes averted to the floor. She rushed out of the door without a word.

"Call me," the man called after her. He set his arms akimbo. "So, my dear—ah, Esma. How may I help you?" Sarcasm dripped from his words, and though he looked younger than the professor, he spoke to her without a hint of respect. "Why have you brought this boy with you?"

"This is not just some boy," Esma said coldly. "This is Conrad Edison."

The man's eyes locked onto me and he smirked. Beneath his unbuttoned shirt, he was lean and muscular. His pale white skin contrasted with the black hair he wore in spikes to the sides, giving him a rather devilish look. He slowly buttoned his shirt, studying me all the while. "I've heard tales of you, boy." He brushed at the wrinkles in his shirt and walked to the other side of the desk. "It seems you're rather unpopular at Arcane University."

"That would be an understatement." The heat from my face faded, my mortification replaced by curiosity. "Who are you?"

The man grinned and pressed a hand to his chest. "I am your savior. The man who will teach you that which the old phonies at Arcane U. would never allow."

"Your name," Esma said in a tight voice.

He rolled his eyes. "Yes, *Esma*, I will give him my name." He turned back to me. "My dear, Conrad Edison, I am your long lost, disowned, disavowed, and thoroughly despised bastard cousin." He rolled his hand and made a curt bow. "My name is Ansel Moore, son of Astra, sister to your dear sweet mother, Delectra."

Chapter 10

It took a moment for the shock to wear off before I could stutter a reply. "You're my cousin?"

"That's what I just said, isn't it?" Ansel sat on the front edge of the desk and looked down at Esma. "I do hope the boy is potty trained because I don't have time to waste if he doesn't live up to your expectations."

"I should think you'd be happy to have an apprentice." Esma straightened her shoulders but failed to look much taller. Even so, she managed to look down her nose at Ansel. "It seems spell coding and scripting has fallen out of favor with the current generation."

"Oh, you can thank the *Overlord* for that." Ansel spat the name like a curse. "He banned the practice so no one could use it against him. It's taken years to reverse course." He stood. "A shame that some people don't stay dead."

Esma flinched as if he'd struck her, and anger swept across her features. She took a breath and slipped back on the uncaring mask. "Please teach him, Ansel." There was pain in her voice.

Ansel's eyebrows shot up. "Very well." He folded his arms and looked me over. "Do what I say and put in the time I request, or I'll drop you faster than moldy bread, boy. Got it?"

I swallowed hard and wondered what Esma had gotten me into. "Yes, Ansel."

"Excellent!" He patted my head like a dog's. "In that case, cousin, you will stay a while, and sweet Esma will go." The amusement faded from Ansel's eyes as he looked at the professor. "Goodbye."

Esma's lips pressed tight, but she turned and left without another word. After she'd left, I studied the hardness in Ansel's eyes. "Why don't you like Esma?"

He blinked as if waking from a daydream and flashed an insincere grin at me. "You're not remotely ready to hear that story." Ansel rubbed his hands together. "Let's get started." He walked to a desk and held up a flat device with a screen. "What's this?"

I didn't know if it was a trick question, but I answered plainly. "An arcphone."

"What does it do?"

Max had explained it simply to me once, so I repeated what he'd said. "It's like a smartphone that uses magic."

"Precisely." Ansel flicked it on. "These days, most people use them for mundane tasks and games, but some gifted folk use them for spell scripting." He picked up a brass wand, its surface etched with golden runes, and unscrewed the base. A smooth cylinder slid out. "This is an aether battery." He opened a compartment on the side of the wand to reveal chips inside. "This is a magical processing unit capable of focusing scripted spells through the wand."

I peered closely at the arcnological marvel. "Does that make it more powerful?"

"Infinitely," he assured me. "How many spells can you fire off in quick succession?"

"I don't know that many." I tried to count them on my fingers. "Three or four, I think, but they're not powerful spells."

"Demonstrate." Ansel pointed to a blank wall.

I took a moment to compose myself and to decide which spells I could best cast. I looked around for a candle, but of course they didn't use them here. I pulled some parchment from my backpack and set it against the wall. Flicking my wand through the pattern, I cast *Ignitus*. The parchment caught fire. Without pause, I blew out the fire with *Ventus*, levitated the paper with *Levator*, and then threw it aside with *Torsius*. It took a total of more than thirty seconds to work through everything, but I felt proud that I didn't miscast a single spell.

Ansel clapped his hands slowly when I'd finished. "Impressive for a second year student, but watch this." He slid the aether battery back into the wand and closed it, then tapped away on his smartphone. Lines of strange code drifted across the screen and then he put away the phone. "Parchment, please."

I took another sheet and set it against the wall. Ansel flicked the wand, guiding it through the patterns so tightly, I barely had time to make them out. The spells shot from the wand in quick succession, fire, air, levitation, and the last spell ripped the smoking parchment in half—all done in under five seconds.

I stared at the wand and back at him. "How is that possible? You didn't say the magic words or anything."

"I am going to tell you something nobody at Arcane University will say." Ansel sat on the corner of his desk. "Language is form, and little more."

"Form?" I grasped at his meaning. "That's what Esma told me."

"It is a way of putting your will into the form of a word." He indicated the charred parchment. "They train you to think of lighting a fire with *Ignitus*, of making a breeze with *Ventus*, but the words themselves have no magic to them."

89

"Do you mean to say it's simple word association?"

Ansel waggled a hand. "Primarily, yes. It helps those with weaker wills maintain a visual of their goal." He pushed off the desk and flicked on an arctablet. A holographic whiteboard sprang into the air. Using his finger, he drew a stick figure of a person holding a wand. Inside the circular head, he wrote, *WILLPOWER*, and over the wand, *FOCUS*. Ansel inspected his work then tapped a finger on the stick figure's head. "Most of the magic happens here. If you don't possess the will, then you will never find the way."

"What about the wand patterns?" I asked.

"They represent runes," he said. "The only magical language is Cyrinthian and it is with that we can script and program spells. That is why patterns are necessary, but you hardly need to make them large."

"In other words, patterns are important." I traced the pattern for *Ignitus* on the whiteboard.

"The elemental rune of fire," Ansel said. "The only reason the *Ignitus* spell is so weak is because you were trained to believe it so."

"If all you truly need are runes and willpower to cast spells, then why can't everyone do it?" I asked.

Ansel tapped his head and his chest. "Willpower. Though most people believe they have strong wills, they have never been tested, never been put through a crucible that either forges them into iron, or shatters them."

I immediately saw a flaw in his logic. "But noms can't do magic."

"Because they don't believe." Ansel's laughter sounded bitter and condescending. "Just the same as you not believing *Ignitus* could turn a rock into lava."

"In other words, if a nom believed in magic, they could cast spells."

"Yes, provided they had a strong enough will." Ansel turned off the whiteboard hologram. "Now that you know the truth, I'm going to give you a test. If you pass, I will continue to teach you. If you fail, we are done and you can go crying back to Esma."

My stomach knotted with stress and anger. If Ansel was right, he could help me expand my abilities, and perhaps give me the edge I needed to fight my parents when the time came. "What do you want me to do?"

He pointed to a shiny chest on the side of the room. "Burn a hole through the side."

Through that? It looked like metal. I bit back a protest because he might fail me on the spot. Just because he'd told me that *Ignitus* could melt a rock didn't mean I could just as easily believe it. And yet, this was it, my first and only chance. I had to do it. I flicked the wand through the pattern a couple of times to practice then squeezed my eyes shut and imagined the fire rune, imagined that it represented heat so intense, it could melt metal.

"Ready yet?" Ansel asked in a bored voice. "I have things to do."

My fist tightened around the wand. Resisting the urge to retort was difficult, but I managed. "Yes."

"Then do it!" he shouted. "Stop wasting time and do it!"

I stared at him, more amused than upset by his outburst because his handsome face grew mottled with red, making him look like an angry child.

Turning back to the chest, I envisioned the fire rune, flicked the wand through the pattern. In my mind, the rune turned from a dull shade of orange to white hot. I aetherated, drawing in as much magical energy as I could stand, and then focused my will on the chest. I used no words, only the imagery of a hole melting in the chest. *I have to do this. If I don't, I'll never defeat my parents.* Images of them reviving from death flashed through my mind, of Delectra holding a wicked knife to my throat, ready to sacrifice me like a lamb. That was what they'd do to the world if no one stood in their way. I would die and my friends with me. I would never be able to resurrect Cora. I would never again know the love of a mother. I would not be able to redeem Delectra.

My morbid imagination turned my resolve into steel. Nothing would stand between me and completing this test.

You are unstoppable, Della said. *You are of House Moore.*

A solid beam of white fire speared from my wand. The air shimmered and crackled with heat and my hand felt as though I'd held it near an open flame. The spell hit the chest with no discernable effect. I gritted my teeth and pushed harder, forcing everything from my mind but its destruction.

The side began to glow and the end of my wand began to smoke. My fingers felt as though they might blister from the heat. I heard a hoarse shout tear from my throat. The spell abruptly sparked, sputtered and died. My knees went weak as jelly and my limbs felt like lead. The wand dropped to the floor and I nearly fell with it. I caught the table with my arm and strained to hold myself up.

Ansel looked at the chest. The glow had already faded and there was no hole in the side. He stared at me, something bright and malicious dancing in his eyes.

I could barely find the strength to speak or move. Using the table as an anchor, I pushed up on my wobbly legs and stared at the chest. *It should have melted!* I felt so certain about it that I stumbled closer to inspect it. Only the faintest mark of black indicated that I'd even attacked it. Turning, I took a deep breath. My arms and legs trembled with fatigue, but I didn't want to collapse in front of this spiteful man. I carefully bent over and retrieved my wand.

"I'll be going," I said. "Don't worry, *cousin*, I won't trouble you again."

Ansel gripped my shoulders and laughed maniacally. "Going? Going?" He shook his head. "Esma was right about you, my dear beloved cousin. You have the makings of someone great."

"But I failed." My voice was barely above a whisper and something vile squirmed in my guts. "I didn't melt it."

"Oh, you're about to have the most horrific case of magic sickness you ever felt." Ansel giggled, sounding like a mentally unbalanced girl.

I'd had mild magic sickness before, but the nausea twisting my insides told me that Ansel was right. I heaved so hard I would have fallen if Ansel hadn't held me up. He lowered me to my knees and shoved a trashcan under my nose. I soon filled it with everything I'd eaten for the day, and continued sicking up until it seemed a week's worth of food had left my body.

Ansel paced back and forth in front of the chest, laughing and talking to himself like a madman. When I finished heaving, he sat down next to me. "It was a trick test, Conrad." He laughed again. "Oh, you tried so hard, and the amazing thing is, you actually put a mark on diamond fiber!"

"Diamond fiber?" I wiped my mouth with the back of my hand. "I thought diamond fiber was magic proof."

"It's indestructible, cousin." Ansel jabbed a finger at the faint mark. "Every spell I've ever thrown at it has done nothing." He crawled on his knees the few feet to the chest and stabbed a finger at the mark. "But look what you did! Just look at it!"

Impressive, my boy. Della sounded immensely pleased.

You're only happy because I'm strong. I was almost too tired to speak even if only in my head. *If only you could be happy because I'm your son.*

Ansel took a deep breath and calmed down. He stood, grimaced at the sight of the trash can, and then pulled me to my feet. "How did you pull your strength?" he asked. "Did you use an avatar?"

"An avatar?" My voice sounded drunken, and an ocean of nausea buffeted me from every side. "What do you mean?"

"Hold onto this." Ansel leaned me on the table and hooked my elbows on the edge. He rummaged through shelves and drawers and pulled out a glass container filled with pink orbs that looked like chewing gum. Ansel plucked one from inside and shoved it in my mouth. "Chew it."

Somehow, I found the strength. My saliva carried the sweet flavor across my tongue and warmth flushed down my chest when I swallowed. Moments later, I felt less nauseated, but still trembled with weakness.

"You'll be complete rubbish in class tomorrow." Ansel snorted and covered his mouth.

"What's an avatar?" I asked.

"Everyone has a different way of strengthening their will," he said. "For some, it is a lover." His forehead wrinkled. "I think it's safe to say you don't have one of those yet."

I swallowed more of the gum medicine. "An avatar is a person?"

"Or the personification of an idea." He frowned. "I hope it's not either of your parents."

Even though my face was a bit numb, I felt a grimace stretch my lips. "No." *Cora, Ambria, Max*—they were my avatars, but I didn't want to tell him that. It felt too personal to share, especially with this unpleasant man.

Ansel waited on an answer, but frowned when I remained silent. "Unless you're an idiot, you know what your avatar is." He slashed a hand through the air. "Keep it to yourself if you want." Ansel looked at the time on his arcphone. "I have a date with a lovely woman. If you'll kindly let yourself out and lock the door when you recover, I will be grateful."

"When do we start again?" I asked.

"Tomorrow after school." Ansel opened the door. "You'll need an arcphone."

"I have one," I said.

He nodded. "Excellent. How is your Cyrinthian?"

"I know very little," I admitted.

"Do you know the difference between runes and letters?"

My answer remained the same. "Very little."

"I suggest you familiarize yourself." He held out his hand. "Let me see your phone." I took it from my back pocket and handed it to him. He pursed his lips and turned it in his hand. "Well, at least it's an Orange and not a MagicSoft. You realize they frown upon these devices at the university?"

"Yes."

"How did you afford this?"

"It belonged to someone who tried to kill me," I said matter-of-factly. "I killed him with a shovel."

Ansel's lips spread into a pleased grin. "You and I are going to get along grandly." He bumped his phone against mine. The devices beeped and then he handed mine back to me. "You now have the fully unauthorized Cyrinthian Codex. I suggest you not use the Dark Runes, or you might suffer unintended consequences."

"Dark Runes?" Apprehension chilled me.

"Oh yes—demon language." Ansel opened the door. "Wish me luck on my date, cousin. I've been after this birdy for a long while." He left without waiting for a response.

I opened the codex on my phone and scrolled through the contents. It was divided into three main sections: Cyrinthian Language, Cyrinthian Runes, and Dark Runes. I also found another book in the library entitled, *Demonomicon, The Demon Codex of Emily Glass*. A quick look through it revealed patterns and language that defied my ability to pronounce them.

Instinct warned me away from anything to do with demons. Victus had used the infernal creatures to warp Delectra, and he'd used them on me to ensure his resurrection. I'd also seen a demon devour a lycan named Brickle.

If I had any choice, I'd never use demon magic.

Chapter 11

I made it back to the university in time for a late supper in the dining hall. With my nausea gone, I was ravenous and ate two servings. Max and Ambria weren't there, which was no surprise since they'd probably eaten over an hour ago.

On my way out the door I heard a single word that sent chills down my spine.

"*Frigidiosa*!" came the shout from my left.

My wand was already in my hands, torso spinning to meet the attack. Nausea clawed up my throat when I tried to cast a shield spell and a wave of sleet splashed across my face, my body, freezing solid where it hit. Within seconds, I couldn't move. Only a small hole in the ice beneath my nose allowed me to breathe.

Two teenaged boys with platinum blond hair laughed and sprang from the bushes to the side of the door. I recognized Max's brothers at once. Dread mingled with panic as I considered what they might do to me.

"I daresay we got him good, Devon." Rhys slapped his identical twin on the back.

Devon walked toward me, eyes alight with amusement. "Such an elegant stance, Edison." He traced his finger down my frozen wand arm. "Poetry in motion."

"Perhaps in stillness," Rhys said with a giggle.

The boys stood to either side of me, mirror images but for a freckle on Rhys's right cheek. The smiles on their faces turned to sneers, warped by the ice over my eyes. I tried desperately to move, but the ice was too thick on my limbs.

"It's a special year for us, Edison." Devon thumped my frozen nose.

Rhys leaned in from the other side. "Our final year, Edison."

"And we plan to go out on top." Devon circled in front of me one way as Rhys walked the other.

"Perhaps you should sit out Kabash this year," Rhys said.

Devon finished the threat. "If not for your sake, for the sake of your friends."

The pair stood next to each other, eyes glowing with malevolence as they spoke in unison. "This is the year of Tiberius Keep."

My eyes rolled wildly and I tried to speak, but all that came out was a low inhuman moan of pure fear.

They laughed, taking sheer delight in my torture and then walked to either side of me, footsteps fading. I struggled, air whistling through the small hole in the ice beneath my nose. My skin felt numb with cold, and my nose began to grow stuffy. I pushed my tongue through the gap in my frozen lips and tried to push a hole through the ice, but it was no use. Unless it melted soon, I'd be unable to breathe.

My struggles had little effect except to wobble me ever so slightly in my awkward frozen stance. It was late, and there were no other students entering or leaving the dining hall at this hour. I had only one chance to free myself before my nose completely stopped up. Tensing my muscles, I used what little give there was in the ice and jolted myself sideways.

Conrad Edison and the Broken Relic

It was just enough to push me off balance. I toppled, a glass statue meeting the stone pathway hard enough to shatter. My shoulder smashed through the ice with a painful crunch. My head whipped down. The ice on my neck cut into the skin, razors of ice numbing and burning all at once.

With my left arm and leg free, I pushed up and then slammed my ice-armored head into the stone. The ice cracked and broke, sliding from my numb face and freeing my airways. I gasped for air. My arm trembled with weakness so I rolled onto my half-frozen back and gratefully sucked in air until my panicked breathing calmed. I spent the next several minutes freeing my other limbs. The remaining ice soaked my clothes, leaving me frostbitten to the core.

Shivering in a puddle of slush, I stared into the darkness, a coal of anger glowing red hot in my chest. I'd been so busy with things that truly mattered, I'd barely even thought about Kabash. Despite Rhys and Devon's cruel threats, I still didn't plan to play a game that meant nothing even if I enjoyed it.

The jealous shriek and cry their impotent rage, Della said. *The strong of heart press on.*

The only pressing on I wanted to do involved my fists and the twins' faces. Considering my slender physique was anything but athletic, physical retribution was nothing but a dream.

I was simply too tired to stand, so I lay on the stone, shivering in the icy puddle.

Do you truly think you can redeem us? Della asked in a soft voice.

It took an effort to answer. *You and Delectra? Maybe.*

Why? Her voice sounded unusually soft.

Because if Victus forced a good person to do bad things, then that means Delectra is worth saving. I offered a mental sigh. *It means my biological mother is actually a good person.*

Do you love us? Della asked timidly.

I didn't know how to answer that at first. I remembered the memory of Delectra hugging me. Of the smile on her face. She cared for me. It wasn't until Victus touched that creepy doll that she changed. *I love what Delectra could be. I love what she was in that perfect moment before I met Cora.*

A perfect moment. Della's words trailed off as if she were walking into another room, and she said nothing more.

My trembling muscles finally felt as though they could support me. I groaned and pushed to my feet, gathered my wand and broom, and flew back to Moore Keep. There I found Ambria and Max in the common room between the dormitories.

"You look awful, Conrad!" Ambria pressed a hand to my forehead. "You're pale and your skin feels cold."

"Definitely looking ragged," Max said. He frowned. "Did Professor Emoora do something to you?"

I sat next to Max on the overstuffed red couch. "No, your brothers did."

Ambria gasped. "Rhys and Devon?"

I nodded. "Well, not entirely."

"What do you mean?" Max asked.

I told them about Ansel and his test and then my encounter with his brothers.

"You have a cousin?" Max blurted, drawing curious eyes our way.

Ambria clamped a hand over his mouth. "You have a cousin?" she whispered.

Max freed his mouth. "Sounds like he's just as crazy as Delectra."

"He's different." I squinted in an effort to accurately describe what I thought of him. "He doesn't seem mean, just agitated and unbalanced."

"Crazy." Max nodded curtly as if there could be no other explanation. "On the other hand, I find it hard to believe you actually put a mark on diamond fiber."

"I was too weak to defend myself when Rhys and Devon attacked." My clothes were still damp and cold. I couldn't wait to change into something warmer.

"It certainly explains why you're so pale." Ambria reached across Max and touched my knee. "Did you eat?"

"I had two servings." I felt acutely aware of her hand and realized with horror that Ambria's touch made me feel just as strange as Liana's. This was terrible. I already had trouble thinking around Liana, and Ambria was my best friend. Unless I found an antidote to girl magic, I'd never get any thinking done.

"Something wrong?" Ambria pulled back her hand, a hurt look on her face.

I shook my head. "No, I—I'm just concerned about what Ansel has planned for me."

"Will you play Kabash?" Max asked, eyes hopeful.

I shook my head. "No, I won't have time—not with Ansel and everything else."

"Probably for the best." Ambria frowned. "I dearly wish we could make Rhys and Devon pay for what they did."

"In other news," Max said, "I'll find out tomorrow if that potion I made is my invention or not."

"It's nothing but filthy oil, Max!" Ambria glowered at Max. "I don't know why it's anything to be proud of."

I yawned and listened to them argue. Before long, I could barely keep my eyes open and told them good night.

Ambria hugged me and looked up with big brown eyes. "I know you want to be a powerful Arcane to protect yourself from your parents, Conrad. Just please don't kill yourself trying to do it."

"I won't." I hoped so, anyway. I headed up to bed, changed into warm pajamas and immediately drifted into darkness.

Delectra drops to a knee, a smile melting the ice in her features. She hugs me. "Did you have a good time, son?"

Warmth spreads from my heart to my limbs. I feel so happy and light in that perfect moment in between the dark gray moments.

The moment repeats over and over, but I am just as happy each time. On the last time, something changes. Delectra kisses my forehead. "It is a perfect moment." Then she raises her hand and slaps me hard in the face.

I shouted and leapt from bed with fright. Max slumbered on, undisturbed by my exclamation, but there was no one else in the room. Something blacker than the darkness moved to my right. I leapt back. It moved into the narrow shaft of moonlight near the window, an obsidian figure in tight Arcane robes and soft feminine features. I grabbed my wand from the nightstand and held it up protectively.

It spoke, smoky lips taking solid form. "They come for you, son." The voice belonged to Della.

"Am I dreaming?" I pinched hard and winced at the pain.

"They will not rest until the ritual is complete." Della reached out a hand. "Be careful, son."

"Why are you talking like this now?" I said. "You never help me."

"The moment strengthens me." Her voice faded as she spoke, and her form began to drift apart. "Your power gives me voice." Della's shadowy hand touched mine, chilling me to the bone. "Now, run." Her last words faded to a whisper and her body dissolved into the night.

I shivered and wrapped my arms around me. Who was coming for me? The last time Della had manifested like this, I'd still been possessed by the demon preserving their souls. I was too disoriented to make sense of anything.

The susurrus of wind drew my attention to the window. I peeked outside and saw three broom riders silhouetted against the moon as they rounded a nearby turret jutting from the tower. Their trajectory left little doubt they were coming straight for my window. I shook Max. He mumbled and groaned. Tired as I was from Ansel's test, I gathered all my strength and rolled Max off the bed.

Thud.

"Ow!" Max jerked upright and flinched back when he saw me standing over him. "What happened?"

"Don't ask me anything, Max. Grab your shoes, we have to run!" I grabbed his arm and tugged on him, but he didn't need further encouragement. We grabbed our shoes and scurried into the hall. I still held my wand so I tucked it into the elastic band of my pajamas.

A broom zipped through the window at the end of the hall and a figure alighted on the floor only ten feet away. The figure cocked back his arm and threw something. Max and I dropped to the floor.

Something smacked into the wall and hissed as if air was escaping. I took out my wand and lit the tip, revealing green gas leaking from a small green ball.

Max and I held our breaths and ran.

We reached the stairs and raced to the bottom. There was no one downstairs at this hour, and the common room between dorms was empty. I didn't know where to go. I hated myself for leaving our brooms upstairs.

The whoosh of air warned us the instant before two brooms flew through the windows and my pursuers found us. They threw more gas bombs. I flicked my wand and diverted one of them back at the assailant. Max grabbed my arm and tugged me down the main tower stairwell. We dodged through mazelike corridors and lost ourselves in the lower halls.

"In here," Max hissed, and led me into the dimly lit confines of one of the rooms filled with exhibitions from the history of Moore Keep.

A shadow flickered against the wall in the corridor outside, that of a man in robes creeping and peeping, vigilant for hiding prey. Max pressed himself in a corner between the base of a statue and the wall. I ducked behind the neighboring sculpture and tried to keep from gasping air for my aching lungs.

Another shadow joined the first. The pair stepped into the doorway and raked the room with brilliant spotlights shining from the ends of their staffs.

"Check the nooks, Plinth," the taller figure said. "I'll take the room across the hall."

"Yes, sir."

I couldn't see the face, but unless someone shared the same name, it was Seer Plinth. These were the people who'd captured me before, and I certainly wasn't about to let that happen again. I raised my wand, but when I attempted to aetherate more than a whiff of aether, a wave of vomitous nausea crept up my throat.

My body wasn't recovered enough to cast strong spells. Max pointed at the marble bust on the pedestal next to his statue. At first I didn't understand his meaning since it was too large for us to lift. But as Plinth closed in on our location, peeking behind statues and displays as he came, Max braced his back against the pedestal and feet on the wall.

It would take him time to shove the pedestal over, and Plinth had to be in position. I waited for the right moment and leapt out of concealment just as the man stepped in front of the statue where Max had been hiding. His eye widened when he saw me.

"There you are," he hissed.

"What do you want with me?" I said in a hushed voice so as not to alert Plinth's companion across the hall.

"To stop you," he said. "You must be cleansed—oof!" With a loud thud, the pedestal toppled over and the marble bust landed squarely on Plinth's back, driving the wind from him. Max and I scrambled through an adjoining door an instant before the other man raced inside the room.

"What the bloody hell, Plinth?" the other man whispered harshly.

Max and I didn't stick around to find out what else was said and ran for the stairs leading to the main foyer and exit. Two people appeared ahead. They raised shouts and pointed at us. We spun around and into the left hallway, racing at full speed and panting with exertion. The dull thud of running feet on rugs followed us, relentless pursuers unwilling to let me escape them this time.

The lights in the hallway flared to full brightness. An alarm wailed in the distance. I looked back and met the glare of Seers, slowing and backtracking to flee the scene before security appeared.

105

Two men aided a limping Plinth past the end of the hallway and toward the stairwell.

He looked up and saw me. Anger creased his face, but the others jerked him away before he could raise a fist and shout curses at me. Max and I looked at each other and grinned. We were saved!

Max's smiled faded. "What if Professor Grace tries to blame us for tonight's troubles?"

"If he can, he will." I pointed to the end of the hall. "We should get back to our room before security shows."

That was all the urging Max needed. Tired as we were, we ran and ran. The boys' dorm was alive with curious students running up and down the hallways, peering out windows and wondering what was going on while a frantic Rory Culpepper shouted at everyone to remain in their rooms.

"Glad I'm not the resident assistant," Max said as we maintained an innocent façade and made our way upstairs.

Back inside our room, we looked out of the window and watched security swarm the front door, a dozen people in navy blue robes with gold badges on their short conical hats.

Max and I drew our heads back inside and dropped onto our beds. I wiped the sweat from my face with a bath towel and lay on my back. Thanks to the alarm, the lights in the room were at their brightest and refused our commands to dim or turn off.

I wouldn't have been able to sleep anyway. A pounding heart and pumping adrenalin would likely keep me up the rest of the night.

"I wonder who sounded the alarm," Max said.

"That would be me."

I jerked up in bed and Max gasped in alarm, but it was only Galfandor landing a broom just inside our window.

"How did you know there was trouble?" Max asked.

"I took the liberty of placing some wards around the keep," Galfandor said. "Since none of the perimeter wards around the university were tripped, it appears I was correct to assume the Seers might be able to penetrate our known defenses." He set the broom against the window sill. "They did not expect wards around the building."

"They must've chased us around the entire building before the alarm went off," Max said. "What took so long?"

"The wards alerted only me, and I was sound asleep." The headmaster shrugged. "I set off the alarm in Moore Keep the instant I realized what was happening."

"How did you know it was the Seers?" I asked.

"An assumption," Galfandor said. "I suppose it could've been any number of unauthorized visitors, but since they were the last people to kidnap you, I logically assumed it was them."

"I think you need to redo the perimeter security." Max huffed. "This isn't the first time someone bad has gotten through."

"Perhaps," Galfandor said. He turned to me. "My apologies for being late, Conrad. I believe the Seers may be less willing to risk an incursion onto school property now that they know we have more than just perimeter wards."

"I hope so." I put my wand back under my pillow. "Did security catch anyone?"

Galfandor shook his head. "Not yet. I'm rather curious to know why the Seers would so blatantly interfere with you."

107

"Maybe they should be called the Meddlers instead," Max suggested.

The old headmaster chuckled. "Perhaps that would be more accurate." He pursed his lips and made a strange airy whistling noise. A brilliant red spider squeezed through the window and hopped onto the floor, standing waist high to Galfandor. Eight curious eyes looked at me as Shushiel extended a black-banded leg and rubbed the soft fur against my arm.

She spoke in whispers, the sound no louder than rustling cloth and difficult to understand. I listened carefully and made sense of it. "I will watch my cousin. I will protect him."

My father had genetically engineered the ruby spiders and branded the tops of their abdomens with an E to mark his property. They'd escaped him and gone to live in the Dark Forest where many of his other monsters now lived. Unlike frogres and the other beasts, the ruby spiders were intelligent and, thankfully, did not have an appetite for children.

Shushiel had explained that since my father made her kind, we were cousins. I saw no reason why I couldn't have a lovely red spider as my cousin. She certainly seemed nicer than Ansel.

"Thank you, Shushiel." I rubbed my hand on her leg. "How is your family?"

"Perhaps you should use the charm I made for you," Galfandor said to the spider. "It would make it much easier for them to understand you."

Shushiel tapped a small blue pendant nearly hidden in her fur. It blinked once and went dark. "Is this better, Conrad?"

Her voice was soft and almost childlike, but perfectly understandable. "Yes, much." I grinned. "You have a lovely voice."

"Thank you, cousin."

"Brilliant!" Max said. "Will you stay with us, Shushiel?"

She spun on eight legs and bent her front ones to tilt her body in a nod. "Yes, but I will remain out of sight."

"But, aren't you a little large to hide?" Max said.

With blinding speed, Shushiel skittered toward the wall and vanished. Max and I looked up and down, but even with every corner of the room lit, we couldn't see her.

"I am here." We looked toward the voice and Shushiel's ruby fur appeared a little at a time, morphing from a perfect match of the gray stone on the ceiling. She lowered herself on a web and hopped up and down on the floor. "Did you like it?"

"Brilliant," Max drawled. "You can camouflage?"

"Indeed," Galfandor said. "It is a skill only the second generation ruby spiders possess."

Why would the cuttlefish DNA become active in the second generation? Vic murmured in my head. He didn't bother to answer his own question, but a surge of pride told me he was quite pleased with his creation.

"What if people bump into you?" Max asked.

"She is inhumanly nimble," Galfandor said. "While she does have other duties and cannot be with you twenty-four hours, rest assured, Shushiel will be nearby."

"Thank you." I laid a hand on her leg. "I feel much safer knowing you're around."

"I will keep my cousin safe," she assured me.

Galfandor boarded his broom and turned toward the window. "I am glad you're safe, Conrad. I will do what I can to contact the Seers and find out what it is they're up to." He left before I could respond.

When I turned for bed, I realized Shushiel had also vanished.

Max lay back on his bed. "Wow." He yawned. "A ruby spider guardian." Another yawn kept him silent for several seconds. "I hope she scares the crap out of Harris." He stopped talking, and I realized he'd drifted to sleep.

The distant alarm went silent, and the light in the room dimmed. I turned on my side and tried not to think about everything that had happened. Della's shade waited for me when I closed my eyes, the smoky black figure reaching for me one last time as it dissolved.

Della had expressed pride in me, but never kindness. Even then, she rarely spoke more than a few words. What had given her the strength to achieve lucidity? Why did she suddenly want me to survive?

Maybe something had changed, but more likely it was a ploy.

When he is dead, I will at last be reunited with the whole. Vic spoke of me in third person, as if he didn't realize I could hear the thought. It confirmed that at least one of the voices in my head wanted me dead.

Chapter 12

As Max, Ambria, and I went about our day, I often wondered if Shushiel was invisible on the ceiling above us, or walking by our sides. She spoke once during Gideon Grace's class but only to say that she disliked how the professor spoke to me.

During lunch, Max got his certificate of invention, declaring his potion to be a unique mixture.

"Can you believe it?" he told us.

Ambria sniffed. "That they'd award you for a mistake? Hardly."

After classes, I told the others I was going to get lessons from Ansel.

"I cannot follow you there, Conrad," Shushiel said, still camouflaged. "I am too heavy for your broom."

"I should be safe at Science Academy," I told her. "I doubt anyone would think to look for me there."

"Can we come?" Ambria asked.

"I don't think Ansel would like that." I climbed onto my broom. "Maybe you could find out more about the Seers while I'm gone."

"How are we supposed to do that?" Max asked. "Even Galfandor doesn't seem to know much about them."

"Maybe there are books about them." I pointed toward the crystal-domed library in the distance. "It couldn't hurt to check."

"Boring," Max drawled.

"Don't let Ansel mistreat you," Ambria said. "You need to maintain your strength."

Ansel would probably stop helping me if I tried to stand up to him, but I nodded as if agreeing with Ambria and flew off the cliff and across the valley.

Arcnology Lab teemed with activity. Students lined up at tables where distinguished-looking individuals signed autographs and demonstrated gadgets. A banner hanging in the atrium proclaimed: *Arcnology Academic Expo*.

A lovely woman in lab clothes that looked several sizes too small smiled and grabbed my hand. "Have you tried the new rocket broom? It combines all the speed of a magic broom with the sleek technology of a rocket stick!"

"It sounds impressive." I slid my hand free. "Unfortunately, I have to meet someone first."

She waved energetically and bounced on her heels. "Be sure to stop back by for some neat swag!"

I pushed my way through the crowd and down the hallway to Ansel's office. A woman in a scanty red uniform emerged from the room looking rather rumpled and paid me no heed as she hurried back to the expo. Ansel sat behind his desk, feet propped up, and staring at the ceiling, eyes lost in contemplation.

Clearing my throat didn't shake him from whatever thoughts held him captive and neither did snapping my fingers. I walked around the desk and hesitantly nudged him. He blinked, turned to me and a lazy smile came across his face. "Do you think it's possible to destroy that which is indestructible?"

I suspected a trick question, but answered plainly. "No."

"And that is what makes something indestructible." He stood and slapped the desk, the sudden impulse startling me. "Magic is based on faith while science is based on fact." He waggled a finger. "And ne'er shall the two coexist."

"Isn't that what arcnology does?" I asked uncertainly.

"Yes, to an extent." Ansel waved away the conversation. "Musings, my friend. Simple musings. Do not trouble your childlike mind with such things for we must make you special."

"Special?"

He bared his teeth in a grin. "Oh, yes. Aren't we all special, some more so than others?" His fingers twirled the brass arcwand on his desk. "Esma sees you as more than the sum of your parts. Therefore, I must make you more special than your precious little self already is."

I didn't know what to make of his rantings, so I let him prattle on until he finally got to the lesson.

"How do you feel today?" Ansel asked.

"I feel okay unless I try to cast a spell." I had a feeling that wouldn't matter to him.

"Naturally." He handed me his arcwand. "Remember all the spells I programmed into this wand yesterday?"

"Yes."

"You will practice casting them." He showed me lines of code on his arcphone. "I uploaded the script to the wand. To activate it, all you must do is start casting the patterns and focusing your will through the wand." Ansel turned off the screen. "I want you to push as hard as you can, cousin. I want you to impress me." He placed a book on a stool at the end of the room. "Begin."

I swallowed my apprehension and began to draw in aether. The mild effort brought acid into my throat. Unwilling to let him see my discomfort, I steeled myself and aetherated deliberately but slowly. The nausea grew stronger, a slick fat slug trying to crawl up my esophagus. It took everything not to gag. When I had enough aether in my well, I held out the wand and began the rune patterns, keeping them as tight as possible.

Focusing my will through the wand, I targeted the book. The moment I completed the burn pattern, sizzling energy sprang from the wand, burning a hole clean through the book. My gorge rose and I heaved so hard it drove me to my knees. I dropped the wand and projectile vomited everything I'd eaten that day, spewing it all across the floor.

I doubled over, weak and spent. Ansel clutched the damaged book and glared at me. He knelt just outside the puddle of vomit and pointed at the charred hole. "You didn't finish the job, you weak pathetic thing!"

I noticed the title—*Moore Family Genealogy*—just before he threw the book in the vomit and stormed out of the room.

I wiped my mouth with the back of my sleeve and gagged at the acidic odor. A disc-shaped robot with a trunk like an elephant wheeled into the room and vacuumed the puddle from the floor while I watched numbly. It rinsed the floor and polished it, then vanished back into the hallway.

When I was able to stand again, I left the room in search of Ansel. The crowd at the expo made it impossible to find him so I climbed on my broom and rose up to the top of the atrium. I looked and looked but he was nowhere to be found.

I'm pathetic and weak. Ansel would probably never speak to me again.

The next day before class, I went straight to Esma's office to ask her advice, but her door was shut and locked with a note:

Professor Emoora is out sick until further notice. Please direct all questions to Professor Fellini.

What had happened to Esma? Terrible thoughts raced through my mind. What if the Seers knew she was my mentor and kidnapped her? What if Asha was truly evil and had done something to her?

"You look worried," Shushiel said in her soft voice. She faded into visibility, hanging from a thread next to me, all eight eyes looking concerned.

"Professor Emoora is my friend," I said. "I want to make sure she's okay."

"I will ask Galfandor for her address," the spider said. "Go to class and I will meet you there." One of her forelegs gently stroked my hair. "Do not worry, Conrad." She rose back to the ceiling and vanished.

Max and Ambria didn't seem the least bit concerned when I told them Esma was out sick.

"Maybe she just wanted some time off," Max said.

"On the third day of school?" Ambria sniffed. "I'm sure she'll be back tomorrow, Conrad."

We ran into Liana outside Professor Grace's classroom. She took me by the arm and kept me in the hall while my friends took their seats. "Are we still on for tomorrow night, Conrad?"

The touch of her hand made it difficult to answer. "Yes, of course."

Her face lit. "That's great! She asked if you could come without Ambria and Max."

"Why?" I backed up a step to free my arm.

"She thinks it will be easier to talk without interruptions." Her smile did little to soften the request.

My gaze wandered to my friends and caught a questioning look from Ambria. I really needed to talk to Liana's sister, but excluding my friends seemed suspicious. I couldn't afford to trust Liana blindly, especially not after what had happened last night. "I'm sorry, but if Max and Ambria can't come, then I can't either."

Liana's head snapped back. "Oh." Her shoulders drooped. "Well, I'll talk to Gwyneth again. Maybe she'll reconsider."

I hope so. What if Gwyneth was the vital link that could help me find the relic? I smiled to cover a nervous twitch in my lips. "Thank you."

"What was that about?" Ambria whispered the moment I sat down.

I told her and a delighted smile crossed her face. "Oh, really?"

"I hope her sister still meets you," Max said. "You should've agreed, and then Ambria and I could've sneaked in and watched your back."

"That's actually a good idea, Max." Ambria's smile faded, and she almost looked ashamed. "Conrad, tell Liana it's okay for you to go alone."

"Are you certain?" I felt foolish for being so quick to turn down Liana without asking my friends what they thought.

Ambria patted my hand. "Absolutely, though it means a lot to me that you'd insist we come anyway."

"Wands out for a pop quiz," Gideon Grace declared, striding into the classroom, a tall thin wraith of ill tidings. His crooked index finger found me first. "Level two *Illumus*, Edison."

In the scant few seconds since he'd entered the room, I'd anticipated him singling me out and had already aetherated. The mild effort made me queasy, but casting the light spell wasn't enough to make me vomit. I cast the spell properly and Grace's lips puckered like he'd just eaten a lemon. He turned to another student and ordered them to cast the shocking spell, *Zzt*. The day was barely started, and already it seemed grueling since I was hardly recovered.

Asha Fellini taught third period in place of Esma, which came as quite a relief for most students who didn't like Esma's aggressive teaching methods. Asha preferred to have students practice rune patterns instead of firing spells at them.

"Thank goodness," Max said. "Professor Emoora keeps me on edge all class long."

I found her methods boring. Asha was much better teaching history than magical defense.

On our way out of class, a soft touch from Shushiel's invisible leg startled me. Once I realized she was trying to get my attention, I took Ambria and Max aside to get out of the crowd of students heading to lunch.

"Esma lives on campus in the teacher apartments," Shushiel said.

Max made a face. "Those are off limits to students."

"Where are they?" Ambria asked.

"The back wing of the university," Shushiel said. "You must have a pass to enter."

"Do you know of a way in, Shushiel?" I couldn't hide the pleading tone in my voice.

"I cannot help you break the rules," she said. "I am here to protect you, not get you in trouble."

I clasped my hands together. "Please?"

She didn't answer.

"You shouldn't bother Professor Emoora," Ambria said. "And it's rude to ask Shushiel to break the rules for you."

I bit back an angry reply and walked toward the dining hall. If they wouldn't help me, I'd find a way to reach Esma myself.

When I reached Arcnology Lab after school, Ansel wasn't in his office. Instead, I found a note taped to a brass arcwand.

Dear little boy, I left you a portrait in the desk chair. Do not come back to me until you're able to destroy it with the scripted spells.

A man with sharp blue eyes, his chin resting on steepled fingers looked out from the painting. Behind him rose a crooked old tree, its leafless branches bearing skulls. At first I didn't recognize Jeremiah Conroy because he looked much older in the other portraits of him. The first Arcane had taken many identities but was most famous for his origin as Moses, and later as Ezzek Moore, the founder of Arcane University and the Arcane Council.

It was during that time he'd fathered the Moore family tree that spawned Delectra, Ansel, and me. The tree of skulls indicated the distaste the artist had for Jeremiah, though I wondered why he'd chosen the final incarnation of Moses for this portrait. Despite his rocky history, Jeremiah had given his life to save Justin Slade.

I tucked the portrait under my arm, put the wand in my pocket, and left the Science Academy campus. From there I flew straight to the Fairy Gardens. As I soared over the stone wall around the garden, I saw a reminder of Victus's evil. Where there had once been a thick forest filled with dryads, nowstood a graveyard of stumps.

I steered toward the ruins of the mansion in the back—a favorite place of mine to practice in private—when I saw a lithe figure with blue skin and silver hair dancing among the stumps. She jumped up and down, waving both arms when she saw me.

Evadora giggled and spun in circles as I came in for a landing. "Conrad!" I got off and she threw herself against me so hard, I lost my breath and dropped the portrait. Just as quickly, she jumped back, clapping her hands, wide eyes curious. "Are you coming to the Glimmer?"

It took a moment to recover my breath so I shook my head. "No, I was going to practice magic in the old mansion." Movement drew my eye to the field of stumps. Branches with bright green leaves sprouted from the sides of the shorn trunks. "What are you doing?"

"The spirits are still alive." Evadora knelt next to one of the thick trunks and kissed the spiral rings. "I am the Glimmer Queen now. I must care for the forest. The Lyrolai who survived the massacre ran into the Dark Forest. I hope they will return."

"I thought there were dryads here," I said.

Evadora rested her head on a stump as if it were a pillow. The roots shuddered just beneath the soil. "There are many kinds of Lyrolai—tree people, glade people, earth people, and more."

"Do they all look like you?" I asked.

"No, only those who lived in the mountain look like me." She ran a hand on the tree bark. "Others look like dryads, and some are purple like the grass." Evadora held out a hand and it changed from silver to purple. "Most are able to change their appearance like me, or so Naeve said."

I watched her skin in fascination. "She put everyone to sleep, right?"

"No, there are a few who remain awake, though I try to avoid them." Evadora's eyes widened. "I know for certain Naeve left Treek awake to punish him."

"Treek?" It was an odd name. I set my broom and the portrait against a stump. "Who is that?"

"Treek is one of the mountain people—a royal like me." Her eyes grew sad. "When Naeve began putting people to sleep, he rebelled. She was so angry that she turned his skin into bark, and his hair into vines, then filled his mind with madness."

I shuddered. "That's awful."

Evadora nodded slowly. "Now he haunts the crimson forest, forever roaming and killing anyone who dares enter."

"I suppose he doesn't kill many people since they're all asleep," I said.

Evadora nodded. "Yes, I don't think Naeve thought it out very well." She turned onto her stomach, propping her chin in her hands. "I have been learning about my people so I can help them leave the Glimmer."

"Leave the Glimmer?" I rubbed a finger in my ear, not sure I'd heard her correctly. "What are you talking about?"

"Naeve put all the people to sleep, Conrad." Evadora moved to another stump and pressed her small hands to it. "I must wake them and lead them out of the broken world and into the light. There are many forests that need us. We will start here in Queens Gate and find another realm to populate."

I sat on a stump. "What about the creatures in the Glimmer?" Calling them creatures was a kindness. The broken realm was filled with monsters that had no place here in Eden. "It would be dangerous for the people here if you brought them with you."

120

Evadora drove her fist into the soil and closed her eyes. "The earth here is healthy again. Now I can help the trees regrow."

"You didn't answer my question." I touched her arm. "You can't simply bring everything from the Glimmer into this world."

She sighed. "I must find another empty realm for the beasts. I have looked at the realms around the anchor stone, but I do not know how to get to them."

I sighed with relief. Relocating the entire population of the Glimmer to Queens Gate would be catastrophic. "The Alabaster Arches don't work. Are there places where the Glimmer touches other realms? Are there other cracks between your world and another?"

"If there are, they are well hidden." Evadora's forehead wrinkled with worry. "Something bad is coming, Conrad."

My insides knotted. "What do you mean? What's coming?"

Evadora gripped my hand. "Come."

I grabbed my broom and followed the girl around the ruins of the sprawling mansion. Vines claimed most of the stonework and bushes sprouted up in the charred remains of the east wing where a powerful Arcane named Harry Shelton had dropped a flaming meteor on it. Behind the mansion was a copse of trees hiding a crack in the cliff face.

It had been some time since I'd ventured into the crack, especially in the normal world. I rubbed the green pebble on the chain around my neck and remembered the words. *As above, so below.* The rock was a piece of the anchor stone, the great green moon in the Glimmer that kept all the realms of Earth from drifting apart. It also allowed the user to travel to the reflected world.

That was now where Naeve lived, Cora's soul trapped in the flesh that had been her reflection.

The crack in the world was larger than I remembered it. I no longer had to crouch. Once past the outer lip, the rock gave way to a tunnel tall enough to stand in. Black vines writhed like snakes against the walls. The sounds of grinding rock echoed in the space and I realized with a start that Evadora was preparing the way for an exodus.

Whether we wanted to or not, it was apparent that before long our world would meet the lost people of the Glimmer.

Chapter 13

Evadora took me to the rift, a star-filled void where an invisible bridge spanned the gap between Eden and the Glimmer. Three orbs of brilliant light, the guardians of the rift, drifted in the sea of stars, streams of plasma trailing behind them. One of them keened, a ghostly sound that made the hairs on my neck rise.

Evadora repeated the sound and the orbs danced in a circle. She made a beeping sound and the orbs responded, soft cooing sounds echoing through the endless void. They zipped away to the left, vanishing into the starry expanse.

My mouth hung open. "You can talk to them?"

"I sat and listened to them for a week," she said. "Their language is harder to learn than those of animals, and the sounds they make are not quite words."

"They don't attack you anymore?"

Evadora sighed. "They will let me go back and forth between the Glimmer and Queens Gate, but if you came with me, they would attack. They also refuse to let my people leave the Glimmer."

"They didn't let Cora through." I frowned. "Why didn't she ever learn their language instead of risking the dangers in the reflected world?"

"I do not think she thought it possible," Evadora said. "I do not let such things limit me." She stepped beside me. "But that is not why I brought you here." Her arm rose, a finger pointing into the expanse.

At first I saw nothing and then I realized it was the nothingness that was important. Hardly a space existed that wasn't filled with stars or galaxies, or streaking comets. All except for one black void that, from this distance, looked about as large as my hand.

My arms trembled. "What is that?"

She shrugged. "During the week I spent learning the language of the guardians, I noticed it. It grows larger every day and I think it comes for the Glimmer."

"Are you certain?"

Evadora tapped her chin. "I suppose it could be coming for all the realms. Perhaps we are all doomed."

Goosebumps ran up my arm at the thought of being swallowed by a void. "How much time do we have before the darkness gets here?" I asked.

Evadora's eyes grew round, full of fear. "I do not know."

"How do you plan to evacuate the Glimmer if the guardians won't let anyone else pass?"

"The reflected world is the only way." Her eyes glistened with tears. "I fear for my people, the beasts, and the wood."

"You can't bring the trees with you..." I remembered how Naeve had made trees walk and narrowed my eyes. "Can you?"

"I can bring some, but not all." Evadora bit her lower lip. "But how am I to take beasts and trees through the reflected world? Even if they can traverse into that world, it would allow Naeve to escape and take control."

It was a monumental task. One I had no idea how anyone could manage. There was one person that might have a chance, but she was dead unless... "What if we could give Naeve's body to Cora?"

Evadora gasped. "What do you mean?"

"When Cora went into the reflected world, her reflection stole part of her soul." I tore my eyes from the void in the stars. "Her reflection came back to the Glimmer and ruled as Naeve while Cora went to Eden."

Tears sparkled down Evadora's cheeks. "Where she died."

I wiped moisture from my eyes, a knot of grief lodged in my throat. "Naeve said when Cora died, the rest of her soul came to her."

"It does not work like that," Evadora said. "Naeve would have had to touch Cora's body at the moment of death. Since she did not, the rest of her soul is lost."

A vice squeezed my heart. "No, that can't be true. How would you know?"

"Mother told me before she left." Evadora perched on the edge of the rift, feet dangling in the stars. "She said Naeve might have a slice of her soul, but she would never have it all." Tears dripped into the void. "I am glad she was with you her final days, Conrad."

I wasn't brave enough to sit so close to that drop into the void, but I ventured far enough to kneel behind Evadora and squeeze her shoulders. "I thought I had a way to save our mother, but I was wrong."

She spun around. "Save her, how?"

I told her about the Broken Relic, and the relics of Juranthemon. "If there's even the slightest chance it could save her, I was going to search for it."

"Juranthemon?" Evadora's eyes flared. "What does it have to do with relics?"

"It?" I blinked several times. "You know about Jura?"

"It is in our ancient history." Evadora took my hand and started walking back through the tunnel to Queens Gate. "Saila of the great city Juranthemon tried to stop the war of the Apocryphan. She did not succeed."

"Saila?" It was odd hearing such ancient history from a girl who appeared to be my age. "Did this woman live before the Sundering that tore apart Earth and split it into realms?"

"She was the daughter of Kathazal and a Lyrolai woman." Evadora stepped out of the tunnel. Daylight sparkled along her bluish skin and her hair shimmered like polished silver. For a moment, she looked more regal than the simple girl I'd met last year.

I joined her and rejoiced in the warm sunlight. "Who was Kathazal?"

"Kathazal is the father of the Apocryphan." She held up a finger and a yellow bird perched there. "He is in the Abyss with the other Apocryphan."

My heart skipped a beat. "The Apocryphan had children with other species?"

Evadora nodded. "The history only speaks of a few, and even then." She shrugged. "Maybe some of them still walk the realms."

"What happened to Juranthemon?" I asked.

"When the Apocryphan went to war with each other, Saila held peace talks in Jura. Someone sabotaged the meeting." Evadora shook her head sadly. "She was very powerful and tried to stop the fighting, but the city was blown apart." She put her hands together and pulled them apart like something exploding. "One of the histories says the Sundering happened right in that very spot."

I couldn't imagine the amount of raw power that destroyed the city and split the world into realms. It was no wonder the relics created from that destruction were so powerful. "Can I read your history books?" I gripped her hands. "Please, it's very important."

Evadora frowned. "We don't have books. We have the Soul Tree." She touched the leaf on a nearby bush. "It is where the memories of the Lyrolai used to go when they died no matter where they were in the world."

Could that possibly mean—my hopes rose. "Are Cora's memories there?"

Evadora looked down. "After the Sundering, only the Lyrolai who died in our realm took their place in the Soul Tree."

A dagger pierced my heart. Cora had died in Eden and her soul was gone forever.

Evadora leaned on my shoulder. "I wish her memories were with us, Conrad." Her body shook with sobs. "I wish I could listen to her memories and find out why my mother didn't take me with her. Why she left me with Naeve."

I took a deep breath to ease the pain in my chest. "How do you find specific memories?"

"You must search," she said. "The ones who died long ago are on the bottom branches. I found the memories from the Apocryphan war on one of those branches, but there is no easy way." A smile shone through her tears. "Yoghra tends the tree, and even he does not know all the memories."

My face pinched with confusion. "Yoghra?"

Evadora's gaze grew distant. "He protected me when Cora was away. He taught me the ways of life. Now that I am queen, I am granted access to the memories on the tree."

Cora's memories are lost. I squeezed shut my eyes and saw my frail foster mother in the hospital bed, hair gone, flesh hanging from bones, eyes sunken. The green rock on her chain, the fragment of anchor stone should have protected her, but the demon curse I carried killed everyone I loved—even her. Now I carried the last link to her broken homeland, the Glimmer.

My eyes flicked open. "The anchor stone, even a piece of it is like a link to the Glimmer, isn't it?"

Evadora sat up straight. "Yes, I think so."

I held out the stone. "Cora was wearing this when she died. What if it linked her to the Glimmer somehow? What if her soul was able to come back here after all?"

"Yoghra can find out." She leapt to her feet. "Mother's soul would be the newest bloom on the tree."

"Wouldn't he have noticed?" I said.

"He probably thought her soul was lost," she said. "Since she didn't die in the Glimmer, he never checked." Evadora danced in place. "Oh, I hope her memories are there." Her teeth chattered. "What if they aren't, Conrad? What if we're wrong?"

"It doesn't matter." I thought of the piece of Cora Naeve still carried with her. "Even if the rest of her soul is lost, maybe we can fix the part that's left."

Her hands trembled. "Transform Naeve into Cora?"

I nodded. "We need the Broken Relic."

Evadora grew very still. "What are the other relics of Jura?"

128

"I only know of a few," I admitted. "The map and key allow travel anywhere in the world by linking doors. The hands can bind or unbind magical properties." I thought back to the book I discovered in the Seer library. "There's also an Eye of Jura, but I don't know what it does."

"Hands and eye?" Evadora pursed her lips. "Those are body parts."

"If Saila was destroyed in the Sundering, do you think parts of her body became enchanted?" I shuddered at the thought. That might be something Gwyneth could answer.

"I will search the tree for Mother," Evadora said. "If she is there, I can search her memories."

"Can you talk to her?" Desperation hung heavy on my words. "I would really like to talk to her too."

Evadora shook her head sadly. "The memories are like a window into a life, and the pieces are not all there." She tapped a finger on my head. "Even beings with short lives do not remember all their experiences."

My shoulders sagged. "I see."

She hugged me and kissed my cheek. "Cora was our mother, Conrad, even if not yours by blood. If she is there, I will bring you back so you can see through her eyes."

"That would mean the world to me." My tears rolled off the tip of my nose and onto Evadora's gossamer dress. I pushed back and managed a smile. "I should practice my magic."

"I will see you soon." Evadora backed away and twirled before vanishing into the crack in the world.

I flew my broom up to the broken second story of the mansion and set the portrait on a dilapidated chair. Instead of practicing, I stared at the portrait and wondered what Jeremiah Conroy might have done in my place. This particular painting looked oddly familiar and I wondered if it was the same one I'd seen in the lower levels of Moore Keep.

Had Ansel stolen artwork from there and was now asking me to destroy it? Though I didn't know much about the man, he seemed the type to trick me into doing something like that. I gathered the portrait and flew back toward the keep. Instead of flying up to my room, I went through the lower doors and wandered through the halls until I found the room I was looking for.

Inside, I found the image of Jeremiah on his knees while Daelissa, an angel of immense beauty and fury, fired a bolt of lightning at him. Next to it was a painting of a broken world, the Glimmer. The author's initials, S.M. were scribbled near the bottom. The same man, Serpus Mandracorn had painted other landscapes and people here.

I continued down the row and found the one image that still puzzled me—the life-sized painting of a door engraved with a triangle, the sides of which curved slightly out like parentheses. The image was so lifelike, it seemed I could reach out and open the door. I passed several more paintings until I found one that matched what I had in my hand.

Apparently, Ansel had made a replica. The one he'd given me was not a perfect reproduction. There were no skulls hanging from the tree. Instead, there was a door hanging open in the trunk. Something caught my eye and I leaned in for a better look. Carved into the door was a symbol just like the one in the other portrait.

What does it mean?

I looked back and forth from the painting Ansel had given me to this one and noted the obvious difference in quality. The one painted by Mandracorn was flawless, the colors rich and lifelike. Ansel's appeared as though it had been hastily copied and subverted with skulls to add a negative connotation.

In other words, I could safely destroy the fake painting.

The triangle symbol piqued my curiosity, so I continued searching through the strange museum. I found other images of Moses in his guise as Ezzek Moore entering a door marked with the symbol, but it was the fourth one that brought me to a complete halt. In this one, Ezzek and another portly man stood before the open door, apparently in conversation.

It was the background that held me captive. I backed up and peered down the room toward the far end. Statues and display cases partially blocked my view, but even so it was plain to see that this image depicted the corner of the room with the painted door. If that was the case, why did it show the painted door hanging open?

My stomach growled as it was well past dinnertime, but it could wait a few moments more. I started at one end of the gallery and carefully examined each painting. It took the better part of an hour, but I counted four more images with the mysterious triangle doors in them. One was in a forest, and the others in cities I didn't recognize, though a little research might uncover their identities.

The paintings were telling me something important, I could feel it. I just had to figure out what.

Chapter 14

More complaints rumbled from my belly so I left the museum and went to the dining hall. Once again, I was nearly alone in the room except for a few students. I shoveled down a helping of stew and bread and then hurried back to the keep.

I flew my broom up to the room to see if Max was there and found him sitting on my bed reading one of the books I'd stolen from the Seers. He flinched and averted his eyes. "I'm sorry, Conrad. I got curious to see what was in these books."

"It's fine." I patted him on the shoulder. "I've been meaning to read them too. Did you find anything interesting?"

Max looked up, eyes brightening. "Your mum was a real bright student and nice until she got mixed up with Victus."

"Yeah." I took the book and traced the leather edge with my finger. "I wonder if Victus was always mean."

"There was something about that earlier." Max thumbed through the pages, some of them adorned with illustrations.

One of them caught my eye. "Wait." I put a finger in the pages so I wouldn't lose the place and flipped through them until I found it again. Two circles sat side by side, and a third rested on top. In the space between the three circles stood a tree that resembled the one in the original tree painting copied by Ansel.

"Delectra asked to reinstate the original Arcane Council crest," Max read. "She argued for a return to heritage, but Arcanus Primus, Jarrod Sager, refused, saying it was time for modernization in Arcane practices."

The name tickled something buried in memory. "Isn't he the primus who was murdered after he began reforms?"

Max snapped his fingers. "Yeah, we read about it last year in history." He chuckled. "I guess we learned something from Professor Beetle after all."

"Hardly," I scoffed. "There was resistance to modernizing Arcane magic practices, but that wasn't what got him killed." I traced the circles with my finger. The area where they connected formed a triangle with curved sides, just like in the paintings. *What does it mean?*

"What do you see?" Max said.

"A clue." I tried to remember if I'd seen the circle pattern anywhere else, but didn't recall it.

Shushiel blurred into view, dangling from a thread nearly in front of us. Max and I leapt backwards across the bed with cries of alarm.

Max caught his breath. "I completely forgot you were here!"

"Apologies," the spider said. "I have been away on family matters and only just returned." Her eyes seemed fixed on the book. "I have seen this symbol before."

"Where?" I scooted back across the bed.

"In a painting downstairs." Shushiel dropped to the floor with hardly a sound. "Shall I show you?"

"Yes, please." I put the book back in my trunk.

"Since I must remain unseen, go to the first floor museum." Shushiel faded from sight. "I will appear when you are alone."

Max and I raced down the stairs, out of the dorm and into the common room. Ambria looked up from a pile of books at a table in the corner and waved us over.

"Where are you off to in such a hurry?" she asked.

"Not sure yet." Max grinned. "Come with us."

Ambria frowned. "What sort of answer is that, Maxwell Tiberius? Does it look like I have time to run around the keep like an imbecile?"

"Shushiel is taking us to see something," I explained. "It could be very important."

Her eyes flashed. "Well, why didn't you say so in the first place?" Ambria closed her books and set them in a stack on the table. "Let's go."

We reached the bottom floor and went into one of the galleries. I looked up and down the rows, but didn't see one with the circle-tree symbol on it.

"Hello." Shushiel's whispery voice came from overhead. We looked up and found her on the ceiling. "The painting is this way." She crawled across the ceiling and stopped in front of the portrait of Daelissa preparing to murder Jeremiah. There was no symbol to be seen anywhere in the painting.

"Where is it?" I asked.

She came down the wall and stopped just above the frame. Two of her forelegs pried the edge of the life-sized painting from the wall and without effort set it to the side. Painted on the wall behind it were three touching circles with a tree in the space between. Just beneath it were the initials S.M.

"So cool." Max reached out his hand and tentatively touched it. "It looks three-dimensional."

"Amazing," Ambria said. "Just like his other paintings."

I stepped next to Max and looked at the image from the sides just to confirm it was indeed a flat image and not hovering right in front of my face. It was like viewing a hologram when I looked at it from the front. Mandracorn's other paintings were not this impressive.

"Why did they cover it?" I asked.

Shushiel raised her forelegs in what might have been a spider shrug. "I do not know."

I stepped in front of it and backed up until it seemed the symbol hung right in front of me. On impulse, I reached out, expecting my hand to find nothing but air. Instead, it grasped something solid. I pulled and a copy of the symbol formed in my hand, the original remaining in place. It was the size of a pendant, filling the palm of my hand.

"What in the world?" Ambria reached out a hand and touched the copy. "It's real!"

I turned it around in my hands, flipping it over and examining it from all sides. It felt metallic, but light as air. "Amazing," I breathed.

"Let me see it." Max took the symbol and ran his fingers along the edges. "It's hard and cold like metal, but it weighs nothing." The symbol turned to smoke and drifted apart.

"You ruined it, Max!" Ambria pressed her hands to her face in horror. "It's gone!"

I reached my hand toward the painting and pulled free another copy.

Ambria gasped. "You can get another one?"

I laughed. "This is amazing." I gave it to her. "What does it feel like to you?"

She took it and pressed her fingers against the tree. "This part feels like wood, but the rest is like metal." A few seconds later, it misted into nothing in her hands.

"I guess it only lasts a little while," Max said. He elbowed me to the side and took my position. "Let me try." He reached forward and grabbed, but nothing happened. "Huh?"

"Make sure you're right in front of it," I said.

Max tried again and again, but had no better luck.

Ambria shoved him out of the way. "You're hopeless, Max. Let me show you how it's done."

Despite her confident words, Ambria had no more success than Max and finally gave up.

I stepped back into place and drew out a copy. Reaching forward with my other hand, I took another. "Let me test something." I handed one to Max and held onto the other. Seconds after Max took the symbol, it puffed away while mine remained solid. I placed mine on the floor. "Don't touch it."

The symbol remained in place while I counted off a minute. I motioned to Ambria. "Pick it up."

She knelt and took it, and once again, the symbol vanished. I repeated the test, but gave it to Shushiel instead. The spider watched the symbol vanish. "How curious," she said. "Perhaps only you can hold the symbol because you are descended from Ezzek Moore."

Max slapped his palm to his forehead. "Of course!"

"Yes, but what's the purpose?" Ambria motioned toward the symbol. "What use is it if he could fill a sack with the things?"

136

I took another copy. "Let's test a theory." We walked down the aisle to the painting of the door on the wall. The symbol in my hand looked too small for the curved triangle portion to line up with the one in the portrait, but I centered it on it anyway. The symbol stretched wider until the lines matched perfectly.

The door seemed to jump off the canvas, a hologram like the one with the symbol. I reached out and pulled on the handle. With a click, the door opened into darkness.

We stood there, mouths hanging open. Even Shushiel's mandibles hung open, all eight of her eyelids blinking.

"Wait a minute," I said. "Spiders don't have eyelids."

Max snorted. "You just opened a door hidden in a magical painting and that's the first thing you say?"

I took out my wand and lit it with a thought. Holding it at arm's length, I walked toward the door.

Ambria gripped my arm. "Just the tip, Conrad!"

I nodded and let just the wand cross the threshold. Polished wood flooring became visible. Ambria released my arm and I stepped into the dark. Glowballs flickered to life overhead, like a string of Christmas lights spreading into a vast warehouse that seemed to stretch on forever. Shelves towered two stories high, and even higher in other places, like a miniature city of skyscrapers.

The others followed me inside.

"Brilliant," Max breathed. "This must be the legendary Vault of Moses!"

"It would take a lifetime to explore this place," Ambria said. She looked back and forth between the museum and the warehouse. "How does it fit inside the keep?"

"It's not in the keep," Max said. "We just stepped into a magical pocket dimension."

I heard people talking, footsteps echoing down the corridor back in the keep. Without thinking, I pulled the door shut and instantly regretted it. "I hope it opens back in the same place." I put my ear to the door, but couldn't hear anything through the thick wood.

"Who cares?" Max said. "This place is supposedly filled with things the original Arcane Council didn't want loose in the world, not to mention stuff Moses collected."

"Look at this." Ambria walked to a thick book on a pedestal just a few yards from the door. She opened it and traced a finger down the page. "It's an index, but it's in Latin."

My heart raced as I realized what wonders might be hidden here. I flipped through the thick yellowed pages of parchment until I found the J section. Halfway through, I found a listing: *Juranthemon*. Below it were individual items. I had my phone translate the list: map, key, heart, nose.

Ambria wrinkled her nose. "Eww, a nose?"

Max pointed out the lot numbers. "How about we stop talking about it and find out?"

Next to the book pedestal was a pile of musty, rolled up carpets. Max kicked one open with his foot and rewarded us with a cloud of dust. I coughed and backed away until it settled somewhat. As I'd imagined, the carpet levitated off the floor when I commanded it, so we all climbed on board. Despite her size, Shushiel was able to compact herself in a corner with Ambria standing between her forelegs.

"You're so fluffy!" Ambria declared, rubbing the ruby fur. "I hope this doesn't offend you."

"I enjoy having my fur stroked," the spider said. "Much like people enjoy having their backs scratched."

I directed the carpet to the aisle number indicated in the index, and then flew down it. Each shelf tower was about a hundred yards long where space between it and the next shelf was left to allow crossing to another aisle. It looked as though the height of the towers was extended when more space needed to be added, though in some places, the shelves were bare, as if nothing that began with "Je" had been collected to fill the section.

We passed all manner of artifacts, from massive marble statues, portraits, clothing, furniture, and even a rusty tricycle. In some places, items were piled on the floor, labeled with Latin on ancient parchment.

Holding my phone out to one of the labels, I asked it to translate.

"Please adjust shelving to fit new items in proper place," the phone said in its robotic monotone. We came to a section of earthenware pottery covered with warnings.

"Please do not touch the cursed pottery," my phone read. "Material evidence for trial of witches accused of killing the Dafongi villagers."

Max shivered. "Creepy."

"I imagine this place is filled with horrors," Ambria said.

"I feel bad vibrations." Shushiel pointed a leg toward the back. "There are things in here, alive, but barely."

Max shuddered. "Living things?" He took out his wand. "I've got a bad feeling about this."

"Guardians?" Ambria said.

Shushiel remained silent a moment. "I cannot tell if we are getting closer to them, or if they are getting closer to us."

I went from feeling happy and relaxed to a raw bundle of nerves. When we reached the proper section, Shushiel hopped off the carpet. "I will investigate," she said. "Be careful." The spider crawled up the side of the shelf tower and shimmered into camouflage.

I took the carpet forward a few feet and found the exact section I was looking for at floor level. Inside a clear display case, a marble nose sat atop velvet cloth. Next to it was a blank space and a folded piece of postcard with a message written in English.

Dearest Jeremiah:

Perhaps you never check your inventory and my words are wasted, but I cannot in good conscience take the map and key from the Arcane Archives without leaving a note. You think the Slade boy a danger to your plans. I believe he is our salvation. As such, I will put him through my crucible and see if the boy survives. I cannot do this without granting him some tools. The map and key will do.

Sincerely,

Underborn

P.S. Perhaps you should keep a closer eye on such important relics. The heart was missing though you have it listed in your inventory.

P.P.S. I also borrowed several blink stones. My research indicates they date back to the time of Juranthemon, but you have them stored separately. You really should hire some help.

"Whoa," Max breathed. "Underborn helped Justin Slade back in the day. Man, I wish I was older back then. It would've been so cool to fight in the war."

"A nose." Ambria sniffed. "What's so special about a stone nose?"

"Looks like it came off a statue," Max said.

I thought back to Evadora's story and realized I hadn't told my friends about the encounter. I corrected the oversight with a detailed summary, including the part about Jura.

"How awful!" Ambria hugged herself and shivered. "In other words, the hands and nose of Jura are body parts from people who lived in Juranthemon?"

Max chuckled. "I wonder if there's a Big Toe of Jura somewhere."

"I'm don't see how anything survived the Sundering intact." I examined the edges of the display case but couldn't find a way to open it. Even though it looked like glass, it wouldn't budge when I tried to lift or push it.

"Look here," Max said, holding his illuminated wand against the corner. Etched into the glass was the Arcane Crest—the very same that opened the door.

"Great," I groaned. "I guess I need to go all the way back and get another one of the symbols."

"Hold on." Ambria took my hand and pressed it against the symbol. The case clicked and slid open. She giggled and raised her arms in victory. "I solved a puzzle!"

Max clapped slowly. "Bravo."

I stared at the stone nose, wondering what magical properties it might have. Could it kill me or my friends? What if it was cursed like the pottery? There was only one way to find out.

John Corwin

Steeling my nerves, I reached for the Nose of Jura and held my breath.

Chapter 15

The nose felt like cold stone in my hand. It was a small nose, quite pert. I wondered if it belonged to Saila or if someone else had lost it in the explosion. More than anything, I wondered if this disembodied nose could do anything special.

Max sneezed. Ambria shrieked and jumped back from me, as if the nose in my hand had just exploded. Shushiel dropped from above and landed between us, much to our shock. Ambria cried out again and fell on her backside. Max tripped over his own feet and grabbed me for support.

Shushiel blinked and her mandibles twitched. I had seen her do that the other times she startled us, and was beginning to suspect it meant she was amused or laughing. In fact, when her mandibles spread, it resembled a spider grin.

"We are safe," she announced. "There are display cases with living creatures inside, but they are preserved, asleep."

Max wiped his forehead. "Whew. I guess the only thing we have to worry about is you scaring us half to death."

"A little warning would be nice," Ambria said.

I pocketed the nose and got back on the carpet. "Get on. We have one more stop before we go." I flew the group back to the index book and tracked down the blink stones. If they had something to do with

Jura, then they might be useful. As I'd thought, they were in the B section.

We found a bin full of rubble, smooth stones of all shapes, sizes, and colors. The Latin label simply said, "Requires further research."

Max kicked the side of the bin. "Maybe these rocks are all that's left of Jura."

"Yes, like parts of buildings!" Ambria picked up a smooth pink stone that fit in the palm of her hand. "How pretty. Can I keep it?"

"It's a bleeding rock," Max said. "What's so special about these things?"

Shushiel tried to pick up one, but lacking digits on her legs, found it difficult to scoop anything from the bin. I plucked the bright red one for her. "Is this what you wanted?"

She bobbed up and down in a nod. "Yes, Conrad." I held it out and she pinched it between her forelegs. "It is very pretty."

"Just like you," Ambria said. Something sparkling further down the aisle caught her attention. "Oh, what's that down—"

Ambria exploded in a puff of shadows, her body instantly annihilated. In the shocked instant it took me to realize my friend had just been obliterated I gagged, felt hot tears burning my eyes, and the world began to fade. A faraway scream penetrated my haze and I tore my eyes from the place where Ambria had stood and saw her staggering thirty yards away, mouth wide with terror.

Max looked at Ambria and back to the smooth black stone in his hand. His eyes widened, mouth spread into a devilish grin, and then he vanished, reappearing in the same instant right next to Ambria. She shrieked again.

Shushiel was the next to dematerialize, appearing several feet above my friends and then dropping right in front of them. Ambria stumbled backwards with a yelp while Max hooted and pumped his fist, even as he wobbled drunkenly.

Understanding penetrated my shock. These stones could take a person from one place to another in a blink. I concentrated on the place my friends stood and wished to be next to them. The world vanished in a blink of darkness. When it reappeared, I stood next to Max. I might have laughed with him had I not felt so dizzy that I could barely stand upright. Even Shushiel wobbled on her eight legs.

Max held up his stone and grinned. "I am definitely keeping this."

After toying around with the blink stones, for a while, we realized that the more we used them, the more they upset our sense of balance. I was ready to toss up my dinner after the third blink and had to stop. Shushiel stuck her stone on her abdomen with a small bit of webbing so she wouldn't have to hold it in her forelegs. Blinking made her less dizzy than the rest of us, but even she admitted it was unpleasant.

"I wonder how far I can go," Max said.

Ambria hiccupped. "I'm done testing. One more time and I'll vomit all over the place."

Max fixed his eyes on something and vanished. He fell to his knees and threw up on the floor about fifty yards away. When he finished, he stumbled back over to us. "I tried to blink to the end of the shelf, but it looks like the limit is about forty yards, give or take." He wiped his mouth with his sleeve. "Man, I'm starving all of a sudden."

Ambria looked like she'd just bitten into a lemon. "Because you threw up dinner!"

Shushiel's mandibles spread into a grin. "This is much more fun than working for Galfandor."

Ambria rested a hand on the spider's back. "That's because you're our friend and we don't make our friends work for us."

Max chortled. "You made me clean up your kitchen plenty of times."

"Because you made a mess, Max Tiberius!" Ambria set her hands on her hips and gave him a fierce look. "That's called responsibility."

Shushiel trembled with spider laughs.

We went back to the magical door. Holding my breath with apprehension, I pushed out. The door opened back into the museum, much to our relief, so we filed out and closed it behind us. The Arcane Crest was gone, the door once again a painting.

Shushiel camouflaged and vanished. Max held his belly and grumbled about being hungry, so we went to the empty dining hall. We had to go to the back of the room and knock on the golem servant door before one of them came out and delivered a plate of steaming roast. As Max chomped happily on a late dinner, I took out the nose and inspected it.

There were no markings or engravings on it. The back was rough and indented, as if it had been torn off a statue, while the front was intricately made, every pore accounted for. The nose was far too perfectly imperfect like a real nose to have belonged to a statue. I wondered if Saila had been somehow petrified before her destruction.

There was so much to discover about this relic and the other related relics. Unfortunately, there was only one place that might have the information, and even if I could find my way back there, it was extremely dangerous.

"What are you thinking?" Max said with his mouth full.

"Max," Ambria said sweetly, "have I ever told you that listening to you chew makes me fantasize about your death?"

He frowned, but began chewing with his mouth closed.

While Max finished his roast, I told them my plan. "We have to find where the Seers held me prisoner. I need to see if they have a book about Jura."

Neither Ambria nor Max looked surprised. If anything Ambria looked resigned. "I thought you might want to do something like that."

"Don't we have dinner with Gwyneth Augustus tomorrow?" Max said. "Maybe she can answer your questions so we don't have to risk finding the Seers."

I'd nearly forgotten about the dinner, but nodded. "Sure. Maybe she can tell us what the nose does."

"I'll tell you what it does." Max took the nose, made a silly face, and put it up to his face. "It makes boogers!" The nose of Jura leapt from his hand and molded itself like putty over Max's nose. His eyes went round and he shouted in alarm. "Help, it's got me!"

I tried pulling it off his face, but it wouldn't budge. "It's stuck!"

Ambria knocked my hands aside and tried to no avail, jerking and tugging hard enough to bring tears to Max's eyes. "What have you done, Max?" She grabbed a serrated knife from the table. "Let me try this."

Max howled like a frightened dog and fell over backwards in his chair in his desperation to escape. He covered the nose with his hands. "Leave me alone, Ambria!" Something popped, and Max's fear turned back to surprise. He held up his hand, displaying the nose pinched between thumb and forefinger, his own face returned to normal.

"It came off just like that?" Ambria still held the knife at the ready.

"Yes, so you can put the bleeding knife away." Max handed me the nose. "Keep that cursed thing away from me."

"What was it like?" I asked. "Did it hurt?"

"I have a headache, and there was an awful smell." Max pounded his chest with the flat of his fist as if trying to keep his food down. "I certainly don't want it near me again."

I put the relic up to my face. It flew from my fingers as if drawn to a magnet and molded against my nose with a pinch and the sensation of something crawling up my nostrils. An acrid stench filled my nostrils, charred flesh, smoke, and the smell of ozone after a lightning storm. It was so strong, so real, that it nearly overwhelmed me.

The sickening mélange faded, replaced by another. I smelled sweat, vomit, fresh stew, and a sweet scent, like flowers in a field. There were so many odors, I couldn't separate them all. Beneath it all was the acrid scent I'd smelled at first. I rotated in my chair and it seemed to grow stronger when I faced a certain direction.

"You look silly," Ambria said.

Max set his chair upright. "What are you doing, Conrad?"

I gripped the nose and the pressure abated, the heightened sensations faded, and once again, my nose was back to normal. "It's like having a dog's sense of smell."

"You can keep it," Max said. "People smell funny."

"There was something else." I put the nose back on my face. Once again the terrible odors of fire and death filled my nostrils before fading. I smelled everything in the vicinity, but a biting pungence pulled my head ninety degrees. I removed the nose again, relieved to have the intense sensation gone. "When I first put it on, I think I smell the destruction of Juranthemon."

148

Ambria's lips curled with disgust. "How awful." She stared at the nose. "May I try it?"

I handed to her reluctantly. "Stay calm no matter what, okay?"

She nodded. "I will." Despite her assurances, when the nose molded to hers she cringed and said, "Eww! It's gross!"

"Keep it on for a few more seconds." I took one of her hands. "Tell me what you smell."

Ambria blinked and looked at me. "You smell nice, Conrad." A grimace stole her smile. "Max smells like vomit." Her eyes widened. "Oh, they're making bread pudding in the kitchen!"

I squeezed her hand to draw her attention back to me. "What else?"

Her gaze wandered to her left, the same direction I'd looked. "They smell like the destruction of Jura?"

"They?" I asked.

She nodded. "I smell dozens of things that are far away, and four more that are close."

"Four more of what?"

"They're different," she said. "They smell like dirt."

Ambria's sense of smell was certainly more refined than mine.

Max took out his blink stone. "Do you smell these?"

She leaned closer and nodded. "I was wrong. They don't smell like dirt, but more like a cave."

"Whoa." Max turned to me. "The nose enhances smells and can sniff out other relics. It's like a nasal divining rod!"

149

"Not all relics." Ambria turned to him. "I think it only homes in on relics of Jura."

"I couldn't make out half the details Ambria did." I watched as she turned in circles, sniffing the air.

"I smell so many relics, it's impossible to say where they are," Ambria said. She stopped and pointed to an empty spot on the floor. "Hah! I can smell Shushiel." Ambria squeezed her eyes shut and removed the nose. "I have a headache now."

"It's probably overwhelming for our brains," I said.

Max put a hand to his chin. "I wonder why Ambria could identify smells better than you."

Ambria gave me the nose, a worried look on her face. "I know you don't want to hear this, but maybe we need someone who's an expert on smelling."

"Bad idea." Max folded his arms and shook his head. "After what she did—"

"Shush, Max!" Ambria put her hands on mine. "We should ask Blue for help. She's a lycan, she knows more about smells than anyone else we know."

"You can't trust her," Max warned. "What if she tells other people about our quest?"

Blue had betrayed my trust and told Harris about my parents. She'd asked for forgiveness, but it took more than that to rebuild trust. I shook my head. "I agree with Max. It's too big a risk."

"Besides, your sense of smell seems really good," Max said. He wiggled his nose with his fingers. "Maybe you're part lycan."

"Part lycan?" Ambria scowled. "Have you ever seen me howl at the moon or sprout fur?"

Max laughed and danced backwards. "No, but you sure do growl a lot."

She raised her fist. "I don't need a lycan's sense of smell to know you stink, Maxwell Tiberius!"

Shushiel's whispery laughter emanated next to me. "I enjoy being your friend, Conrad."

Max clapped his hands together. "With the nose, we can find the Broken Relic easy!"

"It won't be that easy," Ambria said. "I can't tell most of them apart which means we'd have to travel the world hunting one relic at a time until we found the right one."

Max sighed. "Yeah. And I'll bet some of those relics are owned by powerful people who won't be too happy if we try to steal them."

My friends were right. Even with the help of the nose, hunting the Broken Relic would be a long, dangerous journey.

Gwyneth Augustus spoke as a guest in Professor Sideon's class the next morning. She looked like an older version of Liana, dark caramel skin, lustrous black hair, and piercing eyes that were green instead of hazel. Unlike Liana, she had a serious presence about her and knew how to hold an audience captive with a story.

"There it was, ten feet from me in the middle of the spiral puzzle." Gwyneth projected an illustration from her arcphone showing a glowing amulet on a pedestal in the center of a complex pattern of colored tiles that formed a spiral. "Chris Radford and his team showed up right after me, but they were on the other side."

She swiped the image and two figures appeared on opposite sides. "I told him that his solution was wrong, but he wouldn't listen." Gwyneth shook her head sadly. "He had a snarky tech from Science

151

Academy who just didn't understand magic. He thought his computer program could translate the patterns, but he was wrong."

Gwyneth moved Chris's avatar onto the pattern. "Chris should have skipped the first two blue tiles, stepped on green, red, yellow, and so forth. Instead, he followed the bad advice from a Science Academy geek." Chris's avatar fell screaming into a hole. The view showed him land in a pit where a giant snake bit off his head. "I deciphered the pattern with a spell, reached the center, and took home the Amulet of Orroccoco."

The class erupted into cheers, and chants of "Science Academy sucks!"

Sideon seemed distracted by a book during her presentation and only started clapping when everyone else did. He stood and smiled at the bloody remains of Chris's avatar. "Let it be a lesson children: Do not use pure science on a magical problem."

Max raised his hand. "Gwyneth, is it possible to be an apprentice relic hunter?"

She smiled and the boys in the room, including myself, leaned forward, hanging on her every word. "Yes, but you must have completed schooling at Arcane University to be considered."

Ambria groaned. "Why don't you just ask her on a date?"

Max didn't seem to hear her.

Gwyneth answered a few more questions and left. Her gaze caught mine on the way out, and I wondered if she was evaluating me for the dinner tonight. I looked over and saw Liana smiling at me. My throat went dry, but I managed an uneasy smile in return.

Class ended and the students began filing out of the room. Sideon caught my eye and motioned me to the front. I looked behind me to be sure he wasn't gesturing to someone else, but I was the only one there.

"Yes, Professor?" I tried not to look guilty of anything.

"Conrad, I am thinking of putting together an expedition." He took out a handkerchief and patted sweat from his shaved head. "Would you be interested in tracking down a Relic of Jura?"

His question astounded me. "W-why are you asking me? I'm not a relic hunter."

Sideon leaned forward. "Because, child, I was in the dining hall late last night." He smiled in a kindly, yet sinister way. "I saw what you have in your possession."

Chapter 16

I tried to play innocent. "What do you mean? We bought some things from the joke shop."

Sideon shook his head. "Now, now, dear boy. I clearly heard you talking about the Nose of Jura."

"How?" I backed away a step. "There was no one else in the dining hall that I saw."

"I was in the back helping myself to bread pudding," he said. "Right next to the golem servant door."

Heat flushed through me. I felt so stupid for testing the nose right there in plain sight even if the dining hall looked empty. *He was just on the other side of the door from us.*

Sideon patted me on the shoulder. "Don't be upset, Conrad. I think we can help each other a great deal."

I looked up at him. "How?"

"Ever since you mentioned the Broken Relic, I began to think— what if it's possible to mend the Alabaster Arches?" Sideon dug through his old leather satchel and removed a notebook. He flipped through it and showed me a diagram of a disembodied hand. "As we discussed in class the other day, the Hand of Jura can disrupt and unbind magical properties. What if the Broken Relic could reverse this and make the hand able to rebind and fix magical properties?"

It sounded like a lot of ifs to me. "Can one relic affect another?"

He shrugged. "Who knows? But think of the possibilities if we could repair the arches and restore travel to other realms."

I knew the possibilities all too well. Justin Slade could return and repair the damage done to Eden by my father. He could defeat Victus once and for all. If we found the Broken Relic, I could possibly save Delectra and Cora.

Sideon tucked away the notebook. "I have fantasized about repairing the Alabaster Arches all my life, Conrad. I dream of visiting new worlds and exploring their histories. I heard what you and your friends said about the nose—how it can sense other Relics of Jura. If true, we can fix everything that is wrong with this world!"

The professor's eyes shone with excitement, and the look on his face was so hopeful, I nearly agreed to help him right there. Instead, I forced myself to be cautious. Though he'd been my teacher since last year, I still knew little about him. On the other hand, it would be quite handy having an adult's help.

"I need to think about it, sir." I smiled reassuringly. "Searching for relics sounds very dangerous."

"It certainly is, and that's why you need adult supervision instead of running off all by yourself." Sideon patted my shoulder. "Just be careful what you tell Gwyneth tonight. Someone like her will probably try to steal the nose from you for her own glory."

"How did you—oh, you overheard us talking about her."

Sideon smiled sheepishly. "I assure you it was entirely unintentional until I heard you say Jura, and then I simply couldn't help myself."

155

"I understand." If it had been me and someone mentioned Jura, I probably would have listened as well. "How much school would we miss?"

"None at all." He flourished his hands with assurance. "We'll do extensive research for the next couple of months and have the winter holiday to embark on our grand journey." He leaned forward. "Where did you find the relic, if I might ask?"

I certainly didn't want him knowing the truth, so I made up something on the spot. "Someone left it in my room with a note that said I would need it."

"It was an anonymous gift?" Sideon clapped his hands together. "Fascinating."

While I didn't want to tell Sideon everything, it was apparent to me that having an adult to help us plan this venture might not be such a bad thing. I hadn't thought so far ahead. If anything, it was hard for me to fight impatience. "That sounds like a good idea." I noticed the time and grabbed my things. "I have to run or I'll be late for class."

"Think about it," Sideon called as I rushed out of the door.

I reached class just in time. Asha Fellini once again filled in for Esma who I desperately missed. I trusted her judgement, and if she thought partnering with Sideon was a good idea, then I'd do it.

After class, I took aside my friends and told them about Sideon's proposal.

Ambria was aghast. "He overheard us?"

"Wonderful." Max threw up his hands. "Now we have to worry about a professor telling on us."

"This is awful." Ambria pressed her hands to her cheeks. "What if we say no?"

"I want to ask Esma," I said.

Max frowned. "Why her? What about Galfandor?"

"Galfandor probably wouldn't care," Ambria said. "He's certainly let us go on far more dangerous adventures without lifting a hand to help us."

"I trust Esma," I said. "I hope she's feeling better soon so I can ask her."

While eating lunch, Liana approached our table. "Would it be okay if I join you?"

Ambria's lips flattened into a line, but Max nodded. "Sure, why not?"

Liana sat next to me. "What did you think of my sister's story?"

"Awesome," Max said.

"Horrific," was Ambria's tight-lipped response.

I'd been preoccupied with other thoughts during some of the Gwyneth's presentation, but managed a truthful response. "Dangerous."

"Yeah." She held my gaze for a moment then looked down at the tray one of the wooden serving golems slid onto the table. "My sister is so pretty and adventurous. I wish I could be like her."

"Just go into relic hunting like her," Max said, before digging into a steaming pile of cheese-covered broccoli.

Liana poked her fork into a broccoli stalk, but didn't seem interested in eating it.

Ambria's forehead wrinkled. "Are you jealous of your sister?"

157

"I asked my mum to come visit me at school, but she always says she's too busy." Liana stabbed the chicken breast with her knife. "Then Gwyneth comes here, and now Mum is traveling from London to Queens Gate just to meet us for dinner."

Max winced at the chicken breast abuse, but apparently thought better of saying anything and kept eating.

"How often does your sister visit home?" Ambria asked.

"Rarely." Liana sighed. "It's just not fair."

I tried to feel bad for her, but at least she had a living mother who didn't want her dead. "What about your father?"

"He vanished on a relic hunt years ago." Liana took a deep breath and began cutting the chicken breast. "Maybe if I disappeared she'd appreciate me more."

"That doesn't make any sense," Max said. He flinched at the angry look Liana threw his way and held up his hands in surrender. "Hey, at least both your parents don't hate you like mine do." He shrugged. "My sisters and brothers are mean to me too, so I just avoid them."

"Are you serious?" Liana said.

"I'm afraid if you're looking for sympathy, this is the wrong group," Ambria said. "Our families are just the worst. Murderers, dictators, liars." She held out her hands helplessly. "I'm sure your mother loves you, but if she rarely sees Gwyneth, then of course she'll come running to visit."

Liana frowned. Cheese dripped from the broccoli perched on her fork and onto the chicken. "Well, now that I think about it, I suppose things are pretty good for me." Her frown flipped upside down. "Thanks! I feel so much better now."

Ambria groaned. "You're welcome."

"So your mother will be joining us?" I asked.

Liana nodded. "Gwyneth said it was fine for Ambria and Max to come as well."

"Lovely," Ambria said sarcastically.

Max finished chewing his broccoli. "Where are we going?"

"The Dancing Pig." Liana looked back and forth between the three of us as if expecting objections, but I simply nodded.

Ambria lifted an eyebrow. "Did your parents support the Overlord?"

Liana flinched. "What makes you ask that?"

"Rumor," Ambria said, keeping her eyes locked on Liana's.

"My father was forced into relic hunting by the Overlord." Liana dropped her fork, chin trembling. "I remember hearing my parents talking about it, wishing they could run away and escape." Her shoulders drooped. "Unfortunately there was nothing they could do."

Ambria's hard gaze turned sympathetic. "I'm sorry to hear that."

"They were cleared by the tribunals who prosecuted Overlord sympathizers." Liana twisted the fork, gathering more cheese on it. "Unfortunately, the nasty rumors continue, even to this day."

Max snorted. "Hey, my parents loved the Overlord and somehow they weren't tossed in jail." He cut into the chicken breast. "Just goes to show you that there's no justice in the world."

"Amen to that," Ambria said.

After lunch, I told the others to go ahead to class and stepped into a quieter part of the hall. "Shushiel, are you there?"

"Yes, Conrad." She brushed my arm with her camouflaged leg.

"Can you get a message to Esma?"

"I will ask Galfandor," she said. "He often asks me to carry messages to those areas, so I think he will allow it."

I smiled toward the place where I thought she was standing. "Please tell her that I really need her advice on something."

"About Professor Sideon's request?" Shushiel had apparently been present during my conversation with the man.

"Yes, I need to know what she thinks."

"I will tell her, Conrad." Shushiel touched my arm again and then probably left, though I couldn't tell.

During my other classes, I waited impatiently, hoping Shushiel would let me know she'd successfully delivered the message, but by the end of the school day I still hadn't heard from her. I went back to the keep to get ready for dinner with Liana and her family. As I changed clothes, my thoughts wandered to Cora. Since I had time to spare, I decided to take a side trip and see if Evadora was in the Fairy Gardens.

I had low expectations. That made it easier to climb on the broom and fly out to meet her. If I didn't have any hopes to dash, then they couldn't sink any lower. It was a lie I kept telling myself—that so long as I kept my emotions in check I wouldn't cry like a baby when Evadora told me Cora's memories weren't on the Soul Tree.

Evadora was back to dancing among the stumps again when I reached the gardens. She smiled and waved happily when I circled in for a landing. I couldn't help but feel optimistic. Why else would she be so excited?

"Yoghra said he will search the tree," Evadora said. "If anyone can find her, he can."

My optimism evaporated, but I felt relieved not to have an answer right away. It would only postpone the inevitable disappointment, but at least I wouldn't have to deal with it today. "Thank you."

She touched the tender shoots of a newly formed branch and accelerated its growth. "I also asked him to find more memories of Juranthemon. He said he would look."

I didn't have time to talk much longer so I told her goodbye and flew back to my room in Moore Keep where Max was just getting dressed.

"Where did you go?" he asked.

I told him. "Yoghra still doesn't know if Cora's soul is on the tree."

"I'm sorry." He shrugged into a gray shirt. "I really hope she's there."

I put on a brave face and tried not to think about it.

When Max was ready, we flew out of our window and around the keep to Ambria's. She waved, climbed on her broom, and flew outside.

"Do boys always take so long to get ready?" Ambria looked us up and down. "You're certainly not wearing anything special."

I flashed a grin. "Blame Max. He takes the longest showers."

"Do not!" Max shot back.

"You were in there twenty minutes!"

Ambria giggled. "I must say your hair looks particularly silky, Max. Did you condition it?"

"Bah!" Max waved us away. "Don't be jealous just because I look fabulous."

We burst into laughter.

The Dancing Pig sat in the far northeast corner of town in one of the districts hardest hit by the economic downturn in the Overworld. The restaurant was easy to find since it was the only place with lights on outside, and also the only one in town with a giant pig dancing on its hind legs, a mug of beer on its hoof. The other buildings in the area looked rundown, peeling paint and crumbling brick on a rutted road where the cobblestones hadn't been repaired in some time. Most of the glowballs in the street lamps were out.

"What an awful place for a business," Ambria said. "I'll bet the vampires pick off people as soon as they leave at night."

"Yeah, bad location." Max surveyed the streets below. "We'd better stick close together when we leave."

A burly man with a thick beard and shaved head waved when we came inside the otherwise empty pub. "Welcome to the Dancing Pig. I'm Jack Lamont, the owner." His American accent sounded out of place, but no more so than a restaurant in this part of town. "What can I do you for?"

"We're meeting friends," Ambria said in a businesslike tone.

"Gotcha." He pointed to a door in the back of the bar. "They're in the back room."

"How would you know?" Ambria said.

He chuckled. "Because they're the only other people here right now."

We went into the back room and found Liana, Gwyneth, and an older but attractive woman sitting at a large round table. Liana

162

laughed at something Gwyneth said, and didn't look the least bit upset that her mother was fawning over the older sister.

Gwyneth stood and walked over to meet us, hands outstretched. She shook Ambria's hand first. "It's a pleasure to meet you all." She gave my hand a firm shake. Despite the businesslike demeanor, my knees felt a bit weak when she smiled at me. "Nice to meet you, Conrad."

"Likewise, I'm sure," Ambria said in a knowing voice before she and Liana burst into giggles.

Max grinned stupidly at the Gwyneth when she took his hand, and seemed to forget that a handshake was only a temporary thing by holding onto her longer than was necessary. "Hi," he said in a dreamy voice.

Gwyneth smirked and looked at the other girls, looking rather girlish as well. She turned to the older woman at the table. "This is our mother, Janice."

"Pleased to meet you," I said, trying to recover control of my body. Esma had certainly been right about female magic—there was no way to counter it.

We took seats around the table and Jack Lamont appeared a moment later to take our orders. The food was mostly American fare: hamburgers, corn dogs, and a variety of fried dishes. I chose a hamburger with chips—French fries—on the side.

I didn't know when it was polite to start grilling Gwyneth about Jura, so I simply started after the small talk died down a bit. "What can you tell me about the Relics of Juranthemon?"

Gwyneth smiled as if expecting the change in subject. "They are considered the golden standard for relics in power, versatility, and rarity. There are at least a twenty related relics that are known, though it's suspected there are close to a hundred total."

Max choked on his water. "A hundred?"

She nodded. "The Reliquisti have studied many of them, the least valuable. They believe a magical explosion several magnitudes greater than nuclear bombs is what infused the artifacts with enchantments in the first place." Gwyneth leaned her forearms on the table. "Any people caught in the blast were petrified before their bodies were smashed to pieces."

Ambria's mouth dropped open in horror. "How could their bodies become petrified?"

"Probably had the life force sucked out of them by the initial implosion." Gwyneth balled up her fist. "Something at the center of the attack most likely absorbed all the energy until it collapsed in on itself and burst."

Gwyneth's assessment seemed to mirror what Evadora had told me, but I was a little disappointed she didn't know more. "What relics are there?" I asked.

"Most relic hunters have heard of the map and key," she replied. "The less known ones are the sandal, plate, chair, and even a silver hairbrush."

"What in the world do they do?" Max asked.

"The sandal leaves no footprints and allows you to walk on nearly any surface." Gwyneth smiled sadly. "By itself, it's a bit useless because hopping on one foot up walls just looks silly."

Ambria laughed. "How do you even stand upright while walking up a wall?"

"The sandal makes it easier." Gwyneth squeezed a lemon in her water and stirred with her finger. "The plate never needs cleaning because nothing sticks to it, the chair can start fires, and the hairbrush makes your toenails grow."

"Eww." Ambria tucked her feet under her chair. "Why would a hairbrush do that?"

"The plate sounds handy," Max mused. "You're saying I could eat off it all the time, but never have to clean it?"

"Of course you'd like that, Max." Ambria pointed to the discarded lemon peel from his water. "You're always making a mess."

That brought a round of laughter from the others.

"Delightful children," Janice said. "I do miss having the girls around the house."

"Even me, mother?" Liana smiled hopefully.

"Of course, dear." Janice held up her water. "To delightful children."

We raised our glasses to the toast.

The food came and conversation died down. After the meal was done, Gwyneth stood. "Conrad, might I have a moment in private?"

"Ooh," Ambria said. "Do go gentle on him."

Liana giggled when she saw the look I gave Ambria. "Behave yourself, Conrad."

Max frowned. "Where are you taking him?"

Gwyneth pointed to a door leading into the bar. "Just up there."

Ambria leaned over and whispered in my ear, "Shout if you need help."

I didn't think Gwyneth posed a threat, but I didn't plan to let my guard down. I followed her into the bar section. She took out a small brass key and unlocked a door. It seemed strange she'd have a key to the bar, but I assumed she'd borrowed it from the owner. We stepped into a small office and she closed the door behind us.

The door on the opposite side opened and a lean man with a deep scar running down his cheek entered. He flashed a predatory grin and walked around the desk in the middle of the room.

"Good day, Conrad Edison." He held out a hand. "My name is Underborn."

Chapter 17

I shouted for help, spun around and pounded on the door.

Underborn didn't seem the least bit concerned by my cries and sat on the edge of the desk. "I'm not here to hurt you, young man."

The door wasn't locked so I opened it and was shocked to see a closet with a broom and mop. Gwyneth held up the key she'd used. "This is the Key of Jura. We're thousands of miles from your friends right now."

"I knew I couldn't trust you!" I felt for my wand, but it wasn't in its holster.

Underborn held it up, a smile on his face. "I don't expect you'd be able to do much to me, but there's no need for nastiness." He set the wand next to him. "I would like to propose a deal."

There didn't seem to be any immediate danger to my wellbeing, so I closed the closet door and leaned against it, mind searching for avenues of escape.

Listen to him, Della said. *Use him to get what you need.*

Will he harm me? I asked.

No, because he needs you more than you need him. She sounded confident in her assessment, so I took a deep breath and tried to lower the rush of adrenalin in my veins.

167

"What do you want?" I asked.

"I would like the Heart of Jura," he said. "I know where it is, but unfortunately, you are the only person who can reach it."

Several questions sprang to mind, but Della interrupted. *Do not speak. Let him continue. Everything the man does is a test.* I wondered how she knew that, but remained silent and tried to look patient even though I was eager to know more.

Underborn raised an eyebrow and looked at Gwyneth. "It seems our young guest is smarter than he looks."

"I told you," Gwyneth said. "He has a depth to him most children his age don't have."

"Yes, well you're barely an adult yourself." Underborn chuckled. "Ah, to be nineteen again."

I didn't know if I should say anything or not, so I just kept quiet and waited.

"The relic is in the Glimmer," Underborn said. "It was taken there by Ezzek Moore."

I sensed surprise from Della.

What is it? I asked.

The old man was full of surprises, she said. *What better place to hide something than in a realm most don't even know exists?*

I had more questions for her, but remembered I was also talking to Underborn in the real world. I wasn't sure what to say, but Della gave me cues. "What's in this for me?"

"I will help you find the Broken Relic," Underborn said. "I have information that will greatly narrow your search."

If that was true, then it would make finding the relic much easier than if I had to rely solely on the Nose of Jura. "What does the heart do?" I asked, at Della's urging.

"An excellent question," he said. "It is rumored the heart can heal scars." Underborn traced a finger down the scar on his cheek. "I received this trophy from the war. It is a magical wound with an ache that never subsides. I hope the heart can heal it."

I wondered if it was because he was vain.

Yes, he is vain, but magical wounds can cause lasting pain as well. Della went quiet a moment. *It seems beneficial to help him. Perhaps he can speed your search for the Broken Relic.*

Why do you care? Della had never shown such concern.

The perfect moment awakened something in me. Della sighed softly. *It is as if the darkness was sifted away. I—I want you to be happy.*

Does my real mother—does Delectra want the same thing? I asked. While Della was a fragment of Delectra's soul, I hoped they shared a similar sentiment about me.

"Your answer?" Underborn prompted.

"Can the heart heal other wounds? Can it heal bad illnesses?" I asked.

He held out his hands like a half-formed shrug. "I don't know. It may be limited to only scars."

I was certain he knew far more than he was telling me, but it didn't matter. If he could make finding the Broken Relic easier, I'd help him. "I'll help," I said. "And then you promise to help me find the Broken Relic?"

169

"Absolutely." He unrolled a parchment and placed it on the table. "We will sign this agreement and bind ourselves to the terms set forth within. This way we can both be sure neither of us will betray the other."

Do not sign, Della said. *Underborn is a man of his word even if he is a vile assassin.*

I read the contract so I could clarify what Della meant. *So I just take his word for it?* The wording was simple and brief, essentially reiterating what Underborn had said:

Conrad Edison hereby agrees to provide assistance to Underborn and his proxies in securing the Heart of Jura from its location in the Glimmer. Upon receiving the heart, Underborn will provide assistance to Conrad Edison and help him locate the Broken Relic.

Della's answer was curt. *Shake his hand instead.*

What's the harm in signing? I asked.

Spoken words are form, Conrad. They can be molded into other shapes. She scoffed. *A contract is not as pliable.*

I decided not to question her wisdom on the matter. "I don't see a need to sign, Underborn. I've heard your word is good." I held out a hand.

Underborn raised an eyebrow, but took my hand and shook it. "Deal," he said. He picked up my wand and handed it back to me. "I trust you won't try to use that now."

I tucked it away as my answer.

Gwyneth frowned. "How do we know your word is good?"

"If it isn't, a piece of paper won't change anything." Della didn't tell me to say that, but a smug sensation from the back of my mind told me she rather liked the response.

Underborn chuckled. "As you said, Gwyneth, he's more mature than he looks."

I tried not to be overly pleased by the flattery, but it was difficult to control my emotions. I compensated by asking another question. "Where in the Glimmer is the heart?"

"We don't know precisely," Gwyneth said. "You have connections that might help us."

"Even my connections might not help us get past the rift guardians." I also didn't think a journey through the reflected world was worth the risk. What if Naeve waited just on the other side? What if she could control the trees in the reflected realm?

"Getting us into the Glimmer is your primary part of this endeavor." Underborn rolled up the contract and tucked it away. "What can you tell us about it?"

Della gave me a counter question to ask. "What do you know about it?"

Underborn pursed his lips and gave me an unsettling stare before answering. "Very little. I knew of its existence from my research into the Relics of Jura, and that it is a broken realm filled with dangers."

"It's the anchored world," I told him. "It keeps the realms from drifting apart."

Gwyneth's eyes glittered. "How do you know this?"

Tell him about Cora and Naeve, Della said. *Make him realize there is no hope of gaining entrance without you.*

I didn't know exactly what to say, so I answered simply. "My foster mother was once the Glimmer Queen. Her reflection, Naeve, took control of the Glimmer and her name before I banished her to the reflected world."

Even Underborn's eyes flared at this. "The reflected world truly exists?"

I nodded. "It isn't safe to use now, not with Naeve trapped there." My hands trembled at the thought of her, so I folded my arms to keep them still. "Cora's daughter, Evadora, is now queen of the Glimmer. She is like a sister to me."

Gwyneth's mouth hung open, her mature mask replaced by open curiosity. In that moment, she looked nearly as young as Liana. "How did you banish Naeve? What sort of powers does she have?"

"She controls nature," I said. "If you fight her, trees and plants are also your enemy."

"Remarkable." Underborn eyes shone with excitement. "I would love to know more."

No more, Della said. *Information is valuable to him. You have given him a taste and now he wants it all. Tell him there is much more, but it will have to wait until the mission is complete.*

"My information is valuable," I said. "I can't just give it away for free."

Underborn's forehead creased with disappointment. "Very well. I'm sure we can work out an arrangement at a later date." He nodded at Gwyneth. "In the meantime, I suggest you return Conrad before his friends grow suspicious."

"One more thing," I said. "What led you to believe the heart is in the Glimmer?"

"Ezzek Moore was a clever man," Underborn said. "He hid the heart and tucked away the clues in a place he thought no one could ever reach."

The vault. I kept my thoughts to myself since I didn't want him to know I'd been inside the Moore's vault.

Conrad Edison and the Broken Relic

Play to his ego, Della said.

I gave him a disbelieving look. "You outsmarted Ezzek Moore?"

Underborn flashed a grin. "Indeed. I found one of the secret entrances to his vault and realized that only one of his blood could open it. It took me a while, but I tracked down one of his descendants and bribed them to let me inside."

I shrugged as if unimpressed. "Sounds easy enough."

"For me, perhaps." Underborn gave me a smug look. "I could have spent months inside that wonderland. I discovered his small cache of relics, particularly those pertaining to Jura and discovered that the heart was missing. I took the clues he'd left, unaware at the time that I would be wounded in the war and consequently, desire to track down the heart."

"Have you been back since?" I asked.

Underborn held out his hands in a helpless gesture. "Alas, the next time I tried, the entrance no longer worked. I suspect Jeremiah Conroy must have discovered the intrusion and locked down the vault."

I felt relieved that he couldn't waltz in there at any time, but I kept my expression stony. "So you followed the clues he left behind."

"Oh, it was a maddening search." Underborn flashed an unsettling smile. "We eventually arrived at the final clue which pointed us to the Glimmer. Before you ask, no, I won't reveal the details now."

I had plenty more to ask him, but I'd been here long enough and wanted to get back to my friends. I turned to Gwyneth. "I'm ready."

"Okay, let's go." She unlocked the door with the key and opened it. The closet was gone, replaced by the bar once again.

Jack Lamont flashed a grin when he saw us emerge, leading me to think he knew exactly where I'd gone.

We returned to the dining room. Ambria and Max gave me curious looks while Janice continued telling a story that had something to do with Liana making a mess as a baby. I tried to listen patiently but was eager to let my friends know what had happened. Unfortunately, Janice seemed intent on putting a great deal of detail into embarrassing Liana.

Sometime later, Janice stood and stretched. "Oh my, it's gotten late. I really must get home."

Liana looked nearly as relieved as I felt. We left the restaurant and the girls hugged their mother goodbye. Janice boarded a driverless carriage sitting in front of the restaurant and it rolled away toward the entrance of the Queens Gate waystation where an elevator would return her to the surface and London above.

Gwyneth's smile faded and she became all business. "Conrad, we should meet and go over the details."

"My friends will be there," I told her, "because they're coming with us."

Liana's eyebrow rose. "Coming where?"

"Bad idea," Gwyneth said. "There's no telling what we might run into and I can't take care of you and two other kids."

"Kids?" Max's chest puffed out. "I'll have you know we've seen more danger than most adults."

"We made a demon eat a lycan." Ambria folded her arms and stared down her nose at the taller girl. "We killed a frogre and defeated an evil queen. Can you say the same thing?"

"You did what?" Liana looked even more shocked. "What's all this about?"

174

Gwyneth huffed. "We're going on a relic hunt, sis."

Liana's eyes lit up. "Can I come too?"

"No." Gwyneth stared me down. "Just you and me, Conrad. That's the deal."

There is no need to bargain with her, son. Della chuckled. *You have the nose. If you can reach the Glimmer, you can find the heart yourself.*

Apparently, Underborn didn't know I had the Nose of Jura, nor did he know what it did. Why else had he left it in the display case, unless, of course, it had been added after he'd stolen the map and key? Della was right. I didn't have to do what Gwyneth wanted outside the agreement I'd made with Underborn.

"Ambria and Max are coming, period." I pounded the flat of a fist in my palm.

"I'm coming too," Liana said.

Gwyneth ran a hand down her face and adopted a pleading voice. "Don't you understand how dangerous this will be? I know you've had some adventures—"

"Adventures?" Max said incredulously. "We had to save the world from the Glimmer Queen! Have you ever saved the world?"

"Yeah, have you?" Ambria said.

I waved away their protests. "Look, it's not about what we've done, it's about knowing that my friends have my back no matter what." I put my hands on Ambria and Max's shoulders. "This is my family and I know that no matter what, they'll be there for me." I tried to harden my gaze, but it probably came across as squinting. "I don't know you, Gwyneth, and you haven't earned my trust."

Precisely. Della seemed rather pleased.

Liana's lower lip trembled. "Does that mean I can't come?"

Gwyneth squeezed shut her eyes and took a long deep breath. She opened her eyes and blew out the air. "Don't blame me if your friends die."

Her words filled my stomach with knives. Taking my friends put them in danger, but I wouldn't dare go alone with Gwyneth. "Then it's settled."

"What about me?" Liana said.

"No!" everyone shouted at once.

The poor girl shrank away. "Why not?"

Gwyneth looked at her tenderly. "Let's talk about this later, okay, sis?"

Liana looked down. "Okay."

Ambria, Max, and I hopped on our brooms and flew away, leaving the sisters behind to make their own way home. I told my friends about my meeting with Underborn.

"Are you kidding me?" Max shouted. "You made a deal with that man?"

"Della convinced me to," I admitted.

Ambria's wide eyes and tone conveyed her disbelief. "Your mother's soul fragment? Since when has she ever helped you?"

"Ever since I showed her a perfect moment." I told them about the memory of Delectra smiling and greeting me after my first visit with Cora.

"I don't know," Max said. "Getting mixed up with Underborn sounds exactly like something Della would convince you to do so you get yourself killed."

"No." I shook my head. "Something has changed." I hesitated to say what I felt, but put it out there. "I think she's proud of me."

"I'm sorry, Conrad." The corners of Ambria's eyes turned down in time with her lips. "I just don't trust her."

Perhaps you shouldn't trust me, Della said. *Perhaps I am just as bad as your real mother.*

I will trust you until you give me reason not to. I hoped I wasn't trusting her just because I wanted a mother so badly, even if she was just a voice in my head.

Trust no one but yourself, Vic snarled.

Is that all you have to say? I shot back. Vic didn't reply which prompted another question. *Why doesn't he speak as much?*

Della didn't answer at first and even when she did, sounded unsure. *I don't know. We are part of you, but separate. I cannot always hear his thoughts.*

"Are you angry?" Ambria reached across the gap between the brooms and touched my hand. "I hope I didn't hurt your feelings, but I need to be honest."

I'd become so engrossed in the conversation inside my head that I'd forgotten about the real world. "I'm not angry," I told her. "But I think you're wrong." Or maybe I just hoped she was.

A lone figure on a flying broom rose from the streets below and approached us. He held a wand with a white handkerchief flapping in the wind. Shadows concealed his face, even in the bright light of the moon.

"What in the world?" Ambria said. "Is that a flag of surrender?"

Dread filled me. I drew my wand. Max and Ambria did the same as the figure drew closer.

"Conrad Edison," the man called out.

"Stay right there," I commanded him. I looked up, down, and all around to make sure no one else was sneaking up on us. "Identify yourself."

The man's wand glowed, revealing a face I knew all too well.

Chapter 18

Seer Plinth waved his small flag. "I wish only to talk with you, Conrad, I swear it."

"Talk?" Max shouted. "You kidnapped our friend and covered him in blood!"

Ambria waved her wand threateningly. "You come near us and I'll knock you off your broom!"

It seemed I was the only one who wanted to hear the man talk. "Why did you kidnap me?"

"Conrad, we are Seers, sworn to never interfere unless"—he swallowed hard—"the consequences of inaction would result in a dire outcome."

"That's not an answer," I said. "Tell me why you kidnapped me and covered me in blood."

He cleared his throat. "You must be cleansed of darkness."

"Darkness?" I tried to make sense of his words. "What do you mean?"

Plinth's face contorted, as if he were fighting an internal battle that physically hurt him. "I cannot reveal too much or it will change things."

"If you don't tell me enough, then nothing will change at all." I lowered my wand a fraction. "Explain what you mean."

"Darkness weighs heavy on your soul," he said after a moment. "The remnants of your parents must be cleansed. Otherwise, we could all be doomed."

"That's a bit melodramatic," Ambria said.

Max scoffed. "Did you finish the ritual?"

"Yes, but it was not successful," Plinth said. "We must try again."

"One big problem," Max said. "The only way to cleanse his soul is through death, and we're not going to let that happen to our friend."

"His death would be equally ruinous." Plinth's face pinched with worry and his grip tightened on his broom.

"Sorry." I shrugged. "There's nothing you can do to cleanse my soul."

Ambria waved her wand to get his attention. "Can you be more specific about this doom you mentioned?"

"I'm afraid the foreseeance isn't very specific." Plinth blew out a breath. "In any case, I certainly can't tell you what's in the text."

"Why not?" Max said.

"Foreseeance forty-three eleven was never supposed to be known to any but us." Plinth bared his teeth. "Justin Slade discovered the text and likely changed the future of the Overworld in unintended ways. We swore to never let that happen again."

"Then we'll be on our way," I said. "You've done nothing to prove you can cleanse my soul. I'm sorry, but I just don't think you're capable." Though I'd be happy to rid myself of Vic, Della was another matter. She'd warned me when Plinth and his people tried to kidnap me from Moore Keep, and she'd helped me with Underborn. It was odd, but I was becoming rather attached to my mother's soul fragment. It was almost like having a guardian angel.

"Please, just come with me." Plinth clasped his hands together, a man pleading. "Let us try once more."

"No deal." Max pulled his broom up just in front of mine as if shielding me. "Now let us go on our way."

"I'm afraid I can't." Plinth tugged the handkerchief from his wand and rotated his broom sideways. "I will not let a child doom us all."

I held out my wand. "Don't try anything."

Sparks fired from the end of Plinth's wand and into the air. Two more brooms rose above the rooftops directly below us and rose toward his position. It appeared the negotiations were over.

Ambria shot forward on her broom and spun it sideways, smacking Plinth on the bridge of his nose. Blood spurted and he cried out, both hands going to his face. I twisted the back of my broom into him and knocked him off his broom. He fell screaming right toward his comrades. They had no choice but to catch him. Burdened by the extra weight, they were in no position to pursue us.

"Stay away from me!" I shouted. I looked around to make sure there was no other pursuit, and then my friends and I sped away for home.

We landed in front of Moore Keep and hurried inside the main door. I went directly to the painting of the Arcane crest and took a copy of it in my hand then hurried to the door painting. Shushiel shimmered into view on the ceiling overhead.

"I thought you might come this way," she said. "I spoke with Esma."

"Let's go inside first." I opened the magical door and ushered everyone inside before closing it behind us. Safely inside the secret vault of Ezzek Moore, I finally breathed a sigh of relief.

"What is wrong, Conrad?" Shushiel stroked my forearm with her leg.

"The Seers again," Max said grimly. "Plinth tried to convince Conrad to come with him so they could cleanse his soul of darkness."

"When Conrad wouldn't do it, they attacked!" Ambria scowled. "Conrad showed them, though!"

"Conrad?" Max said in disbelief. "You broke the man's nose with your broom, Ambria. When did you learn to fly like that?"

She flinched as if caught off guard. "I—I just flew forward. I didn't mean to hit him like that."

Max chuckled. "So it was an accident? Considering how poorly you fly, that makes sense."

Ambria scowled. "I don't fly poorly."

I ignored the argument and patted Shushiel's leg. "You spoke with Esma? Is she feeling better?"

She waggled her abdomen side-to-side. "Esma looks very bad, even for a human. Her skin is damp and there are dark circles around her eyes. At first, she refused to see me until I said it was about you."

"Poor Esma," Ambria said.

"What was her message?" My eagerness made me sound unsympathetic, but I had to know.

"Esma said you may visit tomorrow after classes." Shushiel blinked her eyes.

Max leaned closer. "And what else?"

"That is all she said." The spider blinked again. "She did not answer your question, Conrad."

I felt disappointed but also elated that I could see Esma again. "I wonder what's wrong with her."

"Must be serious if a healer can't fix it," Max said.

My elation tanked. "Serious, as in life-threatening?"

"Wonderful, Max." Ambria slapped him on the shoulder. "Now you've worried him!"

Max shielded himself with his hands. "I'm just telling him the truth!"

I am sorry, but he is right, Della said.

Vic seemed happy. *She will die.* His maniacal laughter echoed in my brain.

I closed my eyes and covered my ears but couldn't block out the voices in my head. *Shut up! Shut up!*

A hand gripped my shoulder, a spider leg touched my neck, and a soft hand squeezed mine. I opened my eyes and saw twelve concerned eyes looking at me.

"Please don't worry, Conrad." Ambria took my other hand. "I'm sure Esma will be okay."

Max didn't looked convinced, but he nodded. "Yeah, she'll be fine." He flashed a fake grin. "Promise."

"Perhaps the Broken Relic can fix her too, Conrad," Shushiel said.

For a moment, I worried that the effects of the curse my parents used on me still lingered and made Esma sick. But if that was the case, Max and Ambria would surely be even sicker. Maybe Shushiel was right. Maybe the Broken Relic could heal her. Then again, if the Heart of Jura did as Underborn suggested, maybe it could heal sickness as well as scars.

"I'm going to sleep in here tonight," I told the others. "I don't feel safe in my room."

"Nothing will touch you," Shushiel said. "I will set a sentry web. Nothing will get to you, Conrad. I promise."

"You'll be safe with her protecting you," Max said. "Besides, I doubt the Seers will be able to get past the outer perimeter again."

I had far more faith in Shushiel than in the campus wards. Her protection was security enough for me. I took the Nose of Jura from my pocket and set it on the pedestal with the book index. "I think this is safer here for now."

"Agreed," Ambria said.

"Della is right that we could use it to find the heart more quickly," Max said, "but we should be careful not to let Gwyneth know about it, or you can bet Underborn will try to steal it."

"Underborn?" Shushiel's whispery voice sounded startled. "What happened tonight?"

"Something crazy as usual," Max said.

I brought Shushiel up to date and she immediately declared herself part of the expedition.

"I still don't understand how we're supposed to get past the guardians," Ambria said. "Evadora even told you she can't do it."

Max nodded his agreement. "When are we going?"

"Not until we figure out how to cross the Rift without dying," I said.

"We should check out the reflected world," Max said.

Ambria flashed a horrified look. "Naeve is there!"

"She can't be everywhere," Max said. "Maybe there's another lake or pond we could use to get inside."

"Maybe," I said. I wondered if Naeve was still screaming next to the wishing pool in front of the keeps, or if she'd returned to the reflected version of the Glimmer. There was only one way to find out and just the thought of it frightened me. Unfortunately, I had to take the chance because it might be our only way in. Crossing into the reflected realm would require planning just in case Naeve waited there. She was probably angry enough to wait for all of eternity if it meant killing me the instant I ventured into the reflected world.

Secure in the knowledge that Shushiel would watch over me in my sleep, we returned to our respective dorms. My spider friend hung invisible threads in the window and door, and linked them to a web she spun on the ceiling. If anyone tried to get in, she'd be instantly alerted.

It was apparently enough to calm my nerves because I woke up without any memory of having gone to sleep. My first thought the next morning was about Esma. It had only been a few days since I'd seen her, but it felt like a week. I wished that I had thought to buy her a gift while in town, but I didn't think she'd mind if I showed up empty handed.

Professor Sideon was eager to speak with me after enchantments class and asked if I'd considered his proposal. I'd already decided to keep him out of the loop for my Glimmer expedition. If all went well, I might have the Broken Relic much sooner and without needing his help at all. Once I used it for my purposes, I could let him borrow it to fix the Alabaster Arches.

"I haven't decided if I'll look for it," I told him.

His jaw tightened, but a quick smile erased the disappointment. "Perhaps you'll allow me to use the nose to find it then."

I nodded. "If I don't go, then I could probably loan it to you."

He seemed to accept that answer and let me leave without further ado. My last class finally ended and Max, Ambria, and I followed winding passages to the residential wing of the university. A man in loose teal robes sat behind a desk reading a novel with a shirtless man on the front. He looked up with alarm and slid the book out of sight.

"No students allowed," he said. "Professors and their children only."

"I'm here to see Professor Esma Emoora," I told him. "She's expecting me."

The man narrowed his eyes and looked me up and down. He opened a worn leather-bound book and flipped to the middle. A grunt and a sigh later, he nodded. "I see authorization for one Conrad Edison."

"That's me, sir." I smiled politely.

"She's in the Gondor Suite." He pointed down the hall. "Straight down the hall, two lefts, up the stairs halfway then take a right into the door." He took a breath and continued. "Second right and down a ramp, and her door is the green one."

Ambria looked aghast. "How does anyone find anything in this place?"

The guard flashed her a smile. "Miss, there are rooms in this place no one has seen in centuries."

"I can only imagine," she said.

186

"Your friends will have to wait here," the guard told me.

"Don't worry about us," Max said with a wink. "We'll sing songs to pass the time."

Ambria clapped her hands together. "Oh, I know just the perfect thing."

The guard groaned and likely wished he could send them along with me.

I followed the instructions and reached the green door without too much trouble. Esma didn't answer my knocks at once, which made me wonder if she'd fallen asleep or was feeling worse today. The door creaked open to reveal a very pale and tired woman in a pink bathrobe.

Esma managed a weak smile. "Come in, Conrad." Black lines underscored her eyes, and her usually round cheeks looked sunken. Even the color in her eyes had dulled.

I couldn't help it. Seeing her like this reminded me too much of Cora, and sent sharp pains into my heart. I wrapped my arms around her and pressed my face into her robes. "Please, Esma, don't die." Hot tears stung my cheeks. "You can't die."

She stiffened for a long moment, and then it was as if her defenses finally broke. Esma put her arms around me and squeezed me tight. "I'll do my best, son."

I looked up at her and couldn't help but smile. "Son?"

Her smile and tears were at once replaced by a mask, a shield slamming down. "A figure of speech. I'm sorry, I meant to say Conrad." Esma gently separated from me. "I'm not going to die." She offered a tiny smile. "I'll be back to class soon. I have a chronic condition and the only cure is bedrest."

I didn't care if she wanted to protect our student-teacher relationship by pretending not to care. She was my mentor and seeing her so sick made me feel like a frightened little boy in the hospital all over again. "I know I shouldn't tell you this, Esma, but I care for you so much." I wiped away tears. "You're like a mother to me."

A breath caught in her throat and she looked away. "I don't deserve that distinction, Conrad." She squeezed shut her eyes and paused. When she opened them again, she was all business. "I hear you've embroiled yourself in yet another dangerous situation."

I told her about my two problems. "At first, it was only Professor Sideon who wanted to go with me in search of the Broken Relic. Now Underborn is involved if I go into the Glimmer and retrieve the Heart of Jura."

"What does the heart do?" she asked.

"It heals scars." I shrugged. "Underborn said it may heal more, but he'd have to test it." I tried to touch her hand, but she backed away. "Maybe it can heal your illness."

Esma seemed lost in thought, a blink the only indication she'd heard me. "Underborn is not one to be trusted. Tell me every detail of your encounter."

I recounted my memories the best I could, including how Della had helped me.

"Della has had quite the change in heart," Esma said. "Can she be trusted?"

"She helped me a lot with Underborn." I shrugged. "Maybe she really has changed."

I waited for some confirmation from Della, but she didn't offer an opinion.

"I'm proud of you, Conrad." Esma praised me in a dull monotone. "It is vital you not let Underborn know about the Nose of Jura and that you tell him and his surrogates as little as possible."

"That's what Della said."

Esma sat on a plush divan and seemed to sink into the folds of her robe. Dark veins and bones pressed against the thin skin of her hands. "Perhaps she can be trusted."

"She's been surprisingly helpful," I said.

"Does she trust me?" Esma asked.

Yes, Della said firmly.

I couldn't help but grin. "She said yes."

Esma gave the barest of nods. "Conrad, I advise that you delay visiting the Glimmer for as long as possible. Use extreme caution if you test your welcome in the reflected world. Naeve has had plenty of time to lay traps for you there."

"I know." I resisted the urge to step closer to her. "I don't even know how to get in yet anyway."

"Promise you'll let me know your plans." Her eyelids fluttered. "Don't do anything without telling me, please."

"I promise." I knelt next to her chair and gently took her hand in mine. "May I visit again?"

She nodded. "Next week." Took a ragged breath. "I will help you plan." Esma pressed a hand to my cheek. "Don't worry, Conrad. I'll be better soon."

I reluctantly left her apartment and closed the door behind me. When I got into the hall, all the strength vanished from my legs. I slid down the wall and choked back sobs. Esma looked worse than I

189

wanted to admit. It looked as if she was dying, and it tore me apart inside.

Chapter 19

When I caught my breath, I smoothed over my emotions and dried my face. By the time I returned to my waiting friends, I hoped it wasn't obvious that I'd been crying. Ambria gave me a worried look and a big hug.

"Everything will be all right," she said. "We're here for you, Conrad."

"Yep." Max patted me on the back.

Ambria sighed. "Boys are terrible at comforting."

The guard chuckled. "That's the truth."

I told the others about my conversation with Esma on our way to the dining hall. "Maybe the heart can heal her condition."

"Worth a shot," Max said. "Hopefully Underborn will let you use it."

"First things first," Ambria said. "How are we supposed to get into the Glimmer?"

"No idea," I admitted. "I need to talk with Evadora."

"Evadora," Ambria said softly. She stopped in the middle of hall and clapped her hands. "Evadora!"

191

"Uh, that's her name," Max said.

"Shush, Max." Eyes glittering with excitement, Ambria grabbed my hand. "I just came up with a brilliant plan you're going to love!"

Even Max was impressed by the simplicity of her idea and we were beyond excited to try it out. We went to the Fairy Garden after dinner but Evadora wasn't there. We checked for her the next day and the next, but by the end of the week we hadn't seen a sign of our friend.

We finally found her the following Tuesday, once again dancing among the recovering forest. She jumped up and down, waving happily as we circled in for a landing.

"Isn't it pretty?" Evadora ran her fingers along newly formed branches. The stumps had grown taller by at least a foot.

"How wonderful!" Ambria said. "Will the entire wood recover?"

"I think so." Evadora danced and spun. She circled behind Max and leapt high enough to land squarely on his shoulders. "You're bigger!"

Max grunted and stumbled but kept his balance. "So are you!"

Evadora kissed him on the cheek and hopped off, nearly shoving him to the ground in the process. "Big Max and Pretty Ambria. It's lovely to see you again." She curtseyed and burst into laughter.

Ambria blushed. "You think I'm pretty?"

Evadora nodded enthusiastically. "Inside and out."

"Dunno about inside," Max said. "She's kind of mean."

"Maxwell Tiberius!" Ambria pushed him.

Max's eyes widened innocently. "See what I mean?"

Evadora laughed.

I tried to be patient, to let the fun moment continue, but I was too worried about Esma and too preoccupied with finding the heart. I couldn't wait any longer. "Evadora, there's a Relic of Jura in the Glimmer that I need to find."

She snapped her attention to me, forehead arched with curiosity. "A relic?"

"Yes, the Heart of Jura."

Evadora wrinkled her nose. "Ooh—I did not know there was a heart. What does it do?"

"It heals scars." I told her about my deal with Underborn and then told her Ambria's brilliant plan for retrieving it. "The Nose of Jura seems to smell other relics. Can you go back to the Glimmer and use it to find the heart?"

Evadora jumped up and down, clapping her hands in glee. "Of course!"

Max and Ambria cheered.

"I can't believe we didn't think of it sooner," Max said.

Ambria sniffed. "You never would have thought of it."

I took the nose from my pocket and instructed Evadora how to use it.

Evadora inspected it curiously, rolling the stone nose in her fingers. "Does it hurt?"

I shook my head. "No, but there's a strong odor when you first put it on."

She hesitantly held it up to her nose. The stone molded to her face like clay, retaining the marbled look even as it covered her nose. Evadora's forehead creased and her eyes watered. "Oh, it smells terrible!" She danced from foot to foot, face twisted in pain. "When does the smell go away?" Tears leaked from the corners of her eyes as she endured what I imagined was the strong acrid odor.

Nearly a minute passed and Evadora began gagging. "Smells like death." Whimpering, she practically tore off the nose and dropped it on the ground. She sat on a stump and inhaled deeply, sighing in relief.

"Didn't you sense the relics?" Ambria asked.

"Do they smell rotten?" Evadora said. "It was like putting my nose in a dead animal with maggots and flies."

Max gagged and put a hand over his mouth.

"That's not what it smells like," Ambria said. "At first, it's like something sharp and burning, then that goes away and the relics are a distant odor."

Evadora shook her head. "No, it was terrible."

Ambria put the nose on and sniffed experimentally. "I don't smell anything rotten."

"Maybe it works differently for everyone," Max said. "Neither me nor Conrad could smell the relics as clearly as you."

"Please try again." Ambria held out the nose to Evadora.

The other girl sighed and nodded. Taking a deep breath, she put on the nose and sniffed. She coughed, made a choking noise and threw up. "Stinks so bad!" She endured it for several more seconds before taking off the nose again. "I am sorry, but it does not work for me."

"No!" Ambria wailed. "It was such a perfect idea, too."

"Back to the drawing board," Max groaned.

I couldn't believe it hadn't worked. I stared at the stone nose, guts twisting with regret. Evadora could have retrieved the heart in no time at all. I could heal Esma and then trade the heart to Underborn for the Broken Relic. Now it seemed we had no choice but to do this the hard way. I put the nose in my pocket and tried to ignore the churning worry in my stomach. "We need to get into the Glimmer, Evadora. Can you help us get past the guardians?"

She frowned. "They won't let you even if I ask."

"There must be some way," I said. "Can you make them go away like last time and we can run across?"

"Oh, they don't go away." Evadora stood and waved her hands in warning. "They are always nearby and would kill you before you could run halfway."

"What about if we're cloaked?" Ambria asked.

"The guardians do not have eyes." Evadora used thumbs and index fingers to hold open her eyelids. "They will sense you."

"Zap!" Max clapped his hands and made Ambria jump. "We'd be toast."

"What about a shield?" I suggested.

Evadora tapped her chin and looked up. "That might work, but it would need to be very strong."

Max looked doubtful. "How strong?"

"Very, very strong," Evadora said with certainty.

"That's not an answer." Ambria threw up her hands. "I don't know if even your strong shield is enough for the guardians, Conrad."

I didn't need to test my shield against the guardians to know she was right. That left only one route for us to take—the reflected world. While the landscape looked the same in that upside-down realm, the only inhabitants were reflections of people in the real world who would steal part of your soul with a mere touch if you were foolish enough to brave their realm. The rift in that realm was free of guardians which meant you could cross the divide and then return to the normal world once you reached the Glimmer.

Unfortunately, Naeve might be waiting for us.

"We have to visit the reflected world and see if it's safe." I rubbed Cora's green pebble in my fingers. As part of the anchor stone, it allowed the bearer to jump into water and travel to the other realm. "Is there a way I can look into the other side?"

Evadora nodded. "Say the words and put your head in the water. I will hold onto you so you don't slip through."

Max gave her a dubious look. "How long does the passage stay open after you say the magic words?"

"I think until you are all the way through," Evadora said.

"You think?" Ambria grimaced. "What if it closes while Conrad still has his head inside?"

Evadora slammed the side of her hand into a palm. "Chop! His head would come off."

"Gah!" Max made a sign of the cross and backed away. "You are a twisted girl."

Evadora giggled and hugged herself. "It's funny!"

"No, it's not!" Ambria shouted. "It's horrible."

The other girl kept laughing. "I wouldn't let Conrad get chopped up."

I touched my neck and tried to imagine my head rolling off in the mirror dimension and sitting on shore. Would that world be my last memory? I shook off the feeling and walked toward the pond sitting just outside the recovering forest. "Let me see what's on the other side."

Evadora skipped after me. "Chop, chop, chop, the head rolls off! The head rolls off! The head rolls off! Chop, chop, chop, the head rolls off—"

"Stop it!" Ambria shrieked.

Max grabbed Evadora's arm. "Want me to sing about your head getting chopped off?" He made a slashing motion with his hand toward her neck.

Evadora's eyes lit with delight. "Yes, yes, yes!"

He groaned and shook his head sadly. "You sure about this, Conrad?"

I took the stone in my hand. "Yes." I got down on my hands and knees at the edge of the water. "I'm ready."

Evadora grabbed my ankles and lifted me off the ground, holding me upside down and just above the water. She grunted. "You are heavier than last time. I won't be able to hold you long."

"I won't need long." I rubbed the stone and said the magic words. "As above, so below." The dark water met my face as Evadora lowered me. Instinct made me hold my breath, but there was no damp sensation, only a twisting in my brain and then I was looking at the same place, except this time I wasn't upside down.

My body felt oddly disconnected from the rest of me, my clenching hands felt foreign, distant. I tried not to think about what

197

might happen if the magic stopped working and twisted my head for a look around. There were no people as far as the eye could see. No malevolent trees or vines waited to attack, and no signs Naeve lay in wait. Everything looked exactly the same here as it did in the normal world.

I slapped my leg to signal Evadora and she pulled me back into the normal world. My brain felt as though it flipped upside down and then everything was back to normal. Evadora dropped me on the ground. I thudded onto my back with a grunt and got a good look at the blue sky.

Evadora stood over me and shook her arms. "That hurt. You eat too much, Conrad."

That earned a snort from Max.

Ambria knelt next to me. "What did you see?"

"It looks safe. I think we can explore further." I rolled onto my knees and pushed into a sitting position. "Evadora, do you have more fragments of the anchor stone?"

"Yes." Her head tilted. "Why?"

"We'll need three more for Ambria, Max, and Shushiel. I want to make sure we can all escape independently in case something happens."

Her head tilted the other way. "Shushiel?"

"Our giant spider friend," Ambria explained.

Evadora's eyes lit. "Oh, how wonderful! When can I meet her?"

"Soon." I stood up and brushed off my pants. "Will you be able to help us find the relic in the Glimmer?"

"Of course." She bounced on her heels. "I am still learning how to control the land since Naeve never taught me."

"Can you control the trees and vines?" Ambria asked.

"Yes, a little." Evadora bent over and touched a plant that hadn't reached full bloom. She squinted and clenched her teeth. The plant shivered and the flower burst open. "I am able to make the plants heal faster, but making the trees walk and the vines move is harder."

"You had those vines digging in the crack of the world," I reminded her.

"That was only a few vines," Evadora said. "Controlling more at once is very hard."

"What about the animals?" I asked. "You'll be able to keep them away like you did the last time we went, right?"

She nodded. "Of course, but you must stay near me or they might attack."

"Well, that's a relief," Max said. "I hope this adventure doesn't take long."

"When can you bring me more stone fragments?" I asked.

"I will return in"—Evadora looked up and seemed to count on her fingers—"two weeks. I will bring more fragments then."

"Two weeks?" My voice rose with shock. "I need to find the heart sooner."

Her large eyes blinked with surprise. "I have many things to do, Conrad. When Naeve tried to kill you, she unbalanced the animals and many of them are in the wrong places. Unless I guide them away, travel will be very dangerous."

"Can't we just fly our brooms?" Max said.

199

"Naeve left commands so the creatures of the air will attack anything in flight," Evadora said. "Even I cannot keep so many away."

Ambria's eyes narrowed. "How much control over the animals do you actually have?"

Evadora looked down. "Not enough. That is why I must learn more and try to restore balance to the realm. Then it will be safer for you."

Two weeks. What if Esma's condition worsened? I couldn't stand the idea of waiting, but I didn't want to put my friends in unnecessary danger. I just had to hope Esma would be okay. There was one last matter on my mind. "Did Yoghra find anything on the Soul Tree?"

"Not yet." Evadora sidled up next to me and put her head on my shoulder. "There is so much to search that even Yoghra cannot find it quickly."

I looked down at my hands. "Please hurry. My friend might be dying and I need to find the heart to save her."

"If I can return sooner, I will." Evadora squeezed my hand. "I promise."

"How will I know if you return sooner?" I asked.

"I will find you."

I watched her go, my heart growing heavier with every step she took. *If only Ambria's plan had worked.* Esma's pale face and skeletal hands played back in my mind. If it came down to it, I'd go into the Glimmer alone and find the heart.

Do not risk going alone for Esma, Della said in a pleading voice. *Your life is more precious.*

Her tone was so caring it made me flinch. There was a vast gulf between Della's attitude now and how Delectra had behaved shortly after her resurrection. I remembered the sick, evil gleam in her eyes, the razor-sharp knife she aimed for my throat. All I saw in her eyes was endless dark.

Was Delectra always evil? I asked her soul fragment.

Beautiful, young, naïve, Della said wistfully. *I—she was too proud of herself, too driven to be the best. Victus fell in love with her power and used her weaknesses to taint her.* She went silent and offered nothing else.

Della's advice was sound. I shouldn't attempt this journey alone, but if Esma's condition worsened, I would gladly risk death to save her.

Chapter 20

After returning from the Fairy Garden, I sat down on my bed and opened the dossier on Delectra Moore.

Delectra was born the daughter of Damien Shelton* and Sasha Moore. Damien took the name Moore since it was the only name many considered worth handing down.

I looked down the page and found a reference to the asterisk in the text: *Brother to Alfred Shelton, the biological father of Harry Shelton, one of the most powerful Arcanes.*

Harry Shelton had gone to Seraphina with Justin Slade. Apparently, he was my cousin. I continued reading.

Though known for her kindness, Delectra was popular for her beauty and her prodigal Arcane skills. This streak of narcissism is what Victus exploited to warp her into a monster.

A collection of observations detailed what had been found in Victus's journals and how he'd manipulated her. How he'd wooed her into a relationship and convinced her to let him use demon magic on her to increase her powers.

Though not possessed, exposure to so much caustic demonic presence in Delectra's soul corrupted her gradually. Victus delved into aspects of demonic magic that allowed him to imbue inanimate objects with a presence. It is believed he used similar methods on his son, Conrad, the only child known to us that was not sacrificed for more demonic powers.

Bile bit the back of my throat. *Sacrificed?* Delectra had said as much after resurrection, but I'd pushed it from my mind in the hopes it wasn't true. I felt physically ill and had to put down the book.

I half expected Della to say something, but her presence was absent. I wondered if she felt ashamed for Delectra's terrible past. I sensed satisfaction, but it was from Vic. I shuddered to think how monstrous Victus must be.

Max looked up from his enchantments textbook. "What's wrong?"

I told him, and his face went pale as a ghost.

"I thought I knew evil," Max said in a strangled voice. "Victus is way past evil."

Though my hands shook and my stomach roiled, I continued reading. The remaining summary was light on details, but made clear that when Victus had sunk his claws deep enough, there was nothing Delectra wouldn't do for him. The writer described Delectra as the most powerful Arcane of her time, rivaling even Harry Shelton.

Raised as an orphan, Harry Shelton never realized he was related to Delectra.

I started to read Victus's dossier, but the writer did an in-depth psychological profile that quickly bored me.

Victus's parents, once extreme rivals, were Mallory Edison and Jelena Tesla. They married to unite against what was seen as the scourge of magic that threatened to spill into the mortal world and forever change the paradigm. Both vanished shortly after Victus's third birthday. It is theorized that supernatural agents may have been the cause.

It is also unknown who raised Victus to adulthood. Even his journals have a gap in his early years. Either he never wrote of them, or he tucked them away in a place we have never found.

I skipped over more in-depth analysis of his psyche and read how Victus successfully revitalized the Edison name and became one of the most powerful people at Science Academy.

Victus revealed what was to be his greatest creation—a hybrid robot-golem that so successfully mimicked organic beings, that it caused an uproar. Arcanes and scientists alike denounced the invention and ruined his reputation. It was at this point Victus likely began to plot his revenge and stepped onto the road that led to his coronation as Overlord.

The revelation that Victus had created such creatures should have sent chills down my spine, but my father was guilty of far worse sins against nature. The dossier detailed how Victus became obsessed with splicing together supernatural creatures, his creation of the tragon, and his secret expertise in demon magic.

After his death, investigators discovered a secret lab where Victus had sacrificed hundreds of supernaturals and regular people with his experiments. Some wondered if they'd found everything or if it was just the tip of the iceberg.

How can I possibly be related to such a horrendous person? I felt guilty by association even though I was his child. A part of me felt it would have been better had Victus never been born, even if it meant snuffing out my own existence.

By the end of the week, I was able to cast spells without feeling sick. Even so, I didn't attempt Ansel's test right away because I was too busy with schoolwork. Monday came and I began to count down the days until I could see Esma again.

Professor Sideon wasn't in class, which came as a relief to me since I didn't want him to ask me about relic hunting again. His class was taught by Rhonda Podge, a stout woman with no sense of humor. Though she apparently knew next to nothing about enchantments, she kept us busy by asking random questions from the textbook.

It was a joy to escape that class, though my heart hung heavy as we went to Magical Defense. Esma's smiling face met my shocked expression when we walked in. It took all my restraint not to run over and hug her.

"You—you look great!" I said, unable to hide the joy. "I don't understand."

"As I said, it's a chronic condition." She offered a faint smile. "Now, take your seats. I'm eager to get class back on track."

Esma wasted no time putting everyone through their paces, zapping us randomly during her lecture to see who could protect themselves from various attacks. Despite being on edge the entire class, I was beyond relieved to have Esma back and healthy.

The good news kept me energized throughout the rest of the day. When classes were over, I went to the mansion ruins behind the Fairy Garden and practiced with the brass arcwand Ansel had given me. Focusing on a rock the size of my head, I flicked the spell patterns as tightly as possible, focused my will, and let the wand handle the rest.

My timing was much improved over doing it manually. Instead of thirty, seconds, it took me half that time to run the gamut of spells on the rock, and the aether battery seemed to add a little extra zing to my spells.

The spells, fire, air, levitation, and the kinetic power of *Torsius* didn't do much to the rock except leave it a bit blackened and chipped, but I felt confident I could destroy the portrait Ansel had given me by the time I finished practicing.

I wondered if I could use an avatar to increase my power and actually destroy the rock. I flicked through the pattern for *Ignitus*, firmed my resolve, and focused on Cora, Max, and Ambria. An orange beam speared from my wand and into the rock. Sparks scattered across the floor and the stone glowed, but it was nowhere near as intense as what I'd achieved in the first test.

I imagined Cora on her deathbed. Grief pooled in my gut like molten lead. Rather than increase my power, the spell sparked and fizzled out. My arm fell to the side, the wand dropped from limp fingers. I felt weak, incapable. Trying to grasp at my avatar was like gripping a double-edged sword. It had worked for me and now against me, but why? What had I done differently?

There was obviously a lot more to it than I realized. Despite the setback, I felt ready to perform Ansel's latest test. I took the portrait and set it against a crumbling wall. Banishing all thought of avatars from my mind, I imagined the face staring out at me from the canvas was Victus. I picked up the arcwand and flicked through the pattern.

The next day after class, I went to Ansel's office. He looked annoyed to see me, but his eyes brightened when I tossed the charred remains of the portrait on his desk. "What next?" I asked.

He laughed and rubbed his hands together. "Very nice, my boy." He waved his wand over the painting and nodded in satisfaction. "Just making sure you didn't cheat and burn it with matches."

"Of course I didn't!" Cheating had never occurred to me. "How am I supposed to learn if I break the rules?"

Ansel ignored my outburst. He rummaged in his desk and withdrew the Moore genealogy book with the hole burned through the middle and set it on a stool in the corner. "Now, finish what I asked you to do."

I'd anticipated this and produced the brass arcwand. Without a word, I flicked through the patterns. Within seconds, I reduced the book to a blackened, torn corpse.

"Brilliant!" Ansel roared with laughter and nearly tumbled from his perch on the edge of the desk. "And not a drop of vomit to be found."

"Why do you hate Ezzek Moore?" I asked.

His laughter died away. "That's none of your concern, boy. You're here to learn, not ask."

"Do you blame him for Delectra?" I asked.

Ansel's eyes grew dark. "Ask me one more time and you're done."

My face grew warm with anger and frustration. *What isn't he telling me?* What had warped Ansel into this angry creature? I changed tact. "You'll be happy to know Esma is feeling better."

"Better?" His forehead pinched.

"You didn't know she was sick?"

"You're a curious lad." Ansel plucked the arcwand from my fingers. "Perhaps you'll put that curiosity to good work and learn something. He handed me a blank piece of parchment. "You will write a spell script to fold this into an airplane and make it fly."

"Write a script?" I couldn't hide the surprise in my voice. "I wouldn't know where to begin."

"I sent you the codex, sweet cousin." Ansel patted my head. "I'm certain you'll figure it out."

"You won't show me?" I asked.

"As I said, put your curiosity to good use." He lunged forward until his face was an inch from mine, eyes glowing with madness. "Read and learn!" he roared. "Don't be a useless child, Conrad! Make something of yourself!"

For the span of seconds, I forgot to breathe, held in thrall by the insanity in the man's eyes. I suspected he'd had a difficult childhood. "Yes, cousin," I whispered.

Ansel blinked and straightened, face a smooth mask. "Do not return until you've completed the lesson." He rolled the wand across his desk to me and waved his hand in a shooing motion. "Now go."

I tucked the arcwand into my back pocket, rolled up the parchment and left. As I neared Arcane University, two people on brooms whisked around one of the towers and zipped toward me. For an instant, I thought the Seers had breached the defenses, but recognized the tall ebony frame of Elliott Cobain and the stocky form of Jenna Nash, the captains of the Moore Keep kabash team.

"Hey, Conrad." Elliott performed a perfect sliding stop and halted parallel to me. "You're a hard person to track down."

"Probably has a girlfriend," Jenna said with a teasing smile.

"Sorry, I've been taking some extra classes," I said.

Elliott's gaze wandered across the valley. "At Science Academy?" He shrugged. "Hey, doesn't matter. What does matter is Kabash tryouts." He leaned on his broom's saddle horn. "Jenna and I are graduating this year and we want to go out on top. Can we count on you to join the team again?"

"You'll be a carry just like last year," Jenna said.

I already felt like a mountain of work sat on my shoulders. Ansel expected me to learn how to code spells without his help, and I had to plan the expedition into the Glimmer. With my normal school work, it didn't seem possible to fit in a sport as well. "I'm really overwhelmed with school this year. I don't know if I can devote the time necessary."

Elliott's smile faded. "I see. We could really use you. Rhys and Devon Tiberius are graduating this year. Their keep is favored to win the cup."

"Do you really want them to go out victors?" Jenna said. "They were such asses to you last year, I thought you might want some revenge."

My face heated with anger as I thought about how they'd threatened me to keep me from playing Kabash. I could help turn the tables and make sure they had a miserable season. But then they'd only come at me harder the next time and divert me from what really mattered—finding the Broken Relic.

I let the anger melt away. "I'm sorry, I just don't have time."

Elliott nodded. "Well, think about it. Max already said he'd rejoin the team this year."

I was a bit surprised to hear that and it must have shown on my face.

"He didn't tell you?" Jenna said.

I tried to play it off. "Like I said, I haven't had a lot of free time." I angled my broom for the keep. "Thank you for the offer." I couldn't manage a smile before flying away.

Max and Ambria were just leaving for dinner when I arrived.

"Didn't know if you were gonna make it," Max said. "We're starving!"

Ambria rolled her eyes. "Did you go see Ansel today?"

209

"Yeah, I passed his second test." I told them about the new challenge.

"Scripting spells?" Max scratched his head. "Now that's something I'd like to learn."

I snorted wryly. "I don't even know why I need Ansel. He doesn't teach me anything. All he does is give me orders."

"Let's learn together." Max clapped a hand on my back. "Maybe it'll be fun."

"I'd like to learn too," Ambria said.

Their enthusiasm lifted my spirits. "Sure, let's all learn together." After putting my broom away in the room, the three of us walked to the dining hall.

Max ate with his usual gusto and finished well ahead of the rest of us. He opened his mouth as if to speak, took a sip of tea and tried again. "Elliott Cobain paid me a surprise visit earlier. He asked me to join the Kabash team and then said I should make sure you're going to play too."

"Oh, I completely forgot about Kabash," Ambria said.

Max snorted. "As if you care a whit about the game. You can barely stay up on a broom as it is."

"I have too much to do." I broke a piece of bread from the bun on my plate. "Playing a game won't get us any closer to the Broken Relic."

Ambria's expression grew concerned. "Don't you enjoy Kabash?"

"Sure." *It was the most fun I've ever had.* Unfortunately, fun wasn't something I could afford right now.

Why not? Della said. *What's the purpose of life if you can't enjoy it?*

I can't enjoy life if I'm dead. The Seers wanted to purify me, and there was no telling when Victus might try to kill me again. I certainly didn't need threats from Rhys and Devon added to my list of worries.

Competition improves you and makes you strong. Della sounded like a mother teaching her child life lessons. *All work and no play makes Conrad a dull boy.*

I threw up my hands. "But I have too much to do!"

Max and Ambria reared back at the outburst.

"I didn't argue with you," Max said.

Ambria's eyes narrowed. "Is Della talking again?"

"She wants me to enjoy life." I stuffed a piece of bread in my mouth. "Apparently, I don't get enough play time."

"That's for sure." Max sighed. "Conrad, if you're not trying to pass one of Ansel's tests, you're studying or practicing spells. When was the last time you forgot all that and had some fun?"

I thought back to the race against Esma when she took me to see Ansel. That had been fun. Everything else since then had revolved around school and finding the Broken Relic. "Joining the Kabash team means I'll have practice in addition to everything else I'm doing. I just don't think I can manage it."

Managing your time is as important a skill as casting spells, Della said. *I played Kabash, raced brooms, and was still the best student.*

Were your own parents trying to kill you? I asked. *Did you have a secret society breathing down your neck so they could put you through a purifying ritual?*

She had no answer for that. There was only so much time in the day and adding one more responsibility would simply be too much. I had to concentrate on what was important and Kabash was not.

Chapter 21

"What a shame you won't be playing." Ambria patted my hand. "But I understand."

Max sighed. "Tiberius Keep is gonna wipe the field with us."

"I'm sorry." I checked the time and groaned. "I need to start reading the Cyrinthian Codex, and then we've got all that homework from Professor Grace." A poisonous cloud of hopelessness swelled inside my chest. The realization that I wouldn't play Kabash dragged my spirits to the gutter.

Since the codex was on my phone, the only way for all of us to read it was to project the screen in holographic format which wouldn't be wise to do in the keep. We went to Moore's vault for privacy and used a table there. The codex arranged runes based on power and usage with a brief explanation for each one. A separate section contained syntax and usage. At the beginning was a brief definition of the programming language itself.

.ARC is an object-oriented arcnological programming language. All syntax is Cyrinthian with assistance to prevent usage of incorrect runes that might end with disastrous results.

We started plowing through the basics first—how to link wand patterns to start scripts and how to avoid creating a rune paradox which could result in the arcwand or other device exploding.

"Goodness, this sounds terribly dangerous," Ambria said. "Are there any tutorials?"

"Doesn't look like it." Max banged his head on the table. "I'm going cross-eyed just reading this stuff."

I scrolled through the index. "I don't see any walk-through guides, just usage examples."

"Man, if only we had—" Max went silent and looked at the shelves behind us. "Are we stupid or what?"

Ambria sniffed. "No, but you certainly are."

Max ignored her and went to the index book. He thumbed to the front and flipped a few pages before jabbing a finger. "Got it!"

I jogged over and looked at the page.

Arcnology resources – See Nosti, Adam and Shelton, Harry.

Max flipped to the first name and whooped at the listing. "This is just what we need."

We took one of the flying carpets to the proper aisle and found a dusty stack of arctablets on the second level of the shelves. Max picked up one and inspected it. "This is one of the original Orange tablets!" He blew off the dust and sent Ambria into sneezing fits.

She backed away from him. "Max, you little devil!"

He chuckled and turned on the device. "Good thing these aether batteries last a long time." The main screen appeared and Max hunted through various icons. "Wow, this looks like he used it as a development tablet."

"Development?" Ambria said.

"Yeah, for testing scripts and stuff." Max touched an icon and the screen went blank. "Oops."

"What did you do?" Ambria crowded over his left shoulder for a look. "You broke it, didn't you?"

"Who dares access my arctablet?" The apparition of a man dressed in black robes and thick glasses appeared in the air before us.

Max yelped and nearly knocked the rest of us off the carpet in his haste to back up.

I steadied him. "I think it's a projection from the tablet."

"Oh, it is." Max smiled sheepishly. "Scared the crap out of me."

The hologram stared blankly ahead, apparently waiting for an answer to its question.

"Well, what do I say?" Max asked.

Ambria looked at the shelf and squinted. She reached over and pulled a parchment stuck between two of the tablets and unfolded it. "I am the dread pirate Roberts."

"Welcome, Dread Pirate Roberts!" The man held out his hands in welcome. "What is the password?"

Ambria looked at the parchment and frowned. "Um, twue wuv?"

"Access granted." The holographic man bowed and vanished. The table screen turned on and displayed a list of videos below the title, *Mr. Smith's Complete Guide to Cyrinthian Programming.* Ambria raised an eyebrow and looked quite pleased with herself.

"Nice work!" Max stared at the videos. "Looks like we have plenty to watch."

Ambria handed me the parchment. "You might want to hold onto this."

It appeared Ezzek Moore had numbered the tablets and provided passwords for each one, along with the dates each one had been copied. There were summaries of the information on each one as well.

I skimmed through them. "It says that tablet seven has the finalized version of the programming guide on it."

Max grabbed the other tablets and set them on the carpet. "Makes sense. Number seven is the last one."

We flew back to the table and dusted off tablet seven. This one prompted us for a password before the screen even showed up and the name of the guide was different. Instead of Mr. Smith, it said Adam Nosti.

"I wonder if Smith was a fake name," Ambria said.

Max shrugged. "Probably an online name." He scrolled to the first video and played it back. A young man with thick glasses looked back at us.

"Welcome to my guide on Cyrinthian programming. I've tried to keep this updated over the years, so expect to find the latest and greatest information." Adam pushed his glasses up his nose. "Before we go any further, make sure you understand the risks of magic programming and don't execute a live script without thoroughly testing it in a development simulation." He leaned back and flashed a smile. "In this video, I'll cover the basics of programming."

Max cracked his knuckles. "This is more like it."

"I hope it's easier to follow," Ambria said.

I took out my notepad and let the lesson begin.

We spent the next hour watching the first two basic videos and then had to stop so we could do the homework for our classes. By the time we left the vault it was nearly midnight and I could barely keep my eyes open.

Shushiel revealed herself on the ceiling outside and once again nearly caused us to faint with fright. "I thought you might be in there," she said.

"I never know when you're around," Max said.

"Apologies." The spider tilted forward on its front legs. "I had to attend to family but I am here to watch over Conrad as he sleeps."

"Thanks, Shushiel." I patted her foreleg. "It makes me feel safe."

The entire campus was in a festive mood the next day. Students of all ages sported their keep colors and posters for Kabash tryouts reminded me the deadline to join a team was quickly approaching. Many professors also wore the colors of their keeps and kept the lessons light and easy—Gideon Grace, of course, being the lone exception.

Esma, sporting the black and white scarf of Moore Keep, seemed as cheerful as the rest and refrained from zapping students as they entered the classroom. Instead of a regular lesson, she asked students about their favorite professional Kabash players and spoke about some of the best teams in university history.

It was little surprise that Esma mentioned Delectra among the greatest—a fact that drew scowls from the likes of Harris and his friends.

Liana clapped her hands and smiled at me. "That explains why you're so good, Conrad."

"He's lucky, not good," Harris growled. "Why do you think he's not playing this year?"

"Edison stinks at Kabash." Baxter sneered at me. "Tiberius won the cup last year, and it'll win this year."

Foolish boys, Della said. *In your first year, you were the second-highest scoring carry. That is not luck.*

While I appreciated her support, I decided not to engage the naysayers.

Max couldn't restrain himself. "You don't know what you're talking about! Conrad flew circles around your whole team!"

"That will be quite enough, children." Esma's cold voice extinguished the heated argument. "Belittling another person only shows what a little person you are."

Harris stared daggers at me, but knew better than to challenge Esma, lest he find himself at the receiving end of her wand.

As class ended, Esma gave me a sharp look that made me linger after the other students had left.

"You're not playing Kabash," she said in an emotionless voice when we were the last two left.

I shook my head. "I don't have time."

"You've put your quest above everything else." Again, her voice remained neutral.

"I have to." My reply sounded more defensive than intended. "Kabash is just a game."

"It's an experience." Esma walked around her desk. "It's a memory you'll treasure once you leave this place behind."

"If I survive that long." I fiddled with the straps on my backpack. "I also have all the work Ansel gives me."

"Don't change the subject." Esma put a hand on my shoulder. "Perhaps a game doesn't sound so important to you, but there is so much pain, so much ugliness in the world. Do you not deserve a moment's respite? Do you not deserve happiness?"

All the weight of my quest, the bullying I'd endured, and the faint hope I might be able to save Cora crashed down on me. True happiness might await at my quest's end, but what if I could claim tiny bits of it right now? Kabash would not solve my problems, but it might make me feel better.

Esma stroked my hair. "What is the point of life if you cannot enjoy it, dear boy?" She kissed my forehead and jerked back, visibly shaken, and rushed from the room.

I was so surprised it took me a moment to chase after her. I caught her before she rounded the corner. "Esma, what's wrong?"

She closed her eyes and sighed. "Favoritism is not kindly looked upon."

"You don't show me favoritism!" A wry laugh escaped me. "If anything, you make me work harder than anyone else."

Esma opened her eyes, dark with sadness. "I push you so hard because I want you to succeed." Her voice was low and somber. "I want you to be ready for what you will face." She took my hand in hers. "Enjoy this life, Conrad. Live a little before you run off and get yourself killed."

Her words struck deep. What if my quest failed? What if I missed chances to be happy and passed them up for obsession? I saw this moment as an opportunity to ask her another question. "Why does Ansel dislike you?"

"He does not like what I truly am." Esma offered a sad smile. "He is difficult to like, and deeply troubled by his past, but Ansel will point you in directions you might not have considered." She released my hand and folded her arms over her chest. "I hope it is enough." Esma turned and walked away.

I watched her go as if in a trance. *I'm her favorite!* Somehow I already knew that, but hearing her say it aloud filled me with both joy and dread. What if I couldn't live up to her expectations? Then again, the only expectation she'd expressed had been her desire to see me play Kabash, and even then it was for my own happiness, not hers. Everything she'd taught me, the introduction to Ansel and arcnology, had opened my eyes and given me opportunities I might never have had otherwise.

In the orphanage, the Goodleighs had controlled every aspect of my life. They'd expected me to turn into a strong Arcane they could sell to the highest bidder. My parents had likewise forced me to become the vessel of their resurrection and more recently, the Seers had kidnapped me for their purifying ritual.

They all used me to realize their own expectations.

Esma only wanted me to make my own choices. She showed me the paths, but left it up to me to decide which one to take. It was a far cry from what I'd endured, and a heavy burden, but it was mine to bear or not.

It is hard to let someone you care about make a choice you think is not in their best interest. Della sounded subdued, almost reflective.

But you want me to play Kabash, I reminded her.

Yes, but that is your decision to make. She sighed. *I will support you no matter what.*

I'm happy to hear that, considering we're stuck with each other. I chuckled out loud.

Della burst into laughter as well. *Yes, I'm afraid it might make for some awkward moments.*

I'm glad you're nicer than you used to be. I began to walk to the dining hall. *Why hasn't Vic changed like you?*

There is some darkness not even the brightest light can penetrate. Her words sent chills down my back.

Is he really so evil?

The silence was answer enough.

I searched the dining hall and found Max and Ambria sitting at a table off to the side. It came as a mild surprise to see Liana sitting to Ambria's left.

"There you are," Liana said as I took a chair next to Max. "What kept you?"

"I had to ask Professor Emoora a question." I leaned back as a golem set a plate of steaming roast in front of me.

"Your mother was quite a Kabash player." Liana cut a piece of roast as she spoke. "It's obvious where you get your talent."

Ambria scowled. "Look, he's already decided not to play, so just leave it alone."

Max stabbed a fork into his potatoes. "Yep, we're doomed."

"I'm going to play," I said.

Ambria's eyes went wide. "But you said—"

"Brilliant!" Max shouted.

The hall went quiet at his outburst, heads turning our way, and then the dull roar of conversation picked up where it left off.

Max leaned forward and softly said, "Brilliant."

"What changed your mind?" Ambria said.

I shrugged. "I thought I'd have some fun before this quest kills us."

Max gulped and smiled uneasily. "Let's hope we get to play for years to come."

Liana laughed. "I'm glad to hear you're playing, Conrad. I'm not the only one who doesn't want Tiberius to win the cup this year."

Despite the extra stress Kabash practice would put on my schedule, I felt oddly relieved to have made a decision. Right or wrong, I would do my best to enjoy the experience.

I heard my name mentioned at the neighboring table and cocked my ear to pick up the conversation.

"I just heard Edison say he's playing," said a boy in the black and white of Moore Keep. The girl next to him clapped her hands and said something to the girl next to her. A boy in the purple and red of Tiberius Keep scowled and left the table, apparently unhappy at the news.

"I don't understand why people think I'm the only thing standing between Tiberius Keep and the championship," I said.

"You're too modest," Liana said. "You came close to tying your mother's record in strikes last year, and she didn't get that until her third season!"

Someone had mentioned that before, but the number didn't mean much to me. The feel of the wind, the exhilaration of flying after the discus, of hearing the sound of a strike on an enemy building made me feel alive. Why that was, I didn't know, but now that I'd decided to play, I couldn't wait to feel it again.

Liana waved to her friend, Jessica, and got up. "I promised I'd let her look at my homework for history class. Thanks for letting me sit with you!"

I couldn't help watching her walk away and jumped when Ambria pinched my arm.

"Stop staring, Conrad." She waggled a finger. "It's rude."

My face warmed uncomfortably. I got up and gathered my belongings.

Max swallowed a mouthful. "You're finished already?"

"Yeah, just want to beat the crowd to class." I took a last sip of tea.

"Hang on." Max stuffed the rest of his bread in his mouth and got up.

Ambria gave me a strange look as she rose to her feet. "Are you feeling unwell?"

I faked a smile. "Just fine."

We were headed down the winding halls to history class when a familiar voice called out, "Oh, Edison."

Harris and Baxter stepped out in front of us. I stopped in my tracks and spun around. Rhys and Devon stared back at me, wands at the ready.

Chapter 22

"What do you want?" I said, knowing full well why they were here. Word had gotten around about my decision to play Kabash.

"We warned you," Rhys said.

Devon finished his sentence without pause. "But you didn't listen."

"Afraid of a little competition?" Max's face was pale, but he stuck out his chest in an attempt to appear brave.

"Should've listened, Edison." Harris snarled at me. "One day it's going to be you and me. Until then you need to stay out of my way."

"Because I'm evil?" I felt a surge of anger coming from Vic, but tried not to let it affect my thinking.

I'm sorry, son. Della seemed angry with herself. *I'm sorry we ruined your life.*

I didn't have time to deal with her inner musings and the physical threat at the same time, so I let her keep talking and tried to ignore it.

"Exactly," Harris said. "An evil liar I'm destined to destroy." He cracked his knuckles. "If it were up to me, I'd do it right now."

"I'm certain we could arrange a convincing accident," Devon said.

Rhys giggled. "A broom malfunction, perhaps?"

Ambria's eyes flashed wide. "You wouldn't dare!"

"Of course we'd dare." Devon stepped closer, his mirror image in lockstep.

"You're horrible people!" Ambria shoved Rhys in the chest. "Stay away from us!"

Devon gripped her wrists. "Don't you dare strike my brother, little girl!"

Rhys reared back his hand as if to hit her and something snapped in me. I dove at him, bowling him to the ground. Max roared and crashed into his other brother. I flailed with my fists. Something hit me hard in the face and stars flashed. Ambria screamed. I flipped and a weight crashed down on my chest. I threw up my arms as blows rained down on my face.

Shouts came from nearby. The weight vanished and footsteps stomped away from us.

The taste of iron filled my mouth. I blinked the blurriness from my vision and saw the stone gray ceiling above.

Ambria's face appeared. "Conrad, are you okay?"

I nodded. "What happened?"

"You foolish boy!" She threw herself on top of me and gave me a brutal hug. "What were you thinking?"

"They were going to hit you." I winced at a stinging pain in my lip. "I want to get up, please."

"Yes, of course." Ambria stood and extended a hand to help me up, but I settled for rolling onto all fours and pushing up. "You're every bit as foolish, Max." Ambria gave him a hug as well when he gained his feet. "My brave fools."

Max looked mostly unharmed aside from a red mark on his cheek. The look on his face told me I'd suffered a bit more.

"Oh man, you're bleeding bad." Max stepped closer and grimaced. "Let's get you to the healer."

They took me to the healing ward. Percival, a tall thin man with a neatly oiled mustache frowned when he saw us. "I'm disappointed in you, Edison."

I swallowed hard. "For getting into a fight?"

He blinked. "What does that have to do with anything?" Percival threw up his arms. "Last year you brought me injury after injury." He snapped his fingers. "Ah, and the intrigue. It's not every day I get to treat a Siren."

"Um, well isn't getting injured bad?" Ambria said.

Percival ignored the question and started whistling as he inspected my wounds. "Perhaps you should get in a little physical exercise, young man." He pinched my bicep. "You're a bit scrawny."

I followed him into the back room and stopped in front of a mirror. It showed a pale thin boy with rumpled hair and a face streaked with blood. My arms were bruised and my upper lip was split. I rinsed my face in the sink and was able to determine the source of the blood was just my lip and not another cut.

Percival approached with a small vial with beige liquid inside. "This will stop the bleeding." He poured some on cotton and dabbed the wound. The blood instantly congealed into a scab. It didn't help the pain, but at least I wouldn't look like I'd just walked from a slaughterhouse. I rolled my shoulders and neck. Every joint ached.

Percival looked at Max. "You look fine—just a bit of bruising."

"How do you feel?" I asked him.

Max grinned. "Alive and crazy! Can you believe we attacked my brother?" He clapped his hands together once. "We hit my big brothers!"

I found it hard to share his excitement, though knowing how often his brothers had bullied him, this tiny rebellion probably felt like quite a breakthrough. "I guess we lost the fight."

He laughed. "Yeah, we lost big time, but I don't care." Max shadow-boxed the air. "I punched Devon in the eye. I hope it's black and blue."

"Exciting," Percival said. He motioned us back out into the waiting room. "Perhaps next time you'll bring me something more interesting."

Max grinned. "Next time, we'll send Rhys and Devon to you."

Foolish, brave boys. Della sighed. *It will be the death of you.*

I slapped Max on the back and felt some of his infectious joy forcing a grin on my face. "Wouldn't that be great?"

"The greatest." He pumped a fist and whooped. "Man, that felt good."

Ambria groaned. "You're hopeless."

Percival gave me a vial of potion. "This is a protein potion. I suggest you do calisthenics and drink a vial of this a day."

"Sure," I said, knowing full well I wouldn't dare drink one of his concoctions. We left the healing ward and went back into the hallway.

Ambria wasted little time letting us know what she really thought. "Do you know how much taller and bigger those boys are than you?" She put her hands on her hips. "Well, do you?"

Max's spirit couldn't be dampened. "Aw, it's really sweet of you to worry." He held out his fist and pointed to a speck of blood on the knuckle. "Look at that, will you? I really nailed Devon good."

Ambria's finally gave in to a smile. "It was a thing of beauty, Max."

"I didn't get Rhys nearly as good." I inspected my knuckles, but if I'd had any blood on them, I'd rinsed it off in the sink.

"Well, thank you for defending me." Ambria sighed. "I suppose Shushiel wasn't around."

"It's okay," Max said. "Sometimes we have to take care of ourselves."

Harris and Baxter refused to even look our way when we came into history class. Lily pursed her lips and looked back and forth between us and them, apparently unaware of the incident in the hall.

Asha Fellini's forehead wrinkled when she saw me, but she didn't call attention to me and began the day's lesson. The moment class ended, I left before she had a chance to pull me aside and ask questions.

After school, we returned to Moore's vault and resumed our study of spell scripting. Just before dinner we wrote our first script and ran it in the magic simulation program on the arctablet. Symbols scrolled across the screen and a message flashed: *Simulation Successful.*

Ambria, Max, and I exchanged high-fives and cheered.

"It worked!" Max stared at the tablet in disbelief. "It actually worked."

"I should hope so," Ambria said. "It's rather simple."

"That was just a simulation." I bumped the arcwand against the tablet. A message appeared on the tablet screen: *Transfer to device?* I confirmed it and sent the spell script to the wand. "I'm going to test it for real."

"Well, it shouldn't kill anyone if something goes wrong," Max said. He set a candle on the floor about twenty feet away and then stood next to me.

Using the instructions from Adam Nosti's tutorial, I set the spell script to active and readied the arcwand. Out of the corner of my eye I saw Max stepping quietly back several feet. "Worried, Max?" I chuckled.

"Of course not." Despite his words, he didn't come any closer.

Ambria sniffed. "Show some confidence in our work."

"If it works, I'll be really confident." Max took another step backwards.

I flicked the wand through the pattern. A strand of orange energy about a foot in length burst from the tip and spun lazily toward the candle. I continued the rune patterns. The spell wrapped around the candle and sliced through it. The candle fell into four parts, the wick burning on each one. A bolt of blue erupted from the wand and a water spell extinguished the flames.

I glanced back at Max. "Still alive?"

He whooped and danced in a circle. "We did it!"

Ambria leaned her head against my shoulder and hugged me. "Our very first spell script. How sweet."

She felt warm and soft and, for some reason, I felt the urge to stroke her hair. I patted her on the back instead. "I guess that's enough for tonight."

Max rubbed his belly. "Yeah, because guess what?"

"You're starving." Ambria poked him in the belly and giggled.

"Man, I punched my brother and helped make my first spell script today!" He danced a little jig. "Let's get some food and celebrate!"

Ambria hooked her arms through both of ours. "Yes, let's."

The busy dining hall seemed to grow a bit quieter when we went inside. As the children of evil people, we were somewhat used to being the topic of gossip, but the attention today felt different.

The back of my neck grew warm. I turned and caught angry glares from Harris, Baxter, and the Tiberius twins. A crescent of purple underscored Devon's eye.

Ambria giggled. "You did get him good, Max."

Elliott and Jenna threaded through the tables and met us before we could take a seat.

"Are the rumors true?" Elliott asked.

I nodded. "Yeah, I'm going to play."

He turned toward a table crowded with the black and white of Moore Keep. "He's in!"

A celebratory roar erupted and was quickly countered by boos and jeers from nearby Tiberius Keep members.

I should have felt happy, but this felt like too much. What if I couldn't live up to their expectations?

Do your best, son. Della sounded quite proud. *That's all anyone can ask of you.*

I looked toward the long head table and saw Esma beaming back at me. Galfandor a few seats down caught my eye with a nod. Gideon

Grace's face contorted, as if uncertain whether to display pride or anger that his team would be tainted with my evil.

That sourpuss should have been placed in Tiberius Keep, Della said.

"Tryouts for the newbies are this Saturday at noon," Elliott said. "Just think, you'll get to be on the other side of the fence this time."

"I can hardly wait," I assured him.

The week flew past in a blur of homework, studying, and scripting trials with my friends. By Saturday, I was relieved to have some respite. Ambria, Max, and I flew our brooms to the meeting place behind the keeps where a dozen students waited nervously for their chance to join Team Moore. I remembered all too well that feeling and especially how Rory Culpepper had tried to knock me out of contention. Instead, he'd disqualified himself.

I spotted him and his large friend, Gregory, standing near the front of the group. They stared at me, eyes narrow and unfriendly.

"Looks like Rory is still sore about last year," Max said.

"Then he shouldn't have been so rude." Ambria turned her broom and pointed. "There's Elliott."

Elliott hovered along with the rest of the current team at the front of the group. "Guess we'd better join them," Max said.

"See you at the stadium?" I asked Ambria.

She nodded. "I'll eventually make it down there."

Max chuckled. "All it takes is practice."

Ambria replied with a tight smile. "Indeed."

Elliott gave me a thumbs-up when I joined the rest of the team and then launched his speech about tryouts. "When I give the word, tryouts for Team Moore officially begin. The first part is keeping up with us on the way to Queens Gate Stadium." He gave that a moment to sink in and then nodded. "Let's go!"

We spun around and launched at high speed through the forest.

Another glorious season, Della said. *I do so hope we crush those Tiberius rats.*

I imagined the angry glares from the Tiberius twins and wondered if they were done threatening us or if it was only beginning. I threaded through the forest and dove down the steep cliff leading into the bowl of the valley where the city of Queens Gate nestled. Della continued speaking, droning on about past victories and narrow defeats, and before I knew it, we were at the stadium.

Max straggled a little behind me, but when I turned to talk to him, my mouth dropped open at the leader of the tryout pack.

Ambria gave me a satisfied smirk as she skidded to a stop.

Max saw my expression and turned around. His surprise looked comical. "Ambria?"

I remembered how she'd flown into Plinth and suddenly wondered if she'd been secretly practicing all this time.

Ambria caught my puzzled gaze and gave me a knowing nod.

"Our little Ambria is growing up so fast," Max said wistfully. "I remember when she was scared to death to ride a broom."

She is trouble, son. Della sounded worried. *Don't let her distract you from the game.*

I didn't see how it was possible to ignore girls. *Their magic is too strong.*

232

She burst into laughter in my head. *Oh, my darling boy, you are doomed.*

I wiped my clammy hands on my pants and swallowed hard. A hand touched my shoulder. I yelped and nearly fell off my broom.

Jenna snickered. "Something on your mind, Conrad?"

I shook my head. "No, just waiting for things to start."

Jenna motioned me to the edge of the field where a stone tablet inscribed with symbols sat on a pedestal. "I want you to learn how to do this for next year." She traced her fingers along the runes slowly so I could follow.

The oval field burst into activity. Poles sprang from the ground, forming a treacherous forest to navigate. Next came a series of winding tubes interspersed with flaming rings, swinging mallets designed to knock riders from their brooms, and jets of water shooting up or sideways.

"Did you get that?" she asked.

I nodded. "How do you turn it off?"

"Same pattern," Jenna said. She blew out a sigh. "I'm gonna miss this so much." She turned her sad gaze on me. "Treasure every moment, Conrad. It goes by so quickly, it's over before you know it."

She speaks wisdom beyond her years. Della sounded as wistful as Jenna. *Every moment is a treasure, a memory made, a time that can only be revisited in memory.*

Now you're making me sad. I stared out at the sprawling gauntlet, remembering my own trial, happy I didn't have to relive that particular moment.

As with the previous year, the candidates had three tries to make it through the gauntlet unscathed. Ten checkpoints allowed them to

233

start at the previous one instead of starting over again, but even so, it was a difficult task.

Professors gathered on the sidelines, Galfandor, Gideon Grace, Esma, and many others among them. Percival hovered on a flying carpet loaded down with healing potions, an eager look on his face at the prospect of student injuries. It was only my second year here, but it seemed this was the norm for Kabash tryouts.

The new leader of Graeven Keep, Daphne Blake, led her entourage of candidates to the starting line and smiled warmly at Elliott. "Hello, everyone."

"Missing Velma?" Jenna asked of the former team captain.

Daphne rolled her eyes sarcastically. "Why should I miss our star player?"

"I heard she took an offer from the Krakens," Max said. "Is that true?"

Daphne nodded. "Looks like she'll be in the pro league this year."

"Nice." Elliot's smiled faded. "Tiberius is here."

Max looked confused until he realized Elliott meant Tiberius Keep. Rhys and Devon glided over, conspicuous in their efforts to avoid looking at their brother and me. It seemed Devon had covered his black eye with some sort of cream.

"Well, well, well," Rhys drawled. "If it isn't the definition of futility."

Devon barked a laugh. "Graeven and Moore, have you come to see how a real team is made?"

"Yeah, but we don't need you around here to see that," Daphne shot back. "If you want a lesson in futility, maybe you should look in the mirror."

Devon tutted. "I daresay she's a bit dimwitted, brother."

"No doubt," Rhys replied.

"I guess that blow to your head dulled your own wits," Max said boldly.

Devon's jaw tightened, but he refused to look our way. "Shall we start?"

Elliott chuckled and peered at the other boy's eye. "Love the makeup, Devon. Did Rhys do it for you?"

The twins turned away sharply. "Candidates, to the line!" they shouted in unison.

Thirty-six contenders lined up. I caught Ambria's eye and mouthed, "Good luck."

She smiled gratefully and blew me a kiss that made my skin tingle in the odd way only girls could manage.

Elliott shouted out the rules for the gauntlet and Daphne started everyone off with fireworks from her wand. In a rush of wind, and a chorus of excited shouts, tryouts began.

Chapter 23

We ate at the Copper Goose to celebrate Ambria's tryout.

"Fourth place and only one knockout," Max said in disbelief. "I can't believe you've been practicing behind our backs all these months."

"You wouldn't believe how hard it was not to say anything." Ambria looked entirely too pleased with herself.

"Now we'll all be so busy, we'll hardly have time for anything else." I held up a glass of birch beer. "Here's to the busiest people in Queens Gate."

"I'll drink to that!" Max clinked his glass to mine.

Ambria giggled and clinked hers as well.

School, Kabash practice, homework, and extra-curricular studies blurred the days into one another. The two-week mark since I'd seen Evadora came and went without a word from her. I hoped she was okay and that something terrible hadn't happened to her. Then again, she had a poor concept of time—at least I hoped it was something simple.

I couldn't stop thinking about our quest, but there was nothing we could do without Evadora's help. The only way I could get into the

Glimmer was through the reflected world. Since Naeve might be waiting to kill me there, I couldn't simply pop in and hope for the best. All I could do was wait.

Our first game against Graeven Keep went swimmingly. We knocked down their two towers and the keep before they put a mark on our second tower. With their core players having graduated last year, Graeven was comprised mostly of newbies. Our second game against Lab Tesla from Science Academy was no harder. Their rocket sticks were nearly as fast and mobile as brooms, but the players weren't very good.

It was after this game that I spotted a familiar face waiting outside the stadium. Evadora had changed her skin tone to peach, though her uncommonly large eyes still drew stares from people. I interrupted Max and Ambria's excited post-game chatter. "She's here."

"About time," Max growled. "She's two weeks overdue."

"I'm sure she has good reason." Ambria pushed away the hair clinging to her sweaty face and smiled at the other girl. "It's good to see you."

"Finally," Max added. "Where have you been?"

Evadora's eyes welled with tears. "I have not done a good job." She looked at the ground. "The beasts grow wilder all the time, and the plants sometimes ignore me."

"You're new to it." I squeezed her arm. "I'm certain things will improve with time." *Or at least until I can help Cora.* I hated to rush into business, but the suspense was killing me. "Did you bring more fragments?"

Evadora withdrew something from the pouch at her side. Thin black vines were braided together to form a necklace. Nestled within a flower bud on one side was a smooth round pebble, green as the one on my chain.

"Oh, it's lovely!" Ambria said.

A pleased smile shined through Evadora's tears. "I hoped you would like it." She hung the necklace around the other girl's neck.

"Looks kinda girly." Max groaned. "Oh well, I guess I can keep it under my shirt."

Evadora produced another necklace, but instead of a flower bud, the anchor stone fragment was clenched in a setting of black thorns. "I thought you might prefer this design."

"Wow!" Max gaped at the necklace.

"Manly enough?" Ambria said dryly.

"Definitely." He bent his head and let Evadora place it around his neck.

Evadora unfastened the pouch at her side and gave it to me. "I placed several more inside just in case you need them."

"Thanks. This really helps a lot." I fastened the pouch to my belt and opened another line of inquiry. "Did Yoghra find anything?"

Evadora gripped my hands and her smile grew even broader. "Cora is there, Conrad!" She jumped up and down in place. "Her memories are there!"

I swallowed a lump but couldn't stop tears of relief from streaming down my face. My knees buckled, but Evadora kept me upright. "I'm so glad to hear that."

"Me too, brother." She kissed my cheek. "Me too."

"Did you view her memories?" I asked.

"Yes." Evadora wiped her eyes. "I saw myself when I was born. I felt how happy Mother was to have me, and how sad she was to give me up."

Ambria sniffled. "Oh, you're making me cry."

"Let's get out of here," Max said gruffly as he surveyed the crowd leaving the stadium. "I feel like everyone is staring."

"Agreed." I squeezed Evadora's hand and let it go. "It's time to plan our quest."

We left the stadium grounds and walked down the street, headed toward the house on the corner of Dowling and Bucket nearly a mile away.

Max started things off with a direct question. "What's the deal with your monsters? Will they be in our way?"

Evadora's shoulders sagged. She nodded. "The mewlies won't listen to me, so flying will be dangerous. The bronies and gruffalos keep fighting over territory, the scarfers and hydracorns won't let me near them, and the condors don't come when I call them."

Ambria's forehead wrinkled. "I don't even know what half of those creatures are."

"How are we supposed to protect ourselves?" Max ran a hand down his face. "We can't fly, so we'll have to walk through a mess of rampaging creatures?"

"I hadn't thought of it that way." Evadora straightened and grinned. "It'll be fun!"

This odd girl has a strange opinion of fun, Della said. *I suggest you program several defensive spells into the arcwand so we aren't eaten by one of her monsters.*

I completely agreed. The whine of a jet engine pulled my attention behind us.

Ansel Moore offered a sarcastic smile as he guided a rocket stick to our sides. He wore a gray vest over a purple shirt with a checkered tie. Black pants rode up his calves to reveal purple argyle socks. His flashy clothes only made him look undignified atop the narrow saddle of a rocket stick. "Well, if it isn't young Mr. Edison and"—he looked Evadora up and down—"some very strange children."

"My friends," I shot back. I hadn't seen the man in weeks. With Adam Nosti's spell scripting videos, I didn't need Ansel. "What do you want?"

Ansel made a show of polishing his fingernails on his shirt. "I take it you've not learned how to script spells?"

Max snorted. "We've learned plenty, no thanks to you."

Ansel rolled his eyes. "I am here to teach Conrad, not the rest of you."

"What you do isn't teaching," Ambria shot back. "You assigned him work without telling him how to do it."

"Prove to me you learned anything," Ansel said.

I stopped walking and shook my head. "I don't have to prove anything to you."

"Hah," he scoffed. "Because you couldn't script a spell if you tried."

I shrugged. "Believe what you want. The simple truth is, I don't need you. I don't even know why Esma introduced us except to show me there's more to magic than what they teach here."

Ansel's lips flattened into a thin white line. He whipped a wand from within his vest and aimed it at me. It seemed I'd hardly reached for my arcwand and it was already in my hand, a defensive pattern flashing.

A streak of fire jetted from Ansel's wand. My defensive spell summoned a shield and parried the attack. The fire rushed upward and dissipated in the air. A delighted grin spread across Ansel's face an instant before he was knocked off the rocket stick by a spell from Ambria. He hit the brick road with a grunt.

Ansel picked himself up and brushed dust from the back of his pants. "It appears you have learned something."

"In other words," Max said, "we don't need you."

"Wrong, boy." Ansel deactivated his hovering rocket stick and tucked it under an arm. "Scripting with an arcwand is only one aspect. Casting with arcphones and other devices is different." He seemed to filter out everyone but me and him. "I can teach you those methods."

"You can teach *us*." I waved a hand at my friends.

Evadora laughed. "I can't learn your magic, silly."

"I meant Max and Ambria," I told her.

Her comment drew Ansel's gaze. "What are you, girl?"

I interrupted before Evadora could respond. "Well, Ansel, will you teach us?"

He scowled but reluctantly nodded. "Meet me after school on Monday." Ansel boarded his rocket stick and flew away without another word.

"Creepy," Max said. "Do you really think it's worth going back to him?"

I nodded. "If not, we have plenty more to learn from Adam Nosti's tutorials."

Max's eyes went wide. "Oh, we're right next to a Mr. Nutter's bakery!" Before anyone could respond, he went inside an open shop door and began browsing a display case full of goodies.

"I suppose this is a good place to discuss our master plans." Ambria rubbed her hands together and managed a slightly maniacal laugh. "Did that sound evil enough?"

Evadora giggled and mimicked her, managing to sound like a complete lunatic. She raised eyebrows on a few passersby so I pulled the two girls into the bakery where Max had already ordered cookies for everyone.

We sat down at a small table and munched while we discussed our next steps for retrieving the heart from the Glimmer. Though we all agreed that taking Gwyneth was required per my agreement with Underborn, Professor Sideon was another discussion altogether.

"I think having a professor along might be safer," Max said.

Ambria frowned. "I'd rather bring Esma than Sideon."

"Why not both?" Evadora said. "The more the merrier."

Max shivered. "More people for your monsters to eat."

I wondered if Esma would come if I asked her. Her skillset would be a huge help. Then again, a larger group would be a bigger target. There was no reason to include Sideon in our trip to the Glimmer. Gwyneth was an experienced relic hunter so she could probably take care of herself.

Della inserted her opinion. *Take only who you trust. Such a journey will be risky enough without adding variables.*

I trust Esma, I told her.

Do not grow overly attached, son.

Take Sideon, Vic said. His voice sounded muffled even though it was in my head.

Do not listen to him! Della shouted loud enough to make me wince.

"You okay?" Ambria leaned closer.

I nodded. "The soul fragments are arguing."

Max grimaced. "Yikes. At least when my parents fight I can go away."

Do not listen to me? Vic snarled, voice growing louder. *You're only steering the boy into trouble. Pretending to be a loving mother when you're nothing but a pretender.*

His words chilled me to the core. What if he was right? What if Della had been pretending to be my friend all this time?

Ignore him, son. He is a poison in your mind. Della seemed to whisper in my ear, as if that might prevent Vic from hearing. *I do not wish you harm. I swear it.*

Vic tried to speak but it was like listening underwater.

Are you silencing him? I asked.

For your own good. Della sounded desperate. *I beg you, don't believe a word the liar says.*

But it was too late. What if I'd let my emotions affect my trust? What if Della was leading me into a trap? Then again, why would Vic try to stop her? My death would free the soul fragments and return them to my parents. *Do you want to be free of me, Della?*

If only to free your mind, son. She sighed. *I believe the Broken Relic can release you from us.*

243

Will you return to Delectra? I asked.

Perhaps. Della sniffled. *Otherwise, I suspect oblivion awaits. Our presence in your soul is harmful. I believe Vic is attempting to subvert you from within. I can help you resist, but he is equally capable of silencing me.*

"What are they saying?" Max said. "Your face keeps twisting up like you ate a lemon."

I shook my head and blinked, bringing the world back into focus. "Della thinks Vic is trying to harm my soul. Vic told me that Della is pretending to be nice."

Ambria's eyes flared. "Can you trust either of them?"

"I-I don't know," I admitted.

"What does your heart say?" Evadora asked.

I already knew the answer without even thinking about it. But was it just emotion, or instinct? "I trust Della."

Evadora nodded. "Then trust her."

I took a deep breath to clear my head. Thankfully, the spirits remained quiet. "Let's keep the group small. Gwyneth should be the only other person, but only because we have to."

"When?" Ambria asked.

"During the holidays two weeks from now." I picked up another cookie and broke off a piece for Evadora who nibbled on it like a rabbit. "That should give us enough time to find the heart."

"Agreed," Max said. He looked at Ambria.

She nodded. "Yes, I agree."

Evadora was completely engrossed with eating her cookie and took no notice of our questioning gazes.

"I doubt she cares," Ambria said.

"This is yummy." Evadora's eyelids were heavy with pleasure. "If only life were as sweet as a cookie."

We burst into laughter.

Monday came and my hopes of avoiding Sideon were dashed when he told me to see him after class.

"The holidays will be here soon, Conrad." He flashed a friendly smile. "I believe that would be an excellent time to start our search."

I didn't like how he assumed he'd be included in my quest, but since he was my teacher, I couldn't very well admonish him for it. "Unfortunately, I have some other stuff going on during the holidays."

Sideon sighed and seemed to gather himself. "Then may I please use the nose to search for the relic myself? I cannot stress what a boon such a find would be for the academic community. I promise you would be able to use it for whatever purpose you deem necessary."

"What if I want to destroy the world?" I said in a serious tone.

He flinched. "Surely you jest."

I smiled. "Of course." I tried to think of the best way to put him off again, but finally decided some of the truth might be better. "I have to use the nose to find another relic first."

Sideon looked flabbergasted. "What other relic could be more important?"

"All I can tell you is that a very dangerous individual is involved." I bit my lip and spoke in a low voice. "Underborn."

His eyes flashed with alarm. "Are you in trouble, Conrad? Do you need my assistance?"

I was touched by his concern even if it might be self-serving. "Do you dare risk going against Underborn?"

Sideon smiled sheepishly and shrugged. "I doubt a professor would be much of an obstacle." He sighed. "I hope Underborn didn't discover you had the Nose of Jura because of me."

I nearly told him that Underborn had no idea about the nose, but quickly stopped myself from blurting it. "I can't do anything now, but fulfill the contract I made with him."

"I understand." Sideon shook his head slowly. "I don't know if anyone can help you against Underborn, but you might consider talking to Galfandor about it."

"I'll consider it, but I don't want anyone to get hurt." Sideon seemed resigned to accept my story, so I turned and left before I accidentally gave anything away.

One more complication was now out of the way.

Chapter 24

Esma zapped me with a spell the instant I entered the classroom, much to the amusement of Harris and the others. I drew my wand, but the disappointment on the professor's face made me feel ashamed. I'd been so preoccupied with mentally mapping out the quest that I'd let down my guard.

"It appears you'll be the only person in detention today, Mr. Edison." Esma pointed at my desk. "Please take your seat."

Harris and Baxter snickered, but they knew better than to say anything to me in front of the professor.

Esma drew me aside after class. "Ansel told me you're scheduled to meet him today and that he's impressed with how far you've progressed."

"Yes, Esma." I looked down. "I'm sorry I failed to block your attack today."

"It's fortunate you're alive to be sorry, Conrad." She cupped her hand under my chin and drew my eyes up to meet hers. "It doesn't matter how skilled you are. One attack could kill you or knock you unconscious. You must strive to be ever on guard."

"It's not easy."

"Nothing worth doing ever is." Esma smoothed back my hair from my face. "How are you doing, child?"

Her motherly touch sent a shiver across my scalp. Somehow, I remembered to answer her. "We're going to the Glimmer during the holidays. Hopefully we'll find the heart and then Underborn will hold up his bargain to help us find the Broken Relic." I told her about our small group.

"I think it's wise to keep your party small," she said, continuing to smooth my hair almost unconsciously. "Evadora should keep you quite safe, I think." Esma jerked back her hand and looked at it as if it had betrayed her. "Apologies, Conrad. I should not be so familiar with you."

I gripped her hand in both of mine. "It's okay Esma. I know you're my professor, but you're also my mentor."

"Even so, a mentor should maintain a professional distance." I noticed she didn't try to free her hand and her eyes softened. "You make it rather difficult."

I wanted so desperately to tell her how I felt. How important she was to me. "Your help means everything in the world, Esma. I wouldn't be the person I am without you."

She blinked rapidly, tears welling in her eyes. "I don't deserve such credit."

"No, you do." I gently kissed her hand and let it go. "Please don't take this the wrong way, but you're like a mother to me." I backed away, afraid she'd close up again.

Instead, she gripped me in a fierce hug. "You make me proud, Conrad." Esma released me and backed away. "A mother couldn't ask for a better son." She wiped her eyes. "Don't expect preferential treatment because I'm fond of you."

I smiled. "I wouldn't dream of it." Esma was not the kind who showed favoritism by coddling. I suspected the more she liked someone, the harder she drove them. If that was the case, then I must have been her favorite by far. I dug into my pocket and produced one of the spare vine necklaces Evadora had given me. "In case something happens to me, I want you to have this."

Esma took it, her lower lip trembling. "Is this—"

"Yes." I closed her fingers over it. "It's a piece of the anchor stone. It will keep you alive forever, provided you don't get into a horrible accident." I managed a smile.

"It's the same stone you used to get into the reflected world?" she asked. "The one you used those magic words with?"

I nodded. "The very same." I smiled. "Maybe it will keep you healed when your chronic illness strikes again."

She wiped at the corner of her eye. "I'll treasure it always, Conrad." She kissed my forehead. "I wish I could rightfully call you my son."

I swallowed the knot in my throat and nodded. "That would be the most wonderful thing in the world." Because she began to look distinctly uncomfortable, I backed away smiling. "I'll see you soon, Esma."

She swallowed hard and nodded. "Be safe, son."

I could barely contain my exuberant mood for the rest of the day. Ansel took note of it when my friends and I met him in his office that afternoon.

"You're excited," he said, clasping his hands together. "That's wonderful." Ansel laid out several arcphones. "Today you will be learning advanced casting with these devices."

249

Ansel proved considerably more adept at teaching than he'd previously let on. For the next several days, he taught us methods of scripting and casting that worked even better than what we'd learned from the tutorial videos. While arcwands and arcstaffs required some pattern usage, arcphones and arctablets performed those functions invisibly and even allowed advanced techniques such as spell hacking.

We were scheduled to play Tiberius Keep in Kabash that weekend, but an unexpected hailstorm swept through Queens Gate and the game was postponed until after the holidays. By the start of the final week, snow blanketed the university campus and spread into the valley. Even though I had no family gathering or celebrations to look forward to, the weather put me in good holiday cheer.

I always knew when Shushiel was guarding me, because when I walked through the snow, she left prints as well. Unfortunately, her family problems required her to be away quite often, though she still showed up nightly to guard me.

We met Gwyneth at the Dancing Pig on Friday where we laid out plans for infiltrating the Glimmer through the reflected world.

"It sounds fascinating," she said. "Have you explored this reflected world much?"

Max snorted. "Don't do that unless you want to lose part of your soul."

She frowned. "What do you mean?"

"If your reflection touches you, it'll steal a piece," Ambria said. "It's important we don't dilly-dally at all."

Gwyneth nodded matter-of-factly, as if she'd been through so many bizarre situations already that this was no different than anything else. "I'll follow your lead." She took out her arcphone and projected a list. "These are the supplies I'm taking with us. Everyone will carry a light pack with food, water, and other immediate necessities."

"Climbing gear?" Max looked up from the list. "Can't we just use brooms?"

"I've been places where you don't dare use magic," Gwyneth said. "Even the slightest disturbance might set off a booby trap. Sometimes you have to use ordinary equipment."

Max shook his head. "I won't be climbing any cliffs, that's for sure."

Gwyneth didn't seem concerned by that. "Can you think of anything else we should bring?"

I scanned through it, but it appeared she'd planned for the worst, as she'd probably done many times before. "Nothing I can think of."

Ambria shrugged. "I just wonder how you're going to carry so much."

"Technically, I won't be carrying much of anything." Gwyneth opened her satchel and took out a matchbox-sized piece of wood inlaid with gold. The edges were rough and splintered as if broken from a larger piece. "I'll have most of our extra supplies inside this."

Max frowned. "How are you supposed to fit climbing gear inside a chunk of wood?"

"This is the Lost Room of Jura." Gwyneth stroked the wood with a finger. The air shimmered and an ornate wooden door appeared with a thick golden ring mounted in the center. A divot in the door looked as if the wood Gwyneth held would fit neatly inside. Gwyneth tugged on the ring and the door opened with a creak.

I walked over to it and peered inside. As the name implied, there was a room on the other side with a black marble floor polished to a mirror surface, and walls of white stone. It measured perhaps thirty by forty feet. The room was bare of furnishing other than two doors, two windows, and several shelves along the walls. The aforementioned climbing gear sat on one shelf; bottled water, canned foods, and other supplies on another.

"Whoa!" Max put a foot tentatively through the door. "That's really neat."

"Where do the other doors lead?" I asked.

"Nowhere," Gwyneth said. "I mean that quite literally. One door opens to pitch black and the other to brilliant white. We sent through cameras, but they were unable to record anything."

"Did anyone try going through?" Max asked.

"I did," Gwyneth said. "I couldn't see anything. The white light is too bright even with sunglasses, and no light could penetrate the darkness in the other one." She shrugged. "If I hadn't had a rope on me, I never would've found my way back."

"You're crazy," Ambria said in a horrified voice. "What if you'd died?"

"I felt confident I wouldn't." Gwyneth motioned us inside. "Take a look through the windows."

I expected to see nothing and was shocked when the vista of a magnificent city greeted me. A golden street shined between towering buildings, and at the far end, a palace that dwarfed even the university. It glowed white as if it made of pure light. The area teemed with people. Angels flew overhead, women with fish tails instead of feet swam through crystal-clear canals on the sides of the golden street, and ordinary people walked in between.

I managed to overcome my awe long enough to ask a question. "What are we seeing?"

"We believe this is the final day of Juranthemon." Gwyneth touched a hand to the window. "Hours from now, the sky will turn blood red and the city will be destroyed. This room somehow survived and turned into a relic."

Max pressed a hand against the glass window. "Can you open this and go outside?"

"No." Gwyneth picked up a hammer from the climbing equipment. Before I was full aware of her intentions, she reared back and slammed it against the window.

We jumped back with shouts and cries of dismay. The hammer clinked as if hitting solid metal, leaving nary a mark on the transparent material.

"You cannot destroy relics," she said. "I suppose if they survived the destruction of the world, there's little we could do to harm them."

Max held a hand to his heart. "Maybe a little warning next time?"

She smirked.

Ambria pointed to the chunk of door in Gwyneth's hand. "If you can't break relics, then how did the door break?"

"At the instant of the destruction I suppose," Gwyneth said.

I focused back on the other mysteries of the room. "Those doors must go to a place that no longer exists. That's why they go nowhere."

Gwyneth blinked. "Yes, Underborn thinks so too." She tapped something into her arcphone. "He loves unraveling mysteries."

"Don't we all?" Ambria said.

We left the room and Gwyneth closed the door by swiping down on the door fragment. She tapped on her arcphone for a few seconds and nodded. "I assume everything is set on your end?"

I removed one of the extra anchor stone necklaces from the pouch and handed it to her. "You'll need this."

Gwyneth held it up before her eyes. "This helps me enter the reflected world?"

"Yes. We could hold hands and jump in, but if anyone gets separated, it's important they're to escape on their own." I touched the pebble on my chain. "You say, as above, so below, and jump into water. When you're coming from the other side, it's reversed—so below, as above."

"Interesting." Her forehead wrinkled. "I wonder why it works this way."

Ambria pulled out several blink stones from her satchel. "We also brought these just in case."

Gwyneth's eyes widened appreciatively. "Where did you get blink stones?"

Ambria tapped her temple. "We have our resources."

"I'll bet!" the older girl held one in her hand and rubbed it. "It's been a long time since Underborn let me use one of these. They have the unfortunate side effect of making the user dizzy and nauseous with prolonged use."

"That's for sure," Max said. "Made me toss up my dinner once."

Gwyneth winced. "I can relate." She tapped a finger on the table. "What can you tell me about the environment in the Glimmer?"

"For starters, the world is broken into floating islands." I held my hands apart as if that might convey the shape of the broken land. "There's nothing but stars and void between the islands."

"Floating islands in a sea of stars." Gwyneth paled a bit. "I can definitely say I've never seen that before."

"Giants trees form bridges between the islands." I traced an arch with my hand. "They're relatively easy to cross, but you want to watch out for mewlies."

Her forehead furrowed. "And those are?"

"Flying bat cats," Ambria said. "Evadora says they'll eat anything."

"Like flying piranha," Max added, snapping his teeth for effect.

Gwyneth stared blankly as if trying to imagine the creatures and then took notes on her phone. "What else?"

"The last time I was there, I flew across the islands, but since Evadora is new to controlling the realm, she says flying could be dangerous." I told her briefly about how Galfandor and I had flown to the Glimmer Queen's palace at the top of the crooked mountain and narrowly escaped with our lives.

Gwyneth regarded me with open admiration. "You're a rather fearless boy, aren't you?"

"Hey, I helped fight the Glimmer Queen too," Max said.

"All of you," Gwyneth amended before Ambria could pitch in.

"Even if flying is dangerous, we're bringing our brooms just in case," I said.

"You can keep them in the room if you get tired of carrying them." Gwyneth used a stylus to jot notes on the phone screen. "Anything else?"

"Certainly," Ambria said. "Evadora said she could probably keep us safe from the Glimmer monsters, but that not all of them will obey."

Gwyneth pursed her lips. "What sort of monsters?"

255

We told her about the ones we'd encountered during our previous visit. "Evadora mentioned a couple we haven't seen."

"Scarfers and hydracorns," Max clarified.

Ambria scoffed. "Not that it matters. Everything there can kill you."

Gwyneth laughed. "Sounds like Australia."

"Even worse," Max said. "Imagine spider giraffes with serpent heads."

Gwyneth's lips twisted. "I'll be sure to bring a weapon."

"I wouldn't bother," Ambria said. "I think you'll find running shoes far more valuable."

Everyone laughed.

When the laughter died down, Gwyneth consulted her notes. "Are there other people in the Glimmer we need to worry about?"

"According to Evadora, they're all asleep," Ambria said. "Naeve did something to them."

"How reliable is Evadora?" Gwyneth asked.

Max, Ambria, and I looked at each other. I answered first. "She does her best." I felt certain Gwyneth would write *Unreliable* in her notes and underscore it twice.

We continued discussing everything we knew about the Glimmer until it seemed we were repeating ourselves. Gwyneth seemed to recognize this and tucked away her phone. "I think we're as ready as we'll ever be. Shall we meet at the Fairy Gardens first thing in the morning?"

Max looked at me and shrugged. Ambria gave me a nod. "We'll see you then," I said.

We gathered our things and headed outside. Gwyneth saw us out the door, presumably before she would use the Key of Jura to travel back to Underborn. Thinking about that key made me turn and ask her a question. "Can you link doors between realms with the Map of Jura?"

"An excellent question," Gwyneth said. "Unfortunately, we've never tested it. I stored some blanks in the lost room just in case."

I scratched my head. "Blanks?"

"Free-standing doors," she said. "We link to one of our safe-houses and use them if we need to escape."

"Neat!" Max opened the front door to the tavern and stepped outside. "If we could—" He went silent and tripped over his own feet.

The moment I stepped through the door, I saw why. Seer Plinth waited on us with two dozen of his minions.

Chapter 25

"Conrad, you must come with me," Plinth said. "If you do not, I will take you by force."

"What's the meaning of this?" Gwyneth said.

"If you embark on this quest without cleansing the boy's soul, you'll doom us all." Plinth held up the small statue of a woman with a dozen arms. Some of her hands were clasped in prayer, others raised above her head, and some splayed to her side. Her huge eyes were dark spirals around black pupils. "You cannot use the key to escape, assassin's disciple, so do not try to help him."

"You know, it took me a moment, but I recognize you," Gwyneth said. "You're the one who stole that statue from the Louvre right before I tried to snatch it."

"Indeed." Plinth stiffened. "Your master's penchant for collecting powerful artifacts put us on a path to destruction."

"I thought Seers weren't supposed to get involved!" Ambria said indignantly. "By your own admission, you get involved all the time."

"There are those of us who believe it is necessary at times." Plinth directed his gaze on me. "Conrad, we must attempt another cleansing. The soul shards must be removed and then you'll be free to continue your quest."

"I don't think so." Gwyneth stepped in front of me. "Do you really think Underborn will let this go unchallenged?"

"What has gone unchallenged is your integrity." Plinth glared at her. "Conrad, do not trust this girl. She is bound to him by contract."

"My integrity is solid," Gwyneth shot back. "Yes, I'm under contract with Underborn, and I have never broken a contract."

I stepped in front of Gwyneth and held up a hand to silence the argument. "How do you plan to cleanse me, Seer Plinth?"

"We will use the same magic that bound those souls to you in the first place." He motioned forward a figure in a black monk's cowl and robes. "Explain the process."

Terribly scarred hands reached up and pushed back the cowl to reveal a bald head tattooed with bizarre patterns. "The demon who possessed you must be recalled." He spoke as if his tongue were too thick in his mouth. His next words horrified me nearly as much as the revelation that his tongue was forked. "He will come into your body. Once he has subverted your soul, I will drive him out. The soul shards of your parents will come with him."

Do not allow it! Della shouted. *Conrad, you must run. Allowing that demon back into your body will cause irreparable harm.*

Listen to the demonologist, Vic said calmly. *He will heal you. Go to him, son.*

Quiet! Della screamed. *Return to your pit, foul demon!*

I winced at the volume. *I have no intention of letting them touch me.*

"Your parents again?" Ambria said quietly.

Gwyneth frowned. "Parents?"

"Yeah, their soul shards talk in his head," Max said.

"Come to me boy, and I'll make this quick," the demonologist said. "I already have the pattern drawn and ready to go."

I peered around at the other seers and noticed one other person with a hood drawn over their face. I pointed to him. "Who is that?"

The person seemed hesitant to reveal themselves, but Seer Plinth waved his hand. "Show yourself."

When the hood slid back, my lips peeled into a grimace. "Dr. Cumberbatch!" It was the man who'd helped my parents fashion the demon spell that bound their souls to me. "What is he doing here?"

"I realized the error of my ways, Conrad." He held out his hands in a silent plea. "Let me make amends and cleanse you of the darkness your parents left behind."

My skin felt clammy and cold sweat broke out on my forehead. "I'll *never* let you touch me again, you lying bastard."

"I told you I shouldn't have come," Cumberbatch said to Plinth. "Now the boy's frightened."

"Frightened?" I shouted. "I'm furious!"

That curse of his has put you and your friends in mortal peril time and time again, Vic whispered. *His demon magic killed your Cora.*

Cora. I saw her greeting me on her giant ship. Saw her smiling as she handed me an ice-cream cone. Saw her withered body dying in a bed. The clammy cold melted in a furious blast of heat. Somewhere in the back of my mind I heard Della saying something. Heard her scream, but the words were muffled behind a wall of rage.

My wand came free. I raced forward. Plinth's eyes went wide with alarm at this unexpected move. Cumberbatch held out his arms and smirked. "Now, now, child, what do you expect to do? Singe me with an elementary spell?" He pulled out his wand and whirled it.

My wrist flicked in a pattern and a beam of brilliant orange poured from the end. Cumberbatch's eyes went wide as dinner plates as my spell consumed his shield in an instant. He screamed when the sizzling heat met his hand and burned it to a crisp.

"Conrad!" Someone gripped my arm and jerked it down.

"I will kill you!" I screamed as more hands jerked me back. "You murdered my Cora, you son of a bitch!"

Cumberbatch's screams of pain echoed my own and vanished behind the door to the tavern.

"We've got one chance," Gwyneth said.

"Conrad!" Ambria smacked me hard in the face. I wobbled on shaky legs and dropped my wand. My vision went blurry and hot tears filled my eyes.

"Are you okay?" Max's unfocused form filled my vision.

I wiped my eyes and nodded. The anger faded, replaced by a horrible realization that I might have murdered Cumberbatch. The guilt lessened slightly when I thought of what the man had done to me, but even so, I'd completely lost control of my mind.

Gwyneth opened the door to the lost room and sighed with relief. "Thank god the statue doesn't block this relic."

Jack Lamont ran out of the office door. "What in the hell is going on out there?"

"Seers," Gwyneth said. "We're getting out of here."

"Why not use the door?" he asked.

"They have a portal blocker." She ushered the rest of us inside.

"Son of a—" Lamont blew out a breath. "Get going. I'll hold them off if need be." He ran behind the bar and tugged on a tall bottle on the top shelf. Metal shutters slid down over windows and doors. "I can wait them out forever in here."

Something slammed into the door and a monstrous roar filled the air outside. The roof trembled and a massive fist crashed through. Fingers the size of my body unfolded and ripped the roof completely off. Glowing red eyes stared down at me. The massive demon looked like something right out of a fairy tale—spiraling black horns, a humanoid face, and a mouth full of wicked teeth.

Ambria screamed and Max joined in.

The demon roared, blasting us with hot air that reeked of spoiled eggs. It went silent and looked away, as if something distracted it.

Plinth's shouts echoed from outside. "What are you doing?"

"The boy is mine," Cumberbatch shouted back.

"On second thought," Jack said, "I think we should all leave together."

"Get in!" Gwyneth shouted.

We rushed inside the lost room. The demon roared and its huge fist slammed down outside the door. Burning hot fingers gripped the frame and reached inside. Gwyneth leapt back, narrowly avoiding a razor-sharp claw as it extended from a finger. She frantically swiped down on the door fragment and the doorway vanished. With a meaty thud, severed fingertips hit the floor.

Ambria gagged. "I'm going to be sick."

Max pressed his back against the far wall. "That was the biggest demon I've ever seen."

262

"These people aren't playing around," Jack said in a matter-of-fact tone. He chuckled. "Man, you sure know how to pick 'em, Gwyn."

Gwyneth wiped her forehead with a shaking hand. "Conrad, you have some major-league enemies."

My body trembled as the adrenalin rush wore off, leaving me weak. "Cumberbatch is the one who made the demon spell to keep my parents alive. His spell attached their souls to me."

"Um, what's the plan, Gwyn?" Jack peered out the window as blue skies turned crimson. "You realize that you've just trapped us in a paradox, right?"

"A paradox?" Max's eyes went wide. "What do you mean?"

Jack pointed to the relic in Gwyn's hand. "That box opens the door to this room, right?"

Max nodded. "Yeah, so we can escape whenever we want, right?"

Not precisely, Vic said dryly.

The answer hit me in the gut. "You'll only be opening the door to back inside the room."

"Oh, god, you're right, Conrad!" Ambria covered her open mouth. "If she opens the door in here, it'll only open the door back into this room. It's an endless loop!"

"I probably shouldn't have closed the door," Gwyneth said. "At least not until I tested my theory."

"Always jumping without thinking." Jack sighed and looked at the back wall. "Better hope these blanks work wherever the hell this place is located."

"Everything is connected to Jura," Gwyneth said. "The map, the key, this room." She waved her hand toward the gathering apocalypse outside the window. The sky filled with birds. People screamed and ran. A massive dark shadow appeared from within the palace at the end of the golden street. Its shape was familiar, like the void in the stars Evadora had shown me in the Rift.

The crowd ran out of sight and only a lone figure remained. Four more dark voids appeared in the sky, growing larger as they descended upon the city.

The unfolding drama drew Max's gaze to the window. "What's happening?"

"The destruction of Jura," Jack said. "I've seen it a dozen times, but it never fails to scare the hell outta me."

Gwyneth ignored us and pulled one of the door frames from against the wall. Legs unfolded from the frame and held it in place.

I turned back to the window as the woman in the streets grew to immense size until she rivaled even the shadow figures. She threw up her hands and a translucent shield rippled across the city.

She shouted something in an alien language. A voice filled with many voices spoke back in the same tongue. A shadow flickered beneath the woman's massive feet. Blinding white light filled the window, searing my retinas. I turned away. Ambria shrieked.

"My eyes!" Max shouted.

"Yeah, should've warned you," Jack said with a chuckle.

The glare vanished. I blinked open tearing eyes and saw nothing but a void of black.

"Thank god!" Gwyneth cried out in relief as she cracked open the door. What looked like the inside of a warehouse waited on the other side. She leaned heavily on the doorframe. "We're going to make it."

264

Jack slapped her on the back. "Good work, kiddo." He looked back at the rest of us. "When you're finished looking at the darkness, I'd suggest you get out of here."

I wasted no time exiting the room just in case the doorway back to our world vanished. Gwyneth closed the door once we were all through. She leaned against it and took a deep breath. "Perhaps you should stay somewhere besides the university tonight. It might not be safe."

"You're probably right," I agreed. The sounds of heavy traffic rattled through the metal walls of the warehouse. I cleaned off a dirty window with my sleeve and peered outside. The lights of a large city painted the skyline. "Where are we?"

"Atlanta," Gwyneth said.

Max ran to the window and cleaned off a section for himself. "We're near the birthplace of Justin Slade?"

Jack flashed a grin. "Not far."

"Wow." Max put his hands up to the window as if that might help him see even further. "I'd like to see it one day."

Gwyneth walked toward a heavy canvas with the shape of a car underneath and tugged it off to reveal a mint-green sedan. "Might as well stay in town for the night. One of the doors here is linked to London. We can take it in the morning."

"My bar is probably in ruins." Jack shrugged. "Maybe next time I'll put it in a better part of town to discourage summoning big-ass demons."

Gwyneth drove us to a small hotel. Jack got a room and snuck us in the back door so we wouldn't raise any suspicions.

"We could have posed as your children," Gwyneth told Jack after we got inside.

"No way." He popped the lid on a can of beer and took a drink. "Having kids is too weird. I'm a bartender, not a father figure."

Ambria sat next to me on the bed. "What happened to you back there, Conrad?"

"Back where?" I asked, fully aware of what she wanted to know.

Max dropped onto my other side. "You nearly killed Cumberbatch."

"Never would've guessed power like that coming from a kid," Jack said. "You must take vitamins."

"I got so angry," I admitted. "Vic kept telling me that it was Cumberbatch's fault that Cora died. I just wanted to kill him."

I tried to warn you. Della sounded hurt. *You shut me out.*

"Maybe Plinth is right," Gwyneth said. "Maybe you need to be cleansed of those soul fragments."

My fists tightened. "Cumberbatch had no intention of helping me."

"Did you see that lunatic with the scars?" Max asked Gwyneth in a disbelieving voice. "He certainly wasn't there to help."

"That's for sure," Ambria said.

Gwyneth held my gaze. For a moment, she looked unsure, vulnerable. She might have a few years on me, but I could tell she was wrestling with what to do next.

"Do you always work for Underborn?" I asked.

She shook her head. "Not always, but he pays the best."

I didn't break eye contact. "Are you the best at what you do?"

266

Gwyneth paused. Shook her head. "No, but I can be trusted. Others, not so much."

"Trusted by your employer," Max clarified. "Not necessarily by us."

Jack snorted.

She gave him a sharp look. "You can trust that I'll do what I promise."

Underborn is slippery, Della said. *You may think you heard exactly what you wanted. You may think he is dealing with you fairly. More often than not, you will discover you're wrong just as the deal concludes.*

I had a feeling she was right.

Chapter 26

We took a door back to London early the next morning and returned to Queens Gate by walking into the secret entrance and riding the elevator down to the cavernous way station. We reached Arcane University and went into the dorm to gather our equipment for the journey. On the way in, I noticed tiny divots forming in the snow.

"I'll wait out here," Gwyneth said, shivering in the cold wind. "I don't want to run into Gideon Grace."

"I'd rather freeze than see him too," Max said with a grin.

Once inside, I spoke. "Shushiel, are you there?"

"I am." She appeared. "Where have you been?"

I told her about our small adventure. "We're about to leave for the Glimmer."

"May I still come?" she said.

I didn't even have to think about it. "Of course."

"What if we have to fly?" Max said.

"I saw some flying carpets in the lost room," Ambria said. "She can use one of those if needed."

Shushiel bobbed in a nod. "That would be acceptable."

"Okay, let's get our things." I stroked the fur on her leg. "Don't reveal yourself to Gwyneth until I say so, okay?"

"Agreed." The spider faded into invisibility.

We packed our clothes and our magical gear and ate breakfast in the dining hall.

Gwyneth sighed and looked around wistfully. "Sometimes I miss this place."

Liana entered the room, eyes flashing wide when she saw us. She rushed over, a worried look on her face. "Is today the day?"

Gwyneth nodded. "It's important you keep quiet about this, Liana."

"We were nearly killed by a giant demon last night." Max savagely bit into a sausage. "You definitely don't want those people on your case."

Liana's mouth dropped open. "What have you gotten yourselves into?"

Gwyneth looked at me and I felt the weight of guilt pressing on my shoulders.

"They wanted me," I admitted. "It's a long story."

Liana closed her eyes as if to compose herself. She opened them and nodded. "Please be careful, sister."

"I will." Gwyneth stood and embraced her little sister then motioned us up. "We should go."

I got up, took a last look around the dining hall and nodded. Liana put her hands on my cheeks and surprised me with a kiss right on my lips. She released me and backed away, caramel skin blushing. "Do as my sister says."

"Y-yes," I stammered, for some odd reason wishing she would kiss me again.

Gwyneth burst into laughter and left the room.

"Do I get a kiss?" Ambria asked sweetly.

Liana looked at the floor. "Sorry."

Max elbowed me. "Let's get a move on before you forget how to walk."

I looked at Liana a moment, determined to make it back alive if only to explore why her kiss made me feel so light-headed but good. I was tempted to try for another kiss, but Ambria took me firmly by the elbow and guided me down the hall.

I waved goodbye as we left Liana and we headed across the snowy campus to the Fairy Gardens. The pond was covered in slush, but thankfully not frozen over when we reached it. I suspected it was due to the Lady of the Pond, Mirjana who lived beneath the waters with her husband.

The field of stumps had transformed into a grove of saplings sprouting from the wood of the old trees. Evadora skipped into view and waved with both hands. I introduced her to Gwyneth who seemed entranced by the girl's silvery skin.

"You're certainly pretty," Gwyneth said. "Like a little jewel."

"Thanks!" Evadora beamed and clapped her hands. "I like being pretty."

I stepped to the water's edge. "I need to take a peek at the other side just in case." I held Cora's green pebble in my palm. "Evadora, can you help again?"

"Okay," she said, "but I can't hold you for long. You're heavy!"

Gwyneth frowned. "How is that little girl supposed to hold you up?"

Evadora flexed her arm and failed to display any bulge of muscle. "I'm stronger than I look!"

Once again she held me over the water and submerged my head into the reflected world. The world on the other side rippled with my entrance, like a pebble in a lake. I craned my neck and saw no sign of the evil Naeve.

Evadora pulled me back and dropped me unceremoniously on the ground. "Heavy boy," she complained, rubbing her shoulders.

"You're definitely stronger than you look," Gwyneth said.

I opened the pouch of anchor stone necklaces and held it out. "Shushiel, you'll need this."

Gwyneth frowned. "What?" She shrieked and jumped backwards so fast she fell on her backside when Shushiel blurred into visibility. She pushed to her feet, face red. "Has that ruby spider been here all this time?"

"She's our protector." I calmly looped a necklace around Shushiel's proffered foreleg.

"Thank you, Conrad," she said in her whispery voice. Shushiel rotated toward Gwyneth. "I am Shushiel."

Gwyneth brushed off her pants. "I'm Gwyneth. Nice to meet you."

"Likewise." The spider crawled closer to the water. "Will I have a reflection, Conrad?"

"That's a good question." Evadora clapped her hands together. "Let's go see!"

271

"I'm sure you will, Shushiel." I rubbed her furry leg. "Let's not stay too long and find out, okay?"

The spider shivered from the tips of her legs all the way to her abdomen. "I agree."

"Equipment check." Gwyneth tugged on my backpack and made sure it was closed while Ambria did the same for Max. Then we turned around and did the same for our partners while Evadora looked on with an amused expression.

"Wish we could've put everything in the lost room," Max said. "These packs don't feel heavy now, but they will in a few miles."

"If we get separated, you'll need survival supplies," Gwyneth said.

Shushiel tapped a webbed pouch beneath her abdomen. "I have brought my own supplies."

"What's in there?" Max asked.

"Rodents," the spider replied. "I prefer spider bats, but they are too bulky to pack."

Max grimaced. "Those things look disgusting. I don't know how you eat them."

Whispery laughter emanated from Shushiel's mandibles. "I think the same of broccoli."

"It just needs lots of cheese," Max said with a grin.

Gwyneth gripped the stone in her necklace. "Everyone ready for the jump?"

I took my stone in hand and saw the others do the same. I went to the water first. "As above, so below." I jumped, spinning to face my comrades as I slid into the water. My insides felt as though they'd turned inside out. Dizziness washed over me in an instant. I emerged dry on the other side, my momentum carrying me back on shore. Unlike my first time visiting this strange place, I managed to land on my feet.

One by one, the others followed me through—Gwyneth, then Max and Ambria. Evadora came through atop Shushiel, cackling with laughter at the top of her lungs as the giant spider galloped around with her on its back.

"You are the best!" Evadora cried.

Shushiel pranced around, delighted.

Gwyneth leaned close to me, hand on my shoulder, her breath in my ear. "That girl is an odd one."

The hairs on the back of my neck stiffened with pleasure. I cleared my throat. "You'll get used to her."

"Hmm. We'll see." Gwyneth stepped away. "What now?"

I suffered a mild shock to my nerves when I remembered where we were. "We've got to run!" I made a circling motion in the air with my finger. "Everyone gather up and go!"

"We should've used the brooms for this," Max said. "Remember the last time we ran?"

"One moment." Gwyneth took out the door fragment and swiped the side of it. The door to the lost room opened. We ran in and gathered our brooms and a flying carpet for Shushiel and Evadora to ride.

As she closed the door, I sensed a cold prickle coming from the right. Everyone else seemed to feel it too. We turned and looked across the grassy field to see a group of people rushing our way. They weren't just any people—they were us. A ruby spider leapt over the wall in the distance and skittered our way.

Shushiel unleashed a hissing screech that scared me half to death. "We must go!" she said.

Evadora activated the flying carpet and pointed ahead. "To the crack!"

We zipped away, leaving our reflections far behind. The opening in the cliff wall was just as large in this realm as in the real world, allowing us to fly through, albeit at a slower speed. The Rift guardians weren't present in this realm, so we flew across the starry divide unopposed.

On the other side of the Rift, we flew through the enlarged crack there and emerged in the reflected version of the Glimmer. Still flying low, I raced the broom through a glade of tall purple grass. The scaly blades writhed like snakes. Gwyneth yelped as she encountered the grass for the first time.

Thorny black bushes snagged on my clothes so I rose higher and flew over a copse of crooked leafless trees, their thorny black bark like old leather.

In the middle of the copse was a pool of dark water—our gateway out of this realm. There was no time to waste, so I gripped the green stone. "So below, as above!" I dove my broom into the water so close to edge, I nearly caught my arm on the shore.

Another gut-wrenching yank seemed to turn me inside out. I flew out of the other side and nearly spiraled out of control as the laws of physics reversed back to normal. Max emerged an instant later and narrowly missed a collision with me. Everyone else followed in short order and soon our group of frightened adventurers caught their breath on the shore of the pond.

"I'm going to take a look around," I said, and flew up above the trees. A huge green moon, the anchor stone that bound together the realms, hung above a crooked mountain. Broken islands of land drifted in space against a tapestry of stars and galaxies.

"Wow," Gwyneth breathed. "It's beautiful."

I pointed to the twinkling spheres around the moon. "Those are the other realms." I let my finger drift up toward a swirling black vortex that blotted out the stars above the moon. "That's the Void where the Sirens trapped the Apocryphan."

"You're so young to know so much." Gwyneth blew out a breath. "I wish I could've been alive to travel the realms back when the arches worked."

"Maybe we can fix the Alabaster Arches." I shrugged. "Maybe there's a way to travel to other realms from here."

She turned her broom toward me. "How old are you?"

"Thirteen." Though it was considered an unlucky number, Max and Ambria had made it one of the best birthdays I'd ever had.

"Hmm." Gwyneth rested her arms on the pommel of the broom saddle. "You seem older."

"I guess constant danger made me grow up faster." I looked at the moon and wondered if I could fly all the way to it. Maybe once Evadora had this world under control I could give it a try.

Ambria rose beside us. "Do we plan to dally here all day?"

I looked once more toward the moon and turned to Gwyneth. "Do you plan to share the clues with us now?"

"Yes, but I need to consult with Evadora." She descended back down to the pond shore so I followed her. Gwyneth took out her arcphone. "Evadora, can you tell me if this means anything to you?"

"What means what?" Evadora leapt off the carpet. "Life?"

Gwyneth's forehead wrinkled. "No. I'm going to read a riddle left by Ezzek Moore. Maybe it means something to you." She cleared her throat and began. "Calm though we may seem, we are all this creature."

Evadora blinked several times. "People?"

"Are we supposed to track down the heart using riddles?" Max said incredulously.

Gwyneth shook her head. "Moore left a series of riddles leading us into the Glimmer, but we couldn't understand how this final one fit in with the rest."

"Ducks," I said. "One of my foster parents used to complain about how good their neighbors had it, but his wife would always tell him that we're all ducks."

Max scratched his head. "I don't get it."

"Ducks glide along the surface of the water effortlessly," I explained, "but beneath the water, their legs churn furiously to make them go."

"While everyone looks fine on the surface, they're struggling like everyone else," Ambria said. "It's a neat little saying, but what does it have to do with the Glimmer?"

"We deciphered what it meant, but not where it pointed," Gwyneth said. "I hoped Evadora could tell us."

"Oh." Evadora drew out the word. "We have to go to the other side of the world." She pointed toward the crooked mountain. "We have to find the quackers."

"Quackers?" Max said in disbelief. "That's what you call ducks here?"

"That's what I named them," Evadora said. "That side of the world is weird."

Ambria scoffed. "I think all sides of this world are weird."

I hoped the riddle was pointing us in the right direction. Then again, I had a way to confirm that. I gave Ambria a knowing look and then said, "I'll be right back. I slipped away into the trees. A moment later, Ambria joined me.

"Did Gwyneth notice?" I asked.

"Think she might be jealous that you sneaked away with me?" Ambria puckered up and made smooching noises.

I hadn't thought of that. "Do you think she would be?"

Ambria groaned. "Just give me the nose."

I gave it to her and watched in fascination as it molded to her face. Her eyes watered and she shuddered. "Eww. That first snoot full is so awful."

"Do you sense the heart?" I asked.

Ambria held up a hand. "Hang on; I'm filtering out the blink stones." A few seconds later she gazed toward the crooked mountain. "I smell blood."

"Is it the relic odor?" I hadn't counted on that.

She nodded. "Yes. There's the acrid odor, but that metallic blood scent on top of it."

I grimaced. "I hope the heart isn't pumping fresh blood."

"You and me both." Ambria stared into the distance. "Looks like Evadora is right about where we need to go."

Although cardinal direction didn't have much meaning in the Glimmer, I always thought of the crooked mountain as being north. "Looks like we're following the riddle."

Ambria removed the nose. "I agree." She put it in the side pouch of my backpack. "I just hope ducks in the Glimmer aren't horrific monsters." Ambria glanced back. "I'll rejoin the group first. I don't want them to think we've been out here together."

I answered with an absent-minded, "Okay," still thinking about what might lie ahead.

"Gwyneth might think we were kissing or something gross like that," Ambria said.

I blinked and looked at her, puzzled. "Kissing? What are you talking about?"

"Nothing, *Conrad*." She sniffed and walked away.

I watched her go and wondered if I'd said something to upset her. Then again, Ambria was rather easy to upset. I waited a few seconds and then went back to the pond. Gwyneth looked up from a conversation with Evadora the moment I returned. Ambria already stood next to Max acting as if she'd been there the whole time.

"Anyone else need a bathroom break?" Gwyneth said. "If not, I suggest we move out."

"One sec," Max said. He stood in place, a look of concentration on his face and grunted. "Okay, I'm ready."

I burst into laughter. Ambria slapped him on the shoulder. "Maxwell Tiberius, did you just poop your pants?"

"Pooped his pants! Pooped his pants!" Evadora giggled and danced in circles while Shushiel blinked curiously.

Gwyneth laughed and shook her head. "Boys."

I walked over and patted Max on the back. "Need some toilet paper before we move out?"

He shook his head. "Nah, I'll wait til it dries up."

Ambria made a face. "Gross."

The moment of laughter passed and then we climbed on our brooms while Evadora and Shushiel got on the carpet and flew across the broken land.

Our quest had begun.

Chapter 27

We flew due north until we were forced to land on the third island when a flock of mewlies erupted from a forest, intent on sinking their sharp teeth and claws into us. There were too many to fight in the open so we took shelter in the trees.

The few that forced their way through the thick branches were easy to dispatch with spells. Evadora winced every time we killed one, but she seemed resigned to the violence.

"Why won't you listen to me?" she screamed into the air.

The dark cloud of mewlies swirled above the trees like a swarm of bees, a chorus of hisses and mews sending shivers down my spine. Gwyneth held a wand of her own, a slightly twisted rod of golden wood, polished to a sheen. She zapped one of the cat-bats, knocking it from the air. The creature flopped around on the ground, evidently just stunned.

I finished it off with a dagger of ice from the arcwand. The defensive spells I'd scripted into it made it much easier to use.

Gwyneth watched me dispatch another intruder. "You must get your power from your mother's side."

Of course he does, girl. Della sniffed. *Her spells are rather paltry compared to yours, son.*

"I suppose so," I said, trying to ignore Della as she said unkind things about Gwyneth's magical skills and heritage.

"We're never getting out of here," Max groaned as the standoff continued. "There's gotta be some way to get rid of them."

The branches overhead rustled violently. The cacophony of mews turned to panicked screeches and the swarm dissipated in seconds. Shushiel climbed down a thread and dropped to the ground.

"The mewlies seemed as frightened of me as the spider-bats in the Dark Forest are." She swayed side-to-side in amusement. "They are also quite tasty."

"Thank goodness," Max said. "I thought we'd be here all night."

Gwyneth looked up at the eternal night sky. "Whenever that is."

"We shouldn't fly anymore," Evadora said. "That's why the mewlies came after us."

"It appears we have more company." Ambria stared warily into the sky. "They're a lot bigger than mewlies."

I followed her gaze and saw giant birds with bald red heads and crests circling lazily above.

"Condors," Evadora said longingly. "Naeve used to ride them, but they won't let me come close."

"Maybe you could find how to control them in Cora's memories," I suggested.

"That is what Yoghra told me." Evadora sighed. "I could not find anything helpful."

Gwyneth opened the lost room so we could place our brooms inside, but her mouth dropped open in shock. "How many brooms were in there?"

I looked inside and saw all of our brooms neatly stacked in the corner. I held up my broom and inspected it then walked inside and compared it with the one already there. "The brooms are exactly the same." A chip in the broom handle changed my mind because it was on the wrong side. "No, they're mirror images of each other."

Max compared his brooms. "Are you saying we brought copies of our brooms from the reflected realm with us?"

"It makes sense," Ambria said. "Did you notice that our reflections wore the same exact clothing we have on?"

"I wonder if I actually opened a reflected version of the lost room." Gwyneth shook her head. "I've dealt with weird stuff, but this takes the cake."

Max tapped a finger to his chin. "I wonder if we go back to the reflected world and reopen the room if there will be two copies of our brooms inside or none at all."

"We can figure that out on the way home," Ambria said as she placed her broom next to the other one.

"Too bad we can't duplicate money in here." Max took out a silvery bill of Tinsel, the Overworld currency and put it on the shelf. "I'm pretty sure the words and images will be backwards, but it's worth a try."

Ambria tugged on my arm so I followed her outside. She glanced over my shoulder to make sure no one else had come out of the room and whispered, "Do you think a relic could be duplicated like that?"

It was an excellent question. "It's possible, I guess."

"More than possible," Ambria said. "Perhaps we should test the theory on our way back."

"Not everything shows up in the reflected world," I told her.

"Yes, it does seem inconsistent." She sighed. "So many questions, so little time."

"It keeps things interesting."

Gwyneth closed the door once everyone was outside and we began hiking. When we reached the first tree bridge she stared over the lip of the island and into the vastness of space below. "What happens if you fall?"

"Nobody ever falls," Evadora said.

"No one in the history of the Glimmer has ever fallen into the stars?" Gwyneth asked.

"Not that that I know of." Evadora grinned. "Maybe before I was born."

"Do you float down there or fall forever?" Max asked.

I looked up at the thick arching trunk of the tree bridge. "I don't want to find out."

"Maybe we should keep a broom handy in case," Ambria said. "It couldn't hurt."

Max chuckled. "We have plenty to go around."

Gwyneth opened the door to the lost room and grabbed one of her brooms, strapped it across her back. She closed the door and started walking up the trunk. "Let's go."

The angle of the trunk allowed an easy climb where the top of the tree wrapped around the bough from the neighboring island. We traversed two more islands without event. While descending the trunk of a beige tree that linked us to an island of desert plains and savannahs, a massive cloud of dust and the thunder of hooves warned us that something potentially dangerous lay ahead.

Evadora's shoulders slumped. "The bronies and gruffalos are fighting again."

Gwyneth surveyed the land. The island looked about a mile straight across, though a spine of jagged hills threatened a tougher hike. We were nearly to the bottom of the tree bridge when we spotted signs of conflict. Body parts and blood stained the sands. The fanged trunk of one of the elephant-like gruffalos flailed like a dying snake. A miniature pony lay on its side, steaming guts spilled out, its muzzle splayed open in what must have been a final scream of pain.

Ambria covered her eyes and buried her face in my chest. "It's awful!"

More bodies littered the desert plain, vanishing into the sand storm a hundred yards away.

"We should go around," Gwyneth said.

"Bloody right," Max muttered.

Tears streamed down Evadora's face. "Innocent creatures pay for my failure."

"Is there anything here that doesn't try to kill you?" Max asked.

Evadora didn't answer.

We hiked along the edge of the island, staying well clear of the pounding hooves, the screams and trumpets of monsters battling, and the whirling dust. Even so, some of the animals wandered the fringe of the fight.

A lone gruffalo saw us. It stomped its thick feet, shook its wooly head, and trumpeted a war cry, fangs flashing at the end of its serpentine trunk. Evadora leapt in front of the group and held out her hands. "Stop!"

It paused, a light of recognition shining in its eyes. The moment passed and the gruffalo charged. I took out the arcwand and used a spell I hoped might stop the creature without killing it. When it was only ten yards away, I flicked the wand. A cloud of charged vapors streamed into the animal's face. It trumpeted, lifting its trunk to strike.

Though the gruffalo was only a few feet tall, everyone screamed and leapt out of the way. I wasn't quite fast enough. Inches from me, a red figure pounced, knocking the animal on its side. Shushiel bounded away before the fanged trunk found her. The gruffalo struggled and went still as the sleeping spell finally took hold.

Evadora knelt next to the slumbering animal. She looked up at me gratefully. "Thank you for sparing it, Conrad."

My heart thudded and sweat trickled into my face. "Thank Shushiel," I managed to say.

"Are you okay?" the spider asked.

I nodded. "Just scared."

Gwyneth blew out a breath. "Let's hope we don't run into a herd of these things."

We stayed at the island's edge. Shushiel distracted a small herd of bronies before they saw us. Jaws bared, they whinnied and chased after her. She camouflaged and circled back around to meet us and we continued.

As we hiked a grassy plain on the next island, a herd of normal-sized horses began galloping our way, silky manes fluttering in the wind. Unlike regular horses, they each had straight horns sprouting from their foreheads.

"They're like unicorns, but with more horns," Ambria said.

285

Max looked across the plain toward the next bridge. "They're going to kill us before we reach the other side!"

"What are hydracorns doing here?" Evadora said. "They are on the wrong island!"

"I do not think I can distract them," Shushiel said. "They are much too fast."

The huge condors circled overhead like vultures waiting on fresh carrion. Gwyneth looked up at them. "We can't fly."

We were halfway across the island, so retreating the other way wasn't an option. I came up with the only plan that might succeed. "Run for your lives!"

Everyone sprinted toward the other bridge. The hydracorns angled to cut us off. It became obvious within seconds that we'd never reach the other side before they reached us. Shushiel skittered toward the encroaching herd. "I will try to hold them off. Leave me behind."

"No!" Max shouted. He dug in his pouch. "Everyone stand still."

Ambria gasped for breath. "Are you insane?"

"Just do it!" he said. He stopped running, chest heaving for breath. "I have an idea."

Ambria pulled her wand. "Do you plan to eat them, Max?"

I readied my wand. "What's the plan?"

Max took out a handful of black glass marbles and blew on them three times before throwing them individually at different angles from the group. Glass shattered and darkness crept up the grass, spreading like an oil slick. The hydracorns hit the stuff and went sliding uncontrollably, neighing in surprise and anger before the entire herd landed in a massive heap not fifty feet from us.

"Now run!" Max said, and sprinted away.

Our shock lasted only an instant before we came to our senses and ran. The hydracorns were too busy untangling themselves to pursue. When we reached the next bridge, Ambria leaned heavily on Max's shoulder. Between gasps for breath, she said, "I'm not mad at you anymore about getting us an F in potions our first day."

Max laughed. "I just knew this stuff might come in handy."

"Brilliant." Gwyneth flashed a grateful smile. "I was afraid we were done for back there."

"Absolutely." I chimed in agreement. A chorus of neighs drew our attention back to the hydracorns as the last few gained their feet and began galloping our way. "Looks like we need to go."

We began climbing the next tree bridge. The first hydracorns reached it and took tentative steps after us.

"So that's how they got here," Evadora said angrily.

The whoosh of wings drew our attention overhead.

One of the huge condors swept towards Ambria. "Watch out!" I gripped her and pulled her down. Shushiel leapt to our side, as did Max and Gwyneth, wands drawn.

But the first condor had been a diversion. A second bird swooped down and snatched Shushiel so fast, she was nothing but a blur.

Ambria screamed.

"Shushiel!" I leapt to my feet and fired a blast of ice from the wand, but it fell well short. The condor vanished over hills on the next island, its prey in its claws. Tears burned in my eyes. "No! Give me the broom!" I didn't wait for Gwyneth to hand it to me and yanked it off her back. Before anyone could stop me, I leapt into the saddle and flew in pursuit.

"Conrad, come back!" Max shouted.

Gwyneth called a warning. "You're going to get yourself killed!"

I didn't care. I couldn't let the condors kill my friend. Moments after leaving the tree bridge, three of the massive birds appeared in the twilight and dove toward me. I bared my teeth. "Come get me you bloody damned monsters!"

The condors were large and fast, but nowhere near as agile as my broom. I spun right, threading between two of them and led the third on a chase. Pulling up on the broom, I climbed higher, looping behind the bird, and zapped a wing with my ice spell.

Unable to flap the pinion, it spiraled down toward the island where the other condor had taken Shushiel and crashed through the trees. I was far ahead of the other condors now, but a second threat emerged. A cloud of startled mewlies burst from the branches, their screeches deafening.

Like a hive mind, some homed in on the wounded condor, but nearly half broke off and came for me. I fired off a volley of ice spells. Several of the cat-bats plummeted, but there were still too many to fight. I dove for the gap in the crooked branches below where the condor had crashed. The great bird shrieked, its wings covered with gnawing fangs and slashing claws, a giant brought down by ants.

A mewlie slapped into my face, hissing and mewing. Its claws dug into my neck. I gripped its head and tore it off me. Pain blossomed where its claws tore free. I threw it and saw its small body smack into a tree. I clenched my teeth to combat the pain, weaving my way through the forest.

I reached the end of the trees and pulled up to climb a steep hill. The view on the other side of the crest filled me with dismay. A great crater stretched as far as the eye could see, hundreds of stone spires rising from its flat floor. Massive nests sat atop most of them. Skeletons littered the ground below, and dozens more of the huge birds prowled the starry sky.

Flying higher, I rose where I could see into several of the nests at a glance. Some had eggs the size of gruffalos. Others appeared empty and unused, while still more had broken shells, presumably from the birth of fledgling condors. A chorus of squawks echoed through the crater. In the distance, condors tilted their wings and came toward me.

I clenched the wand. *Let them come.* Nothing would stand between me and my friend. I spotted a nest not far ahead. Three hatchlings chirped as the presumed parent condor circled overhead. I saw no sign of Shushiel in its claws or in the nest. Then I spotted something that stopped my heart.

A furry red leg lay on the side of the nest. One of the hatchlings grabbed it in its beak and gulped it down whole. A scream of absolute fury erupted from throat.

How dare these vile creatures eat your friend, Vic said. *They killed her, Conrad. They should suffer the same fate.*

I dove for the circling condor and hit its wing with the ice spell. The bird squawked and tumbled from the sky. It slammed into the middle of the stone spire supporting its nest and the entire structure trembled. Sobs wracked my body. I summoned all my strength and prepared to destroy the weakest part. I would send those monsters to their deaths.

Conrad, no. A soft voice beckoned to me. *They are not your enemies. They are simply doing what they must to survive.*

It doesn't matter, Vic roared with anger, *they killed your friend!*

I stared at the hatchlings, listened to their hungry cries. They'd eaten my friend and still they craved more. But they didn't deserve to die. The parent condor lay motionless at the bottom of the spire. I had probably already doomed them to a slow death by starvation.

Guilt stabbed into my heart. Hardly a day into the journey and Shushiel had saved my life once. I had been unable to save hers. I circled over the nest, but aside from some bones and eggshells, there was no sign my spider friend had even existed.

The hatchlings lunged, big heads on narrow necks, desperately trying to snatch me from the air. Their shrill cries hurt my ears until I couldn't take it anymore. The other condors were too close to ignore, so I sped away.

The others had reached the bottom of the tree bridge and were headed for the one linking that island to the one infested with condors.

Ambria cried out when she saw me. I landed and fell into her arms, my body shaking with grief. "She's gone," I rasped, voice raw with grief.

Max put his hands on our shoulders, tears streaming down his cheeks. "She was such a good friend. Always there for us."

Evadora dropped to the ground, face buried in her hands as she rocked back and forth. I'm sorry, I'm sorry, I'm sorry!"

Gwyneth stayed a distance away, biting her lip and looking troubled, but she hadn't known Shushiel like we had. I didn't expect her to shed a tear.

Ambria backed away from me and slapped my cheek hard. "Don't you ever run off like that again!"

My face stung, and the cuts from the mewlie burned like fire, but none of it hurt so much as the agony of loss hollowing out my guts like a carving knife.

At least Gwyneth waited several minutes before saying what was on her mind. "Shushiel knew the dangers. She wouldn't want us to lose sight of the goal. We should push on before something else finds us."

A forest of blue trees loomed before us, a narrow tunnel between the boughs offering a dark passage. I took one last sad look toward

Condor Island and put a hand over my heart. "I love you, Shushiel. I will never forget you."

"She will always be in my heart," Ambria said.

Max choked back a sob. "I hope there's a spider heaven. She was such a good person."

Evadora screamed at the top of her lungs, "I'm sorry!"

Her voice echoed through the forest. Something inside roared back.

I looked up at the sky to make sure there was no other aerial menace and said, "I don't care about the mewlies. We're flying over that forest."

Gwyneth nodded. "Agreed."

Chapter 28

We flew high above the branches to avoid startling any flocks of mewlies. Other more solitary hunters still found us. An owl the size of a horse nearly took Ambria, but a zap from my ice spell hit it in the eyes and sent it fleeing and hooting in pain. A swarm of fist-sized locusts pelted us like hail. They weren't interested in us, but in our brooms, gnawing on the wood and straw and forcing us to land and drive them off.

Evadora tried her best, but without an experienced queen, the creatures of the Glimmer had taken on the role of disobedient, murderous children. We alternated between walking and flying for hours, finally reaching the crooked mountain. The eternal twilight and bright light of the green moon never changed, but the tired muscles in my body knew it was late at night.

We followed Evadora to the base of a cliff and stood next to it.

Gwyneth peered up at the formidable peak. "Why don't we just fly to the top?"

"No need." Evadora ran a finger against the rock and we hurtled upward as if on an invisible levitator.

Gwyneth shrieked and gripped my shoulder.

I might have laughed if not for the sickening yank of gravity on my insides and the dizzying view spreading out before me. When we reached the top, I quickly stepped to a stone terrace I remembered all too well from my first visit with Naeve. Despite my exhaustion, the bird's eye view struck me with its terrible beauty.

To the south lay the broken islands floating in a galaxy dusted with twinkling stars. The land to the north was mostly unbroken, vanishing into the distance. I wondered where it ended and what waited out there. More importantly, I wondered where I could find a bed and sleep.

Ambria looked straight up at the moon. "It seems close enough to touch."

"Hard to believe those are the realms." Gwyneth took pictures of the small planets orbiting the moon. "Have you ever tried to fly up there?"

Evadora nodded. "To get pieces of the anchor stone." She shivered. "There's no air and it's so cold."

"Like outer space?" Max asked.

Evadora tilted her head curiously. "Outer space?"

His forehead wrinkled. "Yeah, the void outside the atmosphere."

I tried to measure the distance, but what looked like a mile could just as easily be twenty. "Did you touch the moon?"

"No. I went there, there, and there." Evadora pointed out small asteroids of green rock drifting overhead. "Back when the condors listened to me, they would fly me up there and fling me at the rocks." She smiled wistfully. "My skin would freeze, and my eyes would become frosty." She reached out a hand and closed her grasp. "I always fell short."

"Absolutely fascinating," Gwyneth said. "I'd love to fly the broom up there."

Evadora pointed to the south where a flock of condors circled at the shimmering edges of the atmosphere. "I wouldn't try it."

Gwyneth sighed. "I could spend months exploring this place."

I looked to the southeast, toward twinkling lights that weren't stars. Though I had never been there, I knew that was the Soul Tree. *I'll see you soon, Cora.* I wished I could go there and see myself through her eyes. If the Broken Relic couldn't bring her back, at least I would have some small part of her, a living grave I could visit.

We followed Evadora into the mountain palace of the Glimmer Queen. The last time I'd been here was when Galfandor and I came to fight her. Naeve had demonstrated just how futile it was to confront her in her home where she commanded the very grass we walked on.

We stepped through an arch and into the throne room. Gwyneth gasped as she beheld the cavernous domed room, its ceiling laden with every precious stone known to man and more. Light from the jewels shone bright as daylight, a nice change from the moonlight.

There were many more levels to this place: hundreds of rooms, rotting furniture, and faded tapestries. I'd wandered many of them with Galfandor during our search for Naeve. Since there was no reason to go inside, I requested a halt.

"Are there beds in this palace?" Gwyneth asked.

Evadora shook her head. "Nothing nice. It's all rotten and stinky."

The relic hunter looked around and sighed. "I guess we'll use the sleeping bags." She opened the lost room and brought out sleeping gear and food. We helped her set up tents that would block the bright light from the jewels. I was so tired I could have slept in broad daylight.

During supper, I couldn't stop thinking about Shushiel. Judging from the other downcast looks and minimal conversation from my friends, it seemed they were as preoccupied as me. I finished eating and told the others good night.

Every time I closed my eyes, I saw the condor swooping in and taking Shushiel. Saw my friend's last desperate struggles as the bird took her to feed her young. I'd always thought such birds to be carrion feeders—vultures who wouldn't bother the living. Then again, the creatures in the Glimmer didn't follow the same rules as those elsewhere.

"Why did it have to take her?" I whispered to myself.

I am truly sorry for your loss, Della said. *To think a creature born of an evil mind could be so good.*

The ruby spiders seem to be the only good monsters Victus ever created. I'd fought a frogre before—part frog, part ogre—and it was a beast bred for mindless destruction.

The power of creation was his obsession and his downfall. An image of Della appeared in my mind's eye. She smiled sadly at me and I flinched at how vivid it was.

When I opened my eyes, she vanished, so I closed them and once again saw a pale gray shadow of Della regarding me. *Why haven't you done this before?*

"It never occurred to me until now." Della clasped her hands together. "I wanted you to see me for who I am, son." She closed her eyes, lips tight with concentration. Color flushed her cheeks, spread down across a loose red gown hanging from her thin frame. She smiled and stepped closer.

Though I had no body inside my mind, I felt her touch, cool soft skin against my cheek. Without opening my eyes, I touched the affected cheek and whimpered with the desire for this to be real.

Della kissed my forehead and embraced me, and it felt as real as any hug I'd ever had before. "Whatever happens, son, I want you to know that you saved this part of me."

I stepped back. "Saved you how?"

She held out her hands helplessly. "I don't know, Conrad. Perhaps it was when you grasped for an avatar. Perhaps it was showing me that perfect moment. You revived me. Something reminded me of the person I once was." Della wiped a tear from her cheek. "I was alone in the dark, but you showed me the light, dear boy."

I felt hot tears rolling down my cheeks in the real world. "I wish I could save the rest of you, Mum."

Della choked on a sob. "You called me Mum."

I'd said it without even realizing it. "You are my mother, even if only a sliver."

She hugged me quickly and stepped back. "I can't hold onto this much longer, Conrad. I'll need all my strength for what's to come."

"What do you mean?" I asked.

The color drained from her dress, brilliant red turning gray. "Your quest, of course." She kissed my forehead. "Sweet dreams, son." Her fair skin faded and her form turned to mist before dissipating into darkness. Once again, she became just another voice in my head. *Good night.*

I must have instantly fallen asleep because when I opened my eyes, I felt wonderfully refreshed. My arcphone told me it was seven in the morning Queens Gate time. I used one of the magic pans Gwyneth brought to cook some sausage and eggs while her magic teapot boiled water.

The others woke to the smell of freshly brewing tea, or so I imagined, since it seemed particularly fragrant this morning. Max stumbled from his tent, rubbing his tummy and staring intently at the sausage. Evadora dashed from within the tent she'd shared with Ambria and prepared herself some toast. Ambria appeared several minutes later, not a hair out of place, and took a cup of tea.

"Good morning, Conrad." Ambria smiled sweetly. "Did you sleep okay?"

I answered with a heartfelt smile. "It was much better than usual."

Max grunted. "Feels like I barely slept a wink. Couldn't stop thinking about Shushiel."

Evadora stopped chewing her bread and her entire body sagged. "Don't make me sad again."

I slashed a hand through the air. "This is not what Shushiel would have wanted. She'd want us to finish this mission She knew how important this is." I pushed back the sorrow threatening to rise. "We can be sad when we get back home. For now, we need to keep going." A part of me wondered if Shushiel hadn't died for my own selfish reasons. Finding the heart was just a stepping stone in the path of finding the Broken Relic. Even it might not transform Naeve back into Cora or cure Delectra of the demonic poisoning in her mind.

I prayed Shushiel hadn't died for nothing.

"Where's Gwyneth?" Max looked toward the relic hunter's tent.

Evadora dashed across the room and poked her head inside the flap. "She's not here."

We went outside to the terrace and looked around, but there was no sign of the girl. Max shouted and pointed toward the sky where the silhouette of a figure on a broom stood out against the moon.

"She's trying to reach the moon!" Evadora said.

It was difficult to tell how far away Gwyneth was from her goal, but her body contorted violently and the broom drifted back down. She lay down against the saddle horn and I imagined she was probably catching her breath after trying to breach outer space.

"Do you know how hard it is to hold your breath in cold water?" Evadora said.

"It's impossible," Ambria said. "And it's even harder to catch your breath."

"That's what it's like when you hit the blackness," the other girl breathed. "It makes you lose your breath."

I looked around and saw no sign of the condors that had hunted us yesterday which was probably why Gwyneth had chanced going up there. Moments later, she touched down and smiled as if everything was just fine.

"Sorry, I couldn't resist trying." Gwyneth stared longingly up at the moon. "I had an underwater breathing spell I thought might work, but it collapsed."

"Your arms are covered in goose bumps," Ambria said with a note of disapproval. "Perhaps you should've bundled up before going into outer space."

Gwyneth's eyes turned once more skyward, brimming with wonder. "There's nothing more amazing than discovering new places and things. When I was a child, I wanted to be an astronaut more than anything else."

"The Overworld doesn't have astronauts," Max said. "Not even Science Academy goes into space."

"Why is that?" Gwyneth said. "Why do we limit ourselves to this planet?"

I circled my finger in the air to indicate the realms around the moon. "There's plenty to explore right here if we can find a way to get there."

"That's what I hoped." Gwyneth sighed. "Every night I dream of the other realms. After the Grand Nexus was repaired, I thought I'd finally have a chance. But then the Alabaster Arches stopped working again, and all I can do now is dream."

Max patted her shoulder. "If it makes you feel any better, I know what you mean."

Ambria scoffed. "Says the boy who hardly leaves Queens Gate."

He stuck out his tongue. "Oh, shush, Ambria. I'm here now, aren't I?"

"I suppose you are," she said with a curt nod.

We packed up our gear, keeping out a spare broom just in case, and took the invisible elevator back down the mountain. Though the forest was nearly as thick, the violent beasts of the broken islands were few and far between on the northern side of the mountain, replaced by ordinary looking goats, cows, and wild chickens.

The reason for the free-roaming livestock became evident a half mile from the mountain where we found a village. Some houses were carved into the trunks of huge trees, while others were hewn of stone and mortar or even ordinary wood. Black vines as thick as my leg ran through stone-paved streets. Thorny creepers grew from the main trunk and into houses and other buildings.

"Don't touch the thorns," Evadora warned. "They'll put you to sleep."

Ambria flinched back from one of the vines. "For how long?"

"Forever," Evadora hissed.

It was then I saw the first Glimmer folk that weren't Naeve or Evadora. The woman was a little taller than me, her skin coppery, hair dark green and down to her shoulders. She lay snug in a nest of vines as did a man of similar appearance just a few feet away. Black creepers were wrapped around their torsos, the thorns digging deep into the flesh.

We saw dozens more people held this way, all so still as to be dead, but actually asleep.

Evadora stopped in front of one couple who shared the same bed of vines. "I wish I knew how to wake them up."

"It's a wonder their muscles haven't atrophied," Gwyneth said. "Do the vines feed them, or does the sleep spell preserve them?"

Evadora shrugged. "Naeve never told me. She didn't like people, so I stayed away from her as much as possible."

Gwyneth shuddered. "What a horrible childhood."

We made our way carefully through the village, avoiding the thorny vines, and the path ended at a dense forest of black-barked trees with leaves as red as blood. Evadora stared at the blocked path for a long time. "This is the Crimson Forest."

"Where Treek lives?" I asked softly, almost afraid he might hear his name.

She nodded.

"Treek?" Max gave us a questioning gaze.

"Someone who crossed Naeve," I explained. "She turned his skin into bark and made him go mad."

Ambria looked at the lone broom on Gwyneth's back. "Perhaps we should fly."

300

Evadora shook her head. "The night birds will get us."

Max groaned. "More giant birds?"

"No, they are small, very quick, and do not like anything that invades their territory." Evadora made a pecking motion with her finger. "Their sharp beaks could pluck out your eyeballs before you even knew what happened."

"In that case, I want the giant birds back." Max watched the air and flinched as a score of small shadows darted across the sky, bodies whistling through the air.

"Be prepared to run," Evadora said. "We do not want Treek to catch us." She clenched her teeth in concentration. Two trees trembled and broke free of the earth, stepping aside to reveal a foreboding tunnel through the trees.

Gwyneth seemed to steel herself and stepped inside.

Ambria gripped my arm. "Spooky."

I swallowed hard. "Let's hope we make it through before Treek comes after us."

Max took out more of his glass marbles filled with the slick potion. "He won't be able to stand up if he does."

When we stepped into the forest tunnel, tall mushrooms glowed, lighting the path for several feet in front of us. The tree branches and roots grew thick on both sides, shrouding what lay beyond in mystery. Insects chirped, the night birds warbled back and forth, and the hoots of the giant owls echoed from somewhere above. The forest sounded alive with hidden activity.

A centipede nearly six feet long slinked across the path and vanished into the thick undergrowth on the other side. Light bugs blinked off and on in random patterns, their faint illumination drowned out by the glowing mushrooms. Something buzzed past my nose and landed on a mushroom. A tall flower struck like a snake, its petals clamping over the insect and devouring it.

Ambria gasped and jumped back, nearly knocking me over. Gwyneth spun and looked at us. "What is it?"

"Nothing," I said. "Just a big bug."

She nodded and turned around, treading cautiously down the path.

"You should get your wands," Evadora said softly. "Just in case."

Gwyneth held hers high, a beam of light piercing the forest shadows. Mine was already in hand, though I didn't remember drawing it.

Max whipped out his wand. "Why would he want to attack us if Naeve is the one who hurt him?"

"I think his punishment drove him mad." Evadora spoke softly, large eyes darting back and forth.

The faint crackle of twigs came from somewhere in the darkness. Gwyneth held up her hand and shined the light all around while the rest of us held our breaths. "See anything?" she hissed.

There didn't seem to be anything out there. Then her narrow beam of light caught movement. Gwyneth jerked it back, but whatever it was had gone. She bit her lower lip and shook her head. Another crackle drew our attention forward. Something glowed just beyond the light cast by the mushrooms. Gwyneth sucked in two quick breaths and shined her light.

A massive silhouette towered over the path, shadowy snakes dancing atop its crown. Gwyneth whispered something and the light on her wand brightened just enough to penetrate the dark.

Glowing green eyes glared from within a mask of twisted black bark. A jagged mouth opened, and a roar like a forest of trees snapping in half crackled through the forest.

Treek had found us.

Chapter 29

All the mushrooms of the forest burst aglow at once.

Flesh of bark and hair of vines, Treek looked absolutely terrifying enough, but it was the madness in his green eyes that turned my knees to water. He was part man, part tree, and brimming with insane rage. Gwyneth held up her wand but a vine on his scalp snatched it from her grasp while another snared her foot and jerked her to the ground.

I took out my arcwand. A vine whipped toward me. I leapt backward before it got me and fired a blast of ice. Several vines froze and snapped off at their midpoints. Treek bellowed. Several vines looped around Gwyneth's waist and jerked her off the ground then hurled her at Ambria and Max.

In a chorus of grunts, my friends went down. The black marbles filled with Max's potion scattered into the forest.

"Stop, Treek! It's me!" Evadora danced around the grasping vines, waving her arms. "I'm Evadora!"

He didn't seem to hear her. One of his gnarled arms knocked her flying into the woods. I cast another ice spell at his head and broke two more vines, but there were dozens more and I was the only one in my party left standing. I had no desire to kill a person who'd once served Cora, but I had no choice if we were to survive.

I flicked through the pattern and unleashed fire. Bark caught flame and Treek roared in pain. Human screams mingled with his crackling bellows. He rolled on the ground, vines and arms flailing. Sap oozed from the bark, extinguishing the flames, but leaving parts of his skin blackened.

I readied another blast.

"No!" Evadora screamed. "You'll destroy the forest too!" She raced to the fallen Treek. "Please, listen to me!"

Ambria, Max, and Gwyneth struggled to their feet, shaking their heads woozily.

I stepped closer to Treek, wand at the ready. "We're here for Cora."

"The Earth Mother!" Evadora shouted. "The true Glimmer Queen."

The glow in the tree man's eyes faded ever so slightly and he seemed to actually see Evadora for the first time. "Earth Mother." His voice rumbled like a great oak in the wind.

"Your queen needs you." Evadora knelt beside Treek. "Her daughter needs you."

"You are her daughter?" More sap leaked from his wounds, covering the burnt bark. He moaned with relief. "But you are so big now."

I knelt next to him, and even though the sight of his skin repulsed me, I touched it. "We are here to save Cora—the Earth Mother. We need your help."

The phosphorescent glow in his eyes dwindled to brilliant silver. Treek gasped as if awaking from a long nap. He held up an arm and stared at it with disbelief. "Where is the false queen?"

"Trapped in another world," I said. "We're on a quest to save Cora, the true queen."

"Yes, she called herself by that name after Naeve banished her." He tried to sit up and groaned in pain. That didn't stop him from trying again. Treek's bark skin creaked, and the burnt sections crumbled even as more sap poured in to seal the wounds. "I will help you."

"Just like that?" Max said. "You tried to kill us a moment ago."

"Naeve's spell drove me mad," he said in a low ponderous voice. "The daughter has brought me back." He looked around. "Is Cora still banished?"

I met the uneasy stares of the others. "She's dead," I said.

Treek's mouth fell open and a tear ran down his rough face. "Dead? How are we supposed to save her now?"

I told him how Cora had been my foster mother, and how the living curse had killed her. He listened patiently as I recounted my dealings with Naeve and the information I'd discovered about the Broken Relic. "It might be possible to bring Cora's memories together with Naeve's body and restore her."

As I told my story, roots grew from Treek's feet and spread into the ground. His bark skin began to heal faster, and the broken vines on his head grew back out. When I was finished, he nodded sagely. "With love and devotion, anything is possible."

"Oh, spare me," Gwyneth said. "Love doesn't restore life. Magic does."

"Magic is will. Love strengthens will." Treek turned to me. "Where are we going?"

"North," I said. "Something to do with ducks."

"Quackers," Evadora corrected me.

"The aenids." Treek shook his head with the creak a tree in the wind. "Dangerous territory. I will make sure you reach it safely." He closed his eyes and the roots shrank back into his feet. "I am ready."

Ambria held her ribs and winced. "I think you really hurt something when you threw Gwyneth at us."

Max nursed his shoulder. "Yeah, nothing being hit with a hundred and fifty pounds of flesh."

Gwyneth's eyes flared. "I am *not* a hundred and fifty pounds, Max!"

He frowned "One-sixty?"

Her mouth dropped open. "I'm one-twenty, thank you very much!"

"I am sorry." Treek towered over them, but managed to look small and ashamed with slumped shoulders and sagging limbs. Leaves rustled in the wind and Treek tilted his head as if listening. "I will miss you too."

Max leaned over and whispered to me, "Did he just talk to the forest?"

"Looks like it." I watched the tree man and hoped his madness didn't return. We couldn't afford to fight him again.

We continued walking for miles, through villages with slumbering denizens, across hills and dales, over rivers and through forests. The unbroken land ended in a vast marshland of dark waters, mud and waist-high grass.

Treek brushed his hand over the grass and closed his eyes. "It refuses to talk to me."

Evadora tried, squeezing shut her eyes, gradually clenching her teeth. She slapped the grass in frustration. "Why won't the land listen to me?" She sat down and stared into the distance as tears streamed down her face. "Why is it so hard to control the land?"

"There is another force at work," Treek said. "I feel its pull."

"Another force?" I looked around. "Like Naeve?"

He stared into the distance. "I do not know. It is not strong, but it is enough to disrupt the land."

"Do you think Naeve can affect the Glimmer from the reflected world?" Ambria said.

Max blew out a sigh. "Man, I hope not, or we're cooked."

Gwyneth walked along the edge of the marsh a hundred yards and came back. "We'll have to make our own path or fly."

I turned to Evadora. "Is it dangerous to fly?"

She looked up and turned in a slow circle. "I don't know. Maybe."

Gwyneth opened the door to the lost room. "I'm willing to risk it." She grabbed our brooms and the flying carpet.

An image of Shushiel crouching on the carpet next to Evadora flashed through my mind and sorrow choked me. *How will I tell Galfandor or Shushiel's family that she's dead?*

Clear your mind for the present, Della said. *If Ezzek Moore hid the heart out here, he would have set protections in place.*

Like what? I asked.

Tread carefully. He was no one to be trifled with.

Treek climbed onto the carpet with Evadora after she assured him it was safe. The rest of us mounted our broom saddles. We rose into the air, wands at the ready, but there were no signs of airborne threats. In fact, the only life I saw were some ducks floating peacefully in the water some distance away.

"Quackers," Evadora said.

Treek agreed. "Beware the aenids."

"Are they flesh-eating ducks?" Max asked.

Evadora frowned. "I don't know. Yoghra didn't tell me much about the quackers."

"I have only heard they are dangerous," Treek said. "Be on your guard."

Max snorted. "Yeah, we'll do that."

The marsh stretched to the east and west for miles, but ended a half mile to the north in what could only be described as a field of rubble floating in space, quite similar to a belt of asteroids. Unlike the islands to the south that hovered in place, these were much smaller. Some resembled miniature planets no larger than a hundred yards in circumference. Grass, trees, and other vegetation grew on the larger ones. Smaller asteroids rotated like miniature moons around the larger ones and even smaller meteoroids filled the gaps between.

"It's like the land was smashed up into bits and pieces here," Max said.

Ambria shook her head slowly. "The end of the world."

Some sections of the asteroid belt were violent, great rocks crashing into each other, rebounding and scattering. Before they traveled too far, an invisible gravitational force pulled them back in where the process started once more.

"I know it's quite the sight," Gwyneth said, "but we have a lot of ground to cover." She looked up and down the marsh. "Let's form a search line and fly east over the marsh until we reach the end."

"What are we looking for?" Ambria said.

Gwyneth held out her hands helplessly. "I guess we'll know when we see it."

Ambria gripped the pommel of her saddle. "What a marvelous plan." She waved a hand at the vast marsh. "How are we supposed to see if the heart is underwater or perhaps buried in mud?"

"I have just the thing for that." Gwyneth pointed to a pouch secured to her broom. "Each of you have a pouch filled with divining stones." She caught a questioning look from Max and clarified before he could ask anything. "They send aether waves into the water and mud and send a signal to my arcphone that allows me to build a map."

As Gwyneth explained I pulled up next to Ambria and spoke in low tones. "Maybe you can sniff it out with the nose." I slipped the relic to her, blocking Gwyneth's view with my body.

Ambria stayed to my side so Gwyneth couldn't see her face and put on the nose. She sniffed, frowned, and sniffed some more. "That's odd."

I glanced back at the others, then turned to Ambria. "What is?"

"Now I smell two relics. One is close, somewhere to the northeast of us, and the other is distant, somewhere south." She bit her lip. "The other one definitely wasn't there before."

"Please stop talking and listen," Gwyneth said, drifting closer to us.

Ambria's eyes widened and she quickly pulled off the nose and handed it to me. I fumbled the handoff and the relic fell to the ground.

"What's that?" Gwyneth zipped lower and picked up the nose before I could react. She rolled it between thumb and forefinger, confused at first, then her eyes flashed with anger. "Is this the Nose of Jura?"

I flew closer and held out my hand. "It's mine."

"You've had the Nose of Jura all this time and failed to mention it?" Her voice rose. She clenched the relic in a fist. "You obviously know what it does or you wouldn't have just used it."

"Yes I know how to use it." I held out my hand. "Now kindly return it."

Gwyneth reluctantly handed it back. "I don't understand, Conrad." Her tone changed from angry to hurt. "Why would you keep that from me?"

"Because you work for Underborn, and you're a relic hunter." I tucked the nose back in my pocket. "He stole the map and key from Ezzek Moore, you know. Why he left the nose, I don't know."

"Yes, he told me how he broke into Moore's vault," Gwyneth said. "He claimed the map and key were the only two relics inside. Moore must have added the nose later."

"We had no reason to tell you," Ambria said. "We checked to make sure we were headed in the right direction at the start of this journey, and we planned to use it closer to the relic as well so we wouldn't have to search all over the place."

Gwyneth folded her arms. "Then where is it?"

311

Ambria pointed in the direction the nose indicated. "Somewhere over there."

"Perhaps you could put on the nose and guide us there." Gwyneth leaned back in her saddle and waited.

I gave Ambria the nose and she put it back on.

Gwyneth couldn't seem to help leaning forward and watching. "How interesting." She looked at me. "Why did you give it to Ambria instead of using it yourself?"

"She smells things better," I said. "I don't know why."

"I can't smell anything but yuck," Evadora said.

"Fascinating." Gwyneth sighed. "Let's go."

Ambria led us northeast out over the marsh. As we drew closer to the muddy creek wending through the pointy reeds, a bright red duck flapped its wings and rose from the water. I took out my wand and the others followed suite.

Evadora hugged herself. "Oh no, a quacker!"

Though its eyes were larger than that of a normal duck, the bird had no fangs, no claws, and seemed otherwise ordinary. "Don't worry," I said, I'll—"

We were nearly to the last village we'd passed on the way to the marsh and heading south. "Have to get home," I mumbled. "Not much farther." It was vitally important to get back to Arcane University and forget all about coming back here.

Conrad! Della shouted. *Stop this instant!*

I jerked to a halt and shook my head. Max nearly bowled me over, marching purposefully toward the dark path in the forest, Ambria and the others right behind. I gasped when I saw their eyes.

Their irises were frosted over, faces slack. I gripped Max by the shoulders but he wouldn't stop walking. I shook him. "Max, wake up!"

No response.

Try this, Della said. The image of a pattern hung in my mind. *Concentrate on their foreheads.*

I wasn't sure what to expect, but I pulled my wand and while marching backwards in front of Max, waved the wand and focused on his forehead. Pale suffuse energy drifted out and funneled into his head. He blinked his eyes, stumbled, and jerked to a halt.

Ambria plowed into him and fell on her hands and knees. She pushed up robotically and began to walk again. Max gained his feet in time for Evadora, Treek, and Gwyneth to shove past him.

"What—what's going on?" He looked around, completely bewildered.

I didn't have time to answer. I cast the spell on the others one at a time and was soon surrounded by disoriented comrades.

"Beware the aenids," Treek groaned.

Gwyneth bit her lip. "Now we know why."

Max squeezed his eyelids shut and shook his head like a wet dog. "What happened?"

"They brainwashed us," Ambria said.

"I was going home," Evadora said. "I wonder where I would have ended up."

It was a good question. Would we have ended up at the house on Dowling and Bucket, or Moore Keep?

"This is rather vexing." Ambria looked around. "Where are our brooms?"

"Probably back near the marsh." An unpleasant thought sent a jolt into my system. "I hope we didn't drop them in the water!"

Gwyneth looked at my feet and shook her head. "Our shoes are dry—no mud. We probably landed the brooms and started walking."

"Why didn't they command us to fly home?" I said.

"Probably didn't want us turning around and flying right back when we realized what happened," Gwyneth said. "How did you snap out of it so quickly?"

I tapped my temple. "Della got my attention. She gave me a spell to cast."

I used to use that spell to aid my study, Della said. *It clears the mind of distractions.*

I relayed what she'd said. "The question is how do we get past the ducks without them using another mind trick on us?"

"Maybe we can blast them out of the air," Max said.

I waved my hands defensively. "Don't even think about it. The next time they might tell us to drown ourselves."

That warning sent shudders through the group.

"You do realize we would have surely died trying to walk across the southern islands?" Gwyneth said. "They didn't kill us outright, but the bronies and gruffaloes would have made short work of our mindless bodies."

I hadn't thought of it that way, but unless we'd come to our senses by the time we reached the crooked mountain, we probably would have walked right to our deaths.

314

"Again, how are we supposed to beat mind-controlling ducks?" Ambria said.

No one had an answer.

Chapter 30

We stared blankly at one another until Della spoke in my mind. *You need to test the perimeter.* She told me how.

I told the others her plan and they agreed it was the safest way to proceed. We turned around and trudged several miles back to the marsh. We found our brooms and equipment in a pile at the edge of the reeds.

"I'll go first," Gwyneth said as she boarded her broom.

I climbed into my saddle. "I'll be your backup." I'd taught the others the mind-clearing spell during the walk so anyone could cast it.

We flew out over the marsh. I hung back while Gwyneth tried to make it past the ducks. Another red aenid met her in the air. She hovered for a moment, then turned around and made a beeline for land. The aenid settled back into the water, apparently unconcerned with me. I caught up with Gwyneth.

"Can you hear me?" I said.

Her glazed eyes stared into the distance. I cast the mind spell and held out an arm to steady her when she blinked from her stupor. Even so, she nearly tumbled from her broom.

"It got me," Gwyneth said.

"Yeah." I motioned further down. "Let's try the next spot."

"Your turn?" she asked.

I nodded and steeled myself against the unpleasant thought of losing my mind again. We traveled a quarter of a mile east and tried again. Once more, I saw a red duck leave the water and come for me. The yellow and green ducks remained where they were.

I jerked back to my senses after Gwyneth cleared my mind of the spell. Once the disorientation fled I groaned at what lay ahead. "Let's get Max and Ambria started."

It took us several hours, but we came to the realization that not an inch of the border wasn't guarded by one of the red devil ducks, as Max called them. Aside from quacking at our approach, the green and yellow ducks did nothing to stop us.

We even sent Evadora out on the carpet to see if she could talk with them, but the ducks ignored her pleas and sent her away as they did everyone else.

"I don't know what we're supposed to do," Max said. "Even if we zap one of the devils, there are more of them just waiting down there."

"The red aenids swim in groups," Ambria said. "There are just too many to take out before they get us."

"Where do we go once we get past them?" Max threw up his hands. "This is hopeless."

I hovered on my broom and stared into the distance, hoping inspiration might strike.

"I think I know where the relic is," Ambria said. She jabbed a finger due north toward a group of colliding planetoids. "Look."

At first I didn't see what she meant, but then I saw a barren rock with a lone tree growing from the top. It rotated in a circle with two other planetoids, deviating from its pattern only when it reached the

317

bottom of the circle. Once there, the three spheres knocked against one another, placing the tree perfectly in the center.

Three connected circles with a tree in the middle.

"It's the Arcane Crest!" I said. "The heart must be on one of those asteroids."

"Might as well be on the moon," Max groaned.

We landed and made camp for the night. I couldn't stop thinking about the red ducks, about the look in their strange, large eyes when they approached. It was the last thing I remembered every time one of them reached me. It seemed there was a flash, and then nothing. I bit into a biscuit and chewed on it slowly.

They fly up, make eye contact, and then—a brilliant idea slapped me in the forebrain. I jumped up and searched for a loose article of clothing, but couldn't find anything suitable.

Ambria clapped her hands to get my attention. "Conrad, what are you looking for?"

"I think I know how to get past the ducks." I put my hands over my eyes. "I need a blindfold."

Gwyneth jumped to her feet. "Brilliant!" She pulled a scarf from her satchel and handed it to me. "How are you going to see where you're going?"

"I need someone to shout directions," I said. "Let me know if I'm past the ducks."

Max grabbed his broom. "We'll all go and keep you on the straight and narrow."

I slung the satchel over a shoulder, mounted my broom, and lined it up with the three planetoids then throttled up. Gwyneth, Max, and Ambria followed close behind. They drifted to a halt thirty yards from the duck zone. I tightened the blindfold over my eyes then kept my hands steady on the broom and accelerated.

"Slight right!" Max called.

I followed his directions.

"Now back to the left a bit," Ambria shouted.

"The duck is coming," Gwyneth hollered. "It's staring at you."

"It's on your broom!" Max said. "It's trying to pull off the blindfold!"

I felt the weight of the bird settle on the broom handle and then a questing duck bill trying to grasp the cloth. I held it firmly to my face with one hand and used the other to knock the duck off the broom. It quacked angrily, beating me with its wings.

"Leave me alone!" I covered the left side of my face as powerful wings slapped it. "I'm here to retrieve the heart for Ezzek Moore!"

That didn't convince the duck to leave me alone. The air grew distinctly colder. With one last quack, the beating wings faded into the distance.

"You're on the other side!" Max said.

I lifted a corner of the blindfold and saw the edge of the world and beyond it, the asteroid field. The target lay at the outer reaches of the belt. Being closer gave me a different perspective just how big some of the rocks were. They varied in size from head-shaped meteoroids, to oblong asteroids larger than a house. The ones I deemed planetoids were perfectly round, even larger, and some had vegetation.

My broom drifted toward the ground at the edge of the world. I tried to keep it steady, but no matter what I did, it wouldn't stay aloft. I checked the aether battery in the handle. It had a nearly full charge.

"Why aren't you flying?" Max shouted, his words echoing over the hundred yards of marshy plains behind me.

"Something's wrong with the broom." I pulled up again, but it was to no avail. The broom halted a foot off the ground and refused to rise. I got off and pulled the broom away from the edge and tried once again. Only when I was twenty yards from there did it once again work.

Gravity does not operate the same here, Della said. *You cannot fly, so you must walk.*

Walk? I stared at the expanse and shivered. *What if I fall?*

You will not fall, Conrad.

I wondered how she knew that. I picked up a rock from the ground and threw it towards a group of smaller asteroids. It floated through space, arcing gently to begin orbiting around them. It struck one and bounced away only to return and begin another unstable orbit.

"Gravity," I murmured.

"What's happening?" Ambria said.

I turned to the others and shouted back. "The broom won't fly. Gravity is different, so I'll have to walk."

"Are you mental?" Max called.

"I have climbing gear and ropes," Gwyneth said. "Give me a moment and I'll join you."

Ropes and gear will do nothing here, Della said. *Look at that stone embedded in the ground near the edge.*

I found the one she meant and saw the Arcane Crest engraved on the top. Beneath the crest it said: *Only the stout of heart may walk this path. Only my blood will pass.* Ezzek Moore had left a trail of crumbs. Who had he expected to come this way?

I think Ezzek meant for you to find this, Conrad. Della sounded very sure of herself. *I think he left a path of stepping stones through this starry expanse for you to follow.*

Me? But he put the heart here centuries ago. I couldn't fathom what made her think I had anything to do with it.

The Seers spoke of the foreseeance—of you finding the Heart of Jura.

I thought back to my last confrontation with Plinth. *I thought he meant the Broken Relic.*

He spoke of your quest—never anything specific. I caught a mental image of Della tapping her ethereal chin. *Throughout history and all his many disguises, Moses, Ezzek Moore, and Jeremiah Conroy, very few foreseeances escaped his notice. I don't think he would have left a trail if he didn't mean for someone to find it—just as you found his vault, Conrad.*

How am I supposed to breathe in space? I asked.

Della laughed. *Magic, of course. The Glimmer is a broken realm. These asteroids are simply smaller chunks of the land itself. I suspect the atmosphere extends all the way to the edges of the asteroid field, and I also believe Ezzek enchanted this path so that only one of his descendants could cross it.*

I didn't know if she was right or not. All I knew was that the heart lay out there somewhere and I needed it if I was to find the Broken Relic. I needed it for my Cora, and for Delectra. I stepped to the marked stone, gauged the distance to a rock floating in space and leapt.

Della cried out in my mind just as I shouted in surprise as the weight of the world vanished. I was floating free, drifting without

321

gravity and the temperature dropped to nearly freezing. Slowly but surely my trajectory arced down toward the small rock. My feet touched it. It wobbled and rotated. Had it not been flat, I might have fallen off it like a man trying to walk on a rolling log in a river.

As Della thought, I could breathe as easily here as back on land. The only difference was the cold. *Why didn't my impact cause the asteroid to start drifting?* I asked.

Della made a thoughtful sound. *These asteroids seem to be charmed to remain in place. That is why the normal laws of gravity are not functioning here.*

It made sense. Moore had created a path of stepping stones not for the faint of heart. I kept balanced, heart pounding like mad, blood racing through my veins, sweat trickling down my forehead despite the cold. My breath frosted into sparkling crystals that drifted away like miniature stars.

The next rock was even farther away. I braced myself and threw myself forward. Since there was no gravity between the rocks, I flew forward, landing on my stomach. The rock was lopsided and rolled with my added weight. I grasped desperately at the sides and managed to stay on it. I crawled to the middle it, balancing it like a seesaw until I could climb unsteadily to my feet. I looked at the vast distance still separating me from the goal. I pictured Cora standing beneath the tree, orange hair drifting in the breeze, her hands beckoning me to come rescue her.

My lips trembled. *What if I don't make it?*

Della spoke firmly. *You are brave. You are strong. You are a Moore.*

It was as if she lent me her own courage. I needed every ounce to make it.

I leapt from meteoroid to meteoroid. After a long while I reached the asteroids. They were easier to aim for, but harder to hold onto.

During my leap to the third one, I smacked hard into the side and nearly lost consciousness. The world dimmed and blinked back into focus. I felt myself sliding off the edge, falling away into space.

I grasped desperately at the rough surface, but my fingers slipped free and I floated away. "No!" I shouted. I spun slowly around the asteroid, its surface just out of my reach. Moments later, my erratic orbit decayed and I skidded back to the surface.

Their gravity will always catch you, Della said. *Just take care not to fling yourself too far away.*

There were meteoroids orbiting just out of reach of this asteroid. I didn't want to join them in that eternal orbit.

I pushed onward and reached the first planetoid. I had no problem reaching it since its higher gravity gripped me at once. I stood and watched the rest of the world go upside down as the planetoid rotated with me on it. A field of bright green grass covered the ground—a strange color for the Glimmer—and on the other side of the tiny planet was a single red rose growing from a plot of soil. A misty shield hung over the flower, protecting it, preserving it.

I knelt next to the rose. "Where did this come from?"

Ezzek must have planted everything here himself. Della sounded astonished. *Why he would do such a thing, I have no idea.*

It must be a very special rose, I said.

Della didn't reply.

Three more planetoids stood between me and my final goal, each one with a unique surface. Trees were scattered on the surface of the next one, and the last looked like a desert with a small hill. I leapt toward the tree world but instead drifted back to the surface of the rose world. I tried jumping several more times, but I wasn't strong enough to break the spell of gravity.

John Corwin

I sat on the ground next to the rose, forlornly looking at the tree planet as the rotation of this planetoid brought it in and out of sight. I took out my arcphone and scrolled through the spells, but I had nothing that would propel me into the air.

Unless I came up with something brilliant, I was trapped.

Chapter 31

I closed my eyes to ward off the dizziness I felt from seeing the edge of the Glimmer go upside down so frequently. The rotation of this planetoid, while not incredibly fast, was probably several miles per hour.

Science, you buffoon, Vic growled. *Escape velocity already exists on this bloody rock.*

I flinched, surprised to get advice from the devil himself. Then again, he'd already inserted himself several times, if only to cause rage and mayhem. I suspected he had an agenda of his own.

I shook off the foreboding feeling and reviewed what he'd said. *How does escape velocity already exist?* I watched the edge of the Glimmer vanish two more times before it hit me. *The rotation of the planetoid!* It could slingshot me. I shut my eyes to ward off the dizziness, then stood and ran with the rotation.

The rose world was perhaps a hundred yards in circumference, but running with the rotation made me feel like I was practically flying as stars and heavenly bodies blurred overhead. As the tree world came into view, I realized with dread certainty that if I miscalculated, I might fly completely out of the asteroid belt and to my doom.

This had to be perfect.

I waited until the next go-round and jumped. The extra velocity shot me toward the tree world like a rocket. I smacked hard into the top of an oak, gripped it, and felt it torn from my grasp. The very same slingshot effect that had carried me to the tree world, flung me out into space. I flew toward the desert world, but missed it by fifty yards.

I continued my flight, arms flailing, body spinning, and smacked into a meteoroid. My body bounced away, leaving me just out of reach of the rock. I kicked my feet and flapped my arms, all to no avail. The final worlds taunted me with their proximity, several hundred feet away, but I was too far for them to pull me closer.

My rotation brought the Glimmer back into view. From this height, the marsh looked beautiful and the forests spread out forever. I suddenly realized my friends were no longer hovering on their brooms. On the next rotation, I realized why. A score of robed figures stood around our camp. I couldn't quite make out how many, but there were more than enough to outnumber my friends.

The Seers had somehow followed us into the Glimmer and they had my friends.

I twisted around to keep the land in sight, but it was useless. Without help, I was stranded in space and my friends were prisoners. I dug into my satchel for the arcwand, trying to think of some spell that could get me out of this situation.

My hand found something smooth and hard. *A blink stone!* I'd completely forgotten about it. Even if I'd remembered, I couldn't have used it to travel all this way, at least not without making myself dreadfully sick like Max. Its limit was about forty or fifty yards. That was enough to bring me in range of the planetoids. I just hoped it didn't make me too dizzy to make a safe landing. The rotating planetoids would crush me between them if I wasn't quick on my feet.

I held the blink stone, stared at the small worlds, and willed myself there. Everything blinked away in shadows and suddenly I was only feet away from the planetoid forming the upper left side of the Arcane Crest. My stomach felt queasy and a horrendous belch that tasted like yesterday's supper erupted from my mouth.

Gravity yanked me down before the dizziness wore off. I smacked into the smooth surface. There was no time to recover as the planetoid's rotation carried me toward the narrow zone between it and the next one. I scrambled to my feet and ran against the rotation, like a hamster in a wheel. Thankfully, this world's rotation was slower than that of the rose world; otherwise, I would have been ground to bits between the two grindstones.

I made it to the relative bottom of the barren rock and saw the world with the single tree. It bobbed up and down, the tree narrowly missing the other two planetoids during its slow rotation. On its journey up, it met the other two worlds, perfectly aligning the tree in the middle. I suspected it was further proof of Ezzek's magical prowess. Who else could have created a puzzle that altered the law of physics? Then again, this was the Glimmer—a broken realm that seemed to defy the very basics of physics.

The timing to the lower world was tricky. I ran fast enough to keep pace with the rotation of this world then leapt for the tree as the lower world bobbed up into position. I grasped its branches and hugged the trunk as it bobbed up into the space between the three tiny worlds.

I ducked, but there was no chance I would have hit my head. I scrambled down the tree, fighting disorientation with the constant bobbing and rotating motion. Once I reached the bottom, I closed my eyes and took a deep breath. The motion wasn't as noticeable if I didn't see the horizon moving.

Keeping my eyes on the tree, I knelt in the dirt at the base and dug with my hands. But the soil was shallow, and there were no roots beneath it. The tree was embedded in the bedrock, not actually growing there. I looked up at a low branch and plucked a leaf. It felt

327

and looked real, but this tree couldn't be alive—at least not in the traditional sense.

I paced around the thick trunk to the other side and there I found the Arcane Crest painted on the wood. Standing in just the right spot, it looked holographic, like the one in the keep. I reached out and grasped it. Instead of a copy coming free in my hand, something clicked and a section of the trunk opened, revealing a spiral staircase.

My stomach grew queasy as I thought of walking downstairs with all the rotation and movement of the planetoid, but I steeled myself and followed them down, ignoring the centrifugal push on my stomach. At the bottom I found a small room carved in the center of the world. In the middle of the room was a pedestal. In the middle of the pedestal sat a crystal in the shape of a human heart no larger than my hand.

It was perfectly smooth and clear all the way through but for a crack running from the top and deep into the center. Beneath the heart was a piece of parchment that read, *Only one power can mend a broken heart. Only one power can change the world.*

The power of magic, Della said, her voice cracking with emotion. *You have found the heart, Conrad.*

Another sentence beneath it read, *Let one who is without darkness take this heart, lest the world be destroyed.*

I swallowed hard, thinking about Plinth's warning. Were the soul shards considered darkness? Would I destroy the world by taking the heart? If I wanted to save Cora and retrieve the Broken Relic, I had no choice.

I stared at the relic for a moment then hesitantly reached for it. The moment my fingers touched it, the room began to quake. I took the heart and put it in my satchel. The parchment fell to the floor. Rock cracked and chunks fell from the ceiling. I stuffed the parchment in my satchel and raced up the stairs.

328

The three planetoids came together again, but instead of a narrow miss, they slammed into each other. The worlds cracked, broke, and shattered. I shouted in alarm as the tree snapped in half. The planetoids collided again. Something struck me in the midriff and my feet left the ground.

I pushed a leafy branch out of the way and realized I was on a broken section of trunk, hurtling away from the three worlds. A chunk of one planetoid struck the desert world. It careened into the tree world which smashed into the rose world. All three crumbled to dust and rocks.

"No!" I reached my arm toward the planetoids as if by some miracle I could hold them together. My path back was destroyed, but even if it had survived, the broken tree was carrying me out and away, toward the chaotic sections of the asteroid belt that had not been tamed by Ezzek Moore.

I crawled onto the trunk and looked toward stable land. My trajectory would take me closer, but not close enough before I reached the violent section of space. Even now it took me lower, beneath the edge of the glimmer until I saw only the raw bedrock of the shattered realm.

The asteroid belt came to an end not much farther below. I suspected that was where the atmosphere left off and the airless void of space took over. If I didn't stop myself in time, I might carry the heart beyond the reach of everyone.

A spinning asteroid drifted at an acute angle to my direction. When it was close enough, I sprang from the tree trunk and grabbed hold of an outcropping. My impact slowed the rock and sent it drifting slightly west, if direction had any meaning in this place. It plowed through a clumped group of meteors, sending them scattering like billiard balls, and then gently bumped into a larger rock, causing little change in direction due to its superior mass.

I transferred to the larger rock and stared up at the expanse between me and solid land. I was hundreds of feet below the surface, standing on the cusp of the atmosphere. I studied the asteroid field, drawing a mental path from here to the top. I could blink across the spaces too large to bridge with a jump.

Wishing I had Gwyneth's climbing gear, I began my ascent, first climbing this rock and then another one hovering just above. I ascended fifty feet before reaching the first gulf. The closest asteroid was thirty feet to the west and ten feet above my current position. I found a spot, focused on it, and blinked.

My face rested on the other asteroid, but nausea clenched my guts. I gagged, somehow having the presence of mind to grasp a handhold before a convulsion launched me out into space. I took deep breaths and held still until the sickening dizziness passed. There was still a ways to go, so I swallowed hard and climbed.

I was still over a hundred feet below the edge of the world when I came to the final hurdles. There was nothing but the rubble of meteoroids between me and the last few asteroids that bridged the gap upward. That meant I couldn't climb. I'd have to blink at least four more times. From there, I could reach the cliff on the edge of the world and hopefully climb it the remaining distance.

My first blink drove me to my knees when I reached the next asteroid. Once again, I barely held in the contents of my stomach. I gave myself some time to recover, but it wasn't enough. The next blink made me so dizzy and sick, I nearly tumbled from the boulder-sized asteroid. Vomit spewed into space, drifting in chunks and joining the astronomical company of meteoroids. Cold sweat broke on my skin and frosted in the bitter cold. I curled into a ball until the worst of it passed and then rolled onto my back, staring up at the lengthy journey ahead.

"I'll never make it." My throat felt raw from the acidic vomit. I hadn't thought to bring water or food. I probably wouldn't die, but there wasn't much chance I'd make it to the top anytime soon. I'd have to give myself at least an hour before blinks. I hoped that would be long enough for my body to recover.

I took out my arcphone and stared at the time. Several minutes had passed when movement above caught my eye. At first, I thought it was a small red meteor coming my way, but as it took shape, I saw it was something else entirely. Tears burned in my eyes—tears of absolute joy.

Shushiel launched herself from an asteroid nearly fifty feet away, leaving behind a strand of web and landed next to me. She was missing one of her forelegs, but looked otherwise unharmed.

I buried my face in the soft fur of her head and sobbed. "I thought you were dead. I thought the birds ate you."

Her whispery laugh lifted my spirits. "I bit the condor. It released me, but the fall tore off a leg. I camouflaged and hid so I could seal the wound with webbing, then came after you."

"We flew a good ways, so we probably left you far behind." I backed away. "I'm so sorry. I flew after the bird and tried to find you."

She bobbed a nod. "I know, I saw you. I tried to yell, but I have little enough voice as it is."

I laughed through the tears. "We should get you a better amplifier."

"Indeed." She looked up at the asteroids. "Are you ready to go?"

I nodded enthusiastically. "Oh, yes."

"And the heart?"

I patted my satchel. "In here." My joy faded as I remembered what lay above. "How are the others?"

"The Seers thought you died when the planetoids exploded." Shushiel bound a web to me and began to climb the web she'd strung between here and the last one. The webs reached all the way back to stable land, binding the rocks together like a chain. "They are escorting them out of the Glimmer."

"Even Evadora and Treek?" I asked.

We reached the next asteroid and Shushiel transitioned to the next web. "I did not see Evadora, and I do not know who Treek is."

"They must have escaped," I said. "When did you find us?"

"I arrived sometime after our friends were captured." She sighed. "There were too many for me to fight. They spoke of the planetoids and asteroids and how to reach you, but then the planetoids crashed together and exploded. They thought you died, but I have eight eyes." Shushiel chuckled softly. "I saw you vanish below. Keeping camouflaged, I crossed the marsh and reached the edge of the world. From there, I was able to find you."

"You're amazing." I felt like dead weight dangling from the web attached to her abdomen, but we were nearly to the top of the cliff.

"Thank you, Conrad. I feel the same about you." She crossed the thread to the cliff, and using her sticky spider feet, crawled up and over the edge where she released me.

I got down on my hands and knees and kissed the earth. "It feels so good to be back on solid ground."

"What happened out there?" the spider asked. "Why did the small worlds explode?"

I gazed across the marsh and saw no signs of my friends. "We can talk about that later. For now, we need to catch up with the others."

"Agreed."

332

I motioned toward my broom where it sat on the ground a few hundred yards away. "I'll get my broom. Maybe you should get started crossing the marsh again and meet me on the other side."

Shushiel bobbed. "I will see you soon." She shimmered into camouflage. The reeds spread apart as the invisible spider crawled through them.

I ran over and got my broom, took it away from the edge until it was able to rise into the air again, and affixed the blindfold once I oriented myself properly. Then I jetted forward. The ducks didn't so much as quack on my return trip. I assumed they didn't care about me returning to the other side, or perhaps Ezzek had told them to guard the asteroids until someone successfully retrieved the heart.

Shushiel reached the other side twenty minutes after me, and then we set out on foot since the broom couldn't support both of us, and the night fliers in the next region made it dangerous anyway.

We reached the Crimson Forest and continued onward into the dark tunnel of trees. We hadn't gone far when Shushiel stopped me.

"Something comes this way," she said as she shimmered into invisibility.

Chapter 32

I looked around, but whatever it was probably lurked in the dark.

A huge figure burst from the foliage, a small girl perched on one shoulder. Recognition stifled my cry of terror.

"Evadora?"

"You're alive!" She leapt from Treek's shoulder and landed on me, knocking me over backward. As if nothing were the matter, she sat on my chest and spoke rapidly. "Treek got hungry, so we went into the forest so he could root and feed. When we came back, the robed people had captured everyone and there were too many for us to fight. Then the planets exploded!" Evadora balled her fists, smashed them together and made an exploding sound. A tear trickled down her cheek. "I thought you died." She kissed my cheek. "I'm so happy you're alive."

"Can I get up, please?" I asked.

She giggled and jumped up, pulling me to my feet with ease. "Of course, silly."

"Where are the others?" I asked.

"Not far ahead. Some of the robed people wanted to eat on the other side of the forest, so they stopped." Evadora patted Treek's leg. "We're gonna try to rescue them near the mountain."

Shushiel shimmered into view. "Hello, Evadora."

The girl squealed with delight, wrapping the spider in a fierce hug. "I thought you died! I thought you died and it was all my fault!"

"It was not your fault," the spider said.

"Is Cumberbatch with the Seers?" I asked.

Evadora looked puzzled. "Oh, those people are the Seers?"

"Yes, they're the ones trying to capture me," I said. I described Cumberbatch. "He's tall, pale, and very thin with thick black hair."

"Yes, that man is with them," Treek said. "He was very upset when he thought you died. He left long before the others did."

I opened my satchel and took out the heart. "I found this inside the planetoid with the tree."

Evadora's huge eyes grew wider. "Ooh, what does it do?"

"According to Underborn, it heals scars." I shrugged. "I don't know how to use it."

"Perhaps all of us together could free your friends," Shushiel said. She rotated, looking at the forest. "We should try to stay close to the Seers."

I checked what gear I had in the satchel and readied some spells on the arcphone and the wand. "We have to try."

"Yes!" Evadora cried. "Let's save them."

We headed down the path in pursuit. It wasn't long before we reached the village on the other side. Shushiel scouted ahead, returning to tell us that the way was clear, so we continued onward. It wasn't until we were nearly at the crooked mountain that we found the Seers.

Men and women, mouths open in silent screams, eyes wide with terror, lay scattered across the road, robes and flesh charred. I raced among the dead, heart in my throat, deathly afraid of what I might find. There were thirteen bodies. None of them were my friends. I didn't know whether to be relieved or concerned.

"What could have happened to them?" Treek said.

"I don't think Max and the others could have done this." I shivered and backed away from a corpse so badly burned I couldn't tell if it was a man or woman.

Shushiel twitched and skittered off into the woods without warning. Moments later, she returned, pushing Seer Plinth in front of her.

He held a burned hand to his chest and walked with a limp. His eyes widened when he saw me. "You survived?"

"I had help." I grimaced at the sight of his hand, red and swollen. "What happened here?"

He shook his head. "It happened so fast. Spells hit us from behind. Before we could turn and face the attackers, half of my people were dead or dying." He nodded with his head toward a tree. "I saw a hooded person standing there. They hit me with a fire spell and knocked me off the path. I heard screaming, but there was nothing I could do, so I ran and hid."

Anger swelled in me. "Where are my friends?"

"The last I saw of them, they were running down the path, away from the attack." His shoulders sagged. "I don't know if they survived or not."

"How long ago was this?" I asked.

"Perhaps ten minutes," he said. "Not much more."

336

I stared forlornly into the distance. If we'd been a little faster, we might have caught up and prevented the ambush from happening. I wanted to rush after them immediately, but whoever had set up this attack might still be lurking nearby. Perhaps even now they waited to spring another trap on us.

Yes, caution is wise, Della said. *Assess before you jump.*

That's what I'm trying to do. I calmed myself and tried to think of what to do next.

"Let me see your wound," Treek said to the Seer.

Plinth backed away from the tree man. "What are you?"

"An abomination of Naeve's making." Treek stepped closer, his bark-like skin creaking. "Let me see your wound."

Plinth looked from Treek to Shushiel and then at me. "You keep strange company."

"I keep good company," I told him. "Now, let Treek see your wound."

The Seer held out his hand tentatively. Treek held his hand over it and sap dripped onto the skin. Plinth cried out and just as suddenly stared with surprise at the tree man. "It soothes."

Treek nodded and dripped more sap on him. "Cover the wound and you will recover."

Plinth did as he was told and sighed with such relief it brought tears to his eyes. "Thank you."

"You are welcome." Treek withdrew his hand and looked at the dead. "I can do nothing for your comrades."

Plinth nodded silently, more tears forming. "I know you don't want to hear this, Conrad, but this is proof that you should have been cleansed before taking on this quest."

I resisted the urge to punch him—not that my small fists would have hurt him. "Enough of that, Plinth! We're going to save my friends from whatever trap you walked them into." I took a deep breath to ward off the dark building anger. "Shushiel, can you cloak and scout ahead? I need to make sure we're not walking into another trap."

"Of course," she replied. The spider skittered ahead and rippled into invisibility.

I gave her a few seconds to get a good lead then set off at a brisk pace.

The others hurried to catch up.

"I would not approach the attacker lightly," Plinth said. "Whoever it was is extremely powerful."

I looked around at the dead littering the road. "I'm already aware of that."

As we walked, Plinth kept looking at my satchel. "Did you find anything out there?"

"No," I lied. "Just a piece of parchment."

His eyes flared. "Might I see it?"

I shook my head. "It doesn't say much."

"Please tell me." He looked at me so pleadingly that I gave in.

"Only one power can mend a broken heart," I said. "Only one power can change the world." I didn't tell him about the final sentence for fear it would only strengthen his resolve about cleansing my soul.

"That's it?" Plinth's forehead pinched in disappointment. "Why would anyone take such care to hide a simple piece of parchment?"

I didn't answer.

Shushiel found us as we neared the base of the mountain. "I saw five people going up the side of the mountain. Two of them wore robes and I'm certain the others were our friends."

I looked toward the crest. "How long ago?"

"Moments ago." She rotated to face the mountain. "They flew up, but without brooms or carpets."

"There's an invisible levitator." I started walking toward the way up. "You said there were two people in robes?"

"The killers must have had others waiting ahead of us." Plinth limped alongside me. "They killed my companions from behind and drove your friends forward into another trap."

"Who would do this?" Possibilities raced through my mind. "Who else has access to the Glimmer?"

Evadora began listing people with her fingers. "Nobody except you, Ambria, Max, Gwyneth, me, and Shushiel." She frowned and looked at Plinth. "How did you get here?"

Plinth looked away from her. "We have—or had—a relic. The Dagger of Jura allows all who touch it to become perfectly invisible, though at a price. We used it to pass through the Rift not long after you vanished into that pond."

"You followed us?" I stopped and glared at him. "What kept you from catching us sooner?"

"It took me five trips through the Rift to bring everyone through since only a few people can touch the dagger at a time." He seemed to sag inward, eyes taking in the brick road. "By the time we were all through, we'd lost your trail."

Evadora walked up to him, her eyes curious. "What's the price for using the dagger?"

"Imagine being stabbed in the gut, the blade twisting in your organs." He shuddered. "The pain is constant, every step torture. I endured it so many times I thought I might go mad."

"That's awful!" She patted his uninjured arm. "Do you feel better when you release it?"

"Immensely." Plinth breathed in relief. "I can only imagine how the dagger became a relic in the first place."

"Where is it now?" I asked.

Plinth looked to the east. "We found a tree unlike any other I've ever seen." His eyes filled with wonder. "It was so huge, it filled the sky. Its boughs were filled with strange wisps. A mere touch gave me visions of other lives, other times."

"Yes, the Soul Tree," Evadora said.

I scowled at the thought of Plinth touching the tree where Cora's memories resided. "You didn't answer my question. Where is the dagger?"

"A massive furry white creature chased us." Sadness returned to his eyes. "I dropped the dagger between some roots and couldn't retrieve it for fear the beast would kill us."

"Yoghra probably would have just ripped off your arms," Evadora said matter-of-factly. "He doesn't like killing."

Plinth looked horrified.

The dagger is at the Soul Tree. I knew now why Ambria had sniffed two relics with the nose. I began walking toward the cliff again. "We're going to rescue the others and find out—"

Evadora tilted her head. "Find out what?"

My skin went cold from the inside out. "Two people in robes. Two kidnappers." I met Evadora's gaze. "How did Victus and Delectra get into the Glimmer when they were working with Naeve?"

She shrugged. "I don't know."

"They must still have a way, because the only people powerful and evil enough to massacre all those people are my parents." I trembled with fear and anger. "Shushiel, we need to take Delectra alive. We'll kill Victus if we have to. Can you sneak in and incapacitate them with my help?"

The spider bobbed up and down. "Yes, Conrad."

"I'm coming too," Evadora said. She scrambled up Treek's body and perched on his shoulders. "We'll make them pay."

"I'll remain here." Plinth's eyes filled with fear. "I'm too injured to be of help."

The rest of us marched for the invisible levitator without acknowledging his response. Evadora touched the cliff. The invisible force lurched upward at incredible speed. Plinth watched us go, craning his neck until he became a speck on the ground.

"Shushiel, I need you to scout the palace and find out where our friends are." I touched her leg. "Be careful."

"I will be vigilant." She rubbed her leg against my arm. "We will not fail."

"What can we do?" Evadora asked.

341

I hid behind the plants growing on the terrace and motioned Treek and Evadora to do the same. "I don't know. You're both strong, so you can help me subdue them."

We waited and waited, the minutes stretching on until nearly thirty minutes had passed. It didn't seem possible that Shushiel would take so long to search. I crept toward the archway leading into the throne room. It was empty, so I ran across the room to the next door. I heard creaking bark and turned to see Treek and Evadora following.

I motioned them to stop and dashed over to them. "Evadora can come, but Treek, you're too noisy."

The tree man looked down. "Very well. I will wait on the terrace."

Evadora patted his arm. "Don't worry. We'll be back soon."

The two of us crept down a winding hallway and through rooms of rotting furniture and faded paintings. We heard footsteps and hid as a man with a vacant stare walked up nearby stairs and into the rooms above.

Evadora opened her mouth to speak, but I put a finger to my lips. If that was one of the two people, then that meant only one might be guarding my friends.

My theory was tested when we saw two more men, each one identical to the last searching the rooms in the next hallways. Evadora's forehead pinched with confusion and she looked back and forth between the twins.

I heard a faint voice in my head, as if Della were trying to say something, but I couldn't quite make it out. I wondered if she knew what was going on.

Once we made it past the men, we descended some stairs and stepped across the threshold into the next hall—or at least we tried to.

My feet suddenly wouldn't move. Evadora grunted, but she seemed as fixed to the floor as I was.

A hooded figure appeared, wand in hand. "New guests. What a pleasant surprise!" His voice didn't sound like Victus's, but it sounded familiar.

"Who are you?" I shouted. "Reveal yourself!"

The man said nothing. He flicked his wand and Evadora gasped and crumpled to the floor.

"What have you done?" I screamed. "Did you kill her, you bastard?" I touched her neck and sighed with relief when I found a pulse. She was just unconscious.

"We are with the Seers," the man said. "One might call us enforcers. Plinth and his people interfered with you and may have altered your actions, so we're here to repair the damage." He flicked his wand again and my feet came free. "Come this way, and don't try anything foolish."

He's not Victus? That meant these robed people weren't my parents. It meant Plinth's interference had cost his people their lives. Numbly, I stepped inside, leaving a slumbering Evadora behind. The man guided me down the hall and into a large room. Max, Ambria, and Gwyneth lay prone on tables, hands folded over their stomachs as if prepared for burial. Something that looked like a translucent crystal coffin lay on the floor in the back.

Ignoring the man with the wand, I ran across the room and touched Ambria's hand. It was warm as was Max's. Something thumped against a closed wooden door near the crystal coffin.

"Your spider friend," the man said. "She is unharmed."

I spun to face him. "What do you want with us?"

343

"We'll need to wipe some memories from your minds and then you'll be free to go," he said. "If I wanted to kill you or your friends, they'd already be dead."

I had no doubt of that. I backed away, thinking desperately for some way out of here with our memories intact.

"Your friends thought you dead," the man said. "Crushed by tiny worlds." He chuckled. "Yet here you are, alive and well."

I stumbled over the crystal coffin and fell on my backside next to it. The top was transparent, offering a clear view inside. My breath caught when I saw the identity of the occupant. *Naeve!* Her face looked gaunt, body thin and frail, but it was definitely the Glimmer Queen.

Conrad, this man is not who he seems, Della said in a strained voice. *Vic is trying to repress me.*

Quiet! Vic roared. *He will listen to me and me alone.*

Pain stabbed into my head. I winced and pressed my temples with both hands. I rose unsteadily and faced the robed man. "How did you capture Naeve?"

"She was weak from her months of confinement to the reflected world," he said. "We found her near the reflecting pool where you imprisoned her."

Della's words rang true. This man wasn't an enforcer. How would he know that I imprisoned Naeve in the reflected world or where I did it? "Who are you? You're not an enforcer for the Seers."

"Clever boy." The man laughed. "I wanted to wait until my disguise wore off, but perhaps this will be an even better surprise." He slid back the cowl and I couldn't believe who it was.

344

Chapter 33

Professor Sideon leered at me. "You poor, poor boy. You still don't get it, do you?" He scoffed. "And here we thought you were brighter than that."

Puzzle pieces drifted together. His knowledge of Naeve. His ability to get into the Glimmer. His last name, Sideon. Even the sound of his last name should have been familiar. I reversed the first four letters in my head to spell his real surname—Edison. "Victus," I growled.

His smirk vanished. "Impressive. Perhaps your mother was right about you."

"Right about me how?" I said.

"I told you," said a voice that broke my heart into pieces. "I know our son better than you think."

Tears burned my eyes as his companion came into the room—my dear professor, Esma Emoora. I wanted to scream that this couldn't be happening. That the woman who'd mentored me, cared for me, told me she'd be proud to be my mother was in truth, Delectra Moore. "How could you?" My voice was a pale whisper, too stunned for emotion.

"I convinced Victus to let me train you," she explained in a cool voice. "I told him you have untapped potential and deserved a place with us."

Esma's pretty face sagged like melting wax and golden locks of hair drifted from her scalp where they piled on the floor, leaving bald ugliness. She convulsed. Bones cracked and a scream died in her throat. She grew taller, her face narrowed, and black hair spilled down her shoulders. Within seconds, Esma was completely gone, replaced by the cold, uncaring face of my biological mother.

She bent down and retrieved her wand where it had fallen during the transformation. "The Eye of Jura disguises one so completely, that no one can tell the difference." She shed her dark robes, now several inches too short, to reveal tight black robes.

"Why go through the trouble of hiding your faces?" I said, still numb with grief and shock.

"Just in case you escaped us," Victus said. "We didn't want our alter egos revealed." His face began to sag. "But now we have you, and you will join us or die." His smile turned gruesome as his lips melted and his face began to reform. He clenched his teeth and grunted in pain as his body began to grow.

Delectra met my gaze, the uncaring cold gone, replaced by fear and emotion. She spun toward Victus and unleashed a searing bolt of magic. The shot threw him across the room where he landed in a heap, body hidden within the folds of the cloak. She fired again, but the magic splashed off a protective barrier.

Victus roared and threw the cloak away from him, revealing his haughty features. "I knew this would happen, you traitorous woman! He pounded the floor with the bottom of his fist. "You let him get to you."

Delectra went white. "Run, Conrad! Run!"

346

I tried to answer, but pain exploded in my head, and a voice not my own used my lips. "I'm here master! Kill the boy and free me!"

You will not have him! Della screamed.

Victus turned to me, teeth bared in a snarl. "Yes, I think it time to end this charade."

Delectra fired a spell at the ceiling above Victus. Rubble fell, crashing against his shield and throwing up clouds of dust. She raced across the room and grabbed my hand. "Son, we have to go now!"

I pressed my hands to my temples as Della warred with Vic in my head. "I won't leave my friends."

Delectra waved her wand over Gwyneth's head, and the girl blinked and woke with a start. "What? Where am I?"

"No time!" I shouted, taking out my own wand and firing it at Victus as his shield sputtered from the onslaught of stone.

Delectra woke Max and Ambria, then fired a blast at the back door to free Shushiel. The spider bounded from her prison and leapt for Delectra.

I threw up a hand. "Shushiel, no! She's with us!"

The spider blinked. "Are you certain?"

"Yes." I gritted my teeth against the war boiling in my head and blew loose another chunk of ceiling, burying Victus beneath a pile of rubble. I grabbed my disoriented friends and shoved them toward the door. "Run!"

Shushiel bounded ahead, Gwyneth, Ambria, and Max staggering behind. We raced up the stairs and down a long hall.

"What's going on?" Max said. "What's with all the explosions?"

"Is that Delectra?" Ambria shrieked.

"Shut up and run!" I yelled.

We reached the doorway where Evadora still lay unconscious. Max skidded to a stop, leaned over, and picked her up without missing a beat. I helped him sling her over his shoulder.

"There are golems ahead," Delectra said. "I should lead."

I grabbed her arm. "You mean the identical people I saw earlier are golems?"

Delectra peered down the hallway, wand at the ready. "Yes. He perfected them years ago—all part of his plan to infiltrate the Overworld Conclave from the inside out." She held up a hand and crept along the wall. One of the men appeared in the hallway, a silver gun in hand.

She smoked the golem with a blistering spell. The creature screamed in pain, clutching at its burnt flesh and went down. Three more raced into the hall, firing azure beams of energy from their guns. I took down one with an ice spell. Shushiel bounded off the ceiling and landed on the next one, binding it tightly with webs. Delectra scorched the third.

Ambria covered her ears. "You're murdering them!"

"They're not truly alive," Delectra said grimly. "Just simulacrum."

"Do they feel pain?" Max asked.

"They are flesh and blood, but instead of a soul, they have a spark of magic." She motioned us forward. "That was all of them. We need to go before Victus comes."

"All of us together can stop him," Max said.

Fear shone in Delectra's eyes. "No, we can't. He has powerful arcnology spells at his disposal." She blinked and tears trickled down her cheeks. "He still has a demon collar on me. If he gets within range, he can cut off my magic."

"Go," I said. I didn't know what a demon collar was, but there was no doubt that Victus could kill us all if he caught up.

Max grunted and jogged with Evadora on his shoulder. "Thank goodness she's light."

Treek was waiting in the throne room, the vines on his head thrashing in agitation. "You made it!" His deep voice resonated in the chamber. "What happened to Evadora?"

"No time to explain," I shouted. "Run for the levitator."

Before we reached the exit, black vines crept across the door, weaving into a barrier. Delectra fired spell after spell, blasting away layers of vines. She finally cleared a path. Max ducked through with Evadora. Gwyneth and Ambria squeezed through after her while Delectra and I aimed our wands across the room.

"He must have woken Naeve," Delectra said. "She is weak, but still capable."

"She'll recover quickly in the Glimmer." I turned and watched Treek ducking through the hole. "When she does, she'll kill all of us, Victus included."

"No, he placed a demon collar on her as well." Delectra's eyes grew haunted. "It was how he subverted me, forced me to his will. Before long, I was his completely, a twisted evil creature."

"But you're not anymore." I grabbed her arm. "The good part of you is still there inside."

"I was supposed to train you, to make you one of us." Tears formed in her eyes. "Instead, you brought me back." She touched my cheek. "Your love saved me, son."

Shushiel made it through and I motioned Delectra. "Go."

"I think not," Victus said, the gaunt figure of Naeve by his side. She held up a fist and a new wall of vines slammed down over the door.

Naeve slumped to her knees, clearly too weak to do much more. "You will die for this, Victus," she croaked. "Your foul bonds cannot hold me long."

He shoved her shoulder, toppling her to the floor. "I don't think you understand demon magic."

Delectra shoved me behind her. "Leave him alone!"

Victus took a worn doll with black hair and fair features, Delectra in miniature, and held it up. "Do you know what this is, Conrad?"

I gulped a knot of fear. "A toy."

"A demonic collar." He removed a spiky ball from within his satchel. "This used to be yours." Victus laughed. "Ah, the good old days."

"The boy is powerful," Delectra said, trying to regain her cold composure, but her hands trembled and tears streamed down her face. "Spare him and I will do whatever you want."

"Oh, I will spare him." Victus stepped closer. "I will collar him again and wean him of his soft heart and then we will overthrow the pretenders and take back power. With Ivy Slade gone, and my other powerful enemies locked away, there will be nothing to stop us this time." He waved an arm around the throne room. "With the power of the anchor stone, we will gain immortality and power enough to topple even human governments."

"Why?" My voice broke. "What good is it to gain power over the whole world? Will it make you complete? Will it make you happy?"

Victus's smile faded. "I'm afraid nothing can bring lasting happiness, boy. That's why you take your time and savor every success. Relish the little things—the death of an enemy, the adrenalin spike as the light fades from his eyes, the screams as his family dies in fire."

"How could anyone be so twisted?" I spat on the floor. "You're not even human."

"Who would want to be?" Victus stroked the hair on the doll. "Humans are weak and pathetic." He palmed the spiked ball. "Take this totem, boy. Let me collar you and I will let your friends live." He nodded at Delectra. "I will let your dear mother live."

Delectra pressed a hand to my chest. "Don't believe him."

Victus held up the doll and sneered. "Bow to me, woman."

Delectra's body stiffened. "No, I won't let you."

"Do it!" he roared, fist tightening on the doll.

Her body trembled, blood trickled from her nose. Still, she shook her head. "I will never bend to your will again."

I brandished my wand and fired a spell at Victus. The magic splashed off a barrier around him. I fired again and again, but it did no good. I tried to hit the ceiling, but the jewels refracted the energy harmlessly.

Victus's face turned dark with rage. "Weak, useless child. You don't deserve the power I offer." He took out his arcphone and aimed it at me.

I had my own ready and started a defensive spell. A bolt of green energy exploded from his phone and crashed into my shield. The shocks ran through my body, down to my core, and shook the source of my power—my will. The shield flickered. I saw my mother standing there, vulnerable, trembling, bleeding and cried out with rage. "You will never take us!"

My shield redoubled with power, reflecting the energy back at the source. Victus roared with rage as his own attack crackled against his defenses.

Somehow, I had to free Delectra of the demon. I reached into my satchel and put a hand around the heart. Underborn said it healed scars. My mother was scarred by demons, but was it the same thing? I didn't even know how to use the heart. Then I remembered the words on the parchment and what Delectra had told me—how I'd brought her back from damnation.

Yes! Della's voice was but a whisper in my head, but it was clear.

I took Delectra's hand and squeezed it while holding onto the heart with the other. "Esma was like my mother," I said softly, "and now I know why." I kissed her hand. "I love you, Mum."

I heard a cracking sound and took out the heart. The crack in the heart glowed brilliant white, slowly mending itself. Power flushed through me and into Delectra. She gasped, dropping her wand and doubled over. Sickly green smoke seeped from the pores of her skin, swirling around her. Malevolent tendrils darted at her, as if trying to penetrate her again. The white power from the heart reflected it. The smoke coalesced into a dark oblong form, a head with only a screaming mouth. Sharp teeth clacked together viciously, but like smoke in a storm, it drifted apart, screams fading to nothing.

"Impossible!" Victus screamed. "You're not strong enough to free her!" He saw the heart. "You have it. You found the Broken Relic."

My own heart skipped a beat. "This is the Heart of Jura."

He saw my confusion and burst into laughter. "Yes, but it is also called the Broken Relic." Victus shook his head. "Leave it to

352

Underborn to hide the truth within another truth." He dropped the doll to the floor. "What did he promise you?"

I felt so foolish even telling him, but a dark impulse prodded me to. "He said he'd help me find the Broken Relic."

"And he made you sign a contract, yes?" Victus barked another laugh at the expression on my face.

I noticed his other hand doing something with his arcphone and realized he was buying time. I heard pounding on the vines behind me, heard Ambria shouting. "We're nearly through Conrad! Are you okay?"

"I'm here!" I said.

Delectra vomited black liquid and gasped.

"An unfortunate side effect. She will be weak for quite some time." Victus stared at me for a long moment and then shouted, "If you can hear me, I need your help right now!"

I abruptly realized he wasn't talking to me. The intended recipient heard the message loud and clear. Pain erupted in my head and I joined Delectra on my knees, screams tearing from my throat. The heart dropped from my hand and back into the satchel.

I heard Della shouting incoherently, heard Vic roaring in my mind. My shield spell faltered and faded. I drew my wand, but the pain in my head swelled. The image of two souls battling flashed through my head. Vic, an oily black form squirmed around Della, choking her.

Victus grinned victoriously and walked across the room, arcphone in his hand.

"Good riddance, boy." A bolt of green speared for me.

"No!" Delectra threw herself in front of me. Flesh seared and smoked. My mother screamed in agony even as she fired off another spell that struck Victus in the knee. He cried out and fell to the ground, clutching blistered flesh.

The battle raged in my head and Della was losing. Blinded with pain, I flailed a hand into my satchel and found the heart. I focused on Della. She was my mother every bit as much as the flesh and blood Delectra. Through the pain, I sent her a simple message. *I love you.*

Della swelled, snapping the black tendrils of Vic. Hands glowing white, she tore him in half. Vic squealed in agony. *Be gone, foul stain!* Della shouted. I felt a horrible wrenching in my heart and ice cold slithered up my throat. My eyes fluttered open to thick black smoke whirling from my mouth. It darted through the air and into Victus's mouth. He made gagging noises, screams stifled by the foulness.

Now his black soul is complete, Della said in satisfaction.

Victus caught his breath and stood, arcphone in hand. He raised it, clearly ready to finish what he'd started.

I pushed to my feet and lifted my arcwand. I fired a bolt of energy but it rebounded off his shield.

"Weak," Victus hissed. "Pathetic vermin." A malevolent grin spread across his face. "Just die already."

Chapter 34

I summoned a shield as the malevolent force struck. My willpower was weakened from the fight. I felt my strength buckling, heard Ambria and the others hacking away at the vines behind me. By the time they broke through, I would be dead. I looked down at Delectra, at the terrible burn mark on her chest, at how still she'd become.

Tears blurred my vision. She'd sacrificed herself for me. My love had freed her from the demon, but her love had saved my life. This evil man had taken Cora from me and now Delectra. After he killed me, my friends would be next. I closed my eyes and saw the smile on Delectra's face when I called her Mum. Cora appeared next to her, orange hair tied in a loose bun, tears on her cheeks. It was the first time I'd told her I loved her.

I shook my head. "No, Victus, you can't have one more soul." I opened my eyes and glared at him. "You won't take anything else from me."

"What did you say boy?" Victus clenched his teeth. "Begging for your life?"

"You'll take nothing more!" I shouted. "Nothing!" I released the shield and fired a crimson beam from the tip of my arcwand. My willpower met his and exploded in a ring of yellow fire. I looked inside my mind and took the hands of my two mothers. One had

355

borne me, the other had molded me. I'd saved them, and they'd saved me. Together, we could defeat anything.

I heard Victus scream and opened my eyes as my willpower, bolstered by love he could never understand ripped through his magic like paper. He threw himself to the side and my spell blew a hole in the wall behind him. Still screaming in fright, Victus ran. I aimed for him, but he made it through the hole and out of sight.

I dropped next to Delectra and turned her on her back. She gasped for breath, still alive, but the burn causing her terrible pain. I remembered Treek's sap and turned to the vines. "Back away, Ambria!"

I heard her shout at the others and then she said, "All clear!"

I cut a hole through the vines with focused fire and my friends rushed in. Ambria gasped when she saw Delectra. "What happened?"

"Treek!" I shouted. "I need you!"

He lumbered through. His eyes went wide when he saw the grievous wound. "I will help her." He dripped sap on the flesh, spreading it gently with his hand.

Delectra's body shook. She seemed to see me as the pain faded from her eyes and she gripped my hand. "Thank you, Conrad. Thank you, my son." Tears trickled down her cheeks.

Tears of my own rained down on her. "You're going to be okay, Mum." I kissed her forehead. "You're going to be fine." I reached into my satchel and held onto the heart, sending love toward her.

Instead of healing her wound, I felt Della stirring inside me.

It's time for me to go, son.

I flinched at the sound of her voice. *What do you mean?*

356

An image of her formed in my mind, looking down at me with teary eyes. "We have to leave you, son."

Delectra spoke in unison with Della. "You cannot save my life, but you have already saved my soul." She gripped my hand tightly and kissed it. "Lean down and give me a kiss goodbye, Conrad."

I couldn't stop blubbering like a baby. "No, I can't let you go now."

"Do it quick," she gasped.

I bent down and kissed her forehead, her cheeks. "Please don't die," I whimpered.

"I cannot live remembering the monster Victus turned me into or the horrible things I have done," she rasped. A sad smile flickered on her lips. "Death is my peace."

"No, no, no." I pressed my forehead to her lips. "Stay with me. Be my mum."

"I am and always will be." She kissed my forehead. "Now go, son. Go find her." Delectra released one last breath and her body went limp.

I left you something, Della whispered, her voice fading. *Goodbye.*

I suddenly felt all alone inside my head and out.

I looked up. Ambria and Max were on their knees next to me, tears streaming down their cheeks. Evadora huddled in Treek's lap, face red and sad. Gwyneth stood a distance away, her eyes on the fallen Glimmer Queen.

For a moment, I considered tracking down Victus and killing him, but it would be foolish. He could still kill me or my friends. For now, there was only one place to go.

357

My heart felt so broken, I didn't think anything could mend it, but I had to try. I walked over to Naeve. She looked so fragile, a small pretty thing with an ugly heart. She truly was a reflection of Cora, but reversed in every way that mattered.

Fighting back more tears, I summoned Treek. "Can you carry her?"

He nodded slowly as was his way, and touched me gently. "I am sorry for your loss."

Fresh tears broke free. I put my hand over his, rubbing the rough bark. "Thank you, Treek."

I turned to Gwyneth. "Where's the equipment?"

"Everything is in the satchels in the room you found us in." She looked fearfully down the hallway. "Do you think Victus is still there?"

"He probably took another exit," Evadora said.

"I will retrieve the equipment," Shushiel said.

"I still can't believe you survived," Max told the spider. He looked at me, hope buried in his gaze. "I know it feels awful right now, but we have a lot to be thankful for."

"Yes," I said numbly. "We do." Where was the burning anger, the crushing sorrow I should have felt in that moment? I didn't know. I felt empty, numb. I had lost my mentor and my mother all in one terrible blow. Perhaps I was in shock, or perhaps losing the voices in my head had scrambled my emotions. I felt certain that when it hit me it would be a terrible tide.

Shushiel camouflaged and returned moments later with the satchels. Gwyneth retrieved the lost room relic from within and summoned the door. Treek placed Naeve and Delectra on the flying carpet. Evadora climbed on board and steered it.

We should have rested, but I didn't want to chance Victus returning, nor did I want to waste any time. We took the levitator down where Plinth waited. I told him what had happened and that my soul was officially cleansed of my parents' soul shards.

"So you did find the heart!" Plinth said in an accusing tone.

"And the world didn't even end," Max shot back.

Ambria tapped a finger on her chin. "In a way several worlds ended." She flashed a sad smile. "The small planetoids were all destroyed."

Plinth stared blankly at her for a moment. "I supposed that's one way to interpret it."

Gwyneth glared at the man. "Just stay out of our way from now on."

"That will not be a problem," he said.

I motioned forward and we began the trek south. With Naeve in our presence, the beasts stayed far away, but our group stayed close just in case.

"I wonder if Naeve was the reason Evadora had problems controlling the animals here," Ambria wondered. "Maybe Victus captured her and was trying to control the Glimmer."

Evadora smiled. "I think you're right, because the world feels different now."

I couldn't stop looking back at Delectra's still, pale form. She was beautiful, even in death, like an ice princess under a spell. I could hardly believe I'd found my mother and so quickly had her taken from me. It made me treasure the moments I'd had with Esma even more. Her actions and reactions made more sense in retrospect. She'd tried to remain distant, but something had grown between us, something too powerful for even her to resist.

In the end, no infernal force or work of man had been able to overpower the bond between mother and child. I just hoped the same could be said for Cora.

Max looked uneasily at Naeve. "If we don't bring back Cora, then what?"

Ambria met my eyes, her own deeply troubled. "We can't set her free, and we can't hold her prisoner. Keeping her in the reflected world must have been absolute torture, slowly wasting away like that."

"She's a reflection," Max said. "I don't understand how staying there would hurt her."

"Because she has a soul," Treek said. "Souls do not abide well in the reflected world. It is a place for the hollow, the fake."

"What he said," Evadora added.

Max pursed his lips. "So, I guess Naeve didn't have a reflection in that world."

"Another copy?" Evadora raised an eyebrow. "I don't think people have more than one."

"Actually," said a voice that I hadn't heard for quite some time. "It's possible—" I shot a glare back at Plinth. He stopped talking and looked down at the road, drifting further back from the group.

Gwyneth spoke as if she'd resisted asking a question for too long. "When are you going to tell us what happened out there in the asteroids?"

I stopped walking and turned to the others. "I found the heart." I removed it from my satchel and held it in the palm of my hand.

"Ooh, pretty," Ambria and Evadora said simultaneously.

"That's a big diamond," Max said. "Too bad it's cracked."

Gwyneth stepped closer. "I'm sorry for your loss, Conrad, but now that you've found the heart, Underborn will help you find the Broken Relic."

I offered her a sarcastic smile. "He doesn't need to. I already have it."

Ambria and Max gave me confused looks. Evadora's mouth dropped open in delight.

I ran a finger down the crack. "The Broken Relic is the Broken Heart of Jura." I stared hard at Gwyneth. "You knew it all this time. You probably hoped I wouldn't find out until Underborn revealed his little trick."

Gwyneth backed away, jaw hanging open in shock. "B-but no— that can't be true." She leaned against a tree, eyes losing focus. "That bastard lied to me."

Evadora burst into laughter. "Ha, ha, ha! He tricked everyone."

Gwyneth shook her head. "I'm sorry, Conrad. I truly thought—" she looked at the ground. "I didn't know."

I tucked the heart back in the satchel. "I believe you."

She looked up hopefully. "You do?"

"Yes." I looked to the east. "No matter what happens over there, Underborn can have the heart when I'm done."

"You're just going to give it to him?" she asked incredulously.

I smiled, nodded. "Yes, because I doubt he has the ability to operate it." I wiped at my suddenly wet eyes. "It takes the most powerful kind of magic to work the heart."

"Love," Ambria breathed.

I nodded. "I doubt Underborn knows the meaning of the word." I took a deep breath, turned, and started walking again.

Evadora giggled. "I love you, Conrad. You're the best."

Ambria took my hand. "I hope with all my heart you can bring back Cora."

"Me too," Max said. "Me too."

We reached the Soul Tree a day and a half later. Its branches spanned the sky, wispy white leaves streaming in the breeze, the ghostly remains of Glimmer folk. Cora's leaf was up there somewhere, precious memories, and hopefully a part of her soul. My body trembled with fear. *What if this doesn't work?*

My thoughts seemed to echo in my head, a tiny voice all alone in a house that had once held three. It was as if roommates had packed up and left unexpectedly. Despite his dark soul, I even missed Vic's occasional commentary.

A huge beast with shaggy white hair loped down the side of the tree and met us near the bottom. It stood on hind legs and tenderly took Evadora in its arms.

"Oh, Yoghra, you're too sweet," the girl said with a giggle. She ran her fingers through his fur. "We're here for Cora."

He grunted and pointed up the tree, speaking in a rough language I didn't understand.

"We have to go up there," Evadora said. She clambered onto Yoghra's back. "You'll probably want to fly up."

"I will climb as well," Shushiel said.

I walked over to the flying carpet where it hovered with its silent riders. Naeve stirred and mumbled, as if suffering a bad dream. We'd kept her asleep with spells, knowing if she woke up, she could unleash havoc.

I'd need the carpet to fly her to the top. "Can someone help me with Delectra?"

"We can put her in the room," Gwyneth said.

I nodded and wished we'd thought of that earlier. Gwyneth opened the door and Treek gently cradled the body of my mother and carried her inside. He placed her inside a sleeping bag and put a pillow under her head.

"She looks comfortable," he said softly. "So peaceful. Sometimes I wish for death, if only to end my freakish existence."

I squeezed his arm. "Maybe Cora can fix what Naeve did to you."

Treek ran a hand over his rough tree-bark skin. "It is my hope she can restore me to my normal form." Treek rested the same hand on my shoulder. "I wish you success, Conrad."

I swallowed the knot in my throat. "Thank you." I walked outside and climbed onto the carpet.

Ambria and Max drifted over on their brooms.

"We'd like to come," Ambria said.

Max nodded. "If that's all right."

"I want you there with me," I said, my throat suddenly dry. "I'll need all the moral support I can get."

We flew up and around the massive tree and found Evadora near the top with Yoghra, waving her arm to get our attention. I parked the carpet just beneath the wisp Evadora pointed to.

"How do you see memories?" I asked her.

"You simply have to touch it." Evadora balanced on the thick bough, completely unafraid of falling. "Would you like to see her memories, Conrad?"

I was so eager, I reached out and touched it without answering.

I watch the small boy walk down the gangway with his father. He is so precious, but a dark influence hovers over him. I do not trust this Victus, or Delectra. They are doing something to the boy. If I could, I would take him with me now.

The memory faded and I was back next to the tree. "That's amazing."

"I know!" Evadora looked at Naeve. "I hope this works, Conrad." She held onto a branch over her head and swung closer. "Yoghra says that the wisp holds part of the soul, so if this works, the wisp will vanish."

"Well, at least we'll be able to see if it works," Max said.

I probably could have relived Cora's memories for hours, but Naeve wouldn't remain asleep forever. I had to do this now. I took the heart from the satchel and held it in my hand. I touched Naeve with that hand and Cora's wisp with the other.

After so much searching, Conrad is my foster son! He looks up at me with his great innocent eyes and my heart melts. I will be the best mother for him, and one day I will adopt him.

For the first time, Conrad smiles at me. I have finally reached through the dark haze around his soul.

I saw Cora giving me ice cream. Saw us stealing food from a grocery store. Watched Cora kill the man who abused her.

Love swelled inside me as more memories drifted past, some with me and some without. The heart blazed white and the crack began to heal. Naeve groaned and made retching sounds. Green smoke poured from her mouth, as the heart cast out the wailing demon Victus had used to control her.

Ambria and Max cried out with surprise, but Evadora watched with amazed curiosity. Yoghra gripped her hand to keep her from trying to touch the demon before its smoky form vanished.

The heart dimmed to a dull yellow glow and the crack reworked its way through the diamond surface. More memories flashed into my mind, but Cora's wisp remained on the tree. "It's not working." I loved Cora with all my heart, but it wasn't bringing her back from the dead.

I closed my eyes and pushed with my entire soul, remembering Cora's warm smiles, the sacrifices she'd made for me, and her gaunt form as she breathed her last. "Please come back," I sobbed. "I love you Cora." I opened my eyes and looked at the heart. The glow had faded to nothing.

Chapter 35

I failed. Sobs racked my body, but I didn't stop trying, didn't stop pushing. Somehow, I had to make this work.

"I'm so sorry." Ambria drifted right next to me and touched my hand where it rested on Naeve. She wiped tears from my face with the other hand. "You saved my life when you could have left me to die, Conrad. I love you with all my heart."

The Heart of Jura flickered and pulsed a deep red glow.

Max came to my other side and pressed his hand over Ambria's. "Before I met you, I never had a best friend or anyone who really cared about me." Tears filled his eyes. "I love you too, Conrad." He smiled. "And I know I'll love Cora too."

The hard diamond softened and began to pulse in my hand.

Shushiel touched my hand with her leg. "I love you as well, my friend."

The pulse quickened.

Evadora beamed brilliantly through her own tears. "I barely knew my mother, Conrad, but you helped me know how much she missed and loved me even after Naeve banished her." She knelt on the branch and touched my hand and Cora's wisp. "I love you and I love her."

The heart burst into a brilliant red glow, and beat with a steady thumping so loud it was all I could hear as the broken heart began to heal. The wisp dissolved like water, coursing down mine and Evadora's arms and into the heart. Naeve gasped, eyes flaring open. Her skin glowed a golden color that soon faded.

The beating heart grew slower and slower, the glow fading, until once again, it was a hard, cracked diamond in my hand.

Naeve—Cora?—blinked slowly and looked up at us. "Where am I?"

"Cora?" I asked, fear crackling in my voice.

She smiled. "Yes, that is one of my names." She sat up and looked around. "Why am I at the Soul Tree, and who are all of you people?"

Evadora touched her hand. "I'm your daughter, Evadora."

Cora's eyes flared. "But—but you're too old to be my daughter."

"You died, Mommy." Evadora patted her arm. "I grew up while you were dead."

Cora stopped breathing for a moment and then saw the great white beast on a branch nearby. "Yoghra, is this true?"

He nodded and spoke in his language.

Cora replied and touched her head. "I'm so sorry, but I don't remember dying or much before that."

Evadora bit her lower lip. "I know you don't know me, but could I have a hug?"

The resurrected Glimmer Queen smiled broadly. "Of course, my sweet."

I slid aside, feeling somewhat awkward as Evadora leapt into her mother's arms and squealed with delight. "Oh, Mommy, I hope you remember me soon. I have so much to tell you."

Cora looked at me. "Don't I know you?"

I nodded. "It's me, Conrad."

Her eyes filled with regret. "You look familiar, but I'm sorry, I don't remember you."

I choked back a lump of sorrow and forced a smile. "It's okay. All that matters is that you're back." *Cora is alive!* I tried to take comfort in that, but couldn't help feeling immensely sad that she didn't remember me.

We flew back down to the ground where Gwyneth paced expectantly. She looked at Cora and then at me, an unasked question in her eyes.

I gave her a wistful smile. "She's alive, but she has gaps in her memory."

Gwyneth's forehead pinched into a sad look. "Give her time, Conrad." She blew out a breath. "It's absolutely mind-blowing that you resurrected her from the grave in the first place." Gwyneth squeezed my shoulder. "I'll bet once she has some time to recover, memories will start flooding back."

I hoped she was right.

We spoke with Cora for a while, trying to help her remember, but she quickly grew tired.

"I must sleep," she said. "I suppose being raised from the dead is quite tiring." She curled up in the roots of the Soul Tree, and Yoghra covered her with a blanket that looked as if it were woven from his own fur.

I saw Plinth looking around, probably trying to find the dagger he'd lost in the roots. I gave Ambria the Nose of Jura and she sniffed it out within seconds, lodged too deep between the huge roots for us to reach. I didn't tell Plinth where it was, instead asking Evadora to make sure it stayed there, safely away from most hands.

I would have dropped the heart in as well, but I'd made a deal with Underborn.

Since there wasn't much else I could do here and Cora needed time to remember, I decided it was time to return to Queens Gate.

I hugged Evadora goodbye. "Take care of our mum," I told her. "I'll be back to check on her soon."

The girl smiled hopefully. "She'll remember, I just know it."

"Does anything feel different about the Glimmer now that Cora is back?" Ambria asked.

Evadora closed her eyes and held out her hands. After a moment, she nodded. "I don't know how to explain it, but everything feels better—like the madness is going away."

I hoped she was right. For now, I felt happy just to know Cora was alive and well. I looked up at the great tree silhouetted against the moon. The Glimmer was beautiful and peaceful here and I realized there was one more thing I should do before leaving.

"May I bury Delectra here?" I asked.

Evadora nodded. "Of course. Would you like me to do it?"

"Yes, just tell me where."

Evadora led me to a grove of trees that stretched into the distance. Every tree was distinct in its own way, whether by the color of bark and leaves, or the unique shape of the trunks. None were much taller than me, and some were barely up to my knees.

369

"This is where we bury our dead." She knelt next to a tree. "We plant a seed on top of the grave, and the tree uses the body for nutrients." Evadora looked up at me. "Is that okay?"

I smiled gratefully. "I think my mum would like that."

Evadora spread her hands over an open plot and the roots spread the soil open into a neat rectangular hole. She breathed in relief. "I'm so glad my powers are working again."

My friends and I placed Delectra in her grave. I looked at her still form, but didn't know what to say. I thought back to what little I knew about my mother and the words finally came.

"You were a good person. A kind person. Thanks to you, I am good at broom flying and magic." Images of Esma flashed in my mind and the reality that I would never see her again stabbed my heart. "I feel as if I have lost two people today—a mother and a mentor. I will remember the good times we had, how you zapped us mercilessly to teach us magic."

Ambria smiled through her tears. "She was a wonderful teacher."

"Even if she frightened me to death," Max said.

Shushiel bobbed up and down. "It amused me greatly to watch her torture the students."

I picked up a handful of dirt and dropped it into the grave at Mum's feet. "My regret is that we didn't have more time. I think we could have become the best of friends." My eyes stung, but I still smiled. "Even so, I'm so thankful for the time we shared in this world. One day, we will meet again."

I cried silently for a moment, then turned to Evadora and nodded. She moved her hands together, and the earth buried my mother. Yoghra dug into his fur and handed her a small black seed.

Evadora held it over the grave. "With this seed, I give you life evermore." She dropped it into the dark soil and looked at me. "Water it with your tears, Conrad."

I leaned over and let them drip into the dirt. *Goodbye, Mum. Rest in peace.*

We returned to Queens Gate where a new dawn was breaking over a crisp snowy day. I took a detour from the Fairy Gardens and went to Moore Manor. Galfandor opened the door before I knocked. He didn't seem surprised by the motley crew with me and simply said, "Won't you come in for tea?"

"I should be on my way," Plinth said.

Galfandor shook his head. "I think you should stay for at least one cup, Seer Plinth."

Plinth sagged, his weary face creased with sorrow and regret. "My actions led to the deaths of many of my comrades, and yet, all my good intentions were for nothing. I do not think a cup of tea will help."

"I think conversation and rest will do you well." The headmaster patted his shoulder and motioned us in. "Come, now."

Galfandor seated us around a table in his tea room and a wooden golem in butler livery served us tea. I told the headmaster our tale from beginning to end, telling him of my mother's fate, and Victus's deceit. He said nothing, enduring the interruptions from my friends as they added their own flavor to the story and my moments of silence when I grew too choked up to speak.

When it was over the headmaster looked into his tea for a long moment, as if formulating precisely what to say. First, he turned to Plinth. "You are not to blame for the deaths of your comrades. If there's anything I've learned about prophecy, it's that nothing is set in

371

stone and sometimes the terms are so vague, there are many interpretations."

"In other words, our interpretation was far from the mark," Plinth said miserably.

Galfandor nodded, but added nothing more. He looked at me. "Conrad, I'm proud of you, Ambria, and Max. While I'm profoundly sad for your loss, you rid your mother of Victus's demonic influences, and touched her heart with love she had long forgotten." He smiled kindly at me. "You gave her a greater gift in death than Victus ever gave her in life. For that, she can truly rest in peace."

"Truth," Gwyneth said.

I wiped my eyes and nodded. "I just wish I'd had more time with her."

"As do I." Galfandor sat back and stroked his long beard. "I must say I'm immensely glad to hear Cora is once again among the living. I was uncertain if Naeve would flourish in the reflected world and continue to plot until she broke free."

"It seems that once you have a soul, the reflected world is not a place you want to live," Ambria said. "She was still immortal, but I suppose there's nothing you can actually eat there so she withered away."

"As for Victus, it would appear the Eye of Jura allows him to perfectly mimic anyone, thus slipping through our protections." The headmaster's forehead pinched with worry. "The people he and Delectra replaced are real. I only hope they are still alive."

Gwyneth offered an assuring nod. "The eye can only replicate living people, so they would have had to keep them alive." She bit her lower lip. "I would send someone to their addresses immediately."

"It appears Victus and Delectra used two people for the eye to duplicate their appearances, and then created fake identities."

372

Galfandor stroked his beard. "I remember how impressed I was with their skills when they applied for positions here. In retrospect, it's hardly surprising that they surpassed our expectations."

"So the people they mimicked aren't even real professors?" Max asked.

Galfandor met my gaze. "I doubt it."

In other words, the real "Esma" would never be a professor here. I shook off the strange feeling accompanying that thought and told him what concerned me most. "With the eye, Victus could still be here somewhere."

Galfandor looked to Gwyneth. "Is there any way to detect someone using it?"

"Not that I know of." The relic hunter took a fresh cup of tea and a lump of sugar. "The eye physically alters the person, so they wouldn't even have to carry it with them."

Ambria took out the nose. "Well, we can find anything with this."

"Yeah!" Max bumped the table with his knees as he jolted to his feet, and nearly spilled all our tea. "We can go on a relic hunting expedition."

"I would caution against doing anything right now," Galfandor said. "Victus will likely retreat to lick his wounds after suffering such a brutal defeat at the hands of his son." He offered me a smile. "In the meantime, I think it best if Conrad does whatever he can to help Cora regain her memories. She could be a powerful ally against Victus."

Galfandor succinctly stated exactly what I planned to do. Despite winning a battle, trying to hunt down Victus would be foolish of me. Having Cora back was the only thing that mattered to me right now. "I agree."

Galfandor rubbed his hands together. "Excellent. I will review security protocols and see if there's another way to keep Victus from impersonating someone else." He turned to the ruby spider. "Shushiel, would you mind guarding Conrad for a while longer?"

"It would be my privilege to keep my cousin safe." Her mandibles spread wide into a spider grin.

"What about those golems?" Ambria said. "Victus could replace real people with them!"

"Our security wards can detect golem sparks," Galfandor said. "It troubles me to think that he may have used them."

"He claimed to have locked away all his powerful enemies," I said. "There's no telling what he might have already done."

Galfandor drew in a deep breath. "We will have to remain wary until we determine the depths of his deceit. I will warn the Templars. Perhaps they can ferret out his forgeries."

We said our goodbyes and left for the keep. Plinth gathered his belongings from the lost room once we reached our destination.

"I am sorry for all the trouble I caused you, Conrad." Plinth rubbed his red eyes. "Perhaps Cora will allow me to return to the Glimmer and give my people the burial they deserve."

I managed a tight smile. "I'll speak with her about it soon."

"Very well, then." He looked as if he wanted to say more, then abruptly turned and left.

Ambria yawned and staggered in place. "I'm going to get some sleep. I feel as if I haven't had a wink in days."

"Me too," Max said.

"Go ahead," I told them. "I'm going to complete my deal with Gwyneth."

Ambria hugged me. "I'll see you soon."

"Yeah, don't make a racket when you come into the room," Max said with a grin. "I'll be asleep before I hit the pillow."

After they left, I reached into the satchel and took out the heart. I looked at the flawed diamond for a long time before reluctantly handing it to Gwyneth. "Is this Saila's heart?"

She took it and traced her fingers down the crack. "No one knows for sure. Some think she sacrificed herself with the thrust of a magic dagger to her heart in an attempt to shield Juranthemon from attack, but her magic failed, and she died with a broken heart."

I thought of the dagger Plinth had used and wondered if it might be the very same. "What does Underborn really want with the heart?"

"He's a collector." Gwyneth put it into her satchel. "The only relics he uses regularly are the map and key."

"I suppose he'll want the nose now," I said. "Tell him I won't appreciate it if it goes missing."

"Perhaps he doesn't even need to know you have it." She winked, but her expression grew serious. "He fooled all of us, Conrad. While I'm not surprised, I do find his deceit where you're concerned rather harsh."

"I guess I'm getting used to all the lies." I managed a wry chuckle. "Thank you for not telling him."

"Of course." She stepped closer. "You're a good person, Conrad. I'm glad I met you." Gwyneth leaned in and kissed my cheek. "Now I know why my sister has such a crush on you." She laughed and backed away. "Don't tell her I said that."

My face burned and my brain seemed to lose control of my body parts. "Um, yes, okay." I wiped the beading sweat on my forehead. "Your secret is also safe with me."

Gwyneth winked once more, turned, and walked away.

Chapter 36

The holidays ended and I spent what little time I had outside of school and Kabash with Evadora and Cora, sometimes in the Glimmer, and sometimes in the Fairy Gardens. Cora was almost like a child in some ways, having lost many of her memories in the transition from life to death and back again.

The real Professors Sideon and Emoora were found, though of course they were not professors at all, but ordinary folk Victus and Delectra had kidnapped in order to mimic their appearances with the Eye of Jura. Galfandor told me their real names, but I didn't care. Simply seeing the woman who I thought of as Esma would be incredibly painful.

Even now I couldn't stop thinking of her as a person separate from Delectra. She had been as real to me as any other person, and I missed her. Magical defense class was a pale shadow of its former self. Meanwhile, Asha Fellini substituted for both magical defense and enchantments. Seeing the woman who looked so much like Delectra every day was painful at first, but soon turned surreal.

When I met with Ansel and told him the tale of Delectra's death, he burst into laughter. "You finally figured it out."

My heart froze. "You knew?"

377

He bared his teeth. "Yes, I knew. I figured it out immediately, but only because I knew Delectra too well." Ansel spat on the ground. "She threatened to kill me if I didn't keep quiet."

I remembered how bitter he seemed toward Esma and now it made sense. "I'm sorry she did that."

Ansel threw up his hands. "Now that you've told me how she really felt, her threat was probably empty." He shook his head slowly. "I should have seen that she truly cared for you, but it's a feeling that is somewhat foreign to me."

I couldn't disagree with his assessment.

Every day, I missed having Della in my head and wished to have Delectra back. Sometimes I cursed having ever gone on the quest in the first place. Each day I struggled to push forward through the depression and hide my true emotions with a smile.

We won the Kabash championship, beating Tiberius Keep handily. The win gave me a brief respite from the miseries of day-to-day life, but even that high was temporary.

Weeks turned to months, and Cora showed little sign of improvement. Even Evadora was worried that she might never be her old self again. Two weeks before finals, Max, Ambria, and I went to the Fairy Gardens to meet with Cora and Evadora for a celebration of life.

We brought a large picnic and spread it out near the pond and in front of the slowly recovering forest. Some of the dryads had returned now that their trees were tall and strong. Even the Lady of the Pond, Mirjana, and her husband, Klave, joined us to celebrate the restoration.

Cora kissed Evadora on the cheek as she gazed at the forest. "It's marvelous, daughter."

"My magic is strong!" Evadora leapt into the air and clapped her hands.

"It's beautiful," Mirjana said. "I am glad the Lyrolai magic is powerful in you, child."

Cora turned to me and held out her hand. "Would you like a walk, Conrad?"

I was so tempted to call her Mum, but resisted and simply nodded. "I'd love to."

We walked down the trail, dryads with their barky flesh peering shyly between the trees. Treek lumbered from within and waved happily at us. "How fare you, Conrad?"

"I'm great," I told him. "It seems you have new friends."

"And new responsibilities," he said. "For the first time in a long while, I am happy." He bowed to Cora. "My Queen."

"For now, that title belongs to my daughter." Cora touched his arm and smiled gently. "Perhaps one day I will remember enough to earn it back."

Treek bowed deeper. "As you say." He turned and went back into the forest. Laughing dryads danced around him, running their hands in his vine hair and over his bark-like skin, much to his delight.

I was too busy looking at him to watch where I was going and tripped, nearly falling flat on my face.

"Oh, are you okay?" Cora took my elbow and helped me up.

"I'm fine." I laughed at my clumsiness. "I was curious what the dryads were doing with Treek."

Cora blushed. "That is at least one thing I remember." Her gaze caught on something on the ground. She leaned down and picked up my chain with the green stone on it. "You must have dropped this." She put the pebble in her palm and her eyes flashed wide.

"Are you okay?" I touched her hand, but she didn't respond to my touch.

She abruptly leapt back and the pebble fell to the ground. Cora blinked slowly and looked at me.

"Are you okay?" I asked. "Did something happen?"

Her eyes filled with tears and she cupped my cheek. "I remembered something when I touched the stone. It was as if it shined a light on memories long forgotten."

My breath caught in my throat as I cherished her gentle touch. "What did you remember?"

"The moment I knew I wanted you to be my son." Cora leaned over and kissed my forehead. "I remember it. I feel it in my heart as if it was yesterday."

I looked up at her and finally dared say the word desperately tearing at my heart. "Mum?"

Cora nodded. "Yes, son, it's me."

I hugged her, my heart swelling until I thought it might burst. "I love you, Mum."

She held me tight. "I love you too, son."

There was still evil in the world, and sorrow in my heart. But today, in this moment, I had found my ray of sunshine. For the first time in a while, I felt as if I had the strength to go on.

Victus could hide, but soon, I would find him and finish this.

####

I hope you enjoyed reading this book. Reviews are very important in helping other readers decide what to read next. Would you please take a few seconds to rate this book?

For the latest on new releases, free ebooks, and more, join John Corwin's Newsletter at www.johncorwin.net!

Books by John Corwin:

The Overworld Chronicles:
Sweet Blood of Mine
Dark Light of Mine
Fallen Angel of Mine
Dread Nemesis of Mine
Twisted Sister of Mine
Dearest Mother of Mine
Infernal Father of Mine
Sinister Seraphim of Mine
Wicked War of Mine
Dire Destiny of Ours
Aetherial Annihilation
Baleful Betrayal
Ominous Odyssey

Overworld Underground:
Possessed By You
Demonicus

Overworld Arcanum:
Conrad Edison and the Living Curse
Conrad Edison and the Anchored World
Conrad Edison and the Broken Relic

Stand Alone Novels:
No Darker Fate
The Next Thing I Knew
Outsourced
Seventh
Mars Rising

For the latest on new releases, free ebooks, and more, join John Corwin's Newsletter at www.johncorwin.net!

Meet the Author

John Corwin is the bestselling author of the Overworld Chronicles. He enjoys long walks on the beach and is a firm believer in puppies and kittens.

After years of getting into trouble thanks to his overactive imagination, John abandoned his male modeling career to write books.

He resides in Atlanta.

Connect with John Corwin online:
Facebook: http://www.facebook.com/johnhcorwinauthor
Website: http://www.johncorwin.net
Twitter: http://twitter.com/#!/John_Corwin

www.ingramcontent.com/pod-product-compliance
Lightning Source LLC
Chambersburg PA
CBHW051521250626
47156CB00001B/176

9781942453086